PARADOX BOUND

ALSO BY PETER CLINES

The Fold

The Ex-Heroes Series
Ex-Heroes
Ex-Patriots
Ex-Communication
Ex-Purgatory
Ex-Isle

PARADOX

A NOVEL

BOUND

PETER CLINES

B \ D \ W \ Y
BROADWAY BOOKS
NEW YORK

Published in the United States by Broadway Books, an imprint of the Crown Publishing Group, a division of Penguin Random House LLC, New York. crownpublishing.com

Broadway Books and its logo, B \ D \ W \ Y, are trademarks of Penguin Random House LLC.

Originally published in hardcover in the United States by Crown, an imprint of the Crown Publishing Group, a division of Penguin Random House LLC, New York, in 2017.

Library of Congress Cataloging-in-Publication Data
Names: Clines, Peter, 1969– author.
Title: Paradox bound / Peter Clines.
Description: First edition. | New York : Crown, [2017]
Identifiers: LCCN 2017028545 | ISBN 9780553418330 (hardback)
Subjects: LCSH: Time travel—Fiction. | Science fiction. | Suspense fiction. | BISAC: FICTION / Science Fiction / Adventure. | FICTION / Horror.
Classification: LCC PS3603.L563 P37 2017 | DDC 813/.6—dc23 LC record available at https://lccn.loc.gov/2017028545

ISBN 978-1-101-90703-0
Ebook ISBN 978-0-553-41834-7

Printed in the United States of America

Book design by Elina Nudelman
Cover design by Tal Goretsky
Cover photography: (car) Anthony Asael/Art in All of Us/Corbis

10 9 8 7 6 5 4 3 2 1

First Paperback Edition

For my dad, Dennis,
who's done so many things that make it
into these stories

Men like women with a past because they hope history will repeat itself.

—MAE WEST

PARADOX BOUND

The First Time Around

1

Eli Teague was eight and a half years old the first time he met Harry Pritchard.

That morning, Eli's mom had tossed him out the door with a bag lunch and told him to find something interesting to do. It was summer, and she didn't want him inside watching cartoons or reading comics. She insisted a young boy needed fresh air and exercise.

Eli insisted what he really needed was to know how Voltron was going to form and beat the Robeast when one of the five lion keys was missing, but he was told in no uncertain terms that he did not. He was upset in principle more than in fact. They didn't have cable, and there was only so much picture the television's rabbit ears could coax out of the air from the distant Boston stations.

The bag lunch was a dry granola bar, a peanut butter sandwich on wheat bread with the crusts still on it, a green apple, and a thermos filled with cold water. No jelly, because it had too much sugar. No Ho-Hos, because they were nothing but sugar. Not even a juice box. Eli's mom had been on a health kick for a few months now, and he'd been forced to spend part of his hard-earned allowance on Pepsi and snack cakes down at Jackson's. It cut into his comic-book budget, but his mom hadn't left him with much choice.

He kicked around in the yard for a while, then rode his bike along the shoulder to Joshua's house to see if his best friend had any comics he hadn't read. Joshua had come down with a cold, though, and his mother wouldn't even let Eli come in. And Corey was still away at summer camp, so there wouldn't be any new comics at his house either.

Eli rode his bike out past the old baseball field. He threw a few rocks at the stone wall that separated the outfield from the patch of woods behind the Catholic church, and then hiked out to throw a few more at the old rusted car he and his friends had discovered wedged between some trees one day. He went down to Jackson's and worked his way through the three wire racks of comics, even though he knew there wouldn't be any new ones until Wednesday and the new issue of *Amazing Spider-Man* wasn't due for another two weeks anyway. Then old Mr. Jackson told him to buy something or get out, so Eli bought a Pepsi and a Chocodile and rode back to the baseball field to sit in the bleachers and eat his now slightly improved lunch.

He weighed his options while he ate. Closer to the coast there were tourist attractions like beaches and video-game arcades and movie theaters. One of the towns to the south had a statue of the wrong soldier they'd gotten after the Civil War, while one to the north had a guardian scarecrow. Over in New Hampshire were all the malls with tons of stores and shops. None of these were close enough to reach with his bike.

Sanders didn't even have a library. Or even a school. Eli was bussed across the town line when school was in session. The old high school was used as a police station now.

Not for the first time, Eli came to the inescapable conclusion that Sanders had to be the most boring town in the state of Maine. Possibly the most boring town in New England. While he didn't have a lot of worldly experience and had traveled very little, if asked, he would be willing to bet a whole dollar Sanders was the most boring town in the entire United States of America.

Eli finished his Chocodile and hid the evidence in a rust-flaked trash can next to the bleachers. It had been almost three hours since his mom had tossed him out, according to his calculator-watch. He could probably sneak home and hide in his room until afternoon cartoons started. He took a big bite of apple, moved it around his mouth with his tongue to hide any scent of chocolate, then spit the mouthful of fruit into the can. The apple itself followed.

He shoved the empty paper bag and full thermos into his backpack, swung his leg over his bike, and headed for home.

A little ways away from his house, he saw the car on the side of the road. It was old and small, but still took up too much room on the shoulder for Eli to squeeze by on his bike. He was either going to have to come to a stop, drag his bike into the woods and around the car, or go into the street. Being in the street was forbidden, and he would never risk it this close to home where his mom might see.

Still, Eli toyed with the idea of taking his bike onto the gray pavement anyway. It would only take a moment. His mom said he was too young, but he knew he was more than old enough. Just last month, well after his eighth birthday, he had to insist his grammy stop getting him Duplo bricks and only get regular LEGO from here on in.

The old car had spindly wheels like Eli's bicycle and a funny roof like an old wagon. The windows in the back were stretched-out ovals. The whole thing was new-jeans-dark blue.

A car like that didn't belong on the side of the road. It didn't belong on the road, period. Not in Sanders, for sure. Even for a town that still didn't have cable television, it was too old. Too old for anyone in town, even old Mr. Jackson, who was almost fifty.

And then, as he mashed his pedals backward and the bike crunched to a stop in the sand and rocks, Eli saw the older boy, who he would soon learn was named Harry.

Harry stood next to the car—up *on* the car, on little platforms that ran along the bottom—and stretched out across the hood, yanking on some kind of lever. He wore one of the old-timey outfits (even older than the car) that people wore for Fourth of July parades down in the Yorks or sometimes in Portsmouth. A blue coat, not as dark as the car, covered his body and swung back and forth with every movement.

Eli stepped off his bike, dropped the kickstand, and took a few steps toward the old car. "Hey," he said. "Whatcha doin'?"

Harry responded by tossing a big wrench over his shoulder. It clunked headfirst on the side of the road and tipped over into the gravel next to an old toolbox. Then the older boy hopped down, clutching something round and silver in his hand. A vest that matched the coat wrapped around the teen's torso, and his oversized, off-white shirt poofed out around the vest's edges. He had long hair like a girl, but it was done up in a wide ponytail, like old-timey hair in schoolbook pictures.

Eli found this outfit odd—although still not as odd as the car— because usually only adults wore the Fourth of July costumes, or very young children (even younger than Eli, who felt quite old nowadays). On a guess, Harry was closer to eighteen or nineteen. Tall and slim, but not quite old enough to get the pinprick whiskers of grown men. Smooth as a baby's bum, as Eli's mom liked to say.

"Kind of busy here," Harry said. "You should head on home."

Eli took another step forward. The car's front glass—the windshield—was all cracked and broken. "Is something wrong with your car?"

The teenage boy nodded. "Just out of fuel," he said. He gave the car an awkward pat. "We'll be on our way soon, hopefully."

Eli pointed back down the road behind him. "There's a gas station in town," he said. "They can help."

Harry shook his head. "No, thank you," he said. "I've only got a few minutes to get back on the road."

"I could go get some gas for you," said Eli. He waved his arm back at his bike, thrilled with the idea something even slightly interesting was happening right on his street. "I'm really fast."

"I don't need gas," said the older boy. "My partner's off taking care of things." He glanced over his shoulder, then past Eli and down the road. His face was slack, the look of someone waiting to get back a quiz they knew they didn't do well on. "You should get out of here, child."

"I live right over there," said Eli, pointing the other way. "It's okay."

"It isn't. You should head home. Bad things are coming."

Eli glanced over his shoulder, but the road was empty as far as he could see. "What's your name?" he asked, desperate to stretch out the encounter.

"I'm Harry," said the teenager. "Now, go home."

He said the name in his head three times to make sure it stuck. "Hello, Harry," he said. "I'm Eli."

The older boy nodded, his gaze still on the road. Then his eyes went wide and looked down at Eli. He squeaked out the name again, like a high-pitched echo.

Something about the look worried Eli. "Yeah," he said, cautiously confirming his name.

Harry dropped to his knees and grabbed Eli by the shoulders. As he did his coat flared out and Eli saw two leather gun holsters on his hips, like movie cowboys wore. "Oh my God," he said. "Look at you! You . . . you're so cute."

Eli knew he was not cute. He was, in fact, very mature and grown-up. He no longer read *Richie Rich* or *Hot Stuff*, and made sure to only select comics from either Marvel or DC.

Harry was still holding him by the shoulders and still talking—babbling, really—about complications and Eli not being there and more demands for him to go home. It didn't make a lot of sense. It felt like Harry was rushing through stuff, the way adults would give quick answers when they didn't really want to explain things.

One word stood out at the end of the older boy's speech, and Eli latched onto it. "I have water," he said.

Harry froze. His fingers tightened on Eli's shoulders. "You what?"

"Water," said Eli. "I've got some if you're thirsty." He wiggled his arms until Harry let go, and then the pack slid down his back. He swung it around, unzipped it, and pulled out the bright-red thermos. He'd stopped carrying the plastic Transformers lunchbox last year, but his mom still made him use the thermos. The picture of Optimus Prime was chipped and worn away by hundreds of washings.

Harry's eyes got even wider. He snatched the thermos out of Eli's hands, tossed the cup-lid aside, and unscrewed the top. He pushed his nose into it and sniffed hard. His brown-green eyes locked on Eli's as he hefted the thermos.

Then he leapt off the ground and raced to the front of the car. "It's better than nothing," he said.

Eli ran after him, clutching the backpack to his chest. "What are you doing?"

Harry stretched across the hood. Near the center of the windshield sat a small opening that reminded Eli of the top of a jar. Harry carefully emptied the thermos into the tank, shaking the last few drops in, then resealed the cap with a few quick twists of his wrist.

He tossed the thermos back to Eli and dashed around to the other side of the car. He reached in and flipped a few switches on the dashboard. There were a lot of switches, and some lights, and it all looked a bit more like a spaceship than a car.

The car puttered to life.

"Hey," Eli cried out. "You said you were out of gas." He gave Harry a well-practiced glare, the look of a child lied to by an older person.

"I said I was out of fuel," the older boy said. "And you gave me close to a pint."

"I just gave you water."

"Yes," he said. "You're a lifesaver, if I haven't mentioned that yet." He slid into the driver's seat and settled behind the wheel.

Eli stared at the dashboard again.

"Hey!" someone yelled.

Eli looked up and saw a shaggy man jogging toward the car. He had a Bond-villain hat and wore a scratchy-plaid jacket over a pale-blue sweatshirt, even though it wasn't cold out. He had dark hair and a scraggly beard, like people on TV who got lazy and didn't take care of themselves for a couple of days. His mom said it was how homeless people looked. He held a red gas can in his arms, a big square one like they sold down at the station.

"How'd you get it running?" the man asked.

"Quiet!" yelled Harry. He ran back to meet the older man in front of the car.

"I couldn't get anything, the faucet was rusted solid," the man said. He looked at Eli. "Who's the—"

"Quiet," the older boy told him again. He knocked the gas can away from the homeless man and muttered some quiet words to him.

The man stared at Eli's bike, then at Eli. Eli stared back. He wondered if the homeless man was Harry's older brother. Or just some hitchhiker Harry was giving a ride to. Or if he was going to try to take Eli's bike.

Harry hit the man's arm. "Now!"

The scruffy man got in the car.

Harry slipped past Eli and raced around the car to slide behind the steering wheel. The homeless man held out an old-timey triangle hat, which Harry yanked onto his head. "Hey," said the older boy. He snapped his fingers and pointed down at the pavement under Eli's shoes. "Your mother doesn't want you in the street, yes?"

Eli glanced down. He'd followed Harry around to the driver's side without thinking.

"Get off the road and stay there," Harry told him. "In fact, stay there for a few minutes after we go, just to be safe." He pointed back to the sand-and-gravel shoulder where the bike stood.

Eli nodded and looked back at his bike. Something moved on the edge of his vision, down the road. There was another car coming. Coming fast. He could hear its engine.

Harry looked at the mirror mounted on the door. "Time to go," he said. "See you in a couple of years, Eli."

"What?"

The old car lunged forward. Eli was showered in loose grit and dust as the wheels spun and hurled the vehicle up onto the road. The tires squealed and left thin black tracks against the gray pavement. He coughed twice and the older boy's car was already past Eli's driveway and zooming away.

He watched the car vanish down the road and around the far bend where it stopped being Mill Road and became Abbot Drive. The sound of its engine faded, but even as it did another sound grew. A growl like an angry dinosaur or a werewolf or something else that should only be on the Channel 56 *Creature Double Feature*. It was so loud it almost hurt.

Eli stepped off the road. His shoes crunched in the gravel and the last swirls of dust settled around them. He breathed out and took new air into his lungs.

The summer before, somewhat against his will, Eli had been enrolled in peewee baseball and somehow ended up playing third base. It had been almost fun until the day Zeke the Freak, an oversized kid with a jaw like an ape, had sent a line drive right at third. Eli had been looking at something else, heard the crack of the bat, and turned to see the baseball hanging in the air a foot from his face. Each individual red stitch stuck in his memory, along with the curly letters that spelled out WLINGS and a scuff of dirt that crossed one of the stitch lines. Then the ball had struck him in the cheek and knocked out his last three baby teeth. Blood had flowed and Eli had shrieked and Zeke had cackled and a year later he could still remember that moment of the ball hanging in the air.

Eli turned around on the side of the road, and time froze.

The black car was caught in mid-pounce, like it didn't drive so much as lunge forward along the strip of pavement. It seemed heavier in the front, and a thin line of silver ran along its side. The windows were short and rounded on the corners.

Across the width of the car, the driver stared at Eli. His face was shadowed by a black hat, but there was enough sunlight to see his chin and nose and forehead glisten. His cheeks were pink, "a little color to them" Eli's mom would say, and his eyebrows and mustache were dark lines on his face. His smile didn't show any teeth.

Both of the man's eyes were closed. Not blinking or winking. Closed. But his head was turned to point right at Eli.

Past the man's face was a black gun. It was huge and blocky in the man's hand. He was in the process of putting it out his window. The man was driving, and getting ready to shoot his gun, and staring at Eli.

All with his eyes closed.

The moment passed.

The black car rocketed past him. Dust and leaves whipped at Eli. He grabbed at his ears to block the roar, but the sound was already fading. He turned and caught a last glimpse of the car before it screeched around the distant bend.

A sharp sound echoed back to Eli. A distant bang like fireworks. It happened again.

The road went quiet. Dust settled down over the toolbox, the wrench, and the red plastic fuel can. He didn't think they were coming back for any of them.

Eli's left leg was clammy. His jeans were wet. He didn't remember Harry or the homeless man spilling any water on him, but then the smell hit his nose. "Oh, no," he whispered. He snatched up his backpack and held it to hide the stain. He looked back at his bicycle and thought of several different ways to get the bike home until he figured out an awkward one that would let him keep the backpack where it was.

He stared down the road as he struggled home. He'd seen enough episodes of *Knight Rider* to know what had happened. The man in the black car had been shooting at Harry.

A breeze carried the smell of urine to his nose again. Eli cringed with the thought of Zeke the Freak spotting him. Even Josh and Corey would laugh at him for wetting his pants. All other thoughts were pushed away and Eli lumbered the last few dozen yards home with his bike and backpack.

2

Eli was thirteen years old the second time he met Harry.

He'd hit the ugly phase in every child's puberty where his body had to decide whether it would gain height or weight first. Eli's body had chosen the second option. He still hadn't reached five feet, but he'd passed 130 pounds last summer. He hadn't stepped on a scale since, despite his mother's assurances it would all even out in the end.

Mr. Jackson let him go half an hour early that day, because he'd sorted all the shelves and there was nothing to do. There was little chance of a last-minute rush this early in the season. Honestly, no matter what season it was, there was almost never a chance of a rush at any store in Sanders. If it wasn't for last-minute goatropers (his grammy's favorite term for tourists) who couldn't get a motel closer to the beach, Eli was pretty sure Sanders would've vanished like a fart in the wind long before he was born.

He still had a decent chance to catch up with Corey and Josh, though. They'd stopped by Jackson's an hour earlier to grab some magazines, a few comics, and a six-pack of Mountain Dew. They were heading to hang out on the bleachers for a while, until it got dark. Josh hinted there may be girls there too. Not girls like Robin, who was pretty much cool and one of the guys, but maybe someone like Nicole, who was already on the cheerleading squad as a high school freshman and wearing miniskirts and long socks to school at least once a week.

Eli dragged his ten-speed out of the storeroom, pumped the pedals, and cut down behind the Video Emporium toward the Founders House. It was a roundabout way to get to the baseball field, but it beat going by Pizza Pub and the fire station. The little lawn between the two was Zeke Miller's favorite hangout, and Eli didn't feel like dealing with the local bully today.

Really, there weren't any days he felt like dealing with Zeke. Eli's size made him an easy target. In many ways.

The Founders loomed in front of him. The building sprawled across the top of a small hill, its white paint yellowed with age and three or four of its windows cracked, but none actually broken. Eli could never decide if it looked more like a big mansion or a high-end hotel. He'd never seen anyone there to ask, and wouldn't have been interested enough to ask if he had. The Founders just sat there, not quite at the center of town, getting older every year and doing nothing else. There weren't even any good rumors about it. No suicides or hobo murders or angry ghosts or anything.

Sanders was too boring to even have a plain-old haunted house.

Then, as if on cue, one of the windows burst with a crash of breaking glass. Eli clamped down on the brakes and his bike skidded to a halt. He heard the snickering laughter just a moment before the next rock pinged off his handlebars. He yanked his hands away and the laughter increased.

"What are you looking at, Flea-lie?" Zeke bounced another rock on his fingertips, eager to send it flying. For every inch Eli hadn't grown over the past few years, Zeke had grown two. He was already being prepped for the football team, even though school rules said he couldn't play until next year.

Zeke's best—probably only—friend, Dougie, was with him. They stood at the base of the Founders House hill, in the gravel side road that led over to the baseball field. Their own bikes lay in the tall grass behind them.

"Nothing, Zeke." Eli sighed. He glanced at the road and wondered if he could get away before catching a rock in the back of the head. Zeke's aim wasn't fantastic, but it was good enough.

And Eli was an easy target.

A wisp of smoke curled from Dougie's hand. Eli's eyes went to it. It wasn't the first time he'd seen a classmate with a cigarette, but it was still something that caught him off guard. It was foolish, but in his mind smoking was something for college students and adults.

Dougie saw his eyes move. The other boy's face hardened. "You're not going to rat us out, are you, tubby?"

Eli shook his head. If he hadn't stopped his bike, he'd have been past them and heading down the alley toward the baseball field. He probably would've been able to see Corey and Josh by now. And maybe Nicole.

"Well?" snapped Zeke. His free hand flexed open and closed, open and closed, like it did whenever he got overexcited. Everybody called it his spaz fist. "Answer him. You going to rat us out or you going to keep quiet?"

"Yeah," Eli sighed.

A grin spread across Zeke's broad jaw. "Yeah, you're going to keep quiet, or yeah, you're going to rat us out?"

Eli's chest sagged. His belly flexed against the waistband of his jeans. He'd played this game with Zeke before. Too many times. Which is why it caught him off guard when the rules changed.

The rock hit him just above his right eye, on the brow. The blow echoed through his skull, and, for a moment, his neck and back and legs wobbled. He grabbed at the handlebars of the bike to steady himself, but it tilted with him.

Zeke and Dougie snickered. "I think he's gonna cry," said the ape-jawed boy.

"Cry like a chubby little girl," Dougie said.

Eli's legs became solid again. The world stopped swaying. He flexed his knees and the bike straightened out between his legs. A few raindrops hit the back of his hand.

Zeke's eyes went wide. "Shit," he muttered. He shifted his fingers and another lump of gravel dropped to the ground.

Eli glanced up at the gray but cloudless sky. He looked down at his hand. The raindrops were dark red.

He reached up to wipe his forehead. His eyebrow was sore and sticky. The fingers came back streaked with more red.

"Hey," said Zeke. He cleared his throat. "Hey, Eli. You okay?"

Insults, punches, tripping kids in the hall between classes, shoving them around. These things weren't pleasant, but they were accepted. Drawing blood was not. Everyone knew there were rules, even to being a bully.

Eli's body trembled. Fight or flight, his science teacher called it. Eli knew the feeling all too well.

"I'm sorry," said Zeke. "I don't think . . . I don't think it's bad as it looks."

Eli put his foot on the pedal and pushed down. The bike rolled forward, carrying him across the front of Founders House. The other pedal came up and he shoved it back down with his toes.

Zeke took a few steps. "Eli," he called out again.

Eli stood up on the pedals, pumping hard. Getting away was all that mattered, and he hated himself for running. He was halfway down the length of the Founders House when he heard Zeke shout and another cackle from Dougie.

A few minutes later he stopped pumping the pedals, wiped his eyes, and looked around. He'd followed the road up the hill and around half of downtown, almost looping himself back to Main Street. He was on Cross Road, right between the two churches. The bright-colored Catholic church was next to him, and the dark Protestant one stood kitty-corner across the street. Cross Road wasn't named after the churches, but it was a handy coincidence. It also didn't cross anything else, ending at a T intersection on either end.

His eyelid was sticky, but the wetness on his hand wiped some of it clean. He rubbed his fingers on his jeans and left a dark stain only a mother would see. Some spit in his palm helped wipe off some more.

Eli looked up at the Catholic church. Its doors were big and solid wood, but he knew there was a back door to the cellar that had a panel of glass in it. The sun was already near the trees, so he'd be able to get a good reflection and wipe more blood off his face. If he was lucky, he'd be able to pass it off as a random bike injury. High school was complicated enough for a freshman fat kid without his mother making phone calls and accusations.

"Pissbucket!"

The shout made him cringe. Zeke had decided a little blood wasn't anything to worry about after all, and probably had a pocket full of stones. But the moment slipped away and Eli's breath eased. It hadn't been Zeke's voice. Or Dougie's. A clang of metal followed the shout.

Eli scooted his bike forward, past the line of shrubs, to peer into the

Protestant parking lot. In the back, half hidden in the shadows, was an old car. Eli saw a slim figure standing behind it shaking a hand in the universal gesture for unexpected pain.

Something rolled over in Eli's memories and stretched for a moment. He forgot his wounded eyebrow and Zeke and his mother. His foot pushed down and the bike rolled across the street. Another crank of the pedals carried him into the parking lot.

He remembered seeing a filmstrip on cars like this in history class, one about Henry Ford and assembly-line factories. This car was dark blue, with fenders that wrapped around the spoked wheels. The front seemed to be all chrome, and the round headlights were ringed with polished metal. A red plastic fuel can was strapped to the back, larger than the emergency ones the gas station sold. Panels of dark-blue metal had been stacked on top of the hood.

The older boy stood about five foot ten and thin. He had a soft face with green eyes and a small chin. His blond hair curled on the sides, and a loose ponytail with three ties in it slipped over his shoulder when he looked down at the engine. A collarless shirt hung on him, with a blue vest draped over that. The teen took a few steps away from the car, held a piece of metal up in the sunlight, and gave Eli a view of baggy black pants. The sort of Revolutionary period costume some people dressed up in for holiday parades, except these looked . . . real. The fabric was heavier, and the clothes looked worn-in.

A pair of cowboy belts crisscrossed over the boy's hips. Or maybe it was one elaborate belt. A holster hung on each thigh, just below the waist, and gleaming black steel spilled out of the top of each one.

The older boy's eyes flitted from the square plate to Eli. "Are you okay?" he asked. His voice made the warm thing in Eli's memories stretch again. "Were you in a fight?"

"Sort of," said Eli. He dropped the kickstand on his bike and took a few steps toward the car.

The teenager lowered the metal plate and worked something long and white back and forth along the edge. Tiny bristles scoured the coarse surface. "How do you sort of get in a fight?" asked the older boy. He lifted the toothbrush from the plate and blew some dust away.

"Do I know you?"

The teenager eyed the metal square and pursed his lips like someone working up to an unpleasant kiss. "My father always said it's rude to answer a question with a question."

"I'm Eli Teague." The memories yawned and threw back the blankets. The scent of phantom urine tickled Eli's nose. He coughed it away. "Is your name Harry?"

The older boy raised an eyebrow. "I guess you do know me." He tucked the toothbrush into his belt and hefted a bulky object from the passenger's seat. It looked like two cans stuck together. "So, how do you 'sort of' get in a fight?"

"He threw a rock at me," said Eli.

Harry cradled the football-sized thing in his arm. "You didn't get out of the way?"

"I wasn't ready. He usually punches me in the arm. Or pinches my belly."

The other boy grunted.

Eli watched, then cleared his throat. "What is that thing?"

"This, young Master Teague," said Harry, "is one of the miracles of the twentieth century." He lined up the piece of metal and pushed it down into the larger shape. "It's a modified Garrett carburetor. I had some of the plates replaced with superconductive material to improve the electrolysis rate, but impurities build up and they need to get polished every few thousand miles or so." The plate clicked into place and Harry sealed the metal shape closed.

Eli nodded in a slow, thoughtful way.

"You have no idea what that means, do you?"

"Yeah, I do," Eli insisted.

"No, you don't." Harry crouched down on his side of the car. "It's okay. A few years ago I didn't know what it all meant either."

Eli stepped closer and glanced at the exposed engine. Rather than leaning back toward the windshield, one whole side of the hood folded up and over the center line, becoming the stack of metal he'd seen from the other side. Harry leaned forward into the engine compartment, and Eli found himself looking along the engine and down the older teen's shirt.

While Eli wasn't an experienced boy, by any means, he'd been studying his female classmates' swelling bodies for some time now. The sight of cleavage in Harry's shirt made Eli's breath catch and his temperature flare. They weren't as big as some he'd seen in pictures and on videotapes, but those were definitely boobs. Boobs unhindered by a bra. As the older teen lowered the carburetor into position, there was even a quick flash of dark nipple.

"You're a girl," he squeaked, feeling both ashamed and excited.

Harry looked up and followed his eye line. She shook her head and pushed her shirt closed with her free hand. "Don't be rude, Master Teague. We've only just met."

One finger came free of the shirt and twirled in the air. Eli stared at it for a moment, baffled. Then he turned around.

He heard a rustle of cloth and a mutter. "Okay," said Harry, "you can turn around."

He did. She'd turned her vest around backward. It sat on her like a high-necked apron, hiding any other glimpses from Eli's eyes.

"If you're going to stand here," she said, leaning back into the engine compartment, "you can at least earn that little show you just had. Grab a crescent wrench." She waved at the passenger seat.

Eli looked through the car and saw a battered toolbox. He jogged around the car, rooted through the tools, and came up with a rusted wrench that looked like it might have been last used during World War II. He dragged his thumb across it and the wrench unscrewed by a quarter inch.

"Any day now," said Harry.

"Sorry." He walked over and held up the wrench.

"Good." She slid a bolt home through one of the carburetor's edges and twisted a washer and a nut over the end. "Put it on the nut under this while I tighten this down."

Eli squeezed in and reached over the front fender. He got the wrench over the little hex and tightened it. The engine compartment smelled very clean. "Okay," he said.

Harry's wrist whipped back and forth. Her own wrench grabbed the bolt, twisted it, let go, and grabbed it again. Eli felt the nut shift and tighten itself against the washer. "Next one's a little harder," she told him. The bolt slid through on the other side of the pipe, next to the engine itself. He stretched his arm around and realized he was pressed up against Harry. He could feel her body through the clothes between them.

Eli got his wrench on the nut and tried very hard to think of all the issues of *Amazing Spider-Man* he needed to complete his collection. When Harry leaned forward and shifted her leg, rubbing it against his, he began listing members of the Teen Titans and the X-Men. Her wrist moved again, the nut and bolt snuggled together, and the carburetor settled into position.

She held out her hand for the wrench. "I can get the last ones myself."

"I can help," he said.

"Better if I do it myself," she said.

Eli handed over the wrench.

"Besides," she added, "I think you might pass out if we bump hips again."

His cheeks heated up. He stepped back.

A rattle of metal on metal echoed out of the engine compartment, and a minute later Harry straightened up. She tossed the wrenches into the box with a clang. Now that he knew what to look for, Eli could see her hips shift and the way her clothes hung on her. Not just a girl, but a grown-up woman.

"Why do you call yourself Harry?" he asked. "Are you hiding from someone?"

"Harry's my name," she said, folding down the car's hood and rattling it into place. "Short for Harriet."

"Oh," said Eli.

"I never liked 'Harriet.' It always felt like a scratchy name. Kind of harsh." She lowered the other side of the hood and pointed at the hose coiled up on the side of the church. "Does that work?"

He shrugged.

Harry pulled the hose free and dragged it over to the car. She stepped up onto the running board and reached across the hood to unscrew the cap of the gas tank. The hose went in and she walked back to twist the spigot. Water spurted out around the end of the hose. A rushing noise came from the tank.

"What's that for?" Eli asked.

"Just a top-off," she said. "I've got over half a tank in the main, but my reserve's almost dry. I'd rather take the time now than wish I had when I'm getting close to a lead."

He blinked. "But what's the water for?"

"It's fuel," she said.

Eli frowned. "Cars don't run on water," he said. "That's stupid."

"I'd be careful tossing that word around, Master Teague," said Harry. "You're the one who just lost a fight with a rock."

"Cars run on gas," he insisted, "not water."

"The carburetor breaks water down into hydrogen and oxygen. The engine burns the hydrogen, the oxygen goes out the exhaust pipe." She pulled the hose free and walked around to the back of the car, making a long puddle alongside it. "Tap water's not the best. The impurities build up on the plates, like I told you before." A few twists of her fingers got the cap off the red tank and she shoved the end of the hose in deep.

"But if you really had a car that ran on water," said Eli, "you'd be rich. A millionaire. Everybody would buy one."

Harry shrugged and rapped her knuckles on the red tank. It was a hollow sound.

"Are you rich?" he asked.

She shook her head. "I believe I've got forty dollars to my name," she said, tugging off her backward vest, "and fifteen of that's in Confederate bills. Why would you think I'm rich?"

"Because of how you dress," he said. "Rich people can dress however they want because they've got money. They're not weird, they're eccentric."

She slid her arms through the vest and shrugged it over her shoulders. "Big word for a young man."

"I read a lot."

Harry rapped the tank again and this time it was a dull thunk. She dragged the hose out and spun the cap back on. She pulled the gushing hose back to the church and shut it off. "Well," she said, coiling it against the wall, "it's been pleasant, Eli Teague, but the road beckons. I must be on my way."

"Where?"

"There's a little ghost town out in Arizona called Jerome," she said. "I need to get out there before the copper mine closes so I can talk to a man about a dream."

Eli mulled this over. "But if it's a ghost town," he said, "doesn't that mean the mine's already closed?"

"Which," Harry said, walking back to the car, "is why I need to get there before it closes." She flipped a few switches on the dashboard. The engine started up, purring like a content cat. Harry walked back to the driver's side, pulled her coat off the seatback, and spun it onto her arms. It wrapped around her and hung down almost to her knees.

Eli's heart pounded in his chest. He took a step toward the car as she settled into the seat. "Why do you need to talk to a man about his dream?"

She looked at him. How did he ever think she was a boy? "It's not his dream I'm looking for," she explained.

"What's that mean?"

"It means goodbye, Master Teague."

He tried to think of something that might stop her. Instead he blurted out, "Will I ever see you again?"

Harry took her hands off the steering wheel. "How adorable," she said. She pulled him in and pinched his cheek, the one away from his sticky eyebrow. "It was nice talking with you."

She let him go and he took a step back. Her feet shifted and the car rolled backward away from the church. It curved around, pointing itself at the street, and started forward. The exhaust smelled fresh and clean.

"So will I see you again?" he called out.

"It's a big country," Harry said. "Anything's possible." She gave him a wave as the car turned out of the parking lot and onto Cross Road. The purr of the engine became a low rumble and the car raced away.

By the time Eli ran across the parking lot to the street, the old car was gone.

3

Eli was twenty-nine the third time he met Harry.

He'd finally had his growth spurt and ended up very close to six feet tall, which had spread out his weight and almost made him skinny. Despite his mother's worries, he'd gone to college for computers and minored in history—two fields she couldn't see anyone making real money in. It turned out she was right and he'd ended up living above a garage two streets from the house where he grew up. It was too hot in the summer and very cold in the winter. He drove two towns over every day to do IT work for the local Stahlbank branch and manage their network, which amounted to monotonous busywork nine days out of ten.

The Tuesday evening they met started as a long-overdue night with his friends. Neither of the bars in Sanders had a big-screen TV, Corey's latest guideline for a good hangout. Plus Josh had been living in downtown Dover for three months now, and compared to Sanders it was a sprawling technological metropolis. So Corey and Robin picked up Eli. He sat in the back of their Honda and they sang the songs on the radio and met up with Josh at his new place.

As they all walked down the sidewalk, Robin pulled her arm free from Corey's and pointed at a car across the street. "What's that?" she asked Eli.

He glanced over. "That," he said, "is a 1978 Chrysler Newport. Serious gas guzzler."

"You'll never stump him," said Corey.

"I will," she said. "Someday."

"Not on cars."

They found a bar that met with Corey's approval and began to drink. Josh told them more stories of his miraculous life after Sanders and pushed them all to join him. Robin and Corey said no, as usual. They'd bought the Emporium, building and all, and lived in a spacious apartment above the video store.

"Why aren't you living here?" Josh asked Eli, turning from the couple. "You're heading this way for work every day anyway, right?"

Eli nodded and shrugged. His computer degree was worthless in Sanders. Every business in town was still working with cash registers and calculators. It was almost a thirty-minute commute each way. But it was home.

"Just admit why you're not moving," Robin said. "Things are finally getting serious between you and Nicole."

Eli coughed. "That's definitely not it."

"She still trying to get that festival going?" asked Josh.

"Tried and failed," said Eli. "Couldn't get anyone to back the idea of a film festival at a one-screen, second-run theater. It just sounds too small-town."

"It is small-town," said Corey.

"So nothing between you, still?" said Robin.

Eli shook his head. "Nothing worth talking about."

"Dammit," she said. "We need better friends. I want to go on a double date." She mock-glared at Josh.

"Don't look at me," he said. "The only guys worth dating around here are all straight." He lifted one finger off his drink to point at Eli. "Speaking of which, there's an apartment open in my building. Two floors up. Even better view than my place."

Eli responded by ordering onion rings. Dover might have cable television, cell-phone towers, and actual computers, but Sanders was home. He said so and they all mocked him.

They helped Eli eat his onion rings and then a plate of jalapeño poppers that Robin called bland even though they made Josh gasp. Another round was ordered, but Corey had a ginger ale since he was driving. After finishing her drink, Robin pointed out women for Eli and men for Josh, but both of them laughed off her efforts. Josh and Robin risked some dangerous-looking shots the bartender offered them, but Eli chickened out.

And then watches were checked, jobs were mentioned, and the

night was over. They walked Josh back to his brick-building loft and exchanged hugs. Eli and Corey guided Robin back to the car and they headed for home. Twenty minutes later the car shot past the plywood sign welcoming them to Sanders and imploring them to enjoy their stay.

"Home again, home again," Corey sang.

"Watch out for Zeke," said Eli.

Corey lifted his foot and the car slowed down. Just past the sign they saw the patrol car sitting by the side of the road. The radar gun gleamed in the moonlight. Behind the wheel, Zeke Miller's head turned to watch them pass.

"And a perfect end to the night is narrowly avoided," Eli said.

"I only had one drink," said Corey. "It's fine."

"He'd make you take the Breathalyzer at least five times. Just to be sure."

"Yeah, he probably would."

"He's a jerk," muttered Robin without opening her eyes. "You know he grabbed my boobs at graduation?"

"We all know, hon," said Corey.

"He's a jerk," she repeated, but quieter. Then she perked up in her seat. "Oh, what's that one, Eli? Looks really old."

He straightened up in the back seat. The dark-colored car was almost invisible on the side of the road. Eli caught a quick glimpse of a jack holding up the passenger rear side, lit up by a flashlight beam, and a red fuel can sitting on the ground behind the car.

"Is that a Model T?" said Corey.

Robin whacked him on the arm. "He's supposed to get it."

"Model A, business coupe," Eli said. "Nineteen twenty-nine. Stop the car."

"What?"

His head twisted back again. The old Ford had already vanished into the night behind them. "Stop the car!" he yelled.

"Jeez, man, calm down."

Corey pulled the Honda over. Eli reached around Robin to open the door and squeezed out. "I'll see you later."

"What the hell's going on?"

"I'm sorry I tried to set you up with that woman at the bar," Robin said.

"It's okay," Eli told her. "I'm just going to go check on the car back there, see if they need any help."

Corey looked over his shoulder. "I can back up. It's not that far."

Eli shook his head. "Don't worry about it."

"How will you get home?" asked Robin.

"I'll walk. It's a nice night."

"It's about four miles back to your place," said Corey with a wave down the road. "Are you sure?"

"I'll be fine." He patted the roof of the Honda. "I'll give you a call tomorrow."

Robin gave him an awkward hug through the window and he bumped knuckles with Corey. Then the Honda rolled back onto the road and sped away. Eli watched the taillights fade and wondered if he was doing something very stupid.

He turned and walked back along the shoulder. His heart thumped against his ribs. Despite the early October air, he felt warm. A cloud of steam formed in front of him as he let out a deep breath and sucked in another one. An October night, but his skin tingled like Christmas morning when he was eight.

The tall shape of the Model A appeared out of the night. The round eyes of the headlights stared at him, and beneath them the two straight bars of the bumper made a flat mouth. A few more steps and he could see the details of the radiator and the undercarriage. There were after-market suspension pieces by the wheels. The passenger door was open, and he could see someone moving beyond it.

Two steps to the left let him see around the door. Behind it stood a tall woman, about his age, dressed in dark corduroy pants and a blue frock coat. Her blond hair was half-hidden by a tricorn hat, but the loose ponytail still hung down her back.

A wire-spoked wheel with a sagging tire lay on the ground near the foot of an old-fashioned jack that held up the back end of the car. The woman was trying to wrestle with the replacement tire while holding a flashlight under her arm. A long pole leaned against the Model A, right by its oval rear window.

Eli took another step forward. "Hello."

The tire dropped. The woman lunged at the pole and whirled. It swung up and Eli realized it was an old flintlock rifle. The weapon almost vanished in the flare of the flashlight. She held it under the barrel like a soldier or SWAT officer.

"Consarn it," she said. The flashlight beam went to his chest, the rifle continued down to the ground. "You just scared the life out of me."

"I could say the same thing," he coughed. He'd pictured this moment a few hundred times and ways. None of them had begun with her shooting him in the head like a B-movie zombie.

She raised the flashlight. "Wait a minute," she said, studying his face. "Are you . . . ?"

He smiled.

The light dipped down again. "Eli Teague," she said. "What a fine man you turned into."

"It's good to see you too, Harry."

"Twice in as many months," she said, leaning the rifle back against the car. "Are you following me?"

"I don't think so."

"It'd be quite impressive if you were."

"Maybe a little," said Eli. "For a while I wasn't sure you were real."

"Why not?"

"Well . . . the last time we met I'd just suffered a head injury. It makes you question things."

She snorted. "Be a gentleman and come help me with this wheel, Mr. Teague."

Eli gazed at her as she reached for the spare. The old clothes. The blond hair. The hazel eyes. "You look almost exactly the same," he said. "Just how I remember you."

"It hasn't been that long for me."

He gestured at the low loops around her neck. "I like your scarf."

"I have to wear it," Harry said. She waved her hand at the night. "You might not believe it, but this town's infested with lecherous little boys trying to take advantage of a young woman's virtue."

He bit his lip. "Sorry."

She pointed at the tire. "Lift it into place, please."

Eli heaved the old wheel up. It was heavier than modern cars had led him to expect. He worked it in place while she picked up an old lug wrench.

She fitted the wrench over the first lug nut and spun it. "So, Mr.

Teague," she asked, finishing the nut, "what have you been up to? It's been, what, twelve years for you?"

"Almost sixteen." He shrugged as best he could while holding the tire. "I don't know. Grew up. Went to school. Got a job."

"Doing what?"

"I do IT work at a bank. Mostly it's just keeping their computer network up when one of them downloads a virus or something." He saw her staring and cleared his throat. "A computer's sort of an adding machine that runs on electricity. It can—"

"I know what a computer is, Mr. Teague." She twisted another nut into position. "I'm not an idiot."

"Sorry."

"Married?"

"What? No."

"Why not?"

"I'm only twenty-nine," he said.

"Twenty-nine," she echoed. She spun the third nut with her wrench. "So, not married. Why not?"

"I told you. I'm only twenty-nine. And I'm not even seeing anyone right now."

He thought of Nicole as he said it. They'd been hooking up in the Sanders Cinema at least once a week for three months now. Usually on Thursdays when she stayed late to set up the new films. Nicole was only the fourth person he'd had sex with, fifth if one used a generous definition of what counted as sex. But Eli had enough experience to know the difference between sex and love. It was convenient for both of them. There wasn't anything to it past that.

Neither of them wanted more than that from each other.

"My parents were married at eighteen," Harry said, working on the last lug nut. "Well, father was eighteen, mother was sixteen."

"That's young," said Eli.

"It's old in most parts of the world," she said, "even today. So what are you waiting for?"

"You," Eli said. The word popped out without any thought from him. It hung in the air for a moment before settling.

Her eyebrows went up, but her eyes looked sad. "Me?"

Eli scooped up the damaged tire and carried it to the back of the car. He pushed it onto the small arm that extended up over the rear bumper, and stood there while Harry lowered the jack. The car settled on the ground.

A minute later she walked around and set the jack in the trunk. She went away, then came back with the toolbox. It joined the jack. She closed the trunk, cleared her throat. "I think you were confessing something, Mr. Teague."

"I just . . ." His cheeks burned. "Yeah, okay, I've been kind of obsessed. You appeared out of nowhere when I was a kid and everything about you was just so . . . cool."

"Cool?"

"Neat. Interesting."

"I see."

"Like that. You know about computers but you don't know what 'cool' means. You dress like you're from the late 1700s, drive a classic Model A, and you've got fifteen dollars in Confederate bills."

"Only three now, I'm afraid," said Harry, "but the rest went to a good cause."

"Who are you?"

"I told you." She wiped her hands off on the frock coat. "I'm Harriet. My friends call me Harry."

"Are you just going to drive off again?"

"It's what I do." She walked back to the passenger side, leaned into the car, and flipped a pair of switches on the dash.

"Stay," said Eli.

"Beg your pardon?"

He nodded over his shoulder. "You could stay in town for a day or two, before you take off again. We could . . . I don't know. I could show you around. I have a million questions I want to ask you." He shook his head. "I studied history, cars, anything I could think of that might give me a hint who you are."

"A tempting offer, Mr. Teague. Very tempting." She sighed and looked away. "Unfortunately, one that must be declined at this time."

"Why?"

"Because I'm looking for something. And I'm not the only one looking. And I don't think the others can be convinced to take a few days off just because I might want to."

He rolled the words back and forth in his mind. "So this is some sort of contest?"

"More of a treasure hunt."

He set his hand on the passenger door. "Do you need help?"

"Inviting yourself along, are you?"

"No," he said. "Maybe. I've just been hoping for years that you'd show up again. I don't want it to be over in less than half an hour."

She gazed at him for a moment. Her right hand came up, then settled back at her side. "I'm sorry," she said. "I've already lost one partner. Not again."

"Ahhh," said Eli. "I didn't know."

"How could you?" She patted the car. "Anyway, I must be off. I've got to be in Boston on Friday."

"What's in Boston?"

"Quincy Market. Someone's going to be there at noon selling information. I need to buy it."

"For the treasure hunt," he said.

"Something like that."

"That you don't need help with."

"Again, sorry."

"And that you're carefully not telling me anything about."

One side of her mouth twitched up, just for a second. "It's safer for you if you don't know."

"Well, it shouldn't be too hard," he said. "If worse came to worst, you could probably walk to Boston in three days."

"I don't have three days," she said. "I've only got two hours."

"You just said you've got until Friday."

"I've got to be there on Friday, but I've only got two hours to get there."

"I . . . you lost me."

"Again, it's safer for you that way." Harry reached into the car and flipped a few switches. The engine rumbled to life. She kicked at the dirt with her shoe. "I wish things could be different, Mr. Teague."

"So do I," said Eli.

"You seem very nice and clever, and you're very handsome. I think it could be pleasant, getting to know you better." She gestured at the purring Model A. "But this is a dangerous quest I'm on, and I won't risk anyone else's life."

"Quest?"

Harry stepped closer. She was a good height, just an inch or so shorter than him. Her hands settled against his chest. She leaned in close, her lips brushed his cheek, and warm air flowed across his ear.

"Goodbye, Eli Teague."

She shoved him. He stumbled on the soft shoulder, grabbed at the air, and fell on his ass. He looked up and she was already in the driver's seat, taking the wheel in her hands.

Eli crawled back to his feet as the Model A rolled onto the pavement and made a tight turn, heading back out of Sanders. His stomach churned as the car pulled away, but he raised his hand to wave farewell. Harry waved back, and then she vanished into the night.

4

Eli had been back from lunch for an hour, trying to reconstruct the inventive new method one of the tellers had used to freeze half the bank's terminals. He yawned, still tired from a long walk home the night before. And very little sleep once he got there. He'd spent most of the night staring out the window at the road in front of his garage apartment, hoping to see the 1929 Model A business coupe drive by. Or stop.

He readjusted himself after the yawn. One and a half walls of the bank were all glass, and his cubicle had him with his back to the expansive window. Moving to block the afternoon sun from his monitor had become an unconscious habit over the years.

The freeze probably wasn't that difficult. It just wasn't as interesting as Harry's warm breath on his ear. Or the many possible things she could've done with twelve Confederate dollars that would count as a good cause.

Then a new shadow fell across Eli's cubicle and knocked him out of his memories. "Truss is in town," Bill hissed.

Eli's eyes went wide and any lingering happy memories fled. "What?"

Archibald Truss—never, ever referred to as Archie—owned Stahl-bank. Eighty-something branches in the United States, nineteen in Canada, more than a hundred in Europe, and three in Japan. He also owned a movie studio, a toy manufacturer, and large percentages of several car and computer companies. He liked to travel around and check on his different holdings.

Sometimes people knew he was coming. Often they didn't. He'd dropped in on their branch twice in the two and a half years Eli had worked there. Each time had resulted in someone being fired. The first time it had been the old branch manager.

"Sheila saw him having lunch over at that little bistro place," said Bill. "He was just getting his food when she saw him."

"And she's sure it was him?"

The assistant manager's head bobbed up and down, a shadow against the bank's big windows. "His Caddy was out front."

"Dammit."

"Get it running," Bill said, pointing at the computer. "We can't have the network down if he stops by."

"I can't just turn it on," said Eli, soaking up some of Bill's panic. "I'm still trying to figure out what happened."

"Then just make it look like it's on. Get to it."

Eli blinked the sunlight from his eyes and spent fifteen panicked minutes scrolling through code before he spotted the loop. Simple, like he'd thought all along. A million-to-one mistake. A minute of typing undid the freeze and left a flag so he could find the snippet of bad code later. For now, he just wanted to have things working so he could have a sliver of job security.

Someone cleared their throat behind him.

He turned around, expecting to see Bill or maybe a customer who was looking for someone to talk about loans. Instead he choked on the breath he'd taken in and took a moment to let it wheeze out. He used the moment to decide if he was expected to stand or stay seated.

"For Christ's sake," grumbled Truss.

The old man would've been well over six feet tall, but age had hunched his back and put his head even with his shoulders. His bushy eyebrows were the only hair on his skull, and his teeth were too perfect to go with his leathery lips. He looked like a vulture wearing dentures. If the vulture had rectangular glasses and a good tailor.

His two personal assistants-slash-valets-slash-bodyguards flanked him. The one with the bright-red, chopped hair, Svetlana, had a dark suit and a tie that did not go well with her complexion. She stood three inches taller than Eli and at least fifty pounds heavier. Rumor was she'd been some kind of Russian bodybuilder before coming to work for Truss. The one everyone called Helena had sharp cheekbones and curly blond hair she kept tied back in an almost-topknot. Today she wore a pinstriped blazer with a gray turtleneck that showed her lean figure. Eli knew for a brief time people thought she might be a trophy wife, but the speculation had died quickly. Probably because nobody liked the idea of Truss having sex with someone a third his age and even vaguely attractive.

Much like their ambiguous job descriptions, Eli had never been clear if Svetlana and Helena were actual names, nicknames, or if they even knew this was how people referred to them. He thought Helena might be a reference to something, the way some people snickered about it, but he didn't know what.

Truss glared at him over the rectangular glasses. "You're the computer guy, I take it?"

"Yes, sir," he said. After a moment he added, "Eli Teague, sir."

"Are you one of those bootlickers who's going to say 'sir' after every sentence, Teak?"

Eli managed to bite off the correction forming in his mouth. "No," he said. "Not at all."

The corners of the old billionaire's mouth moved up. "Bigger stones than your district manager," he muttered. "Are we safe from the government?"

Eli blinked. "Sorry?"

"The government. My lawyers say they're looking into everyone's computers now. Can they get into this one?"

"Ahhh, well," said Eli, "I can't really say. I'm only in charge of this part of the network."

"Blaming someone else?"

"No, si—Mr. Truss," said Eli. "I'm in charge of the in-house network, yeah, but that's still linked to the bank's larger, international network. Asking me if it's secure is like putting me in charge of one window of your house and asking if the house is secure."

The old man's bushy eyebrows tensed and relaxed. "Go on."

Eli fiddled with his hands for a moment, trying to build a better metaphor, and decided to stick with the one he had. "I can tell you this window's closed and locked," he said, "or if I see or hear anyone in the house from where I'm standing, but that's about it. Security depends on knowing what state all the windows are in." He gestured at the wall of glass behind the old man. "It only takes one to be open for someone to get in."

"If they happen to look at the right window," said Truss.

"Right," said Eli. "Exactly. But there are so many windows that get opened and closed every day, anyone who's determined could eventually get in. The only person who can answer your question is whoever's in charge of your whole computer network, and even they can only give you a best-case scenario."

Truss crossed his arms. "You seem pretty sure of that, Teak."

"I'm just a realist," said Eli. "There's no such thing as a perfect system. They've all got flaws somewhere."

"Even mine?"

Eli had a quick debate in his mind about the scrap of code he'd found and whether he should mention it. "Probably," he said, not pushing his luck.

Truss stared at him, like a snake hypnotizing a rodent.

"Good to see there's someone here with a spine," the old man muttered. He turned and shuffled away as abruptly as he'd appeared. The two women stepped out of his way, shot Eli a synchronized icy stare, and followed their employer.

Eli stood up to watch them go. Half a dozen other heads poked up from cubicles. Half of them watched the old man's progress, the others stared at Eli. Their eyes sparkled with curiosity. Was he about to clean out his cubicle? Was he their new boss?

He shook his head and gave them what he hoped looked like a confident nod that said everything was going to be fine.

The lights flickered twice, went out, and a loud clack echoed across the office. Every computer screen in sight went black. Eli cringed. He couldn't remember if he'd saved his flag with the line of bad code. After the encounter with Truss, he couldn't even remember where he'd found it.

The customers and employees were already grumbling. The two women guided Mr. Truss toward the front door, keeping him hidden between them. They made it look like they were saving the president. A man stepped into their path and Svetlana shoved him away with her thick forearm.

Eli glanced over his shoulder and watched Truss head out to his car, a 1940 Cadillac Sixty Special. The Imperial Sedan model, in oxblood maroon. The kind of car movie stars got chauffeured around in during the glory days of Hollywood. Expensive then, even more expensive now. Rumor was the old man had one on each coast.

He turned, dropped back into his chair, and listened for the hum of computers waking themselves back up. There wasn't much he could do for the next ten minutes. The OS at the bank desperately needed an overhaul. Once it was up, assuming there weren't any more pressing issues, he'd try to dig up any transactions that might have been caught in the brown-out and—

"Hello."

Eli glanced over his shoulder as the shadow fell across him. He yelped, kicked at the floor, and rolled back in his chair to bump against the desk. "Jesus," Eli muttered. "You scared the crap out of me."

The big man didn't move. He loomed in the cubicle entrance, taller and broader than the redheaded amazon employed by Truss. The light from the windows behind him made him little more than a dark shadow in the bank. A void lurked beneath the brim of his fedora, with only a faint gleam along the edge of his cheeks to show anything solid was there.

The man wore an old suit with lines that made Eli think of pictures of his grandfather from the 1950s. An immaculate outfit with perfect dry-cleaning creases in it, but at least half a century out of date even to Eli's untrained eye.

"Can I help you?" he asked when the man didn't speak.

One of the arms came up. It held a long, thin notepad. "Are you," asked the man, consulting the pad, "Elias Teague?"

"Yeah," he said. "Yeah, that's me. Can I help you with something?"

The shadow checked his notebook again, then lifted the page to glance at the one below it. The movement seemed very rehearsed to Eli, part of a performance the man had given many times. "We're investigating a crime," the shadow said. His other hand came up with a square that fell open to reveal a badge. With the light behind it, Eli just saw a flash of silver and the letters U and S before the man flipped it closed and dropped it into a coat pocket. "I spoke earlier with two of your friends, Cordell and Robin Furber. They said the three of you were driving into town last night around ten thirty when you decided to get out and walk. Is that correct?"

Eli took a slow, deep breath. "More or less."

"May I ask why?"

"I just . . . I felt like walking."

The government man said nothing.

"They were going to drop me off," Eli explained, "but my place is kind of out of the way for them, so I just . . . I figured I'd walk."

The big man nodded slowly. "Have you noticed any unusual vehicles in the area lately?"

Eli glanced past the man and caught a glimpse of Truss's blood-red Cadillac across the parking lot, rolling out onto the street. "What do you mean unusual?"

"Something out of the ordinary," said the man. His face stayed very still while he spoke. His cheeks gleamed where the light hit them. He shifted the notebook pages again. "A classic or antique. An old Model A, for example."

Eli swallowed. The memories of shame and piss danced on the edge of his brain, but he couldn't focus on them. He felt the man's gaze on him.

"You've seen it," said the man in the suit. "Last night, perhaps?"

Another memory joined the other two. Eli felt more drops of sweat on his back. One raced down, the other sank into his shirt.

"What did she tell you?"

"Who?" Eli managed to squeak.

"The woman. Harriet Pritchard. Did she tell you where she was going?"

"I don't know what you're—"

"We know she's been to this town before. Fifteen years, eleven months ago. Did she contact you then, as well?"

The people in the front of the bank kept talking. Eli couldn't hear any voices near him. Someone opened one of the front doors, and the shifting pane of glass sent a shaft of sunlight across the bank and onto the man. The air wheezed out of Eli's lungs.

The man wore a mask. One of the transparent Halloween masks people bought as cheap, last-minute costumes. Two pink dots the size of quarters decorated the cheeks. The eyebrows and lashes were painted on, along with the lips. The molded plastic face showed a faint smile, almost a straight line.

Behind the mask, the man's eyes were closed. The eyeholes revealed two ovals of flesh behind them. The man leaned forward, aiming his face at Eli, but never opening his eyes.

Eli swallowed again as the shaft of light swung away. The memory of raw childhood fear churned in his brain. The image of the lunging car and the man with the pistol filled his mind.

"Did she contact you?" the man repeated.

Eli pushed the memories away and straightened up in his chair. "What's this about?"

The man straightened up and folded his notebook shut with one hand. "We're investigating a crime."

"What crime?"

The notebook followed the badge into a suit pocket. "I'm not at liberty to say." In the shadows beneath the hat's brim, the eyeholes of his mask looked like the empty sockets of a skull.

"Why are you questioning me?"

The man took a small step forward. He was in Eli's cubicle now. "We believe you may have information about the location of a dangerous fugitive." His face didn't move enough when he spoke to shift the mask. This close, Eli could see the man's cheeks and square jaw adjust through the clear plastic, but his mouth didn't . . .

His mouth . . .

Eli swallowed a squeak. His heart raced. Beads of sweat drew lines under his shoulder blades and down his back.

Smooth skin stretched behind the painted-on lines of the sculpted mask. The man had no lips. No mouth. No nostrils inside the transparent nose. No eyebrows or eyelashes hid beneath the ones drawn on the mask.

Nothing but blank flesh.

Wrinkles appeared on the man's brow, between the clear mask and the fedora. He took another step and grabbed Eli by the throat. His finger and thumb stretched back, shrinking Eli's windpipe and pushing into the soft spots behind the jaw. "Where is she?" he growled. Eli could hear the faint muffle to his voice, as if the man were talking through thick fabric. Or skin.

"I don't know," he whispered. "I don't. She drove off like she always does."

The empty sockets of the mask stared at him. The blank face leaned in close. "Where is she going to be?"

Eli paused and the faceless man squeezed. Pain flared behind Eli's jaw and raced through his body. He sucked in air, but the crushing hand let only a few thin wisps down into his lungs. He beat at the man's arm, tried to throw himself out of the chair, but the dark man shoved him back without any effort.

"Where?" snapped the man.

"Bosst," said Eli. Fear pushed the sounds out of his mouth.

The man relaxed his grip. "Boston?"

Eli took a deep breath. Almost a third of it squeezed through his windpipe. He gave a weak nod.

"Where in Boston?"

"She didn't say," Eli lied. "She just said Boston."

The faceless man leaned in even closer. Eli could see pores across the space where there should've been eyes. "When?" whispered the man.

Eli tried to look away and his gaze fell on the calendar pinned to the wall of his cubicle. It was a charity thing he'd bought to support a school's drama club or something. Kids a few years younger than him dressed in period New England clothes. He focused on Friday, then looked back at the man.

The man's lack of face turned to the calendar. "Friday," he said.

The faceless man released Eli's throat and straightened up. He brushed a few wrinkles out of his vintage suit. One hand went up and adjusted his tie, then his mask.

Eli filled his lungs. He could still hear voices up front. His coworkers grumbling about the computers. Bill answering questions and calming customers like a good assistant manager should.

The man pulled a small phone from his pocket. It was black and glossy with chrome trim. He pressed a button and held it up to his head. "Hello," he told the phone. "This is Fifteen. Yes, my target has been located. Yes. Thank you." The phone went back into his pocket.

"What are you going to—"

"Do not leave town," said the faceless man. "Do not attempt to contact the fugitive. If she attempts to contact you, report it immediately to your local law enforcement—it'll be transferred to us." The mask stared at him. "There will be severe consequences if you violate any of these instructions. Thank you for your cooperation." The man reached up, adjusted his tie again, and took two steps backward out of the cubicle. He turned his blank eye sockets to the group at the front of the bank, then swiveled around and took four long strides toward the emergency exit.

Eli heard the clunk of the door's release bar. No alarm went off.

He stood up and saw the faceless man lower himself into a large black car. A show-car-condition 1952 Hudson Hornet. It looked powerful and fast standing still. Like it was waiting to pounce.

The Hornet started up with a growl that shook the bank's windows. It kicked into gear, swung around, and roared out of the parking lot. Brakes squealed as it cut off half a dozen cars. One man with a little girl bellowed after the car, but it was already on the road and gone.

Eli needed to go to the bathroom. He wasn't sure if it was to piss or throw up, but either way he figured it was better to be somewhere without carpet when it happened. He marched to the tellers' gate, slid his key card, and then ran.

As it turned out, he just needed to piss, but he leaned forward and rested his forehead on the cold tile anyway. He washed up and looked at himself in the mirror. Sweat soaked his shirt. His eyes were wide. A faint bruise wrapped around his throat, just above his collar.

He looked weak.

Eli pulled his tie loose and headed back to his cubicle. He grabbed his coat and his all-but-empty briefcase and walked over to Bill. The assistant manager was readjusting the blinds. "I need the next two days off," said Eli.

"Why."

"Something's come up. It's kind of an emergency."

"What's going on?"

"I need to meet someone in Boston."

5

Eli woke up in a cheap hotel bed twice the size of his at home. The sheets were stiff, and the pillow was overstuffed, but it felt luxurious. He felt pretty sure the trip to Boston was one of the dumbest things he'd ever done, so it was good to start the day on a positive.

He checked out of the hotel by eight and the woman at the desk suggested a parking garage on State Street. He moved his car, tried not to panic too much at the garage's day rates, and walked to Faneuil Hall.

Eli's last time at Quincy Market had been almost ten years ago, just before graduating high school. The all-pedestrian area—two broad walkways north and south of the main market building—had felt very exotic and European up against his small-town experiences. It still did. He stood and stared at the brick walkways and the colored awnings and the bubble-like streetlamps as dozens of people moved around him. Most of the restaurants and shops wouldn't open for another hour, when the crowds would only get bigger.

He walked down South Market, looped around the big plaza at the end with the Gap and American Eagle stores, then headed back along North Market. He looked up at Faneuil Hall as he walked past it and started down the south side again. A few people walked out with stacks of chairs and sandwich signs.

More people drifted into the marketplace. Men, women, teenagers. A few men and women spread out blankets on the walkway that led to Commercial Street and displayed just enough wares to not be hassled for it.

Eli watched every face he passed and studied every distant coat.

A bright yellow-and-green booth, not much more than a pushcart, sat halfway down North Market. Its sign said TROLLEY TOURS. The woman inside was a few years younger than Eli, with short, colorful hair and horn-rimmed glasses. White earphones hung on each side of her head as she stared at something below the counter.

"Hi," said Eli. "This is probably a long shot, but . . . could you help me out?"

"I can try," she replied without looking up. Barely into her day and bored.

"I'm looking for someone selling . . . information."

She glanced up at him. Her mouth wrinkled. "You mean like a bookstore or something?"

"I don't think so. Maybe someone in another booth or a pushcart?"

She shook her head, shrugged, and her gaze settled back to whatever was below the counter. "There's Newbury Comics and Teeny Billboards. I think the Best of Boston store has a couple of books too."

"I don't think it's books," he said.

Her focus didn't shift back to him. "Sorry. That's all I've got."

Eli walked around the area again, then cut through the market itself. Another trolley stand sat between the Gap, some pushcarts, and three of the blanket vendors. The crowds thickened, making it harder for him to see anyone more than twenty or thirty feet away. The forest blocking his view of the trees.

It also didn't help that there were a dozen or so people in period dress wandering around Faneuil Hall by eleven o'clock. Various performers and reenactors who'd all come to the market for lunch. At least four of them wore blue frock coats. Eli leaped toward the first two, but managed to stop himself before he did anything that earned him far too much attention.

There were also a fair number of people in dark suits. Many with hats. Hats seemed to be making a comeback. His pulse surged twice as he tried to remember if the faceless man had hair or not. Both times a slight turn or shift of the head would reveal lips that moved or eyes that blinked. Eli kept watch, but felt pretty sure the faceless man would attract a lot of attention and wouldn't be able to sneak up on anyone.

By eleven thirty worry gnawed at him. It crossed his mind Harry might not even be wearing her colonial clothes. Sure, she'd worn them the times he'd met her before, but it hardly meant she wore them all the time. Would he recognize her in a leather jacket and skirt, or a UMass sweatshirt and jeans? What if her hair was down and loose? Or piled up under a floppy hat?

He brushed the thoughts aside. He'd know her. And she'd know him.

The man at Teeny Billboards had nothing for him. The woman at Newbury Comics told him about the cool new *Machine Man* graphic novel, also available in digital for the tablet Eli didn't own. The Best of Boston store, it turned out, only had books during the holiday season, but the salesman seemed pretty sure he could order one for Eli and have it within two weeks.

Eleven forty became eleven forty-five. Eli paced back and forth through the marketplace, past various shops selling coffee and Thai food and pastries and gourmet hot dogs. Another one of the reenactors passed him, a heavy man talking on a cell phone while he chewed through a bagel sandwich. His frock coat was the color of old leaves and rust.

At eleven fifty-five Eli stood at the far end of the marketplace, a hallway intersection between a Japanese restaurant and a pretzel shop. The crowd surged around him, all desperate to squeeze in as much lunchtime as possible. A shoulder bumped his. A handbag hit his hip. He stretched up on his toes and tried to see to the far end of the hall. A dozen shades of blue stood out, but none of them the one he was looking for.

He needed to look outside. North or south. He only had time for one before noon.

He picked south.

Eli marched past Victoria's Secret and Urban Outfitters and a Samsonite store. His eyes flitted from person to person. Some met his gaze. Some glared. None of them were Harry.

The old Faneuil Hall building loomed ahead. Crowds gathered to watch two different street performers. A man played pop music on an electric-blue violin. A woman passed five bowling-pin clubs back and forth through the air in a whirl of color.

Noon approached, slid past him, and vanished into the crowd.

Eli ran across to the north side of the market and speed-walked through the crowd. He passed more shops and a Tex-Mex restaurant and the trolley tours booth and countless people in a variety of outfits. He ended at the plaza. His eyes flitted down to his watch—12:07 p.m.

His feet slogged across the red bricks, and the crowd swirled around him. Tourists. College students. Lawyers and bankers on lunch break.

Eli looked at his watch again. Eleven past, now. He debated walking down South Market again. Maybe whatever transaction Harry had come for was still in progress. Maybe he just hadn't seen her on his last pass.

Maybe she'd already finished her business and was on her way.

"Hey," he said to one of the blanket salesmen. The man had half a dozen paintings spread out on the grass, the kind of generic things that graced the Stahlbank lobby and the hotel room Eli'd woken up in. "Have you been watching the crowd? I've been trying to find someone."

The man glared up from his current masterpiece. Paint covered his fingertips, and Eli realized the man wasn't using a brush. "Does it look like I've been watching the crowd?"

"I'm just asking."

The man snorted and lowered his eyes back to his painting.

"Who you looking for?" called out a seasoned voice. "Man or woman?"

A few yards away, between two benches, another salesman sat beneath a tree. A blue-and-gray baseball cap with a spider logo, smudged with years of use, shaded his eyes. A battered knapsack stretched behind him, and a small panel of slatted wood, maybe twice the size of a Help Wanted sign, balanced beneath his hand. It reminded Eli of an old window shutter, and he wasn't entirely sure that it wasn't one. A dozen necklaces and bracelets hung on the shutter, each one tagged with a little slip of white card on a string. The blanket under the man had been folded into more of a thick pad. Probably easier to scoop up too, if one of the wandering policemen approached to give him a hard time.

"Woman," said Eli. "About my age. Thin. Blond."

The salesman smiled. "Not much to go on." He looked to be in his late fifties or early sixties, with a silver beard that was long but well managed. His limbs were thin without looking unhealthy. He wore five or six layers, starting with a Celtics T-shirt and building out to a black-and-white scarf that looked Middle Eastern to Eli's inexperienced eyes. The man could've been a veteran of the first Gulf War. Maybe even the recent one. He looked like he'd been sitting there between the benches for a while.

"Last time I saw her," Eli said, to the air as much as to the man, "she was wearing colonial clothes."

The salesman grinned. "Reenactor? Woman after my own heart." His fingers slipped between the necklaces and plucked at a few silver strands hanging on his board. His free hand gestured at the crowd. "Is she just wearing a cloak or a full dress and petticoat?"

Eli pinballed between a desire not to be rude to the salesman, a mad urge to keep looking for Harry, and a swelling worry that he might be an idiot.

He took one last look out at the crowd. Older women. Younger women. Indian, black, Asian, white. Tall and short. Thin and heavy. Blond, brunette, auburn, black, one bright green, and another with nothing but dark stubble across her scalp.

None of them were Harry.

"Actually," said Eli, turning back to the salesman, "she wears a frock coat and a tricorn."

The salesman blinked. The edges of his expression shifted just enough for Eli to register it. "What color?"

"Blue," said Eli. "Classic colonial blue." He shook his head and gave the panel of jewelry a final, polite gaze. "It all looks nice. Sorry to waste your time like this."

The salesman's smile shifted a little more. The practiced, polite expression slipped away. The real one left in its place twisted closer to a smirk. "You talking about Harry?"

Air rushed through Eli's nose and into his chest. "What?"

The old man's smirk spread.

"You know her? Harry Pritchard? Is she here?"

"You just missed her. She blew through pretty quick."

"Are you sure?"

"Pretty sure. She was looking for me." He held out a hand. "Theodoric Knickerbocker."

Eli took the hand automatically and shook it. "Sorry?"

"My name," the salesman said with a tug at the brim of his cap. "For friends and the better class of acquaintances, it's just Theo. Knowing Harry bumps you right up."

"Thanks." He shifted on his feet. "So you know where she's going?"

Theo pursed his lips and leaned toward Eli. "Maybe."

Eli waited. "Well?"

"What's it worth to you?"

"Seriously?"

"I'm a businessman, kid. I don't give anything away."

"She's in danger."

"So you say. Harry can take care of herself."

They stared at each other.

Eli broke first. "How much are we talking about?"

"We all have our plans and secrets to keep," said the salesman, "and Harry won't like it if I'm giving out clues to where she's going. Trust is worth something."

"How much?"

"Let's say . . . a hundred bucks."

"That's not much to give up someone's secrets and trust."

"If it's not much, you shouldn't have any trouble paying it."

Eli thought of the parking-lot fees again and sucked in his cheeks.

"Fine." Theo sighed. "How much cash d'you have on you?"

"Sorry?"

"Cash. In your wallet and pockets. How much?"

Eli did some quick math. "About thirty dollars, I think. I could get some more if there's an ATM around here somewhere."

Theo shook his head. "Look at the jewelry, count to five, and then give me twenty-five."

"You're selling her out for twenty-five dollars?"

"I'm not selling her out, I'm just selling relevant information to a potential rival."

"I'm not her rival. I'm trying to help her."

"Well, in that case," Theo said, "I don't feel bad about selling you the information."

Eli sighed, looked at the board, and pulled out his wallet. He only had twenty-eight, it turned out. He'd need to hit the cash machine no matter what. He thought of Harry's shrinking wad of Confederate currency. "Is this how much she paid?"

"Harry's a longtime customer and a friend. She gets special rates."

Eli plucked a handful of bills from his wallet and held them out. Theo extended two long fingers, clamped them across the bills, and folded the cash back into his palm. The hand vanished into his pocket, then reappeared with the fingers spread wide. He reached across to the board and his fingers danced through the array of necklaces and bracelets. He selected a bracelet, glanced up at Eli, then moved on to the next one. A quick twist of his wrist freed it and he held it up.

"Is this some sort of clue?" asked Eli, taking the bracelet. Small gears of brass and steel dangled from it like charms. "Is it a signal for someone?"

"No, it's a cheap bracelet," said the salesman. "If I don't give you something off the board, the cop over there is going to think I slipped you a dime bag or something. They'll leave street vendors alone if we don't give them a reason to bother us."

"Oh."

"You got a car?"

Eli gestured toward the distant parking garage. "A couple blocks away, yeah."

"You should be able to catch her, then. She's headed out to the left coast. Pasadena."

Eli sifted through the hundreds of city names in his head. "Pasadena . . . California? Where they do the Rose Bowl?"

"That's the one."

"On the other side of the country?"

"That's what all the maps say, yeah. She's going to be there on Wednesday next week, four thirty-two in the afternoon." Theo looked at his watch. "That's almost exactly five days from now, with the time change. After that, though . . ." He shrugged. "Who knows where she's headed from there."

"So, where in Pasadena is she going?"

"She'll be at the fork in the road."

Eli waited for more information. "Could you . . . maybe be a bit more specific?"

"What, like an address or something?"

"Yeah, or at least a cross-street or something."

"I don't know. Go to Pasadena and ask somebody."

"Ask them . . . where the fork in the road is?"

"Yeah. What am I, a tour guide?"

Eli switched tactics. "What's she looking for?"

Theo's smirk melted into a frown. "You've got no idea what's going on, do you? You're just chasing her because she smiled at you the right way."

"What?" His tongue stumbled against his teeth. "No, no, no."

"It's okay. You wouldn't be the first young man smitten with her. Although I've never seen one go this far."

"Smitten?"

The smirk returned. "Have the hots for her, dumbass."

"Well, no. I mean, she's hot, yeah, but I'm just . . . I just wanted to warn her."

"Warn her?"

"Yeah. There's a . . . a guy after her. A creepy guy."

The old man smirked and raised a brow. "At least you're honest."

"What? No, not me. I mean, I'm just here to warn her about him. The man with . . ."

"Man with what?"

"You wouldn't believe me."

"Kid, if we both trotted out all the things we'd seen that the other wouldn't believe, I'd bet a million bucks I'd win by a wide margin. What'd this guy have that got you so spooked?"

Eli studied the man for a moment, then shrugged. "It's not something he had. It's what he didn't have that freaked me out."

"Okay, I'll bite. What didn't he have?" The last words slipped from the man's weathered lips and took some of his confidence with them. Realization and worry settled across his brows.

An echo of the expression twisted in Eli's stomach. "This is going to sound freaky and impossible," he said, "but this guy didn't have a—"

"A face," finished the old vendor. He glanced over at the finger-painter. "He was wearing a plastic mask over a smooth face."

Eli stared at the old man, and then he spewed out two days' worth of fear and confusion. "I saw him on Wednesday, but I saw him once before, when I was a little kid. He drove past me on the road when I was on my bike."

A whistle slipped out of Theo's lips. "Bet that gave you nightmares for a while."

"Sort of. For a while. I think I convinced myself it wasn't real, even after I met Harry again."

The old salesman nodded. "You wouldn't be the first."

A shiver shook Eli, and it took him a moment to realize his body had just relaxed. Tension he didn't even know he'd been carrying slipped away and left him feeling . . . free. Reassured. "Seeing him just brought back all these childhood memories. I think . . . I almost wet my pants."

"Again," Theo said with a smirk, "you wouldn't be the first."

"And his voice was just awful. I thought it was the mask, but then I realized it was his skin muffling—what is he? How can he talk with no mouth? Or breathe? Or see?!"

"You heard his voice?" Theo shuddered. "How close were you?"

"He was right there in my cubicle with me," Eli said. "He was asking me about Harry and standing closer to me than you are. He had me kind of blocked in my chair, and then he—"

"Wait," said Theo, holding up a hand. "You talked to him?"

"Yeah."

"An actual conversation?"

The term threw Eli for a moment. "He sort of . . . he asked me about Harry. Interrogated me, I guess. I didn't really tell him anything, but that's how I knew she was in trouble."

"He talked to you," Theo said, considering the words as they slid out of his throat.

"Talked to me. Threatened me. Choked me." The memory of strong fingers prickled the skin of Eli's neck.

Theo dropped the board of jewelry onto the blanket. The pieces jangled against one another. "You stupid rookie," he growled. He rolled off the blanket, grabbed its edges, and tossed them one across the other, folding it around the display board. The finger-painter looked up from his masterpiece.

"What's wrong?"

"Think about it, kid," Theo said. He looped a string of knotted shoelaces around the blanket and pulled it into a tight bundle. "He asked you about Harry, let you go, and you came running straight here. That sound like a smart move on your part? You ever seen a god-damned movie?"

The cool air slipped into Eli's collar and down his back. "I . . . I wanted to help."

"You want to help?" Theo threw his knapsack over one shoulder and shoved the bundle under the other arm. "Get the hell away from me. Managed to stay under the radar for forty years, and now you blaze a trail straight to my . . . Goddammit."

His gaze slid from Eli's face to lock on something behind him.

Eli turned.

The faceless man stood halfway down the market, taller than most of the crowd. His hat added a few more inches even as it shadowed his blank skull from the midday sun. Eli could see a gleam of plastic wrapped across the space where the man's eyes should've been.

No one reacted to the clear mask or the smooth skin beneath it.

Theo's free hand grabbed Eli's wrist and yanked. The salesman ran past the finger-painter, across the plaza, dragging Eli until the younger man's feet started to catch up. They pushed past shoppers and lunch-goers and random wanderers.

"Move," snarled Theo. "We've gotta get out of his range."

"Hello, Mr. Knickerbocker," bellowed the faceless man. "And Mr. Teague. If you could both please remain where you are, it would be ap-preciated! Don't attempt to escape!"

Eli shook free of Theo's grip. Theo didn't hesitate, adjusting his bundles and diving between a man and woman in sharp overcoats. He didn't look back to see if Eli followed him.

Eli followed him. He sidestepped quickly around the couple, push-ing the man aside as gently as possible. "Sorry," he called back over his shoulder.

As his head turned, people shrieked behind him. The crowd scat-tered as the faceless man raised a huge pistol. It came up through the parting crowd like a hungry shark breaking the surface of the water. The faceless man stood in the open space, a black-suited statue with one arm raised and aimed in Eli's direction.

"Last warning, Mr. Knickerbocker!"

"Don't stop, kid," Theo snarled back over his shoulder. His lurch-ing gait carried him toward the wide plaza exit beneath the steel-and-glass roof. "Keep running. Get as far away from him as possible. As long as you're close they'll be certain—"

The gunshot echoed over the crowd, across the plaza, between the buildings.

Theo's baseball cap flipped in the air. The old man dropped his blanket bundle and took three quick steps. He let the knapsack slide off his shoulder and took three more. Eli's momentum carried him past Theo, and he twisted around to urge him to leave the knapsack.

But Theo's next step became a stagger. His knees sagged. His head dropped forward to display a thick, wet line of red spreading out across the salesman's scalp.

Theo crumpled. His skull struck the bricks with a sound not unlike a bat connecting with a well-used Little League baseball. Blood drained out between the cobblestones, a gleaming red spiderweb around Theo's head.

Eli stumbled three, four more steps and paused.

The faceless man strode forward. A few more shrieks and cries bounced in the air. Half the people scattered before him, the rest froze with expressions of horror or anticipation.

Theo vanished behind a grove of legs as some shoppers pushed in for a better view.

"Excuse me," the faceless man called out. He slipped through the crowd without effort, the pistol down, his badge held high in his other hand.

Eli pushed back into the crowd, away from Theo, away from the body. He shifted direction and skirted around the outer edge of the plaza, doubling back the way he'd come, back to where Theo's blanket had been spread out. He guessed he was thirty or forty feet away when he risked a glance back.

"Pardon me, ladies and gentlemen," the faceless man called out. "Please stand aside." The tall figure brushed past the lunchtime diners and shoppers and passersby to stand by the fallen salesman. A few glanced up at the tall man, but then their eyes returned to the body.

Why didn't anyone react? A six-and-a-half-foot-tall man with no face stalked through the crowd and no one stared or screamed or recoiled.

The faceless man's shoulders hunched, and his arms seemed to

tense. Even from thirty feet away, Eli could sense the annoyance waft-
ing off the tall figure. The masked skull turned to the left, then to the
right.

Eli saw two police officers work their way through the crowd toward
the faceless man and a cool wave of relief washed over him. A woman
and a younger man. They seemed to bob up and down through the
crowd like swimmers in rough water. The distance between the police
and the faceless man shrunk, and then the last few shoppers stepped
away to create a space.

The female officer stood near the faceless man. Her pistol was out,
but she didn't seem to be threatening the broad-shouldered monster.
She looked up at the plastic mask, at the thing in the faceless man's
hand, and nodded three times.

She turned to her partner and exchanged a few quick words. Then
they both waved the crowds away from Theo's fallen body, clearing a
space in the plaza. The female officer glanced back at the faceless man
and gave a confirming nod.

"Ladies and gentlemen!" The voice rolled out across the plaza.
Not amplified, but clear and loud. It reminded him of the actors at the
Ogunquit Playhouse, booming out the lyrics of Buddy Holly without
making it seem like shouting.

Eli could still hear the soft, muffled edges on the words.

The faceless man lifted his arm and displayed the object in his
hand—the badge in its leather wallet. "I know this has been disturbing
for all of you, and I'm sorry you had to see this. Rest assured, this is a
matter of national security. We're looking for a dangerous fugitive who
may have spoken to this man in the past half hour or so."

People stared at the tall, blank-faced man in the suit. Some looked
curious. A few squinted suspiciously at the raised hand with the badge.
But still no panic. No alarm.

"The fugitive is a woman," the faceless man told the crowd. "Ap-
proximately thirty years old, five foot ten, blond hair. She is most likely
dressed in a blue coat, like one of the colonial reenactors here, possibly
wearing a tricorn hat."

A few people on the edges of the crowd looked around. They eyed
the distant reenactors. Some of them pointed. The police scanned the
dozens of faces in front of them.

"She may also have an accomplice," continued the faceless man. "Male. Twenty-nine. Five-foot eleven. Brown hair. They were both supposed to meet with this man, a collaborator." Without turning his blank features, he gestured at the body splayed on the bricks behind him.

A cold chill crawled over Eli's skull and slipped down his back. A level of panic he hadn't felt since childhood tingled in his chest and fingertips.

He took a step back and let his shoulders slump a little. He let his chin settle low and hunched a little more. His left foot slid back again and he dragged the right one after it. He took three more steps backward.

Most of the people in the crowd still looked at the faceless man, but a few on the edges glanced around. A few yards away, the finger-painter scanned the crowd, his head swinging back and forth.

Eli pulled his sweatshirt hood up, realized it made him look like every guilty person since the creation of hoodie sweatshirts, and pushed it back down. He turned to his left, parallel to the crowd, and then let his path curve around, away from the faceless man and toward the streets outside Quincy Market.

"Hello, Mr. Teague," boomed the voice. "Good to see you again."

Eli wasn't stupid. It was a trick to make him turn and look. To get him to reveal himself. He kept his shoulders slumped, his head down, and continued toward the road. He passed a few people heading the other way, into the plaza. They looked ahead at the crowd, then glanced behind them. Two or three of them glanced at Eli.

He reached the corner, stopped, and stretched. He filled his tight chest with air and tried very hard to look like a man with all the time in the world. A man definitely not trying to slip away from a crowd that might be turning into a mob.

He looked to his right, down the street, and turned a little more to look over his shoulder at the plaza.

The faceless man had waded through the crowd. The blank sockets behind his plastic mask were aimed at Eli. He took another step forward and raised his arm.

Eli ran.

6

What little Eli knew about being on the run was from half-remembered movies and less-remembered childhood novels about teen investigators. He didn't think either source could be thought of as reliable. He also didn't have much else to go on.

He ran for two blocks, then slowed down and tried to blend into the crowd. He shrugged his dark pea coat off and pulled the sweatshirt hood back up. He thought about tossing the coat but decided to leave it draped over one arm.

He stopped to stare at a flyer taped to a phone pole—something about a band he didn't know playing at a bar he'd never heard of—and used it as a chance to look back the way he'd come.

No one pointed or yelled. No police or enthusiastic citizens or faceless men. A good number of pedestrians strode through his field of view, but none of them seemed interested in him. Or anyone else for that matter. They focused on newspapers, phones, balancing their bags, and just getting to a hundred different destinations.

Eli turned and kept walking away from Quincy Market.

And away from his car too. It sat in the garage north of the market. Probably for the best—there might be someone watching it. Or maybe the faceless man could track it somehow.

So, thought Eli. What now?

Finding out the secrets of the alluring Harry Pritchard and her mysterious life had lost a lot of appeal in the past half hour or so. A few seeds of fascination still tickled his mind, but a much larger part of his brain screamed, *Not worth it!* Truth was, he'd known her for maybe two hours all together. He knew nothing about her, good or bad.

He could go home. Just go back to his car and—if he didn't get arrested right there—drive home to safe, boring Sanders and continue with his safe, boring life. Again, assuming he wasn't arrested and hauled off to some prison or stockade or something.

Maybe the faceless man would leave him alone. He had twice before. If Eli made it clear he didn't know anything—and didn't want to know anything—maybe the blank-faced man would let him go home.

But the faceless man had shot Theo Knickerbocker. In the head. Right in front of a few hundred people. No questions. No hesitations. One warning—bang.

A man with no face and a Halloween mask had shot someone dead in the middle of a shopping mall. And no one had said a thing! The gunshot had caused a few screams and cries, but then . . . nothing.

Going home didn't seem like a great option.

Just like finding system bugs—process of elimination. He couldn't stay here. He couldn't go back.

Stupid as it sounded, he had to go forward.

Eli walked two more blocks coming to this decision. As his chain of reasoning came to its end, so did the sidewalk. And across the street from him sat the bus station.

The hotel room had eaten a good chunk of his dwindling bank balance, and a ticket to California would eat up a lot of what remained. He knew, better than most, that bank withdrawals could be tracked, but didn't see much choice. After a bit of internal debate, he got all the money he could from the bus station's ATM—flinching at the fee— and then paid cash for the ticket. It wasn't much of a screen, but it might slow the police down a little bit.

Or whoever else might be following him.

The route cross-country involved a few transfers, but it would put Eli in Pasadena five hours before Harry's scheduled appearance. By sheer luck, the bus he needed boarded in just forty minutes. He spent the time walking from one end of the terminal to the other, watching every road and door. It probably made him look suspicious, but his nerves jumped too much for him to stand still.

On the fifth time around the station, Eli saw the faceless man standing on a distant street corner. He ducked behind the bulk of a vending machine before the mask turned to aim in his direction.

When he peered around a few moments later, he saw the faceless man's back.

A woman's voice with a thin Boston accent called boarding for his bus. Ten minutes early. He backed away from the corner and followed the signs to his terminal. He stood in line next to the big blue bus as people slung duffel bags and rolling suitcases into the luggage compartment. He glanced over his shoulder three times while the line inched forward, showed his ticket to a bored man with Coke-bottle glasses, then climbed up the narrow stairs.

The inside of the bus looked more like a train. Or what trains looked like in the movies Eli had seen over the years. The seats were set up in groups of four, facing each other two by two. A small staircase led upstairs. The bus had an upstairs.

He found a seat near the window and hunched down low. He should've bought a hat at the bus station's little store. Or a pair of sunglasses. He shifted the hood of his sweatshirt, hoping it settled in a position that hid his face without looking like it was hiding his face.

An older man in a down coat flopped into the seat across from Eli. His skin had the color and texture of a vintage leather jacket. At least thirty years of cigarettes wafted from the man's pores. One rested behind his ear. Wrinkles along its length showed where it had been bent and straightened.

Through the bus window, Eli saw a man in a dark suit step out of the station. He stood fifty feet down the walkway and held no luggage. One of the hanging signs blocked the man's face. His body turned toward Eli's bus, away, then back.

A woman sat down in the aisle seat across from Eli. The cigarette man raised a brow, and a wave of perfume rolled up to sting Eli's eyes. He blinked away the smell of baby powder and chemical roses.

The man in the suit took a few steps toward Eli's bus. Was the suit black or very dark blue? Eli tried to get a better sense of its color and style, but the man was too far away, and the bus window, while not filthy, was far from clean.

A hiss came from the front of the bus. The people around him rumbled. Eli looked forward and saw a few people in the aisle adjusting luggage in the upper racks. The bus trembled. A college-age kid chose between Eli and the cigarette man and sat down next to Eli.

The doors closed. Everyone had boarded and the bus was pulling out. The floor trembled and Eli's seat gave a small lurch. The station outside seemed to slide away.

The man in the suit slid away with it. He took a few more steps toward Eli's bus, trying to keep up. Eli glimpsed a glossy plastic chin and painted lips and then the faceless man vanished as another bus came between them.

The bus swung back in a smooth arc. After a moment Eli was looking at the back of the row of buses, with narrow glimpses of the terminal between them.

Then the seat lurched again and they moved forward.

Eli was California-bound.

7

Four buses, a train, another two buses, and five days later, Eli stepped onto the sidewalk in Pasadena in desperate need of a shower, some clean clothes, and at least one solid meal.

The city reminded him a bit of Dover. A good-sized town with parts of a city squeezed in here and there. There were three- and four-story buildings of brick and concrete across the street from steel-and-glass storefronts.

The weight of his pea coat pressed sweat out of his chest and back. After half an hour he shrugged out of it and slung it over his arm. The sun felt oppressively bright and hot, and once again he found himself wishing he'd bought sunglasses in Boston.

Half the people on the street either had a phone pressed to their head or held in front of them like a microphone. Most of the others wore tiny headphones. Two wore massive, retro-looking sets that covered their ears. Eli tried to catch the two or three people with open ears, but they slipped away in the crowd or into buildings.

After twenty minutes of trying to catch a pedestrian, Eli switched tactics.

He looked around, spotted a chain drugstore, and walked in. Less than a dozen customers, if he counted right, despite the noon hour, and one cashier on duty. A paunchy security guard glanced at the heavy pea coat over his arm, then went back to staring into space. Eli found a granola bar and a Mountain Dew (four of his remaining thirty-two dollars gone at convenience-store prices) and waited until the two customers in line had concluded their transactions.

The cashier looked tired or bored. Possibly a mix of the two. Eli put her at fifteen or twenty years older than himself, not quite his mother's age. A few strands of silver highlighted the woman's hair. Her name tag had a dark, sticky spot in the shape of a *T*, followed by ORI. She took Eli's meager lunch, waved it over a price scanner, and asked if that would be all.

"Ummmm, actually," said Eli, "I don't suppose you know where the fork in the road is?"

The woman blinked and looked at him for the first time. "Sorry?" Her voice had an accent he couldn't place, almost turning her *s*'s into *z*'s

"The . . . the fork in the road. I'm supposed to meet someone there in . . ." He glanced at his watch. "In about an hour. But I'm not sure where it is."

She stared at him for a moment. Then she blinked twice. "Oh," she said. "The fork?"

"Yeah. I guess."

"It's easy." She waved her hand at the door. "Go down Colorado," she said, pointing with one finger. "About six blocks and turn left on Pasadena Avenue. Then just go straight until you see it. Maybe two miles altogether."

Eli smiled. "Thank you."

"Where're you from?"

"What?"

"Your accent. Where're you from?"

"Maine," he said. "A little town called Sanders. You haven't heard of it."

"Near Stephen King?"

"Not really, no."

The cashier shrugged. She gave him his change and pushed his food across the counter without offering him a bag. Her eyes slid to the person behind him.

Eli munched the granola bar as he walked down Colorado. It was a big, wide street, several lanes across, and his gaze kept sliding up the taller buildings to the sky. At Pasadena he tossed the wrapper in a trash can and cracked open the Mountain Dew.

Traffic on Pasadena Avenue all came at him, one way. The road started out with businesses but quickly became more residential. The houses had a very cinematic feel, as if he'd seen the street a dozen times in movies or television shows. Eli kept expecting celebrities to step through apartment doors or out of parked cars.

The woman across the street could've been a celebrity. Her outfit showed either determined eccentricity or a poor sense of disguise. She wore a long trench coat and a swollen hat of brown leather, something between a large bonnet and a plush muffin, with a large brass button just over her forehead. What he'd first mistaken for an odd, heavy collar on her sweater had glinted in the sun and revealed itself to be a huge pair of sunglasses, or maybe goggles. She looked around with quick, nervous glances, waiting to get recognized, and locked eyes with Eli for a moment as they approached each other. She managed a weak smile when he didn't react, as if they'd shared a secret.

He passed more apartments, a big complex that identified itself as the Ronald McDonald House (something he'd definitely seen on television), and a house that declared itself to be an English tea garden, before he reached a wide-open space. The narrow block between two roads formed a small park, with some grass, spiky bushes, and a few trees that included a huge, thick palm. A gravelly path led to an oval of sand and some kind of marker at the park's center—a narrow pillar of aluminum, or maybe steel, that stood twenty feet tall.

Another minute of walking carried him past the park to an intersection. On the other side of the block, the road mirrored his, a one-way street running the other way. The little park was a triangle, not much more than an oversized traffic island formed by the two streets coming together to form a single road.

No. Not where they came together. Where they split.

The fork seemed . . . normal. Houses on either side. A small apartment building at one end. A man worked a lawnmower across a distant lawn. Eli wasn't sure what Harry would be looking for here in just . . . twenty minutes.

Assuming he was even at the right intersection. Theo had made a blanket assumption everyone would know which fork he was referring to. The cashier seemed pretty sure, granted. Could it be possible the roads didn't split like this anywhere else in the city?

What if it wasn't related to street layout? What if "the fork in the road" was the name of some trendy bar or club hidden in one of the nearby buildings? Those supposedly covered Southern California, and it'd make much more sense as a meeting place. Hell, it could be a cutlery store or travel agency or just a little bookshop with a catchy name.

He waited for a cluster of cars to pass by and crossed the street to the corner of the park. What he'd mistaken for grass was a dense, low plant with swollen leaves. It reminded him of the brown-green seaweed that washed up on the beach sometimes.

He wondered what the park looked like from above. What did the points of the triangle aim at? Maybe the short paths or plants formed some kind of symbol or—

The steel monument at the center of the park. From this angle it was less of a pillar and more of a futuristic, one-piece signpost. The shaft flowed up and widened into a rectangular top that reminded him of a huge highway mile marker.

Eli stepped around a few bushes and got a clear view of the monument's base. His mind froze up. Once again he was struck with the surreal sensation of being in a movie.

A Muppet movie.

8

Metal tubing held the giant dinner fork a foot or so above a rough slab of concrete. Two basketball-sized stones and a third, larger one, sat in the sand in front of it, as if some giant had stabbed at them and just missed. A sculpture or an art installation of some kind.

Eli walked up to it. Silver paint gave the fork the color and texture of brushed aluminum. He rapped his knuckles against it and heard a wooden clunk. Thick, but hollow.

He walked around the fork, looking for a plaque or an inscription or maybe a small note held in place on the frame with a magnet.

Nothing.

He turned and looked at the trio of stones. Were they markers? He leaned over the closest one and looked for letters or numbers or symbols of some kind.

He heard a click behind him. Metal on metal. Just loud enough to stand out from the ambient sound of passing cars and the distant lawnmower. The sound probably hadn't made it out of the small park.

Eli turned.

Harry's long flintlock rifle was a dark circle to his eyes, only recognizable from the way her hands held it. Recognition sparked in her eyes, and her glare softened, but not much. "Mr. Teague?"

"Harry," he said. He let his hands drift out, not up over his head, but plainly open and empty. "You're early."

"Not as early as I'd hoped," she said. "What are you doing here?"

"Trying to find you."

"And you have," she said. She took a few steps toward him, but the rifle didn't shift from his head. "You'll please pardon my saying, but I find running into you again on the other side of the country a bit disturbing."

"Imagine what it feels like at gunpoint."

Her mouth twitched, but the rifle still didn't move. "How did you find me?"

"Theo," he said. The salesman's surname popped to mind. "Theo Knickerbocker."

"How do you know Theo?"

"I . . . I went to Quincy Market looking for you and found him. Well, he found me. He tried to sell me a necklace. We talked for a couple minutes and he figured out I was looking for you."

"Did he, now?"

"Yeah. He told me you were coming here."

The rifle shifted in her hands. "Theo doesn't just tell people things," she said. The words were ice.

Eli realized she'd wrapped her finger around the trigger.

"I . . . I paid him," he said. "Twenty-five dollars. Cash. He told me you'd be here now, and gave me a bracelet." He reached for his pocket to pull out the trinket, but stopped as her grip tightened on the rifle.

Harry stared at him. "What were you looking for?"

"What?"

"Just now. When I found you. What were you looking for?"

"Nothing," he said. "I was just . . . looking. Trying to figure out what you were coming here for."

She said nothing.

The rifle barrel wavered between a black dot and a blurred, foreshortened rod. *It's pointed at one of my eyes,* Eli realized. "I thought you'd need—"

"Why are you following me, Mr. Teague?"

"To warn you about the faceless man."

She took in a fast, short breath. "When?"

"Just a few days ago. The day after I helped you change the flat tire. He showed up at the bank where I work. He was looking for you. And then he followed me to Boston and killed Theo."

The rifle wobbled. The barrel tilted down. "Theo's dead?"

"He . . . he shot him. In the head."

"And you got away."

"He was focused on Theo. I got to the edge of the market and ran."
Her mouth trembled for a moment. "Do you have a firearm?"

"A what?"

"A firearm. A gun. A pistol hidden somewhere on your person."
He shook his head. "No, nothing."

"Excellent." The rifle came up and became solid again. "Toward me, please."

"What?"

She tipped her head toward the scrub behind the fork and made a small shooing gesture with the rifle's tip. "This way. Quickly, please."

He walked toward and past the large utensil. Her boots shifted in the dirt, swinging her around the fork so it never came between Eli and the rifle.

He headed to the edge of the dirt oval and paused at the scrub plants. He glanced right, then left. Past the intersection to his left, the Model A business coupe sat against the curb, the andalusite blue all but black on the tree-shaded street.

He leaned his head back. "You're not really going to shoot me, are you?"

"Don't be daft, Mr. Teague. Do you have the time?"

He glanced at his watch. "It's almost one thirty."

"How close?"

He looked again. "One twenty-seven." He looked over his shoulder. "What happens at one thirty?"

She stood a few feet away. Her aim had relaxed and she stared up at the fork. She looked at him, then past him to the scrub. "Close enough," she muttered. "See the fork's shadow? The top of it?"

He looked down at the scrub. His own shadow was a dark blob across the tan-and-green plants, but the fork's long shadow reached past him. Its edge sat almost a yard into the growth. "Yeah," he said. "Yeah, I do."

"Dig there."

"What?"

"Dig," she repeated.

He stepped toward the shadow's edge and the plants crunched under his feet. A few stronger branches scraped at his ankles. He moved to the side, double-checked the fork's shadow, and kneeled. One of his hands pushed into the low bushes. The brown leaves scraped at his fingers and palm. He glanced back at Harry.

"Dig." The words had more emphasis this time.

"What for?"

"Because I have a rifle and you don't."

"No, I mean, what am I digging for? Am I just making a hole or . . . ?"

"Just dig, Mr. Teague. You'll know when you find it."

He looked at the rifle, then her, then back to the muzzle. "I don't suppose you could—"

"If what you say is true, we don't have a lot of time," she told him. "It's best if you just keep your mind to the task at hand so we can both be gone before anyone finds us here. Dig."

He sighed and set both hands to work. He pushed the low branches and leaves out of the way. They moved without effort, lifting up and folding back.

Two or three of the plants had been snapped off and left in the tangle of branches. A rough circle of dirt beneath them was dark and loose. He could see parallel trails where someone had run their fingers back and forth to smooth the ground.

He held back the scrub with one hand while the other pawed at the ground. The soil came up easily. It felt like digging at the beach, although the grains felt larger and coarser. He went down a few inches, then clawed at the sides of his hole to widen it. The ground there resisted, reinforced by a web of threadlike roots.

Another group of cars drove by, and Eli wondered if anyone saw the woman holding him at rifle-point. No one called out or honked horns. Wasn't Los Angeles supposed to be all about guns and drive-by shootings? Did they not notice, or just not care?

He hadn't even dug for two minutes when his fingers brushed something smooth and angled eight inches down. They found the shape again and pulled it from its tiny grave. He flipped it over in his hand, and a few quick swipes knocked most of the dirt from it. "This it?" he asked Harry.

The soil hadn't even stained the little packet of wax paper. It had been cleverly folded into a square envelope, maybe three inches on each side. Through the tacky paper Eli could feel something round, maybe the size of a half-dollar, although the packet seemed too light for a—

Harry snatched it from his fingers. She tugged on one of the folds, and the packet bloomed like a paper flower in her hand. She plucked something from the center and closed her fist around it. She murmured something Eli couldn't hear and let out a deep sigh. The rifle lowered and drifted to the side.

Eli stood up and coughed. "So what is it?"

She glanced at him. "Thank you for the warning, Mr. Teague," she said. "You have my appreciation, although I'm sorry you came all this way for nothing."

"What's that supposed to mean?"

"It means you should run back home. As fast as you can. Forget you were here. Forget you saw me. Go back to your life and be thankful for it."

"Forget . . ." He shook his head. "What the hell is going on?"

"You have, if I understand the phrase correctly, jumped into the deep end of the pool. You should go home now while you can. They haven't directly connected you to me. You're just a witness."

"Like Theo was?"

"Theo'd been playing the odds for a while. It won't be the same for you." She waved the rifle, and the movement made her ponytail swing out from behind her head. "Go."

They both heard the growl at the same time. A rumbling engine that stood out even over the SUVs and sports cars rolling past the traffic island. The sound came from the bend to the south, echoing off the houses.

"Run," Harry whispered. She shoved the mystery item inside her jacket. The rifle came back up. "Run now."

"What about you?"

The growl rose and became a roar. Eli glanced to the side and saw people in the passing cars glancing at their dashboards, then out to the streets.

"Mr. Teague, this is no time for chivalry or nobility. Please, you need to get away from here as fast as you can. Run until you drop and then keep crawling."

"I'm not going to just leave you to deal with—"

The Hudson Hornet ignored the stoplight and shot through the intersection. The black, glossy finish reflected the sky and the sun and the other cars. The roadster aimed itself at Eli and Harry.

"Dammit," said Harry. She backed into him, forced him around the fork.

The moment slowed in time.

The Hornet's tires were already up on the island. The driver's side of the car plowed through one of the pointy bushes. Grit sprayed up from the other tire. Eli saw the faceless man behind the wheel. The plastic mask gazed back at him.

Harry's rifle went off. The Hornet's passenger-side tire exploded.

The car lurched to the side, crushing two more pointy bushes under its bulk before the driver could compensate. The Hornet slid into the dirt oval and came to rest. The passenger door sat just a few feet from the concrete base of the fork.

"I'm sorry," said Eli. "I don't know how he followed me here."

The driver's door opened and the faceless man rose up out of the car. His clear mask now had round cheeks and a wide, cartoon smile like a clown. He had changed his suit too. The deep-blue pinstripe made him look thinner, and a silk handkerchief poked out from the breast pocket. A tiny gray tuft rode on one side of the hat, tucked into the band. It was an old man's hat, or a hat young men wore in old pictures.

"He isn't following you," Harry said. She swung the rifle up, aiming at the sky, and then pushed it into Eli's hands. "This is the one that's been after me."

9

Hello," said the faceless man, turning its mask toward Eli. "Please drop the weapon, Mr. Teague. If you could both put your hands above your head, it would—"

The sides of Harry's colonial coat flapped open. Her hands swung up, each holding a pistol. The guns thundered in the open space—three, four, five, too many shots—and the faceless man staggered back, kicked hard in the chest.

Eli flinched away, glanced back, and saw no blood on the fallen man.

Harry spun, shoulder-checked him, and ran. Three long strides carried her past him, over the plants, to the sidewalk. Tires squealed and horns wailed again as she sprinted across the street.

"Come on," she bellowed over her shoulder.

The faceless man sat up next to his car. He didn't seem to notice the bullet holes in his coat or pale shirt. He reached for his fallen pistol, a movement with no urgency behind it.

Another mirror-black Hudson Hornet roared up Pasadena Avenue, and another chorus of tires and horns echoed across the small park as drivers avoided it. Eli heard the heavy, hollow crunch of two cars colliding as the big sedan charged onto the island and came to rest along the southern point of the triangular park.

Eli turned and ran. He lurched, thrown off balance by the flintlock rifle he clutched and didn't dare release. The leafy plants crunched under his feet.

"Hello, Mr. Teague," boomed a voice behind him. "You were instructed to remain in your hometown. You haven't followed these instructions."

The cars in the street hadn't worked back up to speed, so Eli earned more angry honks than screeching brakes as he dove through traffic. An SUV scuffed its tires and bumped him just hard enough to stagger him. The rifle clattered against the grille. The big truck's driver, a woman with platinum blond hair, shouted at Eli through the windshield.

Then the windshield spiderwebbed with a bang as a gunshot rang out behind him. The driver screamed. Eli barely pushed himself off the big car's hood before she gunned the accelerator and sped away.

Twenty yards ahead, Harry yanked open the Model A's passenger door. She threw herself across the rumble seat and behind the wheel. The engine coughed once and let out a roar of its own. The car lunged forward a few feet just as Eli reached it.

He dove into the passenger space just as Harry slammed the car into reverse. Momentum threw Eli off the seat and the flapping door banged against his shin. The rifle's barrel hit him in the side of the head. Outside the pavement rushed past the car.

He pushed himself back up onto the bench. Harry had her arm over the seat, craning her neck to see out the rear window while she drove full speed down the street in reverse. The transmission whined with the effort.

Through the windshield, Eli could see the faceless men. Two of them. They stood in the middle of the street and stared down the road after the old car.

A horn blared, Harry swerved the car, and Eli grabbed the dash to keep from being flung out the passenger door.

The Model A swerved again, sharp. The wheels on the passenger side lifted off the road, and Eli slid back into the car, bumping up against Harry. She shoved him away and slammed the pedals to the Model A's floor. The vehicle lunged forward, the passenger door slammed shut, and the seat back hit Eli right below the shoulder blades. The rifle shook free of his grip and fell between him and the door.

Harry spun the steering wheel back and forth, hand over hand like she was piloting a ship. The Model A wove through traffic. She ignored the yellow line and earned a few blaring horns and shouts.

It took Eli a moment to recognize the cylindrical speedometer, but it swung back and forth with every sharp turn. He guessed their speed at around sixty miles an hour. Through what looked like a residential area. Maybe even the outskirts of some kind of college. The engine didn't seem to be straining at all.

Harry wove around a pickup and muttered something under her breath. She spun the wheel again, and the passenger door thumped Eli in the side. There didn't seem to be any seat belts. Which made sense for a 1929 Model A, he realized.

"What . . ." Eli flinched as the old car slid between a moving truck and a green sedan. "What just happened?"

The Model A swooped around another corner. Eli braced his feet and pushed himself back against the seat. He didn't slide as much this time.

"Can we slow down a lit—"

"No."

The road ahead was empty. Harry shot straight through the stop sign at the end of the block without hesitation. She glanced over her shoulder without slowing. Eli looked back too. The road looked empty for at least two blocks. But then he caught a glimpse of something black and gleaming. He could hear the growl of the Hudson Hornet's big engine as it closed on them.

"We have to get out of their range," she said.

"Their what?"

"Their range."

Harry turned right at the next corner. There were no other cars, but she still didn't slow down. Eli pushed himself into the seat and managed to not end up pressed against her again. He heard tires screech and skid behind them, and the growl grew louder. He glanced through the rear window and saw the Hornet just a few dozen yards back.

The Model A blasted through another stop sign. This time it got them a sharp bleat from a small blue car. The next cross-street had a full stoplight, which Harry also ignored. Eli heard brakes squeal and flinched away from a close view of a bus headlight and then they were through the intersection.

Behind them he heard a sharp squeal of brakes and the deep growl faded away.

He spread his feet a little wider as they went around the next corner. Again, Harry didn't move. She almost rode the car's controls, standing on the pedals and using the steering wheel to pull herself up off the rumble seat. It made him think of kids on bikes, using their own weight to force every ounce of speed out of the cranks. Her ponytail swung out to the side and then back.

The growl of the Hudson Hornet's engine faded more. Eli couldn't be sure, but it sounded like the car was driving in a different direction. It sounded like a distant freeway.

Harry glanced at Eli, then back to the road. "When people are scared," she said, "they tend to move in straight lines. That's why most people search for them that way."

"They do?"

"Have you ever heard stories of children lost in the woods? When it takes days to find them, how often are they right near where they first vanished? No one can find them because they're in the last place most people think to look."

Eli looked at the houses and cars as they flew past. "Isn't everything in the last place you look, technically?"

"The problem is," she continued, ignoring him, "if we don't make any turns, we just end up going where they expect us to go, and they catch us. But if we make too many turns, we don't get out of their range."

"And they can catch us?" Eli guessed.

She nodded once and spun them around another corner. A small dog on a leash yipped at them twice.

"What do you mean, their range? Can they see somehow? Do they have . . ." The memory of a blind superhero danced on the edge of Eli's thoughts. "I don't know, radar-sense or something?"

"Mr. Teague," she said, "right now I'm spending a small part of my concentration driving this car and a very large part reminding myself I shouldn't kick you out and leave you for them to find. Please consider this before distracting me. Or asking any further questions."

The Model A swerved around a pack of bicyclists, then cut them off to take another corner. Half a dozen angry men and women glared at Eli through orange-lensed glasses as the bikes clattered to a halt. A female voice followed them around the corner: "Asshole!"

He let another two intersections go by before he asked, "Where are we going?"

"East, at the moment."

"No, I mean, where are—"

"I know what you mean, Mr. Teague!"

Eli looked over his shoulder. "Are they . . . do you think we lost them?"

"They're always following. It's just a question of how far behind they are."

He opened his mouth, but closed it before any actual sounds came out.

Harry looked back and cocked her head to listen for a few beats. Her shoulders dropped. "I think we may have done it," she said. "I thought our goose was well and truly cooked when the second one showed up. I've never heard of anyone getting away from two of them."

Her feet shifted. The Model A slowed. The car still moved faster than the speed limit, but not so much it would gather more attention. Almost two minutes passed before she took another turn.

"Can you . . . Are you going to drop me off somewhere?"

She guided them past a gorgeous green 1970 Chevy Chevelle. The lanky driver blinked at them as they went by. Eli heard the muscle car's engine rev behind them. It sounded small after the roar of the Hornet.

He cleared his throat. "Are you going to—"

"I heard you the first time, Mr. Teague."

"Sorry," he said. "You can call me Eli."

"I think it's best if we keep things formal for now, Mr. Teague." Harry sighed. "As tempting as it is to leave you here, I can't do it."

"Why?"

"Because they'd interrogate you and then kill you."

"Ahhh."

"If you were lucky, they'd kill you first."

He managed a nervous laugh. "Yeah, lucky me. Can't question a dead man, right?"

She glared at him. "Of course they can," she said. Her attention shifted back to the road. "It just doesn't hurt as much when they cut the answers out of you."

Eli tried to come up with a response, but it withered in his throat.

She shook her head. The ponytail swished back and forth across her back. "I'm stuck with you, Mr. Teague."

10

They'd been driving for almost an hour. Harry had stayed off the highways. For the past thirty minutes they'd been on a two-lane road which seemed to shift between residential areas and long stretches of plains or almost-desert. If Eli's reading of the sun was correct, they were heading more or less northeast.

It occurred to him he'd seen more types of terrain in the past week than he'd seen in the previous twenty-nine years of his life.

Cars zoomed up and swerved around them. Shiny sports cars, pickups, a U-Haul, minivans, even one big sixteen wheeler. Harry seemed determined not to go over sixty-five. Once Eli got used to reading the cylindrical speedometer, he realized how steady she'd kept their speed once they were out of Pasadena.

"So," he said.

She glanced at him. She'd been giving him quick looks every few minutes, usually as she looked over her shoulder. Her expression shifted between sad and aggravated. She hadn't said much. When she did, it was just short, simple commands. Stop crowding her (a challenge on the tiny bench that made up the rumble seat). Brace for a turn. Adjust one of the mirrors.

Eli knew a 1929 Model A shouldn't have side mirrors. Yet another upgrade. He wondered how many others the car had.

"So," he said again, "is this all about the treasure hunt?"

Harry sighed. "In a manner of speaking, yes."

"The guys with . . . the faceless men . . ." A dozen questions raced onto his tongue and tripped over one another. A dozen more pushed their way to the front of his mind.

"That's what everyone calls them," she said when nothing else came. "It's what they've always been called."

"Always?"

She nodded. "Since the country was first founded."

Three new questions shoved themselves into his forebrain, and knocked a random one off his tongue. "What did you mean about their range?"

She reached up and tugged the point of her tricorne away from him, just an inch. "They're certain of everything within about three hundred feet. Some of them a little more, some a little less."

"What do you mean, certain?"

"Are you wearing stockings right now, Mr. Teague?"

"What?"

"Stockings. Socks."

"Yeah," he said with a confused nod.

She glanced at him, her eyes flitting away from the road. "You didn't check."

"Yeah, but I know I am."

"You're certain," she said with another nod. "Just as you could be certain walking through a dark room you're familiar with. Just as they are. It's how they move. How they drive." Her fingers flexed on the steering wheel. "How they aim."

"So it's some kind of . . . ESP? Telepathy or something?"

She shook her head. "It's just certainty."

"But what does that—"

Harry glanced in the tiny side mirror and raised two fingers off the steering wheel, silencing him. Another engine rumbled up behind them. Eli waited to see the car rush past them, but it hung back. He looked over his shoulder, through the oval rear window.

A police cruiser followed a few car lengths behind them. A Dodge Charger, with an aggressive-looking push bumper. It settled in and matched speeds with them. The morning sun splashed across the windshield and hid the officer. Or officers.

"Consarn it," muttered Harry.

"It might not mean anything," Eli said. "Maybe he's just checking out the car."

"That's what worries me."

Eli tried to picture the Model A from behind as the officers would see it. A blank spot formed in the image. "Does your car have license plates?"

Her chin went up once, then back down. "Yes."

"Are they up to date?"

"Not precisely as such, no."

Eli fought the urge to glance back at the cruiser again. "How out of date are they?"

Harry's fingers danced on the steering wheel as if she was counting. She glanced at the side mirror again. "Seven decades? Maybe eight?"

"Seven *decades?*"

Red light flashed in the side mirror and the cruiser's sirens let out a squawk.

Harry snarled.

"*Pull the car over,*" a voice echoed behind them.

"Hang on," she said, "I'm going to make a run for it."

"What?!"

"If we can find a slick spot, we can lose him. It'll be tough out here, but if we can make it to the next town—"

He grabbed her arm. "Why are we running? He'll give you a warning or a ticket and then we'll be gone anyway."

"The faceless men sometimes use local law enforcement," she snapped, shaking him off. "The police could have orders to arrest us on sight."

"They might not. They might just be—"

The siren squawked again. "*Pull the car over now!*"

Harry glanced from Eli to the mirror. The Model A's engine rumbled. Eli braced his feet.

The cruiser lunged up alongside them. The lights on the roof flashed in their eyes. "*Now!*" shouted the officer through the PA system. Eli could see the figure in the passenger seat pointing emphatically at the highway's shoulder.

Harry reached for the gear shift, but Eli touched her arm again. "They'll run us off the road," he said.

The cruiser's passenger wheels crossed the line. Its doors were inches from the Model A. The officer in the passenger seat pointed at the shoulder again.

She glared at Eli, grumbled something he couldn't hear over the competing engines, and took her foot off the gas.

The car slowed. The cruiser stayed alongside them until Harry angled the car into the dirt and gravel on the side of the road. It dropped back at the last moment to pull in right behind them.

Doors opened. Feet crunched in the gravel. Eli glanced back and saw two officers with their hands on their guns, but neither of them had drawn. He looked at Harry and saw her feet poised over the pedals. "Just so you know," she said through gritted teeth, "there's a good chance we're about to die."

"What?"

"Try to act casual, Mr. Teague."

"What do you mean, die?"

The policemen walked forward and split to come up on either side of the car. The one by Harry stood tall enough that the Model A's roof hid his eyes and hat. Eli's was thick and heavy, with a name tag that read FOSTER.

"Kill the engine," said the one by Harry. With one hand he removed his sunglasses and hung them on his shirt pocket.

Harry glanced at Eli and pasted on a smile. "Of course, Officer." She reached out, flicked two switches, and the car's engine coughed itself to sleep.

"Keys," he said with a nod at the steering column.

"There are no keys in a Model T, Officer," she lied sweetly, moving her hands away from the column. "If I want to start it again, I'll need to get out and turn the crank for the magneto." She gestured at the front of the car.

The officer looked out at the hood, studied the small dashboard, and weighed the information for a moment. "License and registration," he said. Not a question, just a simple command.

Foster shifted next to Eli's door. The posture felt familiar from assorted run-ins with Zeke over the years. Two parts arrogance, one part excitement that he might get to pull his weapon. Eli hoped he was imagining it.

Harry looked up at him. "Is there a problem?"

The officer looked at her, then turned his head to look at the space behind the bench. "Why didn't you pull over when we instructed you to?"

Harry took in a breath. "Well, you see—"

"That was my fault, Officer," interrupted Eli. He looked over and bent his head to make easy eye contact. "We're a little punchy from driving. I bet her she could outrun your Charger for a mile."

The officer bent slightly to meet Eli's eyes. "That's extremely stupid. When an officer gives you a command, you do as he says."

"I know," said Eli. "I realized that pretty quick."

"Not quick enough," said Foster with a snort.

"I hope the bet was worth it," said the other officer. He shifted and the glare vanished from his name tag for a moment. Eli saw what looked like LAZNEY written on the little tile.

Eli looked at Harry with what he hoped was a proper mix of regret and naughtiness. "It would've been."

Foster snorted again.

Lazney's hand came off his pistol and he turned his attention back to Harry. "License and registration, ma'am."

Harry adjusted herself and tried to reach inside her coat and around to her back pockets. Eli pictured her pulling out one of her own pistols and shooting the policeman point-blank. The officer must've thought of it too, because he tensed and set his hand back on his pistol.

But her hand came back empty and moved to reach into the coat at chest height. She blinked twice. "Oh," she said. "Oh, my."

Lazney stared down at her.

She switched hands and reached for the other side of the coat. Her eyes flitted to Eli. "Dearest," she said, "have you seen my billfold?"

"I . . . your wallet? You don't have it?"

"No, I can't find it anywhere." It was a good performance. Better than his. She patted herself down again.

"It was on the nightstand at the motel," said Eli.

Her eyes widened. She looked back out at Lazney. "My apologies, officer," she said. "I believe I've left it behind at the . . . the motel."

Lazney's mouth was a flat line. "Registration?"

"Also in my billfold. Wallet."

"You keep your car registration in your wallet?" Foster didn't bother to hide the sneer in his voice. Lazney shot him a look that confirmed Eli's suspicions about the other officer.

"It's a classic," said Harry. She reached out to pat the small dash and then gestured at all the open space between Eli's legs and the windshield. "There's no glove compartment."

Lazney blew some air out of his nose. "And if I was to ask for proof of insurance, ma'am?"

She put up her hands and shrugged. "Also in the wallet. I'm so sorry."

The officer leaned back on his heels. The flat line of his mouth sank into a frown. He glanced at Eli. "What about you?"

"Sorry?"

"Got any ID? Or d'you leave your wallet at the hotel too?"

Harry caught Eli's eye just before he reached for his back pocket. "Sorry, no," he said. "I don't bring my license when she drives."

"That so?"

"To be honest," said Eli, "I can't even drive this thing. It's her baby."

"What's with the Civil War outfit?" asked Foster.

Eli stopped himself from rolling his eyes. "Revolutionary War, actually," he said.

"So what's with it?"

"Car shows," said Eli. "That's where we're going. Lots of people dress up to go with their car."

"How's a Revolutionary War outfit go with a Model T?" asked Lazney.

"I just like the outfit," Harry said. "Besides, frock coats are always fashionable."

Lazney blew more air out of his nose. His trigger finger slid down and tapped the side of his leg just in front of his holster. "Where are you headed?"

"Like I said," Eli answered, "a car show."

"Where?"

"Las Vegas," he said, hoping they were aimed somewhat at Las Vegas.

"But first we'll have to double back to get my wallet," said Harry. "We're lucky you stopped us, Officer. We might've been stranded in Las Vegas with no money and no identification."

Lazney raised his head to look over the car at Foster. Eli guessed they were mouthing words to each other. Harry caught Eli's eye and gave a small shake of her head

Lazney tapped the Model A's roof twice. "Wait here," he said to them.

"Don't even think about starting the car," added Foster.

"As I said before," Harry chimed, "I can't start it without getting out to turn the crank."

The officer grunted. The two men took a few steps back behind the car and started talking.

Eli leaned in to whisper but Harry held up a finger. She turned her head, aiming her ear back. Her eyes closed. Eli glanced at the two officers through the rear window and tried to catch their words.

"—ole thing stinks," said Lazney.

Foster muttered something Eli half heard, half lip read as *It's Zen.*

Lazney said something about probable cause and warrants.

Foster shook his head again and spoke loud and clear. "They match the description."

Harry's eyes snapped open. She flicked two switches on the dashboard. The engine burped once and turned over.

"Hey!" shouted Lazney.

Eli glanced back as Harry floored it. The officer was in midstride toward them. Foster already had his pistol out and was moving to get a clear shot.

The Model A lunged forward. The first gunshot missed, but Eli shrank down as the second one thunked into the car. A low gurgle came from the back. "Damnation," swore Harry. "He's hit the reserve."

Then they were over a rise and out of sight. She worked the gears again and the Model A accelerated even more. Eli guessed they were close to top speed.

She glanced at him crouching in the leg space. "While you're down there, Mr. Teague," she said, "there's a small package in the door's side panel you could grab. Brown paper, red string."

He blinked and twisted around. What he'd thought was just a mass of crumpled paper for insulation turned out to be four or five small parcels with color-coded string. There were two with red string, each the size of a hardcover book. "Does it matter which one?"

Harry glanced in the side mirror and shook her head. "Quickly, please." The siren grew loud behind them.

He pulled the packet free of the door and sat up. It shifted and bent in his hands, as if loose chain links filled the paper bundle, or a few of the cast-iron bar puzzles that showed up now and then at the tavern across from the bank. "What do I do with it?"

"Throw it up on the roof!"

"What?" he looked over his shoulder. The police cruiser was two hundred yards away, tops, and gaining fast.

"Throw it onto the roof!"

He reached up through the window with the package, balancing it on one hand. The wind whipped at his sleeve. The bag shifted on his fingers.

She slapped his leg. "Throw it!"

Eli tried to judge speed and height and then heaved the parcel into the air. It vanished from sight for an instant and then he saw it through the back window, tumbling away behind them. "Dammit!"

"Perfect," said Harry.

The packet exploded on the pavement, already a good thirty feet behind them. Eli saw what looked like black crosses bounce and tumble on the road. Sunlight glinted on some of them.

Then the Charger ran over them and its front tires exploded. A moment later the driver's side sagged in the back. The rims chewed through the rubber rags and sparked off the highway. Lazney or Foster, whoever was behind the wheel, steered into the slide like a pro. The police car crossed the far lane and came to a halt on the opposite shoulder in a cloud of dirt and dust.

And then the Model A was over a rise and the police vanished from sight.

Eli settled back onto the bench and took a deep breath. "Oh, fuck."

"Nicely done," Harry said.

"What was that thing? The package."

"Just a bag of sixteen-penny nails. A blacksmith bent them all at right angles, and a shipbuilder welded pairs of them into stars so they'd land with a point up."

"There's a word for those," Eli said. "Those spike things that blow out tires."

She nodded. "There is. I've forgotten it."

"Me too," said Eli. He looked over his shoulder. "Why didn't we use them before?"

"Before?"

"When the faceless men were chasing us."

Harry snorted. "There'd be no point. They'd just dodge them."

"You can't dodge a hundred spikes on the road. Not in a car."

"They have certainty, Mr. Teague. You would be truly amazed at what it lets them do."

He shook his head and glanced back again as the Model A crested another low slope. He caught a glimpse of the distant police car and a stick figure moving around it. "We should probably get off the road. Maybe lay low for a while. They're probably on the radio right now, setting up a roadblock or something." He waited for a reaction. "It means they can talk to other officers who are a long dist—"

"I know what a radio is, Mr. Teague."

He bit back his first response. "Of course you do. Sorry."

She glanced at him. "They can't tell other cars about us because it would attract attention. I'd wager they were told to avoid attention." She dipped her head back over her shoulder. "One of them probably walked in, flashed his badge, and just gave instructions to whoever was on duty."

"One of them," Eli repeated. "By which you mean . . ."

"You know who I mean."

He sucked another deep breath in between his teeth. "What the hell are they?"

Harry adjusted her fingers on the steering wheel. An orange light flickered twice on the dashboard and then lit up. Just below it a small gauge bobbed up and down, back and forth between 1/4 and 0. It settled closer to 0. "I'll need fuel soon," she said. She glanced at Eli.

"Okay," he said. "Do you need me to chip in or something?"

"No."

"Do you need gasoline in the car to tell me about the faceless men?"

"The car doesn't run on gasoline."

"That's not really an answer."

She bit back a sigh. "It's not a question that offers simple answers, Mr. Teague."

"Maybe a quick summary?"

She glanced at him. "It's complicated."

He waved at the freeway ahead of them. "We've got time to kill."

"Very complicated."

Eli snorted.

She looked ahead. "Let me find a safe place to refuel," she said, "and I'll tell you what I know."

11

The Model A ate up another mile or two of desert highway. To Eli's eyes, most of the small signs seemed to be random numbers. Mile markers, he supposed. Local highway designations.

The town clung low to the ground, like heat shimmering on pavement. At first, when it came into view in the distance, Eli mistook it for scattered slabs of rock covering the plain. As the Model A got closer and details accumulated, many of the buildings looked like mobile homes that had been converted into oblong cottages. Here and there he spotted two trailers fused together. Low ranch-style houses and a few one-story brick buildings made up the rest of the town, maybe fifty structures in all, laid out in a crooked grid with a decent amount of space around them.

The sun had bleached every building to whites, grays, and faded tans. As the town drew closer Eli could see the skeletal remains of half a dozen or so structures, like the remains of a bomb testing site or some half-forgotten war zone. The phone poles stood apart with no cables connecting them. One close to the freeway had a distinct lean to it.

"Where are we?"

"Unless I'm mistaken," Harry said, "that's the Nevada state line right over there." She pointed at the far side of the plain, where a distant, billboard-sized sign stood near the highway. "If you're asking about the town, I'm afraid I don't know its name off the top of my head."

The Model A crossed over a low bridge. Eli wouldn't have even noticed it except for the sign telling him he was crossing a river with a name he couldn't wrap his tongue around. At least half a dozen holes punctured the sign, the same kind of holes he saw all the time through the isolated signs of his own small town. He turned back and saw a thin stream of water a foot or two lower than the highway. It ran through a wide drainpipe under the pavement.

The road bent and Eli felt a shift. Momentum tugged his stomach to the left. A lifetime of New England winters made him tense as the wheels spun on the pavement for a few seconds. Harry twisted the steering wheel into the skid, and Eli felt the wheels grab, slip, and grab again. Then the Model A seized the road and continued toward the town.

Eli twisted around to look at the road behind them. "What'd we hit?"

"Nothing."

"No, I mean, what was on the road?"

She shook her head. "Nothing."

He sighed and settled back on the rumble seat. The pavement on this stretch looked dark and new. Lines hadn't even been painted on it yet. An oil patch would be almost invisible against the fresh asphalt.

A few more details appeared as they closed in on the town. A small diner-style restaurant sat near the main road. A gas station stood next to it, still displaying the older red-orange circle logo with GULF in dark blue letters. A moment later he picked out a wooden sign that read MARKET on one of the brick buildings. Another one had a bright-white mailbox out front.

A black car with huge tail fins pulled into the gas station ahead of them. Eli tried to get a better look at the front, because the rear window and taillights made him think it might be a 1959 Cadillac coupe in gorgeous condition. He knew old cars lasted better in drier climates, but the Caddy looked amazing. "You just passed the gas station."

"I am aware of that."

"Do you think there'll be another one in a town this size?"

"Help me find a church," said Harry, ignoring the question. "Or maybe a house that looks like no one's home."

His gaze drifted up an approaching phone pole. Three wires stretched across the arms at the top, mere threads against the blue sky. He glanced back, couldn't spot the leaning pole, and wrote it off as an optical illusion caused by the surrounding hills.

The town made a much better impression up close than it did at a distance. About thirty or forty years out of date, but it still looked pretty nice. It probably wasn't that different from Sanders, Eli realized. There were people on the streets. A few carried bags. One had a brief-case. Most of them glanced at the Model A as it drove by, but it held the attention of only a few, and even those for just a few seconds.

A powder-blue car passed them, and Eli craned his head to follow it. The driver noticed and gave a polite smile and nod. "I think that was a '58 Edsel Corsair," Eli said.

"Focus, Mr. Teague."

He cleared his throat. "We're looking for a church?"

"Please."

"Do you remember the time we met at the church, back in San-ders?"

"Of course I do," she said. "It wasn't that long ago for me. Barely two months."

Eli gestured out at the Model A's hood. "You were working on the engine."

"And you were looking down my shirt."

"Well, I . . ." His tongue fumbled in his mouth. "I didn't mean to. I was thirteen and I didn't even know you were a girl. A woman."

She shook her head. "Oh, Mr. Teague, you silver-tongued devil."

He sighed and shook his head. "You told me the car ran on water. That it had a Garrett carburetor."

She nodded. "Yes."

"Yes, that's what you said?"

"Yes to all of it."

Eli shook his head again. "The Garrett carburetor's an urban leg-end."

"An urban legend with a US patent."

"The patent doesn't mean anything," he said. "His design doesn't work."

"Well, then, I guess Eleanor doesn't work either."

"The car's name is Eleanor?"

"Yes."

"Why?"

"Because that's what . . . her original owner named her. He saw it in a motion picture."

"So how does Eleanor have a working Garrett carburetor?"

Harry pointed at a house that looked like a poor man's attempt to copy a Craftsman home. "No one's cut that lawn in almost a month," she said. "Almost a dozen newspapers between the porch and driveway. Someone's out of town."

"Or lazy."

Harry smirked. "I've done this once or thrice before. You get a feel for lazy over absent."

She circled the block, but when they came up on the house again there was a man in a white hat and retro cardigan walking a small dog. They drove past, and the terrier crouched on the front lawn between two tall dandelions. The man yawned and looked at his watch.

"Definitely no one home," Harry said as they circled the block again. "Might even be a bad house."

"Maybe he just hates his neighbor."

Harry shook her head. "If he thought he was getting away with something, he'd be watching out to make sure he does get away with it. He didn't even notice this fine automobile driving by."

"Yeah," murmured Eli. His eyes stayed on the 1959 Dodge Lancer parked in the driveway next door.

They circled around a third time. The man with the dog was at the far end of the block. A woman across the street and two houses down emptied a mailbox. Harry's chin dipped approvingly and she pulled into the driveway.

She was out of the car before the engine stopped rattling. "Open the tank for me, please, Mr. Teague," she called over her shoulder. Her coat fluttered behind her as she strode over to the loose coil of rubber. "Dust and cobwebs," she said, pointing at the hose. "It's a bad house, as I said."

Eli opened the door. "And that's . . . good?" He slid out the door and reached across the hood for the gas cap. It popped off in his hand and he glanced at the rubber seal. Definitely aftermarket.

"Good for me." Harry pulled three, four, five loops of the hose off its bracket and twisted the valve. The house's guts groaned, burped twice, and then spat out some rust-red liquid. The splashing stream mixed with the silt and dirt on the driveway and became a thin mudslide that raced in four different directions. She watered the lawn while the hose ran clear.

Another car approached, a big four-door Mercury with double headlights and a hardtop. The driver locked eyes with Eli, but drove on by.

Eli took in a breath through his nose, then a second, deeper one through his mouth. The air smelled . . . different. The tang of car exhaust and gasoline trailing behind the Mercury seemed stronger, but the air itself seemed fresher. He wondered if the desert climate kept things separate somehow.

A black-and-white squad car rolled by down the street and drove the pleasant thoughts from his head. They stayed gone even after Eli recognized it as an old Ford Fairlane, maybe a '61. Eli glanced back. "You sure it's safe to be sitting here like this, out in the open? What if those cops called ahead?"

"They didn't," she said, dragging the hose to the Model A.

"What if they call ahead to the local station?"

She shoved the hose into the tank. "They won't." It rang and thrummed and sang as the water churned inside it. Harry closed her eyes and focused on the sound.

He walked back to the Model A. "So," he said, "guys with no faces."

"Yes," she said without opening her eyes.

"Who can order police around."

"Yes."

"Do I need to actually ask questions before you'll answer anything?" She opened one eye. "Yes?"

Eli rolled his eyes. "Come on."

Harry opened her other eye. "I'll warn you now, Mr. Teague, I may not be able to give you a satisfying answer. Most of what I know is more of . . . well, stories and general ideas that've been passed along from one searcher to the next. My . . ." She paused to tap the top of the hood and listen to the drumbeat of the gas tank. "My old partner taught me a lot of it, but most of it was what he'd learned from the woman who'd taught him. It's like a childhood game of secrets, where he whispers to me, I whisper to you, you whisper to someone else, but the story changes a little bit every time."

"Telephone game," Eli said. "I remember playing that when I was a kid."

Harry nodded. "There's a great deal to tell, but it's all second- and thirdhand knowledge at best. So, as I said, it doesn't lend itself to simple explanations." She nodded toward the rear of the vehicle. "Would you check the reserve, please, Mr. Teague? I believe it took a shot."

He sighed and walked around the car. "I still want answers."

"You'll get them."

A few drops fell from the base of the red gas can to a puddle under the Model A. Eli ran his fingers across the plastic surface and found the puncture about two-thirds of the way down. The tip of his pinkie could just fit into the hole. "Yeah," he called out. "It caught a . . ." He glanced up and down the street. "It got hit."

Harry muttered to herself. "Straight through?"

Eli checked. "Looks like." He crouched down and peered through. A moment or two of lining up through the gas can showed him a small dimple and a scratch on the Model A's dark-blue finish. "Yeah, clean through. Looks like the water slowed it down a lot, though. Barely dented the car."

She muttered again.

"What?"

"I said we'll have to patch it for now."

The tail-finned Caddy drove past, heading home from the gas station. Eli admired its lines, then found his eyes drifting to one of the small homes. "I didn't know they still made towns like this."

"From your point of view, they don't."

"What's that mean?"

She didn't answer. He walked a few paces back toward the house. His leg muscles flexed and tingled, thanking him now, warning him it would hurt later. He reached for his toes, his hamstrings quivered, and then he stretched back to look up at the house.

Dust and cobwebs didn't just cover the hose—they covered the whole structure. Gray strands rounded every corner of the porch and roof, every window frame and door frame. A fine coat of gray dulled each pane of glass and fixture.

The house wasn't just unoccupied, it was mummified.

Eli took a few more steps and peered in through the window. A wooden chair stood a few feet out from the wall. A piece was missing from its elaborate back. A square cardboard box with sagging corners sat by the room's lone door. An empty bookshelf stood against one wall. Not entirely empty, he realized. A handful of books lay flat on the various shelves, camouflaged with years of gray dust.

Something sprawled on the floor, halfway between the box and the chair. Not quite at the center of the room. His first thought was a bundle of clothes, blanketed with more cobwebs and dust. Then he saw the bones and decided it was an animal that had gotten trapped in the house somehow and died, maybe a large cat or a raccoon.

But the skull looked very round for an animal. And very large for the body.

Harry set a hand on his shoulder. "Best not to look inside, Mr. Teague. These places accumulate history. Rarely the good kind."

"I think that might be—"

"It's long dead, whatever it is," she said. Her hand patted his shoulder, just a faint tap, and she stepped back to the chugging hose.

He looked through the window at the tiny skeleton. It was in plain sight, right by one of the main windows. He could see faint footprints in the dust all around it. Some looked like shoes. Others, like paws.

"Shouldn't we tell someone?"

"About what?"

Eli gestured at the window.

Harry raised an eyebrow. "Do you think nobody knows?"

"Well . . ." Eli looked at the town, than back over his shoulder. "Shouldn't we tell the police?"

"In a town this size, I'm sure some local deputy checks in on empty buildings at least once or twice a month."

"So why haven't they done anything?"

"Because they don't want to know," she said. "Or maybe they already know, and they just want to avoid confirming it. Whatever that is in there, it's been there for years, at least. Perhaps decades."

Eli looked at her face. Her expression reminded him of his mother or a teacher trying to explain some basic truth that just wasn't being understood. Boredom mixed with acceptance, seasoned with sadness, dusted with a few grains of annoyance.

Harry must have seen her reflection in his eyes. Her face softened.

"It's a bad house," she said. "Pretty much every town has one. One of the darker side effects of the dream."

"The dream?"

"Yes."

He waited for her to continue. Instead she walked back to the car, swung the red tank from its bracket, and pulled her toolbox from the trunk. "I just need a few minutes to putty the reserve," she said, "and then we'll be on our way."

"I thought you were going to explain the faceless men."

"We're getting there, Mr. Teague, I promise."

Eli sighed, stepped over the hose toward the door, and then changed course. He kicked one of the rolled-up newspapers around so he could read the headline. Even the top one had the brittle look of newsprint that had been exposed to the elements for weeks, maybe months. The banner named it the *Herald Republican*, established in 1938, which left Eli wondering if "Herald" referred to the paper itself or the name of the town. There didn't seem to be a single main headline, but according to the largest one the president had announced a budget surplus of over a billion dollars, which didn't seem terribly noteworthy, even to Eli's dim understanding of government spending.

Then he caught the first words of the article.

In an official announcement in Washington, President Eisenhower declared a budget surplus of . . .

Eli's eyes jumped back up to the banner, and the date below it.

JULY 20, 1960

He glanced back at Harry, thumbing some kind of gummy material into the hole in the gas can, then at the Dodge Lancer parked across the road. He tried to remember seeing a single car from the '70s or later since they came into town. He'd been distracted by all the classics, but there must've been one. He looked down the road, where the man in the hat and cardigan had gone with his dog.

He walked back to Harry. "Where are we?"

She stopped blowing on the patch, a yellow-clear goop that filled the hole. It already seemed hard. "We're about a mile and half from the Nevada border."

"That's not what I mean."

She blew on the patch again before flipping the plastic tank around. "Then say what you mean, Mr. Teague. No sense pussyfooting about it."

He stared at her. Then at the Lancer. "Did we . . . are we in 1960?"

Harry shrugged and thumbed a wad of putty into the exit hole. "Mid-1960s," she said. "Possibly early 1966, but I don't think so."

"You don't think so?"

She shook her head, then packed a wrinkled tube of something chemical-smelling back into her toolbox. She stood up and blew on the patch one more time.

Eli smelled the air again. Looked back at the papers. "How?"

She sighed and closed the trunk. "That question covers a great deal of ground."

"We traveled through time?"

"Through history, yes."

"When?"

"That's a bit of a brain teaser, isn't it?" Harry carried the gas can over to the hose, swinging it back and forth through the air.

Eli followed at a safe distance. "Shouldn't . . . shouldn't there have been a flash of light or a tunnel or a . . . I don't know, something?"

"Do you recall the tires skidding as we approached town?"

He nodded.

"That was it. That was when we slipped back."

"How?" he asked again.

" 'How' will take a little more to explain." She stuck the hose into the gas can and cranked the spigot again. Water sloshed into the container.

"Can you just give me a simple version?"

"I'm sorry, Mr. Teague, but no. This may be difficult to believe, but the mechanisms of traveling through history defy simple explanation."

He looked at her. Back at the newspaper. Then back at the gleaming Lancer in the driveway across the street.

The street in the small desert town that had looked old and abandoned when they'd approached.

Before the skid.

"Holy shit," he said. "I mean, I kinda knew. I figured it out after the second time we met, but I still didn't really . . . I mean, we actually did it. We're in the past."

"Yes," Harry said, pulling the hose free, "it's very exciting." She watered the driveway a bit more while twisting the spigot off. She tapped the dried plug on each side of the gas can, nodded, and heaved the plastic can up to her hip. Eli reached to help, but she turned away and lugged the reserve back to the Model A. He followed behind her. She lined up the tank, heaved again, and dropped it into the bracket. Its weight made the car bounce once.

"The dream," Eli said again.

"Yes?"

"Back when I was a kid, you said you had to see a man about a dream."

She nodded once and pulled a strap across the plastic tank.

"Is that the thing you're looking for? The dream?"

Harry met his eyes. "Yes," she said. "I'm one of many people searching for it."

"For . . . what?"

She rested her hands on the red container, her back to him. "You've asked about a lot of things," she said. "My search. History travel. The faceless men. What you don't realize is that, in truth, these are all related questions about the same thing."

She looked at him and waited.

"The dream," said Eli.

"Yes. What do you know about history?"

"Ummm, do you mean the Middle Ages or the Renaissance or—"

"American History. How the United States began."

Eli's mind flitted back through grade school and high school and the half dozen college classes that had earned him a minor. There'd also been some casual independent studies into clothing and fashion, trying to learn more about the woman he'd last seen when he was thirteen. The history of automobiles had been his main focus. "More than the basics?" he guessed. "Still less than a lot of people, I guess."

"Words of warning," she said. "Much of what I'm going to tell you will go against what you've learned. Not just in history but in many disciplines. Some of it's just going to be unbelievable, but it's all true."

"Okay."

"We should get going."

"Going . . . where? When?"

"East, for now. I'll explain everything as we go."

"Thanks." He stood there in the driveway, his gaze flitting from the cars to the houses to the fresh pavement.

The corners of her mouth flexed. "Get in the car, Mr. Teague. The road beckons."

Harry flipped the ignition switches, the Model A shuddered, and they backed out of the bad house's driveway. As they headed back out of the town, Eli caught a quick glimpse of the dog walker heading into the small market and someone at the gas station with a blocky red Chevy pickup. Then the highway was under their tires again and the Model A—Eleanor—picked up a little more speed.

12

It had been dumb luck that Officer Zeke Miller had been there at the desk that day. Wednesday was supposed to be his day off, but Captain Deacon had come down with a bad case of food poisoning. It meant double shifts to pick up the slack. Goddamn perfect Barney ended up on patrol and Zeke got called in to man the station's phones and radio. Which was the most boring part of the job, especially in a town like Sanders.

The man on the phone had introduced himself as Agent Fifteen and rattled off a badge number to confirm his authority. He asked for the senior officer on duty. Zeke introduced himself. Agent Fifteen had been looking for a dangerous fugitive, an insurgent. According to him, she'd been seen in Sanders.

Zeke had found this hard to believe. One, that any kind of major-league fugitive would be in Sanders. Two, that a woman could be all that dangerous. There were hot, kick-ass women in movies and stuff, sure, but that was all pretend.

Fifteen had assured Zeke the woman, Harriet Pritchard, was dangerous. However, the agent already had a man dealing with her. He needed Zeke to keep an eye on her accomplice in town. He'd asked if Zeke knew of a man named Elias Teague.

Zeke knew him all right, and had said so. He'd known Eli Teague pretty much his whole life. Fifteen said this was good, and had asked Zeke to keep an eye on Eli until further notice.

That had been last week.

Now Zeke sat at the station's front desk and glared at that same phone. He'd glared at everything for the past few days. He snapped another pencil. Then he snapped the two pieces. He put his thumbs against the short, stubby remains and managed to break three of them. He couldn't get leverage on the fourth.

Barney had been on the phones when Zeke had shown up for his shift. Goddamn perfect Barney. Two years ago Zeke would've thought a man named Barney would need brick balls to be a small-town police officer. Barney's were solid marble all the way through. A walking Greek statue, the people of Sanders called him. He'd transferred up from York Beach with glowing recommendations.

Zeke didn't get along with him.

They'd exchanged a few basic courtesies. Barney offered some news on Captain Deacon, and mentioned a few items in the logbook. Then he grabbed his coat and headed for the door for a night patrol.

And Zeke had settled in behind the desk. The desk where he'd be for the next. Fifty-nine. Nights.

After he'd questioned Nicole about Eli's disappearance, she'd had called Deacon with a bunch of exaggerated stories about intimidation and police brutality. It was all lies. She didn't have any bruises. She was just an uppity bitch who'd had it in for Zeke since he broke up with her in high school.

And, yeah, he'd kicked in the door to Eli's crap little apartment above Tanner's garage. He'd been chasing a fugitive. Time was of the essence and all that shit—he couldn't wait for a search warrant. His only real mistake had been keeping Agent Fifteen's call to himself and not telling Deacon about it.

Now half the town'd turned against Zeke. Just that morning, getting off work, he'd heard whispers at the grocer when he stopped in to get a coffee and a knockoff McMuffin. Robin Furber talking with Thatcher behind the counter about how Eli was too responsible to just up and leave without saying anything, everyone knew that. They'd clammed up when they saw Zeke, but they weren't the only ones. Everybody in town kept wondering what had really happened to Eli. The fact that he'd asked his boss at Stahlbank for a few days off didn't matter. Everybody gave Zeke the eye, like he was some kind of movie maniac with an ax or something. Like he'd done something.

At least Deacon was a fair man. He'd said it didn't look good, but he wouldn't be the one to start a witch-hunt. Zeke just wasn't going out on patrol for two months. Or dealing with the day traffic in the office. Two months manning the phones and radio, every night for the next fifty-nine nights. And counting.

Rookies, cripples, and old men did desk duty. He was young and strong. At the peak of his game, like they said about star quarterbacks. He should be out keeping the town safe with Barney, not sitting in the station. Especially at night.

Zeke left the desk and stomped around the office. His left hand flexed open and closed, open and closed, open and closed. They only got three or four calls a night, and at least two of those were always that old fossil Mr. Moreland, calling to complain about barking dogs or a loud car driving by his house or someone walking by outside. Late shift on the desk equaled punishment, no question about it.

Zeke glared at the wanted posters. A collection of losers the Staties were looking for, plus three or four from the FBI. The real smart criminals almost never got wanted posters. One of the teachers at the academy had told him that. These people backed it up. A bank robber. A few aggravated assaults. One attempted murderer. A car thief from Ogunquit. Seriously, who was stupid enough to steal cars anymore with all the alarms and stuff?

Eli's picture should be up on the board, Zeke realized. It needed to be. Eli was a fugitive. He'd aided and abetted. And he was an asshole who'd been making Zeke's life suck since third grade, whining about every joke or noogie or dodgeball that came his way.

Every Monday morning Deacon cleaned the whole board off, sorted in the new posters, and put them all back in alphabetical order. He tacked them up. Real tacks, the flat metal ones, not plastic pushpins.

Zeke entertained the idea of rearranging the posters now to make space for Eli's poster. This was a federal matter, after all. That's what the voice on the phone had said. There'd be a poster.

He imagined himself prying at the tacks, wedging his nails under them and pulling until they slid out of the corkboard. He could have the board stripped in twenty minutes, put back together in maybe half an hour. Eli's poster would go in the bottom row, but if Zeke swapped it with the FBI Most Wanted guy, Quilt, that'd put Eli up at the end of the second row. It was a good spot. Visible as soon as someone walked into the station.

Maybe they'd get extras of the Eli poster since he was local. Or he could make copies. Some wanted posters only named the one big crime somebody was wanted for, but hopefully Eli's would list everythi—

"Hello, Officer Miller."

Zeke spun around and reached for his sidearm. People should know better than to sneak up on a cop. If they wet their pants at the business end of a Smith and Wesson, well, that's how people learned to respect the uniform.

But he was on punishment desk duty. In Sanders that meant his holster was empty. A shotgun sat in a quick-release mount behind the counter for emergencies, but right now "behind the counter" wasn't the side he was on.

All this rushed through his mind as Zeke registered the man standing behind him. Just a few feet behind him. He hadn't made a sound coming into the station or walking across the small lobby.

The tall man wore a dark suit with a matching hat, like in *Dragnet* or one of those shows about people back in the sixties. He had one hand in his coat, and Zeke's thoughts went back to the shotgun as the hand came out holding . . . a leather square. The wallet flipped open to reveal an elaborate silver badge with gold details and a glossy red-white-and-blue inlay. Zeke registered the letters US and DEPARTMENT OF something that began with D before the man snapped the badge holder shut with a casual display of badassery.

"I'm Fifteen," said the man. All the sharp edges were gone from the man's voice, like his words were coming through a handkerchief or scarf. "We spoke on the phone the other day."

Zeke's mind cleared and he remembered the call and the agent. Then he remembered Eli'd ruined any chance to look impressive on the federal level. Zeke bit back his anger and stuck out his hand. "Good to meet you in person, sir."

Fifteen looked down at the hand, and for a second Zeke thought the agent was going to leave him hanging. Then the man reached out and closed his fingers around Zeke's. He had a strong grip. Not in a macho, asshat, scoring-points way. A solid, dependable grip. He pumped Zeke's hand twice, then released it. "I've come to hear your report on Eli Teague."

Zeke's survival sense awoke in the back of his mind and crept forward. "My report?"

The tall man pulled a long, old-fashioned notepad from inside his suit jacket. "You were instructed to keep Mr. Teague under surveillance. To make sure he didn't leave Sanders."

Zeke's stomach flopped. His survival sense growled, warned him this conversation was a bad place to be. "Hey—"

"And yet, two days after you and I spoke, Mr. Teague was seen in Boston, speaking with a known collaborator of our fugitive, one often used to pass supplies and messages between insurgent groups."

"Look, I did the best I could. I tried to keep an eye on him, like you said, but he's a sneaky bastard. Always has been."

"So you knew this, but still didn't take precautions to stop him from getting away."

A statement, not a question. Zeke had heard things phrased this way many times in his life. By his parents, his teachers, his assorted bosses. Always with that same tired-but-not-surprised tone.

Something settled over Zeke. His skin tingled. His pulse slowed. The noise that always cluttered his mind cleared away. Even his growling survival sense quieted itself. The word "epiphany" would mean nothing to him, but on some primal level Zeke understood this was a major moment in his life. The next few minutes would have a profound effect on everything that happened afterward. He needed to be straight and come clean and not spray his usual stream of protective bullshit over everything.

"No," he said. "No, I didn't. I didn't know what he was going to do, because I was just thinking of him as some wuss from school who was pounding my ex, y'know? I wasn't seeing the big picture." He paused for a moment. "I wasn't given all the information so I could see the big picture. Maybe if I'd known what was really going on, I could've done my job better. But I did the best I could with what I had."

The agent seemed to consider this. As he did, Zeke noticed the mask the man wore. A transparent one with eyebrows and cheeks and lips painted on the plastic. Probably some special government-issue thing. It seemed weird he hadn't noticed it before, but maybe that was the point of it. It made it hard to pick out the details of the agent's face.

Fifteen had his eyes closed behind the mask, like he was thinking. He stood rock still. It was almost as if he'd started daydreaming. He turned his head toward the wanted posters. "Are you a citizen of the United States, Officer Miller?"

Zeke twitched. It'd only been eight or nine seconds of silence, but the agent's voice startled him all over again. Like it was coming from nowhere, even though the man was right in front of him. "What?"

Two fingers flipped the notebook closed. "It's a simple question. I need to make sure before we continue."

Zeke nodded. "Yeah, I'm one hundred percent American. All the way back to my great-great-grandpa. My family's been in Sanders almost the whole time."

"Were you born here?" It was a we're-all-friends-here question. One to keep him at ease.

"Yeah. Well, Wentworth-Douglass down in Dover. It was the closest hospital."

Fifteen gave two slow nods.

Zeke had to admit, the whole mask thing was a little creepy. Now that he was really looking at it, it looked like one of the cheap-ass masks they sold at CVS around Halloween, or the big costume stores that opened over in New Hampshire every September. He'd seen people wear those a few times, once when some losers had tried to rob the Cumberland Farms store on the south side of town. They didn't hide shit. This one, though, blurred all the agent's features so the only thing Zeke could see was skin tone.

Definitely some kind of government-issue thing.

"I would like to offer you," Fifteen said, "an opportunity for personal advancement."

"A . . . what?"

The agent slid his notebook back into his coat, pulled out a white square, and—

The big man was three steps closer, pressing the square over Zeke's nose and mouth. Zeke tried to slam the hand away, but it was like hitting a heavy bag at the gym. Something sharp burned his eyes as something sweet tickled his nose and throat.

"Congratulations, Officer," Fifteen said as the lights dimmed. "You've been selected for service."

13

A few miles rolled by under Eleanor's wheels. On the dashboard, the rotating cylinder drifted back and forth between sixty and sixty-five miles per hour. The broad, flat desert stretched out around them, marked here and there by distant hills.

Harry drummed her fingers on the steering wheel again. She did it a lot. For a while Eli tried humming different songs under his breath to see if anything lined up with the beat of her fingers. Classic rock. Pop stuff. Country. Movie themes. Even a few children's songs he remembered from grade school. Whatever she tapped to was either very obscure or completely random.

A mile marker approached them and flashed by.

"Back in 1764," Harry said, keeping her eyes on the road, "a group of British colonials became frustrated with the Empire. With their lack of representation in their own government. Britain had a Parliament at this point, but the American colonists had very little say in it."

"And taxes," said Eli. "They were upset about taxes."

"Not as much as you'd think. It wasn't the tax itself—they understood the need for it, and taxes were actually quite low at the time. People simply didn't like having no say in when it was levied or how it was used.

"Effectively, they felt like they were being oppressed by foreigners. That they were a country ruled by Britain rather than part of Britain. And, with several of them, this notion took root. That the American Colonies were a separate country." The cadence of her voice shifted, relaxed. The words came out at a comfortable, practiced pace. "The idea grew and eventually it occurred to them that they could be a separate country. That they could declare independence."

Eli nodded again.

"Looking back with the benefit of history," Harry continued, "this seems pretty straightforward. It's what you and I grew up with and were taught in school."

"Wait," said Eli, "you were taught this in school?"

"Of course."

His eyes went up and down her colonial outfit. She looked at him for a moment, then understood. "I was born in 1885, Mr. Teague, I just like the coat." Her fingers flexed on the steering wheel. "But we're getting off point. Don't interrupt."

"Sorry."

"As I was saying, independence seems like a straightforward idea in hindsight. At the time, though, this was revolutionary. In several ways. Nothing like this had happened before. Oh, conquered countries had rebelled, overthrown their rulers, and reasserted themselves. Stolen lands had been stolen back or abandoned to the original owners. But for a colony, an established extension of a country, to just declare itself independent . . . it simply didn't happen. It hadn't happened in hundreds of years of colonial expansion."

"I know all this," Eli said. "More or less."

"I'm setting the stage, so to say." Harry leaned on the steering wheel and the Model A followed a curve in the road around a tall, rust-red hill. "It's one thing for a group of educated aristocrats and upper class to come to this conclusion, but how do you get the farmers and merchants and blacksmiths behind this idea? Keep in mind, many of them were only four or five generations away from feudalism. The idea of nations overall, let alone declaring independence from one of the oldest empires on the planet, was simply beyond them."

"That's silly," said Eli. "People weren't stupid back then."

"They weren't," she agreed. "I've met many of them. But you're looking at it with hindsight again. It seems simple and straightforward to you and me, but they lacked the proper framework."

"So they had to come up with a great sales pitch," said Eli. "And they did."

"Not precisely. They did have a . . ." Harry worked the term on her tongue. "A sales pitch. Thomas Paine and others continued to push the idea of unfair taxes. But again, most people were used to the idea of unfairness and taxes. They accepted it as a simple truth of the world."

"So what did they do?"

She let another half mile slip past them. "They created a dream."

He waited a moment, then waved her on.

"They needed something to inspire people," Harry explained, "for the citizens to rally behind and believe in. Something which could be the base for their whole idea of a fledgling nation. And Benjamin Franklin came up with the idea of forging a dream."

Eli shifted his jaw from side to side. "Okay . . ."

She took another breath. "Franklin was a scholar and a high-ranking Freemason. While he was in Europe, he used his status as a Grand Master to gain access to certain historical documents and religious texts. With these, he designed a ritual, a conjuration of sorts. When he returned to the Americas in 1775, he gathered some of the founding fathers from other lodges to perform it with him.

"They summoned Ptah, the Egyptian god of creation. The blacksmith god. And they came to an accord, which resulted in him forging a dream for them. The American Dream."

She glanced at his face. Eli stared back at her. Another sign appeared on the road ahead. It rushed forward, passed, and vanished behind them. He never registered what it said.

"You can't be serious," he said.

"I can't say if it's the precise, gospel truth. I can only say it's how the story came down the Chain to me."

"This is . . . that's ridiculous. Every part of it is nonsense."

"It's all true."

"Why not throw Santa and the Easter Bunny in there?"

"Don't be absurd, Mr. Teague."

"Absurd?" He shook his head. "The Freemasons aren't some mystic cult. They're a service organization like the Shriners or . . . or Rotary Club. I did night shifts at the Cumberland Farms down in South Berwick every summer through college. They'd stop in all the time after meetings." Even as he said it, Eli pictured the line of rumpled businessmen showing up one after another to buy convenience-store coffee or gasoline.

"A service organization which goes back thousands of years," she said. "One that many of the founding fathers happened to belong to."

He shook his head. "It's nonsense."

She shrugged.

"You're saying the American Dream is an actual, physical thing?"

"Yes."

"It's an actual thing that a group of Freemasons had a god make for them so they could convince everyone in the country to leave England?"

"That's the gist of it, yes."

He stared out at the desert. The shadows of hills and stones and lumpy cacti stretched longer as the sun sank behind them. "That's completely nuts."

"And yet," she said, "like the Garrett carburetor, still true."

Eli crossed his arms. The Model A ate up another mile of highway with its tires before he spoke again. "So the whole American Revolution happened because of an Egyptian god?"

"Such a silly idea, I know," said Harry. "If it was true, there'd be giant obelisks in the nation's capital, pyramids on the currency, noticeable things like that."

Eli opened his mouth to respond, then shut it. "Is this dream in Washington?" he asked, half a mile later.

"I don't think so, no."

"Philadelphia?"

"No."

"Where is it? Can we go see it?"

She shook her head. "I'm afraid not."

"Why not?"

"Because no one knows where it's gone. It was stolen from the place it was kept. I'm searching for it. Many people are."

"Right," he said. "You're all searching for the American Dream." He rubbed his eyes.

"I did tell you it was a lot to take in all at once. And we've barely scratched the surface."

"How," he started. The sentence died after the one word. "Why do you . . . did you make all of this up?"

"Of course not." She frowned and gave him a disappointed look.

"So where's it all coming from? Where did you hear this?"

She sighed and focused on the road. "Around. Down the Chain. The person who brought me into the search told me most of it."

"Most of it?"

"People talk. They trade information."

"So all of this is just stories you've heard?"

"Not just stories. People have been observing and testing this for hundreds of years."

"Hundreds?"

"Yes, hundreds. We travel in history, Mr. Teague. We've spent more years searching for the dream than the country's actually existed."

"How's that even possible?"

"It's a big country," she said, "with a lot of history behind it. If you're going for square footage, it has an amazing amount of history for such a relatively young nation."

"How long have you been searching for it?"

She glanced at him. "Just over nine years."

He blinked. "How old are you?"

"A gentleman shouldn't ask such a thing of a lady."

"I don't think I'm much of a gentleman," said Eli, "and I'm really getting the sense you're not much of a lady."

"And there's that wit again."

"My point is, you can't be much older than me."

"I turn thirty in a few months," she said. "More or less."

"More or less?"

"It's hard to keep track when you don't see the months in order. I may be thirty already. No more than that, though. Maybe just twenty-nine." She glanced away from the road to meet his eyes. "I was nineteen when I first went on the road."

"That's young."

"Old for the time I was raised. I had friends who were married at eighteen. My parents were worried I'd be an old maid."

Eli let a mile go by, and then another. "So, you're searching for the American Dream."

Harry nodded. "Yes."

"And the car, Eleanor, is a time machine. Like in *Back to the Future*."

"What?"

He waved a hand at the dashboard. "Is that what all the switches are? Controls or something?"

"That's the ignition. I don't want to risk losing a key, and we . . . I needed some way to safeguard her against hijacking."

"So Eleanor is . . ."

"Just a car. With some modifications to the engine and the ignition."

"But it travels through time."

Her head bobbed back and forth. "The car travels through history, yes," she said. "But we're not traveling through history because of the car, if that makes sense."

"Not really."

Her fingers tapped out another verse of something on the wheel. "You can put on fancy shoes and run," she said, "but the shoes aren't making you run. You aren't running solely because you're wearing the shoes."

"I think I'm still missing something."

She nodded slowly, and Eli could sense her organizing thoughts as the Model A covered more distance. "Have you ever heard people talk of a town or part of a city that's, say, stuck in the 1950s? Or the 1920s? Or the last century? Sayings like that."

"Yeah, of course."

"Well, sometimes, more times than you'd think . . . they are."

"They are . . . ?"

"Stuck. Trapped in history. A road or a neighborhood or a whole town where it's still 1950. Or 1920. Or 1875."

"You mean they never developed?"

"I mean they never left. History slipped past them and they're still stuck in 1950. It's been 1950 there for decades. You see, the dream was intended to allow people's hopes and beliefs to become true. It allows people to live how they want. In some cases, it can even reshape the world."

"How?"

"For the sake of argument," she explained, back on familiar ground, "let us say a great number of people believe the same thing. That this town or that era is the pinnacle of how things should always be. The mindsets, the culture, the technology—they believe this is a moment which defines the very best of America. Or, in a few rare cases, the very worst of it."

"Okay."

"When enough of these people get together, their belief focuses the dream and it makes these things so. That point is pinned down and stuck while the rest of history moves on past it. Or piles up around it, really.

"That's what the dream does in these places," Harry said. "It brings things to a halt. The people there decide they don't want things to change, so they don't." She paused to glance at him. "These are the slick spots. The places we can skid across history."

Eli looked out at the desert. The sun was on the horizon behind them. Shadows covered most of the landscape, broken by a few fierce slashes of daylight. "When we drove into the town yesterday," he said, "the car skidded on the road."

The corners of Harry's mouth twitched. "Not on the road. On history. As I said, the dream has created hundreds and hundreds of slick spots all over the country. You just need to know how to spot them. And if you know where these slick spots are, if you get a feel for them, you can use them. Go through them. Sometimes slingshot around them for a bit of momentum, so to speak. And they can take you anywhen in America's history."

"Anywhen?"

"Well, within certain limits. Geographically, the late 1700s is all the East Coast. Then there's the Louisiana Purchase, which opens up a lot of territory for us. No Texas until the end of 1849 and no California until 1850. Alaska's a little tricky because it's not connected, but I know a few folks who've done it."

"What about Hawaii?"

"There aren't any roads to Hawaii. Don't be foolish, Mr. Teague."

"Right," he said. "Foolish."

"A few spots are very specific," she explained. "There's a street in Dallas that only leads to November of 1963, and a bus route in Montgomery that goes to December of 1955. A road in Philadelphia will take you to August of 1776. Others are more general and give a little more elbow room once you become skilled at driving them. Washington, DC's filled with them, of course. There's a sort of sweet spot that crops up often across the country, from 1945 to 1957, and that's useful. The decade of ultimate, unchallenged American superiority, from some people's view."

"What happened in 1957?"

"*Sputnik.* Absolute proof another country was ahead of the United States. Kicked the legs out from under a lot of people."

They drove for a few minutes without speaking. The pavement hummed under Eleanor's tires. The engine purred in its coarse way.

Harry cleared her throat. "It took me a week to get my mind around it. Even when Christopher, my old partner, showed me the roads, I was convinced it was a trick."

"It's kind of familiar, actually," he said.

She blinked. "Really?"

Eli nodded. "I took a couple science classes in college. Didn't really want to, but I needed them for requirements, so I tried to find the fun ones. And one of them was an astronomy course."

"Navigation?"

He managed a chuckle. "Not exactly. Not really my thing, but some of it was interesting."

Harry turned her head to look at him. To judge him. "You failed the course."

"No," he said. "I passed. Barely."

She snorted.

He used his hands to sketch a plane between him and the windshield. "Later in the semester the professor talked about how light and gravity and time and space were all related. He had this really great diagram of space, a huge gridded plane, and all the stars made these sort of . . . depressions in space. Their gravity bent space-time in places, so you'd end up with funnels in the plane."

"I believe I've seen similar images," said Harry.

"So, this time travel—"

"History travel," she corrected.

"—it's a space-time thing?"

"Oh, no, not remotely. But if you're looking for a visual metaphor, that one's as good as any." She shrugged and the steering wheel wobbled in her hands. "This is more or less how it was explained to me."

"More or less?"

"As I said, people talk and trade information. I've heard a few different versions of the story. We all have our own examples and metaphors."

Another mile passed by.

"Okay," he said, "I have to know."

"Know what?"

"Why? Why are you searching for this thing? What's the point?"

Harry turned and furrowed her brow at him. "Haven't you been paying attention?"

"Like you said, it's a lot to get your mind around."

She sighed. "At a distance, with a large number of people, the dream can alter the flow of time and reshape the nation. If one person actually possessed it, held it, the entire United States—and all its people— would all be whatever that one person dreamed. They could impose their will on the whole country."

Eli blinked. "How?"

"I don't know the details," Harry admitted. "I just know the person who finds the dream can do whatever they want with the country."

"But how do you know that?"

She shrugged. "As I said, people talk. They tell stories."

"So . . . you heard gossip."

"It's not gossip, Mr. Teague."

He opened his mouth, looked at her expression, and closed it again. Two miles hummed by beneath the narrow tires.

Eli shifted on the bench and rolled his shoulders. "Okay," he said. "Let's assume everything you've been saying is true."

"It is."

"Assuming it's true," he repeated, "shouldn't this happen to lots of people?"

"What?"

"Slipping back in time. Or forward, I guess. Can you go forward?"

"Of course. Some of the slick spots extend decades into what you'd consider the future."

"Okay, so why isn't it happening all the time? What's that joke— 'where are all the time travelers?' If these slippery spots—"

"Slick spots."

"—slick spots are all through history, then shouldn't hundreds of people have slipped back to 1960 or forward to 2020 or where— whenever?"

Harry nodded. "True enough," she said. "To be honest, quite a few do."

"What?"

"As I said before, we've all heard the stories of the towns trapped in the past. Most motorists slip in one side and straight out the other. Then they drive home and tell their friends about the adorable town they drove through with hundred-year-old houses that still looked new.

"There's also a limitation," she continued. "Only American steel goes through. All those foreign cars, the imports, none of them will slide." She reached out and rapped her knuckles against Eleanor's dashboard.

"Why not?"

"I don't know," said Harry. She punctuated it with another shrug. "I would guess because they're not American."

"What about American fiberglass or—"

"I believe I was clear that a lot of this is second- and thirdhand knowledge, yes?"

He closed his mouth. "You were."

"Thank you."

The sun had almost vanished behind them, no more than a warm glow in the side mirrors. Ahead the sky was dark, and he could see a few bright stars in the sky making their presence known. As if hearing his thoughts, Harry reached out and flicked another switch. The headlights flickered once and then surged to life, throwing a bright oval on the black pavement in front of them.

"You said most of the people drive through," Eli said. "What happens to the rest? The ones who don't drive out the other side?"

She stretched one finger up, off the steering wheel, and pushed the point of her hat up away from her face. Her eyes stayed on the road, focused on the patch of light a dozen yards ahead of them. A quarter mile passed by under the Model A's tires.

"Harry?"

"Some of them just become lost for a while," she said, as if she'd never paused. "They spend a few hours, maybe a whole day, lost somewhere else and go home with a slightly stranger story. Some of them never find their way home, and they end up becoming searchers. A woman I know, Monica, hopped into the wrong taxicab. Got into it in 1977, stepped out in 1936."

"And the rest?"

"The rest," she said, "make too much noise. Too many ripples in history. So they're removed."

"From the slick spot?"

"From history, Mr. Teague." She shook her head. "They're eliminated. Killed."

"How many people are we talking about?"

She shrugged. "Two, perhaps three hundred a year. There's no way to be precise."

"Three hundred people a year?" he repeated.

Harry nodded.

"Three *hundred*?"

"Is there a problem?"

"How do three hundred people go missing and nobody notices?"

"Of course people notice. Do you know how many people go missing in this country every year, vanished into thin air? Thousands, since the day the country was founded. Why would those people lost in history stand out more than any others?"

"So how do they explain it when their bodies are found?"

"Their bodies aren't found. Ever. They're removed."

Eli shook his head, trying to make all the pieces line up with the world he'd known just that morning. "But . . . how? By who?"

Harry glanced at him. "I think you can make an educated guess, Mr. Teague."

"You mean . . . the faceless men?"

"The faceless men," she echoed.

14

Zeke heard movement around him. Not just him being moved past things in his wheelchair, but things moving past him as well. Shoes on carpet. Something went by with a squeaky wheel, and it made a picture in his mind of one of those little bookshelf-carts librarians pushed around.

The blindfold was soft cloth, like a T-shirt, but had enough weight to it that it settled across his eyes and cheeks. He couldn't see through it or under it. He'd woken up with it across his face after Agent Fifteen had knocked him out back at the station.

His arms were strapped to the wheelchair, not cuffed. He'd been in cuffs enough times, for enough reasons, to recognize the feel of the double edge, even through clothes. He wasn't as sure about the restraints on his legs, but if his arms were strapped his legs probably were too.

Who had wheelchairs with straps on them? Prisons? Psycho wards? Feds?

He didn't hear anyone talking either. Or breathing. Even when someone moved by in a rush, he didn't hear them gasp for air. Just the sounds of the wheelchair on tight carpet and dozens of bodies moving back and forth around him.

"This blindfold's gettin' really fucking old," Zeke muttered.

"Watch your language," said Fifteen. His iron fingers flexed on Zeke's shoulder. "Not much longer."

"I don't like not seeing where I'm going."

"That's the point of a blindfold."

"This some sort of black-ops thing? I see something I wasn't supposed to?"

No one answered him.

He focused on Fifteen. The big man had a solid grip on Zeke's left shoulder, and his voice had come from the left. But that meant someone else had to be pushing the wheelchair. Unless the big guy was doing it one-handed.

Zeke sensed a doorway around him, then felt it push through the air and heard it latch behind him. The wheelchair rolled forward a few more feet, then settled back and trembled. Did wheelchairs have brakes? He thought they did.

"Free his hand," Fifteen said, "and take off the blindfold."

Zeke felt a finger slide into the blindfold at the back of his head. The heavy fabric dropped down to hang around his neck like a turtleneck. He opened his eyes, blinked a few times, and forced them open again.

The office looked old. Not dusty or worn out, just . . . old. Like the captain's office with all its '70s furniture and out-of-date office phones. Except this place looked like something out of a World War II movie. A typewriter sat on one side of a creepy-clean and ordered desk. An American flag stood in the corner. An old safe with a big dial and a handle squatted against the back wall.

Agent Fifteen stepped around to the far side of the desk and opened a drawer without sitting down. His hat had vanished, but he still had the freaky plastic mask over his face. The badge, notebook, and pistol moved from his coat and vanished into the drawer. He pulled a single file folder from another drawer, centered it on the desk, and opened it to look at the pages inside.

A hand reached down from behind Zeke and unbuckled a thick, beltlike strap. He twisted around and saw another dark-suited man. This one had a feature-blurring mask with round cheeks and a smile, almost like a clown.

Clowns creeped Zeke out. He turned away just as the strap came free. The man kept his hand on Zeke's wrist, pinning it to the wheelchair's wooden armrest.

The wheelchair had the big wheels in the front. Dark creases marked the brown leather of the straps. Somebody'd fought to get out of this thing. Maybe a couple people.

The man released his arm and stepped back. Zeke looked at Fifteen, still reviewing paperwork.

"Who the fuck are—"

The clown-agent behind Zeke rapped his head.

"What the fuck, you—"

The knuckles cracked against his skull again.

Zeke twisted around, trying to grasp at the man with his free hand. His fingers never came close. The clown-agent never flinched.

"Officer Miller," said Fifteen, "I trust we can carry out this process in a professional manner."

"What the hell's going on?" growled Zeke. "You kidnapped me. You abducted a police officer! D'you know how hard they're going to come down on you?"

Fifteen selected a page from the file folder and set it down on the center of the blotter. "I'll need your signature on this before we can continue."

"Fuck you!"

The lights in the room brightened, turning everything white, and an instant later the pain hit, rocking his head forward. He took a deep breath and shook his head until his vision cleared. The back of his skull throbbed where the clown's punch had connected.

He glared at the agent behind him, then at Fifteen on the other side of the desk. "Who the hell do you think you are?"

"We," said Fifteen, "are the faceless men behind the government. Our office served this country before all five branches of the Armed Forces."

He set his fingertips against the sheet of paper and spun it around. His arm stretched out and the paper slid across the desk. "Sign," he said, "at the bottom."

Zeke looked at the blank sheet. "What is it?"

"Your contract."

"It doesn't say anything."

"It says everything it needs to. The conditions and term of your service. Requirements of your position." Fifteen lifted a pen from its precise position alongside the immaculate blotter and held it out across the desk. "Now sign. At the bottom."

Zeke stretched out his hand and took the pen. He could just reach the bottom edge of the sheet of paper. He looked up at Fifteen, then back at the clown-agent behind the wheelchair. He tried to make out any features, any expressions, behind the plastic masks, but they blurred into nothing, almost as if . . .

"What is this?" hissed Zeke, swallowing down a mouthful of fear and holding it down with anger. He retracted his arm, repulsed by the idea of what he might be agreeing to.

He twisted around to stare up at the clown-agent behind him. He couldn't see anything behind the clear mask. The skin wasn't blurred, it was just . . . blank. No eyes, no whiskers, no mouth, no—

"This is a chance to serve your country in the most honorable way possible," said Fifteen. "Sign the contract."

"What the fuck are you?" Another punch to the back of the head rattled his teeth. Maybe not a punch. That could've been a nightstick. Maybe it'd been his own nightstick.

"Sign, Officer Miller."

"Are you going to kill me? What the fuck is this!"

The faceless man in the clown mask stepped forward and grabbed his wrist, stretching it back out to the contract. Something twanged in Zeke's shoulder. He tried to drop the pen, to fling it away, but the man's hand was already there to catch it and shove it back into Zeke's fingers.

"*Sign,*" the two agents said in unison.

Zeke liked to tell himself he was the bravest man in town, but when the two men talked, a couple beads of cold sweat left trails down his back. "Please," he said, "just tell me what this is all abo—"

"SIGN!" Even muffled by skin and masks, the word made the room tremble.

His fingers fumbled with the pen and scrawled his name at the bottom of the page.

"Excellent," said Fifteen, sliding the page away. "Thank you, Officer Miller." He tucked the signed sheet back into the file and set the folder on top of the stack marked IN.

"Now what?" asked Zeke. His shoulder throbbed. Was it dislocated? Dislocated would hurt a lot more, he figured, so he counted his blessings.

The clown-agent spun the wheelchair around. The office had a wooden door with a large window of bubbled glass. Fifteen walked past Zeke and retrieved one of two black hats that hung on a coatrack next to the door. He set it precisely on his head with one hand while the clown strapped Zeke's arm down again. He tried to fight, but it was like being a little kid and fighting with a grown-up.

Fifteen opened the door and stepped out into the hall. The clown pushed Zeke's wheelchair after him. It was an old-looking building. Lots of wood and plaster. Identical doors with bubbly glass, none of them labeled. Not even a number. It reminded Zeke of detective offices in black-and-white movies.

The hallway stretched as far as he could see to the left. Dozens, maybe hundreds of doors. Countless china-hat light fixtures hanging from the ceiling one after another, making endless bright pools on the beady carpet.

To the right, the hall went maybe a hundred yards. It looked like it opened into a larger room, but Zeke couldn't be sure. The faint sounds of conversation and movement crept down to them.

Fifteen started down the hallway and the clown pushed Zeke along right behind him. The noise grew. Zeke thought about asking another question, but held his tongue. He didn't want to look stupid or scared.

The hall ended at a set of double doors, each with a rubber wedge kicked under it to keep it pinned against the wall. Beyond them Zeke could see the big room, a gym-sized room, at least. He glimpsed a press of bodies, a hanging chandelier, and then Fifteen led them into the room without pausing.

Zeke had gone down to Foxwoods Casino a few years back for a long weekend. He'd never admitted it to anyone, but being there reminded him of one of the stories his mom had read him as a kid. The country mouse goes to the big city and finds it all too big and fast. All the people and sounds and lights at Foxwoods had been overwhelming.

A sea of faceless men filled the huge room. Hundreds of them. All in dark suits of black or blue or charcoal, some with pinstripes or a fine herringbone twill. A few wore vests. Others had double-breasted suits, the kind Letterman wore. They sat at dozens of desks and studied maps and marched through aisles in pairs and trios. It was Foxwoods times a thousand, set in a gigantic, old-fashioned office.

"Fuckity Jesus," said Zeke. "How many of you guys are there?"

"Forty-seven," said Fifteen without hesitation. "And again, watch the language."

Zeke flinched, waiting for a blow to the back of his head, but none came. "What?"

"We pride ourselves on being polite and professional."

"No, you dumb—" Zeke bit down on his tongue. Actually bit down and drew blood to make himself stop. "How's there only forty-seven of you if the room's full?"

Fifteen gestured down at the room. "This is all of us. Every version of every faceless man on every assignment at every point in our illustrious history."

"Looks confusing as . . . heck."

"Better," said Fifteen. "It isn't. Confusion comes from distraction. We have certainty and purpose, so we aren't distracted."

"Right," muttered Zeke. "Purpose."

They moved through the crowd. The wheelchair plowed forward, staying a few feet behind Fifteen even as other agents wove back and forth between them and alongside. The press of bodies surrounded them, and from his position Zeke saw nothing but suit jackets, vests, and ties.

A pair of faceless men walked past, heading the other way, and one of them thumped an elbow against the side of Zeke's head. A solid hit, probably an accident, but his cop reactions leaped to the fore, angry at someone for not noticing his uniform even though he was strapped into a wheelchair. He wrenched his head around on reflex and barked after the faceless man. "Hey, nimrod!"

The outburst caught the clown off guard. His hands came away from the wheelchair. Fifteen paused and turned back.

The two faceless men also stopped and snapped around as one, like a pair of targets turning on a shooting range. The shorter one, the one who'd hit him, wore a shirt and tie without a jacket. A dark vest, the same color as the man's slacks, covered his chest. No plastic mask or hat. The smooth curves of his face turned until his brow lined up with Zeke's.

They stared at each other for a moment. Zeke wasn't sure where to look, and ended up focusing his glare on the bridge of the nose, what'd be right between the eyes on a normal person. He could feel his pulse in his throat, but he knew better than to back down. He'd rather die brave anyway.

"That was me," the faceless man said after a few more moments. His muffled voice sounded uncertain, as if he wasn't sure he should apologize or not.

"Damn straight it was, moron. Hittin' a guy in a wheelchair?! What the fuck's wrong with you? Watch where you're going!"

The faceless man's head stayed pointed at him. Zeke realized he'd just told a man with no eyes to "watch." He wondered if anyone else had caught it. A few other faceless men around them seemed to have noticed the exchange. Two in dark suits were hatless. One dressed in tweed wore a round Dr. Watson–type hat on his head, another had an old colonial triangle.

"It's not important," said the taller man. He wore a dark suit, an American flag pin, and a see-through Halloween mask like the rest of them. "He doesn't matter anymore." He set a hand on the shorter one's shoulder and they both turned away.

The words created more beads of sweat inside Zeke's shirt. "What's that supposed to mean?" said Zeke. "Hey, I'm talking to you, jackass!"

"That's enough," said Fifteen. "We're on a schedule."

The clown's hands settled on the wheelchair again.

Zeke turned, a wiseass remark swelling in his mouth. Then he twisted back around and caught a last glimpse of the retreating faceless men before the wheelchair moved on and they vanished into the crowd. The tall man with the dark suit, the pin, and the Halloween mask.

"Was that you?" he called to Fifteen. "You were here and there?"

"Probably," said the agent ahead of the wheelchair. "Like he said, it's not important."

They left the big room through a single door and entered another hallway. This one was darker and more utilitarian. And cold. The chair's tires squeaked on a gray-and-white checkerboard of linoleum tiles. Fifteen led them past a few solid doors, turned a corner, and walked past a few more.

An old stretcher, old like the wheelchair and everything else in this place, rested against one wall. Zeke eyed the thick leather straps and the splashes of blood on the sheet. The stain was more red than brown. Still fresh.

Fifteen turned another corner and stopped at another door. A twin door. Instead of handles, each one had a long steel-and-rubber bumper that ran up and down.

A hospital door, Zeke realized. Made to catch gurneys on their way to . . .

"Fuck a duck," he whined.

Fifteen pushed open the door with one hand and gestured Zeke inside.

Darkness clung to the corners of the operating room. Rolling trays and tanks of gas lurked on the edges of the shadows, along with some '70s-looking machines covered in dials and knobs.

The faint light simmered around the gurney in the middle of the room, held there by a big, mirrored fixture on a mechanical arm. A small pillow and clean white sheets covered its top. Long leather straps dangled about where the head, chest, waist, and ankles would be.

Zeke puffed out a breath and it steamed in the cold air.

One of the trays rolled forward into the light. The scalpels and clamps and saws clattered against one another. Things of chrome and steel sat on the tray that Zeke couldn't identify, couldn't even guess at.

Behind the tray, another faceless man stepped out of the shadows. This one wore a long white surgeon's scrubs and held his hands up to display heavy rubber gloves. A pale-blue face mask hung around the man's neck, and a paper cap of the same color covered his hair. The doctor's white clothes pinched in the middle, and Zeke realized the man wore an apron over his long scrubs.

It made him look like a butcher.

"Hello," said the doctor. "Shall we begin?"

Zeke threw himself against the straps. The chair creaked, the leather bent, but nothing gave. He thrashed back and forth, wrenching his neck and his sore shoulder and his hips.

Nothing budged.

The clown slapped a hand down on either arm, squeezing Zeke's biceps as Fifteen unbuckled the straps across his forearms. Zeke tried to leap again as the buckles opened, but the clown's grip made him wince. He slammed his head back and heard plastic crinkle before he hit something that felt and sounded like a wooden block. A few white spots twisted across his eyes and faded.

The grip didn't budge.

Fifteen unfastened the straps across his legs and grabbed his ankles before he could start kicking. Zeke tried kicking anyway. He thrust his hips up at the faceless man, then threw them side to side.

"On the table, please," said the surgeon. He gestured at the small pillow. "Faceup, head here."

They heaved Zeke up and stretched him across the gurney. The surgeon adjusted the pillow, placing it beneath Zeke's neck. Then he lifted the straps on his side of the gurney one by one, resting them on Zeke's body.

"I don't know what they told you," Zeke said to the surgeon, trying to keep his voice steady, "but I'm a cop. You can't do this to me. People will look for me. They'll find you."

The leather strap across his waist and wrists cinched down, pushing him against the gurney. Another strap compressed his chest. The clown vanished back into the shadows.

"D'you hear me? I'm a cop! A police officer!"

The surgeon set the last restraint across Zeke's forehead, right at the hairline. It creaked against his skull. The doctor paused, then pulled it tighter. His blank face panned back and forth. He nodded once, then stepped away.

Zeke tried to follow the man with his eyes. He flexed his fingers and rolled them into fists. He stared up into the lights over the table and told himself he would get through this. He would survive it and then everybody would know he was not to be messed with.

Especially Eli. None of this would've happened if not for goddamned Eli. Zeke'd still be back at the station, probably eating pizza and—

A faint hiss echoed off to the side, like a gas stove waiting for the pilot to catch.

The surgeon returned. He'd pulled his blue mask up to cover the lower half of his empty face. His hand came up holding a triangle of black rubber attached to a long hose. The hiss came from inside the triangle, and it came down toward Zeke's mouth.

"Take a few deep breaths," said the faceless surgeon. "In and out. Count backwards from ten. And the next time you open your eyes . . ."

Zeke stared up at him as the rubber triangle settled over his nose and mouth. "Yeah?"

"Well," said the surgeon, "there won't be a next time after this."

15

Shadows stretched out and filled in all the space on either side of the road. Two hours after leaving the town, the dark sky rose up ahead and came crashing down like a wave, leaving a foam of stars above them. Eleanor's headlights cast a bright oval on the road ahead of them as they raced along.

Eli remembered his astronomy professor telling a story about Albert Einstein and headlights, but couldn't recall the point of it.

Harry cleared her throat. "The founding fathers were very forward thinkers," she said, her voice falling back into the practiced cadence. "They left ways to change the Constitution because they knew ideas change or fade away altogether. What's dangerous now can be harmless in a few generations, and vice versa. When they created the dream, they understood just how powerful it was. They knew how dangerous its ability to change the country could be in the wrong hands. So they petitioned Ptah to make guardians for it."

"Petitioned?"

"It's how the story's come down the Chain. You're interrupting again."

"Sorry."

"Supposedly Franklin had General Washington ask his best men for volunteers. Dozens offered their lives, but only five of them were found to be worthy."

Eli opened his mouth, but a glare from Harry cut through the dark and killed any words in his throat.

"These five became the first of the faceless men. Their identity, their features, it was all stripped away. All they have is their duty to protect the dream."

"Okay . . . wait."

She sighed. "Honestly, Mr. Teague—"

"You're saying they're not wearing some special mask or . . . or cloaking field or something? Like, a mask under the plastic mask? They actually don't have faces. No eyes or nose or mouth."

She nodded.

"So, how do they talk? Or eat? Or breathe?"

"Nobody knows."

"So how do they see?"

"As I explained before, certainty."

"Yeah, but what does that mean?"

"It means they have absolute certainty of what's around them and what they're doing."

"How, though?"

"Nobody kno—"

Eli sighed and slumped back on the Model A's bench seat.

"What little we do know," said Harry, "comes from one of the greatest searchers, a man named Abraham Porter. He tested their range, learned how far their certainty reached."

"How'd he do that?"

"He used a sniper rifle."

"Oh . . ."

"Abraham is one of the very few searchers to ever kill a faceless man. Turns out they're only certain of things within three or four hundred feet of themselves."

"He killed one of them?"

"He killed eight of them, altogether."

Eli whistled. Then he straightened up on the bench. "Wait. You said there were five of these . . . of them."

"The first five," she nodded. "Since then they've recruited soldiers and agents from across history. The Civil War. Both world wars. Korea. Operation Desert Strike. The One-Day War of 2029."

"Jesus. How many of them are there?"

"There are dozens now. Maybe hundreds. Time flows differently around the dream. I've heard stories that one of the original faceless men is still alive and over a thousand years old because of all his time on the road."

"Wait," he said. "The dream's protected by dozens of these guys?"

"At the least."

"All like the one that showed up at my job? Like in Pasadena? That tough? That strong?"

"Yes."

"Are they all that strong and . . . bulletproof?"

"They're not actually bulletproof."

"They're wearing vests?"

"No, they just . . ." Her fingers tap-tap-tapped the steering wheel, and the rhythm tickled the edges of Eli's brain. "You've perhaps heard stories," said Harry, "where people are shot, but the round strikes at just the perfect angle, in just the perfect place, and they survive with minimal injury. It bounces off a bone without so much as breaking the skin?"

"I think so, yeah."

She nodded. "That's what the faceless men do. Certainty allows them to know just how to stand or move themselves to be in that perfect position where the round will cause the least amount of injury."

"So . . . they're bulletproof."

"No," said Harry. "Abraham proved that. It just takes a great deal of work to stop one."

"And they're guarding the dream?"

"They were, yes."

Eli shook his head. "How the hell did someone get past a few dozen of those guys to steal something? Hell, how'd they get past them and then back out of . . . wherever it was?"

"Nobody knows."

"Do you know who took it?"

She glanced at him and shrugged.

"There's a lot of 'nobody knows' to this."

"Truer words, Mr. Teague. Truer words."

Eli sighed. The headlights of the Model A hit the glossy surface of a roadside billboard, turning it into a white rectangle. They drove past, and he blinked away the glare in time to glimpse ALL-NEW STAR-DUST CASINO in curling letters on the sign.

"The faceless man who first came to talk to me, who followed me to Boston. He had a badge."

"They do," Harry said.

"I think he used it to hypnotize the crowd in Boston."

"Like most badges, it's a symbol of power. It allows the bearer to ignore some rules and laws."

"How?"

"Just having the badge makes them less noticeable. If it's out, they can influence what people see. How they perceive things. It's why people usually don't notice the masks. Or the lack of features."

"And you know this because . . . ?"

"Abraham, again. When he killed one, he tried taking its badge. Experimenting a bit. It worked for a while, but once they realized he had it, they could . . . I don't know, see around it? Ignore it?" She yawned. "He tossed it in a trash can in Times Square on V-Day."

"Why do they wear the masks, then? If the badge can make people ignore them?"

"Once again . . ."

"Wait, let me guess—no idea?"

"One thing we do know," she said, "through hard experience, is that they were fanatical about protecting the dream. Franklin, Monroe, Jefferson, and the other founding fathers—even they weren't allowed in its presence again once it was created. They all knew it'd be too tempting for them."

"Absolute power corrupts absolutely," Eli said with an absent nod.

Harry tapped her nose twice. "Protecting it was the faceless men's only reason for existing. When the dream was stolen, it was their greatest possible failure. They became zealots, obsessed with getting it back."

"Okay," said Eli, "but that's good, right? I mean, if this thing's the foundation of the country, then it can't be a good thing that it's gone."

"Not at all."

"So if they want it back . . . well, why are you even getting in the way?"

She shook her head. "We're not. I said they *were* fanatical about protecting the dream. Their priorities have . . . shifted."

"Shifted how?"

Harry twitched on the bench. She rolled her shoulders, and with her grip on the wheel it swung her body forward and back. "They searched for the dream for a hundred years," she said, "through almost three hundred years of American history. And somewhere in there, amidst all those rumors and stories and sightings of faceless men, the first searchers found out about the dream too."

"Okay."

"Some of the searchers are not, shall we say, as cautious as others. They see the travel itself as a means to an end, manipulating events to serve their own needs."

"But isn't that . . ." Eli tapped his knee. "Isn't that just making more ripples, like you were talking about before?"

"Exactly," she said with a sage nod. "Some of them are more devious, but the searchers who make extreme changes are hunted down by the faceless men as well."

"Okay. So they guard the dream and they guard . . . the timeline?"

"History," she corrected.

"Right. But I still don't get what the deal is. If you're not messing things up in history, and you all want the dream found, they why aren't you—"

"They stopped looking for the dream," she said, shooting another glance at him. "That's what I've been trying to explain to you.

"After a hundred years of being unable to find the dream they—" She paused to clear her throat. "They decided to focus more on the 'protecting history' aspect of their duty. And they decided that anyone traveling through history was a risk."

"Even if you're not doing anything?"

"Precisely."

"Well . . . why keep doing it then?"

"Because someone has to find the dream, Mr. Teague. How long can a house stand without a foundation beneath it? Even in your era, you must be able to see the unity of the nation coming apart."

"I guess, yeah."

"When the dream is found, the country's underlying bedrock will be restored."

"And you'll get your three wishes, or whatever."

"Someone's going to affect the shape the country takes, yes. Would you rather it be someone like me or some greedy little weasel?"

He shook his head. "This is nuts."

"And yet, still the truth."

"As you were told it."

"Yes, there is that."

Eli watched the endless night roll by, then focused his gaze on the bright space the headlights formed ahead of them. "It almost makes sense," he said, "in a weird sort of way. I mean, once you get past the fact it's nuts, a lot of it does sort of line up."

"It does."

"Still, I think I'll leave that part out when I tell people where I've been for the past week." He sighed. "I guess I'll be leaving most of this out."

In the dark, her face shifted.

He saw the movement. "What?"

"You won't be able to tell anyone."

"Well, I'll have to tell them something," he said. He shook his head and pictured the questions from Robin and Corey, from his mom, from Bill at the bank as he begged for his job back. "I've been gone over a week. People are going to ask questions."

The tip of Harry's hat shifted back and forth in the dark. "I thought you understood," she murmured, half to him and half to the road.

"Understood what?"

Her fingers drummed on the steering wheel, the same half-familiar rhythm. "You'd already caught their attention. They'd taken note of you because you'd spoken with me twice before. But once they saw us together in Pasadena—once they saw us *leave* together . . ."

Something twisted low in Eli's belly. Not quite nausea, not exactly a tightening. "What are you saying?"

"I'm not just answering your questions, Mr. Teague. I'm trying to teach you. You need to know all this if you're going to survive on the road."

"No," he said. "No, I don't. I'm not on the road. I'm just . . . I just want to go home."

"I'm so sorry," she said. "You can't. When I said I was stuck with you, I didn't mean for the short term. They're after you now too."

The Second
Iteration

16

Eli'd never been anywhere so dark before. No houses, no streetlights, no moon, only a few faint stars that didn't seem to cast any actual light. The whole world had faded away as the car drove on, leaving nothing but a few dashboard lights and a bright oval of pavement.

He glanced over at Harry. They hadn't spoken in almost half an hour. Even then it had just been twenty minutes of back-and-forth apologies from her and denial from him. Denial that, even he had to admit, had gotten a bit pleading at the end.

He cleared his throat. "Are we going to stop for the night?"

Harry glanced at him. "I hadn't planned on it."

"Are you good to keep driving?"

"I beg your pardon?"

"You aren't tired or road blind or anything?"

She raised an eyebrow. "Road blind?"

"Sometimes, when I have to do a lot of driving, I zone out and go on automatic. Just sort of lose focus and then realize I haven't really registered anything for the last ten or twenty minutes. Especially when it's monotonous like this." He gestured out at the black.

"I know what you mean," she said. "I've just never heard it referred to that way."

"Ahhh."

"I am a bit . . . road blind," Harry admitted. "Road nearsighted, perhaps."

"Do you want me to drive for a while?"

Her eyes flicked toward him in the dark. "Have you ever driven a Model A before, Mr. Teague?"

Eli shifted on the wooden bench. "Once, but the owner was walking me through it. We never even left the parking lot."

"I think we'll preserve her gearbox for a bit longer, then," Harry said, patting the steering wheel.

They came up over a rise and a cluster of red lights appeared in the distance. A big truck, plowing its way across the desert. Harry swung the wheel, brought them up alongside, and then past it. She reached an arm out and waved as they settled in ahead of the truck. Two quick *baaaaahs* from the big rig's horn echoed behind them.

Eli glanced back. They were already past the circle of the truck's headlights. He squinted at the dashboard. "How fast are we going?"

"About seventy. The steering gets wonky past that, so I prefer not to go faster in the dark."

He leaned back and studied the car's dash in the dim light. Harry had added a wooden dashboard over the classic metal one, putting some space between herself and the back wall of the gas tank. A not-uncommon rebuild for a Model A. She'd carried over the steel "clover" of instruments the Model A classically had. The cylinder speedometer and gas gauge. The ignition key had been replaced by a series of silver switches. Nine other switches had been added next to the clover in a three-by-three grid. The small orange light, now calm and dark, sat at the top of the clover, just above the gas gauge. She'd created an interesting design, keeping it balanced even though the car hadn't been designed with much of a dashboard.

"How fast can it go?"

"She can get close to ninety on a straightaway," said Harry. "The speedometer only goes to seventy-five, though."

Eli smiled. "A 1929 Model A business coupe that hits ninety miles per hour."

"Stranger things in heaven and earth," she said.

"You've made other modifications, haven't you? Past the carburetor."

"A few, yes. A carbon-fiber timing gear. Some better electrics. But that's nothing new. People customized Model As for decades, yes?"

They drove on in the darkness. A car appeared in the distance. It flashed its headlights, high-low-high-low as it approached. Then it roared past them in a gust of sound and wind.

"Can I ask you another question?"

"I suppose it depends," said Harry. "What about?"

He gestured at the steering column. "Your car."

"Then, yes, Mr. Teague, you may ask a question."

"The car has a Garrett carburetor."

She glanced at him. "Yes."

"How?"

"How did we get a carburetor?"

"How did you get one that runs on water?"

Harry sighed. "Someone revisits the idea in . . . 2027? '28? The original conversion was done in 2029, and then we had the carburetor upgraded in 2034."

The dates went back and forth in Eli's mind. He tried to think of all the things that could've been invented in the years till 2027.

"Garrett's basic design is fairly correct," she continued, "he just didn't have the right materials. Imagine if you tried to make a catalytic converter with wood and ceramics. It wouldn't function, but that wouldn't mean the basic idea of a catalytic converter is flawed."

Eli let his breath huff out through his nose.

Two more miles slipped by under the Model A's wheels.

"Okay, then," he said, "what about this? Why not just get a better car?"

Harry's eyes gleamed wide in the dark. "Better how?" She patted the steering wheel again. "Ignore him, girl."

"If you can travel into the future," Eli asked, "why not get . . . I don't know, a flying car or something? I thought the future was going to be all electric cars and jetpacks and stuff."

She snorted. "And what would I do with your fancy automobile when it ran out of electrical charge in 1830? How would I repair it when it broke down in 1787? How could I replace batteries or motors or computer-chipped ignition keys? After 1985, automobiles just become too complicated. Too many things to go wrong." Her fingers flexed on the steering wheel. "Older is better. Anything goes wrong with Eleanor, I can fix ninety-nine percent of it with a crescent wrench and a hammer. Tools I can carry with me."

"That kind of makes sense."

"In addition," she said, sounding like a schoolteacher, "there's the blending-in issue. Old automobiles are an oddity, but they stand out much less than future ones. There's almost 130 years of American history where a Model A barely rates a second glance. Something like a Tesla Model X, though? That's going to stick out like a sore thumb. There's barely three decades where it won't attract attention."

Another mile vanished beneath Eleanor's wheels.

"If blending in and attracting attention are real issues," said Eli, "maybe you should rethink your wardrobe."

He saw the tricorne tip down for a moment. "Frock coats are worn for almost two hundred years, Mr. Teague," she said. "Even in eras when they're not fashionable, they're not unheard-of garments."

"Even for women?"

"As I mentioned earlier, the unfortunate truth is that most of American history is not terribly friendly to women, especially those traveling alone. When we first met and you mistook me for a young man, it was not entirely because of your own ignorance."

"Thanks . . . I guess."

"It's a camouflage which has helped me more than once since I started traveling the road on my own."

"Sorry," he said.

"For what?"

"That you have to . . . I don't know, put up with that. That you have to hide who you are."

"It's the way things are. There's no point apologizing for the past. We can only learn from it and try to be better."

Eleanor skimmed over a few more miles. It crossed Eli's mind that, aside from being unnaturally fast, the car ran smoothly on the road. His infrequent experience with Model A's before this had been a lot like trying to ride one of those massage chairs they sold in the big shopping malls over in Newington.

Harry yawned. She bit it off at the end and glanced in Eli's direction. "Pardon me."

He yawned himself. "Are you sure you're okay to drive?"

"I'm just fine." She nodded too enthusiastically. "Don't worry about me."

A thought wiggled into his mind. He cleared his throat. "Is this because of me being here?"

Her fingers shifted on the steering wheel. "Truth be told," she said, "we hardly know each other, Mr. Teague. It would be a bit improper, and all too forward for me to suggest we . . . well, that we . . ."

"Sleep?"

"Sleep," she agreed. "Together. Sad to say, the only real clue I have of your character is from when you were a teenage boy."

"I've grown up since then."

"Yes," she said. "Yes, you have."

Another mile of highway rolled by.

"If you want to stop for the night," Eli said, "I'll sleep on the ground and you can sleep here in the car."

Harry coughed out a grim laugh. "I don't know if you've noticed," she said, "but it's almost impossible to sleep in here."

"You have my word," he said, "you've got nothing to worry about from me." He thought about it, then added, "Miss Pritchard."

The shadows beneath her nose shifted back and forth, up and down. "Very well," she said. She glanced back over her shoulder. "There's been no sign of them. We're probably safe for now."

The rumble of the Model A's engine dropped an octave. She guided them closer to the edge of the road. The point of the tricorne turned toward the road's shoulder.

"What are you looking for?"

"A good place to pull over for the night. No big stones or deep ditches."

Eli looked out at the rolling desert. "Is there a reason we can't find a motel?"

She barked out a laugh. "Even these days, that's ten or fifteen dollars a night."

"I've still got some cash."

"Which won't be printed for another twenty or thirty years, at best. You'd best get used to living tight, Mr. Teague. It's been at least six weeks since I slept on a mattress."

A few different thoughts bounced through Eli's head, which he chose to voice with a simple "Ahhhh."

Eleanor slowed, and after cruising for another two miles they found a spot Harry deemed acceptable. The Model A rolled off the pavement and onto the hard-packed dirt. It continued on for seventy or eighty feet, carrying them far clear of the highway. Harry flicked a few switches and the car shuddered to a stop.

"Here we are," she said. She gestured at the outside.

Eli nodded. "Y'know, after a week of sleeping on buses and trains, the ground doesn't look that bad."

Harry pushed the door open, slipped out, and reached back to pull a battered olive-green bag from behind the bench. A duffel bag. Or a rucksack. He wasn't sure what the correct term was for the upright bag. "Not just the ground, Mr. Teague. When you travel with me, you get all the luxuries." She wiggled the clip loose on the rucksack, unfolded the top, and pulled out a wool blanket. "Would you like brown or gray?"

"Is there a difference?"

"The gray one also has some black stripes."

He managed a smile. "Whichever one you don't want."

Harry tugged out a gray blanket and tossed it at him. She walked a few feet from the car, a slim shadow in the dark. The bag dropped to the ground, and she swung her blanket into the air to open it.

Eli kicked a few stones into the night and spread his blanket on the ground a few yards from hers. The wool was thick enough to hide most of the bumps. He stretched out on one side and tugged the other half over himself as best he could. It wasn't a sleeping bag, but it created a pocket of warmth in the cool night air.

On the other side of Eleanor, a big truck roared by on the highway. They were far enough off the road to muffle the sound of its engine. The headlights raced away, a cloud of light sliding across the desert, never reaching the Model A. Eli wondered if it was the one they'd passed a while ago, and tried to remember if they'd passed an exit or off-ramp of some kind.

Harry shrugged off her coat and balled it into a pillow. She stretched out a few yards away from him, lying on her side with her head far from his. She reached back and pulled the extra blanket up over herself.

The quiet stretched between them, broken by a car zooming by, then another big truck. He could tell she wasn't asleep. Her breathing wasn't right.

"Nice blankets," said Eli. "Good weight."

She made a sound almost like a grunt.

"I hate light blankets. You should be able to feel a blanket sitting on you."

"They're from an Army-Navy surplus store in Tulsa," she said. "Somewhen around 1993, if memory serves."

He thought about it, then repeated the year aloud.

"Yes," she said, and echoed it back to him.

"So you really travel in time."

"In history," she said. "And yes."

"And we're in the 1960s right now?"

"We still are."

Another big rig drove by on the freeway, headed west, back toward California.

"Can I ask another question?"

She let out a sigh. "Of course."

"Your old partner, Chris . . ."

Harry twisted on her blanket, turning to face him. Her eyes glinted in the night. "He preferred Christopher. He considered Chris to be such a common name."

Eli waited a moment. "You talk about him in the past tense."

"Mr. Teague," she said, "you may have noticed I have not brought this topic up before."

"Carefully danced around it," Eli agreed.

"What does that tell you?"

"Sorry. What happened to him?"

She sighed in the dark. "What do you think? They killed him."

"Ahhh. Sorry."

"It was a long time ago."

"I'm still sorry."

"Thank you." The shadowy blob of her blanket shifted again as another truck drove by back on the highway. "Get a good night's rest. We have a long way to drive tomorrow."

He felt a yawn build and let it out. After sleeping upright in seats for so many nights, the firm ground felt remarkably comfortable, and the blanket, luxurious. Sleep tugged at his eyelids and he welcomed it.

"Mr. Teague?"

"Yeah?"

"It's Mrs. Pritchard. Not Miss."

"Oh," he said. He woke up a bit more and said, "Oh. Sorry."

"I wanted to be sure that was clear," she said. "I apologize for any confusion."

"Yeah, of course." He thought of asking another question, decided against it, and then sleep dragged him back down.

"Good night, Mr. Teague," her voice whispered out of the dark.

17

The voices swam in, circled his mind, and prodded him awake.

". . . not an average case," said the faceless doctor, "but I believe all the grafts should take well."

Fifteen nodded. "When will he be ready for fieldwork?"

"As soon as he wakes and has his orientation," said the doctor. "And I believe he just woke up."

Fifteen shifted his attention. "How do you feel?"

He wondered how they knew he was awake when he hadn't moved or opened his eyes. He remembered something about people breathing differently when they were awake and wondered if he'd been snoring or something. Maybe he could get a little more sleep if he didn't react. They might leave him alone.

Fifteen spoke again. "I know you're awake. Please don't waste any more time."

He ignored the faceless man standing at the side of the bed with arms crossed. Ten more minutes would be a victory. It'd show Fifteen who . . .

How did he know where and how Fifteen stood when he hadn't opened his eyes?

Why couldn't he think of his own name?

Why couldn't he open his eyes?

In the back of his mind, he remembered being forced to sign the contract. The scrawl of his signature. His heart speeding, his breath coming in fast gasps. He remembered the faint chemical smell of the gas as it hissed into the mask and he pulled it in through his nose.

Why couldn't he open his eyes?

He flexed the muscles of his face, felt his cheeks and forehead tighten. His head thrashed side to side and he tried to rub his eyes against his shoulder. Straps pulled tight on his wrists and across his chest as he moved.

"This is normal," said Fifteen. "There are always a few moments of panic at first."

"My eyes—" he started to say, but his mouth was all wrong. His jaw felt stiff. His tongue stayed still. His lips didn't . . .

Once he realized the screams were his, he stopped.

He turned his head to Fifteen. "Why can't I remember my name?"

"The procedure involves some grafts and transplants," the doctor explained. "Some things are moved. Others added. And still others removed."

"But why can't I remember my name?" He tried to adjust his face, to grit his teeth, but his features refused to move.

"You're one of the faceless men," said Fifteen. "You don't have a name."

"But I had one," he said.

Fifteen shook his head.

"I did. I was . . ." It danced on the tip of his tongue. "My name was . . ."

"You don't have a name. You'll be assigned a number as identification is required, on a case-by-case basis."

"So who am I? What's my number?"

"You are Zero."

"What?" He tried to sit up, and the straps pulled tight on his chest and wrists again.

"You are Zero," repeated Fifteen. "Every faceless man begins as Zero to remind him he has no identity. Each of us is what we need to be to perform our duty, no more and no less."

A grumble settled in the back of Zero's throat, as did the awareness that he still had a throat. "You were Zero once?"

Fifteen nodded. "We all were. I have been Fifteen for the past eleven weeks. Before that I was Twenty-Three, and before that Eight, Sixteen, Four, and other numbers as circumstances required."

"Zero," he repeated. It tickled his mind, made the name on the tip of his tongue dance just a little harder. Not quite right, but close enough. "How can I see you?"

"You can't. You don't have eyes. You're one of the faceless men."

"But you're right there."

"Yes," agreed Fifteen with a nod.

"So how do I know that if I can't see you?"

"Through certainty," said the faceless man.

"What's that mean?" The phrase lacked something. A word he'd used all the time. A very flexible adjective. Sometimes a verb. One of his favorites.

"Have you ever walked through a familiar room at night? You can still move with confidence, step around objects, reach for light switches or remotes. Sometimes you even notice that something's different."

Zero nodded. "Yeah, okay."

"That's how we see. We are sure of everything, so we move with certainty."

There was more to it, Zero felt certain, but he accepted the faceless man's explanation. This felt out of character for him. Before, he would've demanded more. Demanded with the words he could no longer remember.

How much had they cut out of him?

Enough that it didn't bother him. Not at the moment. He'd deal with it later.

"Let me up."

"Let yourself up," said Fifteen. "And be quick. We have work to do."

Zero turned his attention to the straps that held him down. The buckles sat out of reach, just under the lip of the gurney. The straps . . . he remembered them as heavy canvas, but they seemed thin. Inconsequential.

He stopped struggling against the straps and just sat up. They popped and tore and dropped away. He reached down and ripped aside the lower ones with a sweep of his hand and swung his legs off the gurney. His feet hit the floor and he stood before the faceless man.

"Excellent," said Fifteen.

Zero became certain of the frayed threads at the torn edges of the straps. And the ripples of the sheet on the gurney, also splattered with blood. And the tray of instruments, which had been pushed back. The twenty-one pieces of bloody gauze in a wire trash bin. The tank, which contained anesthetic gas. The green gauge on the tank, which had a black needle pointing precisely at the line after 1/4. The hose on the tank leading to the rubber mask. Fourteen drops of condensation inside the mask.

The room leaned to the side, as if he'd had a few too many boiler-makers. He tried to close eyes he didn't have as more information poured into his mind. He grabbed the edge of the gurney behind him and willed himself to be as solid as it.

His level of certainty dropped. The glut of detail faded away. Zero straightened up.

Fifteen observed it all. He nodded. Then he turned away and walked out the big swinging doors. Zero followed him into the hallway.

They entered a locker room, and Zero went to a locker. It wasn't his, he knew. He didn't have enough of an identity to claim ownership of anything. Not anymore. But he understood the locker had been pre-pared for him, one of the many facts of which he was now certain. Ar-ranged inside he found shoes, a shirt, and a dark-gray three-piece suit, almost black. Brown paper wrappers held black socks, a white T-shirt, and plain boxers. The tie was a deep red, like blood when it first swelled up from a wound. It had a pattern in the fabric to give it texture.

The vest took a long time. He buttoned it crooked on the first try, and it had a lot of buttons. At least as many as the shirt, maybe more. He almost tossed it back inside the locker, but such a show of temper didn't feel right anymore. It'd been a long time since he'd had to knot a real necktie, but after his first attempt he became certain how the band of silk needed to loop and fold. He snuggled it against his throat and looked as sharp and badass as Fifteen.

Yes. Badass.

He left the coat on its hanger, closed the locker, and turned to Fif-teen. "How do we get started?"

"You forgot your coat."

"Are we heading out?"

Fifteen paused. "No," he said. "Not yet. Why?"

"I don't want to wear the coat inside," he said. "I'll be too warm."

Again, his words felt wrong. Edited. They lacked the passionate emphasis he enjoyed.

Fifteen didn't move, then nodded once.

They walked back into the hall side by side. Partners, even if Zero still needed to get his bearings. He took a dozen steps and had to set a hand against the wall. Knowledge of the hall poured into his mind. Details, history, facts flooded his consciousness. The wall was simple and solid. He tried to draw that solidity out of it.

Fifteen waited.

"It is," said Zero, "a lot to get used to."

"It is," agreed the other faceless man.

They returned to the main room. Faceless men filled the space, every square foot of floor. Everything about them echoed and repeated. He could sense every iteration, pick out every detail of each version.

Zero tried to close his eyes again. Then he reached up and covered the front of his head with his hands. Nothing changed. He let out a frustrated grunt.

"It can be overwhelming," said Fifteen. "All the new perceptions. The influx of information. I took almost two weeks to adjust. Some men take days, a few have needed over a month."

"Okay." Zero tried to take a breath. His lungs fluttered, his throat twitched, but no air flowed. He panicked, his heart raced, he tried even harder to suck in air, and then he remembered he didn't have a mouth. His chest muscles spasmed and fought with his lungs.

He forced himself to straighten up, willed his chest and stomach to stop pumping at his lungs. He wouldn't look weak in front of the new boss. He wouldn't mess this up. Just like before a game. No nerves. No worries.

His body responded.

"You're doing very well," Fifteen said.

"Thanks. Thank you."

Two faceless men moved past in the other direction, one pushing something. Zero sensed the angles, the closing gap, the pace of their strides, but he couldn't turn the certainty into motion before his elbow connected with a heavy slap of muscle and bone. His body felt sluggish and clumsy as waves of unfamiliar sensory input hit him again and again. He managed to not stagger and kept himself alongside Fifteen.

Then someone behind him yelled, "Hey, nimrod!"

He stopped. Fifteen stopped next to him. They turned at the same time. Zero wasn't sure who had started the move, if one of them followed the other.

The other two men stood a few yards away. Except there were three men. The two standing were faceless men, with a normal human—eyes, nostrils, mouth, hair—seated in a wheelchair.

Strapped in a wheelchair.

His new senses ebbed, swirled, crashed over him again, and Zero recognized the people who stood before him.

"That was me," he said.

"Damn straight it was, moron," snapped the man with a face. "Hittin' a guy in a wheelchair?! What the fuck's wrong with you? Watch where you're going!"

Watch? Zero remembered being over there, on the other side of the conversation, where he hoped nobody would notice he'd told a man with no eyes to watch it. And he could sense the underlying panic, the fear that he'd gone too far, threatened a monster.

He was a loser.

Had been a loser.

"It's not important," Fifteen told him. "He doesn't matter anymore." The faceless man set a hand on Zero's shoulder and applied pressure. It helped him focus and guided him away from the confrontation and deeper into the crowd.

"What's that supposed to mean?" yelled someone behind him, someone who wasn't important. "Hey, I'm talking to you, jackass!"

Zero tried to calm his thoughts as they thrashed in the churning waves of input. "Did you know that was us? Before?"

"Yes," said Fifteen.

"Why didn't you say anything?"

"What was there to say?"

"You could've told me not to hit him."

The faceless man shook his head. "I couldn't."

"Why?"

"Because you hit him in the side of the head," said Fifteen. "We both observed it and remembered it."

"So?"

"You can't avoid something that already happened. We're not exempt from the rules."

"But it hadn't happened to me."

"It had. Both sides. You saw it."

"That doesn't make sense."

Fifteen raised a hand to the room. "The history of the faceless men—of the country—is all happening right here, right now. All of it. It will happen. It has happened. We know all of the events and all of the outcomes. Especially here. We have certainty."

The words brought all-new thoughts and facts to the surface of Zero's seething perceptions. He grabbed them. Held on tight as they tried to slip back under the waves of input.

"Wait," he said. He stopped and stepped to the left to avoid a pair of faceless men going the other way. "The dream. The American Dream. Our purpose. Did you know all along it was going to be stolen?"

"Of course we did. From the day the home office was founded. We know all the events and all the outco—"

"And you didn't do anything? I would've had every version of every man here armed and standing around the thing."

"Precautions were taken," said Fifteen, "even with the potential risk to causality. They made no difference, as we knew they wouldn't. The dream was taken."

"That's just pathetic."

The faceless man's head shifted. "Excuse me?"

"You knew a crime was going to happen—a crime against the United States—and you just let it happen. I think that's the definition of pathet—"

Fifteen's punch slammed into his chest. Zero slid back and crashed into a desk. The faceless men around him froze.

"Do not *ever*," roared Fifteen, "think to question the ability or dedication of either this office or the men who serve it."

Zero pushed himself back to his feet. "I was just saying—"

"You will say nothing!" Fifteen stalked forward and loomed over the smaller man. "You are nothing. Don't forget that. You're Zero for a reason."

Thoughts and awareness and perceptions raged in Zero's head. Blurry half memories of how he'd react to such words, even without the assault. Just recently, someone had taken an uppity attitude and he'd . . . why couldn't he remember?

Part of him, a small part, screamed at the fact that he'd been lessened. They'd cut so much of him away, he wasn't even sure what was gone. He had no context. He had less of everything.

He brushed the voice away. Or, as far away as he could.

The uppity person hadn't even been important. A minor distraction in the past, before he'd become one of the faceless men. She'd only been important because of the reason he'd been recruited. The one thing he'd hung on to . . .

Zero looked up at Fifteen. "Where?" he said. "Where is Eli Teague?"

18

Eleanor's tires spun, grabbed at dirt that had been pavement a moment earlier, and pulled them out of the second skid in as many minutes.

Eli's stomach recovered from the lurch and took the moment to remind him he hadn't had anything close to a solid meal since the greasy biscuits at breakfast seven or eight hours ago. The grumble faded even as he steadied himself. How did time travel affect stomach clocks? Maybe that was how time travelers told time.

The cold hit him like stepping into a freezer, an abrupt drop of temperature. And it kept dropping. "Jesus," he muttered, pulling his arms tight to his body.

"I did warn you," Harry said. She wore a new shirt under her vest, an ivory one that buttoned up almost to her chin and had ruffles like an old tuxedo.

"You said it'd get cold. I wasn't expecting high seventies to low twenties in half a second."

"Be prepared, Mr. Teague. Don't tell me you were never a Boy Scout."

The road wandered through the forest like a drunk. It didn't seem to be maintained in any way below the dusting of snow, just beaten down by years of travel. To emphasize Eli's observation, Eleanor's tires kicked up a rock that thudded beneath the floorboards.

A few miles off, at least a dozen thin columns of smoke curled up into the air. The smell of burning wood and coal reached through the cold air to tickle his nose.

Harry steered the Model A off the road and parked behind a cluster of tall weeds that probably could've been called saplings. Snow dusted their brown leaves and branches. They walked back to the road.

A few slow, lazy flakes drifted past Eli's face. He'd known many days like this in Maine. Cold enough to snow and sap your heat, not quite cold enough for it to last. As a kid, it was the kind of snow he'd hated—not enough to cancel school or even to be fun when he got out of school.

He stamped his feet twice and rubbed his hands together. Like most New Englanders, he had a set of gloves and a spare wool hat in his car. His car was about a thousand miles away, though. He also guessed at least a hundred years would pass before it was actually built.

At least he'd kept his wool socks. And had real shoes on instead of sneakers.

He pointed at the smoke. "Is that it? Independence?"

She nodded.

"And we're in 1850?"

"Unless I missed it, 1853. Independence is a challenging one. For about twenty years, it was the place tens of thousands of people wanted to be." She tugged a cloak out from behind the bench and wrapped it over her frock coat.

"So it's one of those towns you talked about? One of the ones that got stuck in time?"

"It was," she agreed. "The perfect slick spot. Then the gold rush dries up, the Transcontinental Railroad is finished, and history gets its teeth into the town again. So it's a slick spot, but only during that twenty-year period. We had to go back to a point where we could get to this point."

Eli nodded slowly. "I think I get it."

Harry mashed her tricorne down on her head and gave him a once-over. "Your clothes should pass," she told him. "Put the wristwatch in your pocket. Try to keep the cuffs of your pants over your shoes. Not wearing boots out here will attract attention."

He shoved the watch into his coat. "Anything else?"

She looked him up and down. "That'll do for now."

They headed into town. Trails of dark, slushy mud in the snow—and a few small piles Eli felt sure weren't mud—helped mark off the road. Countless hooves and wagon wheels had pounded it more or less flat, but the mud froze in uneven ridges and furrows that could wrench an ankle.

"How do you know?" asked Eli.

"Know what?"

"That we're in 1853?"

She turned around to face him and took a few steps backward. "Are you suddenly doubting again, Mr. Teague?"

He shook his head. "I mean, how do you get us here? Or now, I guess. How do you get us exactly now and not in 1852 or '54 or the middle of summer or something?"

Harry shrugged. "Practice."

"You said it's not the car. Eleanor's just a regular Model A."

"She is. It's just about knowing how and where to drive. When to brake, how to steer the wheel."

"But how?"

Harry turned back to the road. "Do you know how to ride a bicycle?"

"What?"

"How to ride a bicycle."

"Yeah, of course."

"How do you do it? How do you balance? How do you steer without tipping over?"

He opened his mouth, shut it, then sighed. "Practice."

"Exactly."

They trudged toward the distant buildings. The air nipped at Eli's face and seeped into his clothes. His coat kept out the worst of it, and a few drafts slinked down to pool in his shoes. He paused after ten minutes to stamp his feet again and felt vindicated when Harry stamped hers too.

"Are you looking for another clue here?" he asked.

"Of course."

"Is it hidden in town?"

She glanced over her shoulder. "It, Mr. Teague?"

"The clue."

"We're looking for a man," she said, "not a treasure map."

"Ahhh." He rubbed his hands against his sides to warm them, then shoved them back into his coat pockets.

Harry reached up and tugged the point of her tricorne to the left. The slanted shadow across her face shifted to keep the sun out of her eyes. Her hand slipped back inside her cloak.

"That's a neat trick," said Eli.

She glanced at him, then up at the folded brim. "Learned it from a sharpshooter in 1802," she said. "You could use his hat for a sundial."

Eli chuckled. "So, this guy we're looking for. Do you have a name or a description or something?"

"His name is Gregson Edgar Russk," she said. "He's a somewhat successful prospector. He has black hair, a big bushy beard, and one of his front teeth is broken. He's spending most of his time in two different saloons, drinking and . . ."

She kicked at a rock jutting from the snow. It flipped over twice as it slid through the muck, then came to rest. They walked past it.

Eli cleared his throat. "Drinking and . . . ?"

"Let's just say he's been alone for some time. And now he isn't. On a regular basis."

"Ahhh," said Eli. "Got it. That all sounds pretty specific. Shouldn't be too hard to find him."

Harry snorted. "Here and now, not so much." She waved her arm behind them, then forward at the town. "This is the California trail. It starts here in Independence and leads almost every settler and prospector out to gold territory or back here to proper civilization."

They walked on for another few minutes. He glanced back down the road, but couldn't see the trees where they'd hidden the car. On a guess, they were more than halfway to town. He rubbed his knuckles against his chest before burying them in his pockets. "So what do we need to talk to, uh, Greg Edward—"

"Gregson Edgar Russk."

"Right. What do we need to talk to him about?"

"Same thing as always," she said. "About a dream." She reached up and tugged her scarf higher, covering her nose and mouth.

"What makes you think the dream would be here?"

"Oh, I don't think it is," said Harry. "I think he was influenced by the dream before he struck out on his journey. It's what put him on the right path."

"Okay. Kind of makes sense."

"So we need to find out when he got on that path. Theo told me he struck it rich out in California and I backtracked him to here."

"And then from here to . . . the dream?"

"Perhaps. That's the hope."

"Is this what all the searchers do? Hunt for clues?"

"More or less. We each have our own methods and strategies."

Eli stopped to stamp his feet two more times, and also held his hands over his mouth to blow warm air on the palms and back onto his nose. A breeze slid through his jeans and set off a shiver that worked its way into his thighs. "So how'd Theo know about him? Russk?"

"His specialty is—was—information and rumors about the dream. That's why I met him in Boston."

"Oh."

"Oh?"

He shrugged. "I thought he sent you to Pasadena."

She shook her head. "That was a personal matter. Just a message he passed on. I'd backtracked my leads to Mr. Russk, and Theo found some useful background material for me."

"How?"

"Keeping his ears open. Asking questions. Calling in the odd favor when and where. Theo had friends and informants all over."

As they reached the first buildings of town, a man appeared on a horse. A thick overcoat draped over his shoulders, and a hat of gray fur matched the shaggy hair poking out beneath it. He approached, passed with a nod to each of them, and headed back along the road.

Eli glanced over his shoulder at the man as they headed into town. "You worried about him?"

"Why would I be?"

"He's heading for the car."

"He's heading for Kansas City," Harry said. "In this weather, he won't waste time wandering off the road. If he happens to catch a glimpse of Eleanor in the bushes, he'll just think she's an odd-looking carriage."

They entered the town. Small and simple buildings lined the out-skirts, some of them a step or two above being shacks. They reached a cross-street, and a board by the door of a larger, barnlike building had two horseshoes nailed to it. A few people walked around and alongside and past them. They wore long coats and shawls and one man had what looked like a deerskin wrapped around himself. A few of the women stared at Harry, but only for a moment or two. Eli drew more eyes.

Harry turned, smiled widely at him, and grabbed his arm. She pointed at another store window, this one marked ZION MERCAN- TILE. "Calm down," she murmured to him.

He looked at the window, then back at her close face. A few inches separated their noses. "What?"

She kept the smile wide and squeezed his arm. "You're staring at everyone and everything like it's all new. Just act naturally."

His eyes flitted around at the buildings and the people and then came back to her face. He took in a breath, held it, and let it back out. "Okay," he said. "Sorry."

"No need to apologize," said Harry, just loud enough to be heard. The smile faded as the grip on his arm eased.

She led him to the next cross-street. At the corner, a wooden pole stood on the railing of a porch. Faded and chipped stripes of red, white, and blue paint twisted around the pole. A team of horses trotted by pulling a weather-beaten coach. Eli stepped back and the equally weather-beaten man at the reins gave him a slight glance. The coach made it to the next block, weaving on the snowy road, before a whip snapped and the horses picked up the pace.

"If Theo's got all these contacts and information," Eli asked, "why doesn't he just use them himself?"

She gestured at a shop window. "Why don't the people selling shov- els just go mine gold themselves? It's not where his skills are. Were. He helped to find the dream in his own way."

"But he still charges for it."

"Not as much as some. Theo just tried to keep his business run- ning. He wasn't one of those greedy, money-grubbing weasels like Tiko or—"

"Tiko?"

"Chinese black-marketeer. Started in San Francisco, got on the road. Parts, tools, fuel, whatever you need, as long as you can meet his terms."

Harry looked to her left, then her right. She pulled an envelope from her pocket and unfolded it into a sheet of coarse paper. A few dozen short, handwritten lines marked it. More of a list than a letter, Eli decided.

"Mr. Russk frequents two saloons on this side of town," she said. "We need to figure out where they are." She glanced back over her shoulder, then squinted at the handwritten notes again. "I think that's . . . Union Street? So this would be Ruffner."

Eli stomped his feet again. Icy needles pricked at his toes and calves and thighs. "Is one of those saloons nearby?"

Harry looked up from the paper and glanced down each street again. "I believe so," she said. "Cold?"

"Yeah. Not freezing, but definitely cold."

"Don't mess this up for me, and I'll get you a hat." She studied his face. "You'd look good in a derby."

"Sorry?"

She moved her hands back and forth around an imaginary dome and nodded. "A derby. A bowler hat."

He smiled. "And blend in as well as you?"

"Don't believe all your western films, Mr. Teague. The derby was the most popular hat in America for over a century. Even in the Wild West, it was worn far more than the cowboy hat."

"Or the tricorne?"

"Don't be rude. That won't get you a hat either." She pointed down the street. "This way."

They walked past another dozen buildings. The homes and businesses crept closer together, although they were still farther apart than any "neighbors" Eli could think of back in Sanders. A few had an old New England feel, but he still couldn't name any of the architectural styles. Several of them looked brand-new, as if they'd barely stood up to a year of sun and snow. One had a high, peaked roof, while the two on either side of it looked more like the near shacks on the outskirts of town. A long, mournful hoot echoed twice above the buildings, and it took him a few seconds to recognize the distant sound of a train whistle.

"There." Harry pointed down the street at a large barn. "That's one."

"You sure?"

She folded the corners of the paper in to form the envelope again. It vanished back into her coat. "Yes, I believe so."

"It looks like a barn," Eli said as they marched across the muddy path.

She nodded. "On the outside."

The left-hand barn door had a regular-sized door set into it. Harry lifted the latch and a wave of warm air washed out and over them. They stepped through and pulled the door shut behind them.

Harry tugged off her hat, beat it twice against her thigh to knock some snow free, and tucked it under her arm. Eli took the moment to wipe the snow from his head. Then he looked around, trying to seem as casual and uninterested as possible.

The white planks of the barn floor looked newer than the houses outside, a stark contrast to the shriveled boards of the walls. The fireplace on the back wall also looked like a recent addition. The potbelly stove close to the bar could've been twenty years old, but it stood on a small platform of fresh bricks and mortar. Eli's eyes picked out more bright wood scattered throughout the barn, reinforcing steps and beams.

An American flag had been draped across the far wall. Eli counted up the perfect columns of stars in the blue corner. Four rows of six. A smaller flag hung over the bar, this one with a dense circle of clustered stars in the corner. Colorful blankets and animal skins hung in several places. He guessed their purpose was half for atmosphere, half to cut drafts.

A dozen tables and thrice as many chairs stood scattered around the big room. The chairs had clustered at a few tables, as was their nature. A handful of padded, blanket-wrapped ones had gathered near the fire and the stove, although one sat empty and alone in a corner across from the bar.

Also across from the bar stood an upright piano. With a set of antlers mounted on the wall above it. Eli felt a grin forming at the sight of the old movie standard, but fought it back down.

"So this is, what?" he asked, looking around the barn. "A speakeasy?"

"Speakeasies are during Prohibition," said Harry. "This is just a saloon."

"Doesn't look like one."

"Have you been in a lot of saloons?"

He shrugged. "I just didn't think they'd be so . . . basic."

Eli counted up eight people scattered around the saloon, plus the bald bartender, who locked eyes with Eli in the mirrors behind the bar. A woman in a green dress. An older man with thick silver muttonchops that stood out against the black lapels of his coat. A skinny man in layers of threadbare clothes, younger than Eli, with a bush of red hair and no whiskers.

"I see four possibles," she said.

"Me too."

"Let's wander and look a little closer, shall we?"

"Couldn't we just ask?" He cleared his throat.

She shook her head. "Word could get around."

"And?"

"He's a man who found a rich claim out in California. If he hears two strangers are looking for him, he's just as likely to vanish as to announce himself." She gazed up at Eli. "We can't have him go into hiding."

"Warmer by the fire," the bartender called out.

Eli nodded to the man. Harry flashed him a smile. The bartender went back to dusting bottles with his rag.

Harry led them to a table in the back, just outside a half-circle of chairs before the fireplace. Eli looked back as they passed each of the four dark-haired men.

A pair of cards landed on the table in front of a man with a dark beard that stretched down his shirt. A few strands of brown and gray threaded through the cascade of facial hair. He picked up a card and gave his opponent an evil grin that displayed a full set of teeth. Eli put the man's age at fifty, or maybe a hard-lived forty.

The man who sat alone at a table with his plate of food had a square-cut beard and no mustache. Eli wondered if the man was a Lincoln fan, then tried to remember if Lincoln would even be known at this point in time. He glared when Eli's gaze lingered too long.

The third man, by the fireplace, had a sharp tuft of a beard, a Vandyke. His nose and forehead looked like bronze. A book sat open in his lap, and Eli had the distinct sense the pages hadn't turned for quite a while. The man tapped the left-hand page with two fingers while he stared at a stone in the side of the fireplace.

The last man leaned against the staircase and talked with the woman in the green dress. He had a thick, lush beard and mustache of black hair, but was as bald as the bartender. He kept talking to the woman even as his eyes drifted to Harry and followed her to the table where she sat down. His gaze settled on Eli for a moment before darting back to the woman in front of him.

The bartender leaned over the wooden counter and called out to them as Eli and Harry settled in at the table. "What'll it be?"

Eli glanced at Harry. She gave an ever-so-slight dip of her eyes and he turned to the bald man. "What's on tap?"

The bartender's brow furrowed.

Harry's boot jabbed at his ankle under the table.

Eli coughed. "Sorry," he said. "Thinking of something else. I'll have a . . . a whiskey."

"Bourbon?"

"Yeah, sure."

The man nodded and glanced at Harry. "Just a coffee for me, sir," she said.

He looked over at the iron stove and frowned. "I'll have to put a pot on."

"Ahhh," she said. "If it's too much trouble then, never mind."

He drummed his fingers against the bar for a few moments, then tossed his rag down and pulled a kettle from a hidden shelf.

Harry beamed at him.

"How are we paying for this?" whispered Eli.

"It will only be twenty cents or so. I have some money."

"I thought you'd spent it all."

"I said I'd spent the Confederate bills. I didn't say I hadn't picked up anything else since then."

"Now what?"

"Now," she said, "we'll warm our feet, each have a drink so as not to arouse suspicion, and then go to find the other saloon. Hopefully before nightfall."

"Why?"

Her mouth pulled into a tight smile that was only slightly condescending. "Our situation may appear relaxed, Mr. Teague, but please don't forget we're just one of many teams searching for the dream. They may not be following the same path as us, but that doesn't mean their own investigations won't eventually lead to the same place and time."

"No, I mean, why are we going to the other saloon?"

She sighed. "Because," she said, "Mr. Russk isn't here."

"Yeah he is." Eli tipped his head back and to the left, toward the fireplace and the man with the book. "I'm pretty sure that's him."

"No, it isn't. He doesn't match the description I was given."

Eli nodded. "You said he's been back in town for a few days, right?"

"I think so, yes."

"From what you're telling me, the man comes into town for the first time after, what, a month on the trail? A couple years of mining for gold? He's tired, dirty, a little ragged. But he's got a lot of money now, he feels like splurging. That's what you were saying earlier, right?"

She nodded.

"He'd get some good food and a lot of booze and maybe . . ." He debated a few terms in his mind. "Maybe get some company, like you said. I'd bet he'd probably go to the barber too. Get cleaned up, get his hair trimmed. Maybe even get a shave."

Her eyes widened.

Eli nodded toward the man slumped by the fire. The man with the tanned nose and forehead, but pale cheeks around his Vandyke beard.

"Ahhhh," she said. "Good eye, Mr. Teague."

19

Harry pulled the envelope from her pocket and unfolded it. She reread it, tore off the bottom half, and folded it into thirds. The rest of it went in the small lamp on the center of their table. It flared up and drew a few eyes as it turned to ash.

"Not leaving tracks?"

"You're learning, Mr. Teague." She stood up and moved to stand before the other man. "Mr. Russk?"

He looked up from the fire. "Yes?"

"Gregson Edgar Russk?"

"I am," said the man. His eyes flitted up and down her body, taking in her figure and the clothes hiding it. He glanced over at Eli. "Who might you be, young lady?"

"I'm Harriet. You can call me Harry."

He grinned and showed off a jagged front tooth. It was a triangle of gray in a row of tan-brown teeth. Eli tried not to think about what a break like that would've felt like.

"You seem to have me at a disadvantage, ma'am," said the prospector.

She lowered herself into the chair across from him, creating a triangle between herself, Russk, and Eli. "A friend told me I might find you here. You're from the South, yes?"

"Louisiana man," he said with a nod.

"A Southern gentleman," she said. "Excellent. I was hoping you might be able to spare a few minutes of your time to help me with something."

The prospector glanced over at Eli again. "It's early," he said, "but I'm willing if the price is right."

She laughed and granted him what seemed to Eli like a very fake smile. "No, not that," she said.

He gestured at the bottle. "Want to help me finish this off?"

"It won't change my mind."

"Too bad," said Russk. He tapped the book in his lap. "Don't suppose you can read?"

"I can."

His eyes darted to Eli again. "You could spend the day reading this storybook to me, then."

She shook her head. "It's the best offer so far," she said, "but still not what I'm here for."

He huffed out a sigh.

"My brother and I wanted to talk about your inspiration," she said. "We were wondering what led a Southern man like yourself to drop everything and head west."

"Maybe you haven't noticed," said Russk with a smirk, "but lots of folks are heading west."

"Not really," said Harry. "There must be half a million people just here in Missouri. Most of them aren't going anywhere. Most people in the country aren't." She smiled again. A better smile. "But you did, Mr. Russk. You left behind friends, your job, everything you know. Why?"

He studied her for a moment. This time just her face. Then his gaze shifted to Eli.

Russk stood up. The man stood an inch or two shorter than Harry. "If you'll pardon my sayin', I don't like the path this question leads down."

She spread her fingers wide, but stopped short of raising her hands. "I don't mean to make you uncomfortable," she said, "I'm just curious."

"These ain't curious questions," said the prospector. He brushed back the ragged edge of his coat to reveal a tube of scratched leather on his thigh. His hand settled near it. Eli took a moment to recognize the tube. He'd seen too many custom-shaped holsters of nylon and plastic in movies and on television. The simplicity of Russk's caught him off guard.

Eli leaned forward, but Harry pinned him in his seat with a glance. Her gaze went back to Russk. "There's no need for guns."

"Ma'am, every time somebody tells me that, it means I'm gonna need my guns."

"Well, then, this time will be a pleasant exception."

He shook his head. "Thank you, but no."

"We have no interest in your claim, Mr. Russk," she said. "None at all. I just want to know what made you travel to California."

"And I believe I've been clear. I don't want to talk about it."

"If that's the case," said Harry, "I do have one other thing you still might be looking for. Favor for a favor."

"Ma'am," said the prospector, "I've told you all the things I'm looking for. You ain't offering none of 'em." He stood up and headed for the bar.

"You haven't told me about your sister," Harry said as he moved past her.

Russk took another three steps, giving Eli a cautious look as they came close. Then Harry's words registered and he spun around. His hand came away from the holster. "What did you say?"

"Louisa is your sister, isn't she?"

The prospector leaned in close. "My sister's dead. The redskins got her."

Harry's head went side to side. Her eyes never left his. "Would you like to talk now, Mr. Russk?"

His eyes flitted between her and Eli. For a moment, Eli thought the man would turn and walk away. Or reach for his gun again.

"Gregson," asked the bartender. He had the wary tone of a man used to leaping in, and ready to do so if needed. "There a problem?"

Eli glanced around the bar. More than a few of the patrons watched. The two men playing cards looked eager. So did the woman by the stairs.

Russk's eyes settled on Harry. She leaned back in her chair. With one hand, she pulled the bottom half of the paper from her pocket and tapped her fingers against it.

"No problem, Ray," said the prospector.

In the corner of Eli's eye, the bartender nodded and relaxed. The woman by the stairs sighed and returned her attention to the man with her. The dark-haired man playing cards dropped his hand to the table and chuckled.

"I'm very sorry, my friend, that I must resort to blackmail, Mr. Russk," Harry told him. "Please believe me when I say I want you and your sister to be reunited as soon as possible." She held up the folded piece of paper. "This was intended to be a sincere thank-you for helping me with my own quest."

Russk glanced at Eli. "Thought he was your brother."

"He's like a brother to me," said Harry. "We've known each other for so long. Honestly, if a horse's kick hadn't left him unable to perform a husband's duties, I would've married him years ago."

The prospector looked at Eli again, this time with pity in his eyes. Eli bit his tongue.

"But enough about my problems, Mr. Russk." She held the paper out past her knees, then pulled it back when the prospector reached for it. "I propose a simple trade. My information for yours. A favor for a favor."

"How do I know it's the truth? This could all be some swindle."

She unfolded the paper, leaving the blank side to the prospector. From where he sat, Eli could see four handwritten lines. "Your sister has brown hair and brown eyes. She had freckles when she was younger. There's a scar on her left hand and another one behind her right ear, but she wears her hair loose to hide that one."

Russk's eyes opened wide. Tears swelled at the corners. "I'll tell you where the mine is," he said with a quick nod. "I've got a map to the claim and the papers. It's all yours."

"As I told you before, we have no interest in your claim."

Russk blinked away the tears before they could blur his vision. His eyes darted from Harry to the paper. "What do you want, then?"

"Why did you go to California?"

"For the gold. That's what everyone's headin' out there for. We've all heard the stories."

She shook her head. "But why, Mr. Russk? What set you on your path? What made the decision for you?"

"I don't understand." He leaned close to her, to the paper. "What d'you want me to say?"

"Why did you go? What was the final straw for you? The deciding moment. Was it something you heard or read or saw? Did the thought just come to you, perhaps?"

He shrugged. "I just . . . I d'know. I was in N'Orleans doing odd jobs for a machinist. I'd been hearing some stories about gold, about how people was just plucking nuggets right up off the ground. And then I ended up talking to this one fella who came in about some parts for equipment he needed fixed. Talked with him for almost two hours. He'd come back from California rich as Midas. Was living the dream, you know?"

Harry's fingers trembled. "And it was him?"

Russk shrugged again. "Suppose so. Never really thought of it like that. But yeah, it was that night I decided t'go." He tapped the bottle. "I was sipping a bourbon, thinkin' about what he'd said, and decided to head out to California and make my fortune. And I did. That's all it was."

He reached for the paper. Harry lifted it away. His face hardened.

"The man," she said. "The man you spoke to in the blacksmith's shop. What was his name?"

The prospector's jaw shifted. It clicked each time it moved. Eli pictured the jagged point of the broken tooth tapping back and forth against the lower teeth and tried not to wince.

"Hawkins," said Russk. "Frank Hawkins. He'd done the trail when he was younger, one of the first ones out there back in '48, and struck it rich. He was heading back for another go when I met him, but this time he was taking a boat down to Panama and crossing there."

Harry glanced back at Eli to make sure he was paying attention. "If I was to see Mr. Hawkins," she said, "how would I know him?"

Russk's head went side to side. "It was almost three years ago, ma'am. I don't remember much of anything."

"What do you remember? Anything will help."

Russk stood up and held his hand above his head. He looked at Eli and raised it a little higher. "He was about yea tall. Strong. Shaved good. Nice fella, but he had this way of kinda . . . staring at people. Had a strong gaze." The prospector snapped his fingers. "Had this big buffalo-hide cloak. I asked about it 'cause it was warm out, and he said it was a . . . a 'membrance from his first trip. Said he'd never get rid of it."

Harry nodded. "When was this?"

"I told you. Three years ago."

"Could you be more specific? The month? The day, perhaps?"

He shook his head. "It was March, I think." He snapped his fingers. "It was two weeks before Easter. End of March, '50?"

Harry nodded. "That will do," she said. "Is there anything else you can tell us?"

He shook his head. "Nothing, I swear."

She smiled. "Thank you, Mr. Russk."

She held out the folded piece of paper. He stared at it for a moment, at her, at Eli. Then he snatched it away.

Harry waited while Russk sat down, unfolded the paper, and squinted at the words. Eli watched the man's lips move while his eyes worked back and forth through the handwritten lines. Almost two minutes passed before he looked up.

"This all true?"

Harry nodded.

"Edmunds had her all this time?"

She nodded again.

"Why?"

"I'm afraid I don't know anything beyond what's written there, Mr. Russk. I can just promise you it's all true. She's with Edmunds in Memphis."

He frowned and crumpled the paper in his fist. Then he looked down at it and spread it flat over his knee. He worked at the wrinkles and creases with his fingers. "Thank you," he said.

Harry nodded and stepped back to join Eli at their table. "What was that all about?" he asked.

"Which part?"

"His sister in Memphis with Edwards?"

"Edmunds. And I have no idea. As I told Mr. Russk, I don't know much past what was on the paper."

The bartender barked out "coffee," and set a tin mug down on the bar next to a glass with an inch of amber liquid in it. Harry guided Eli to the bar, where she fished a small coin purse from her coat and slid two coins across to the bald man. Eli went to move back to their table, but she held his arm. "Keep some distance," she said. "We don't want him starting more of a conversation. It leads to questions we can't answer."

Eli nodded and sniffed the bourbon. "So now what?"

"Now," she said, "we need to find Mr. Frank Hawkins in New Orleans."

"He could be anywhere by now," said Eli. "Maybe even dead. He was just passing through on the way to California, remember."

"I remember, Mr. Teague," she said. "That's why we'll be going . . ." She lifted her head higher and looked to the door. Then she swung her gaze to the bar.

Eli looked at the rack of bottles, then tried to figure out if she'd seen something in the mirror. "What?"

"Shhhh," she hissed at him, half closing her eyes.

He shut his mouth. The murmur of conversation still swung back and forth across the saloon. The bartender rustled the coals in the pot-bellied stove. Outside, the wind moaned on the corners of the building, never quite reaching a howl. When it fell to its lowest he could hear the distant sounds of a main road or maybe a highway.

"Wait a minute—" he began.

Harry's eyes snapped open. Her hands came up and pushed him toward the door.

He turned his head, trying to catch the sound again. "Is that a car? Here?"

"It's them," she said, giving him another shove. "They've found us."

20

The cold hit Eli in the face and clawed at his ankles under the cuffs of his jeans. The patches of warmth inside his coat shifted, and the ones in his jeans escaped back inside the bar. It didn't seem to be snowing any harder, but what had earlier been a breeze now qualified as a light wind.

Harry shoved him again and the door slammed shut behind them. "Can you still hear it?" she asked him, tilting her head. "We need to know which direction they're coming from."

Eli closed his eyes. Flakes of snow settled on his ear. The wind groaned across the rooftops. As the groan faded, he caught the last rumbles of an engine—a big, monster engine—settling down. "That way," he said, pointing.

"Pissbucket." She started down the path, glancing back at him. "Come on!"

He took three loping steps and caught up with her on the muddy road. He glanced at the buildings around them. "Do we have time to get back to the car?"

"They're between us and the car," snapped Harry. She elbowed him down a different road. "This way."

"Why?"

"Because if we get too close to them they'll know right where we are." She hooked her arm around his and dragged him along the snow-and-mud street. "A little faster, please, Mr. Teague. And try not to attract attention this time."

"Any faster and we'll be running."

Harry turned right at the first intersection and guided them down a new street. In the distance, a three- or four-story building loomed over the houses. A town hall, Eli guessed, or maybe a courthouse. His shoulders hunched as a man in a black coat and hat stepped out from between two buildings, but the man had a thick beard and dark eyes.

"Where will they be?" asked Eli. "The faceless men?"

"Probably coming in from the same slick spot we used. If we're lucky, there's only one of them."

They speed-walked past a dozen people, four horses, what looked like a stagecoach, and two more roads. At the next corner Harry pointed left. They half-jogged down the street, then she led them back up a muddy road, striding alongside a cart pulled by an ancient horse.

Harry went to turn down the next snow-dusted street, and Eli yanked her back. She fought his grip for a moment, then saw what he saw.

Two faceless men in matching hats stood at the far intersection, questioning a man and a woman. Their plastic masks gleamed in the sunlight. The larger one's mask and build matched the one Eli had first seen back at the bank. His badge was out and raised while he talked with the older couple.

The second one stood a few inches shorter, a few pounds lighter. He wore a vest and dark red tie under his coat. His mask had arching brows, a thin handlebar mustache, and a painted beard so narrow it was almost a line. A familiar design, but Eli couldn't place it. The faceless man's head jerked back and forth, never quite far enough to be aimed at Eli and Harry. The movement looked like part keeping watch, part nervous energy.

Harry took a step back, pressing against Eli, forcing him back himself. Six slow steps put them back around the corner. "Consarn it," she muttered. She looked back at him. "Thank you, Mr. Teague."

"Don't mention it," he said.

"We must be just on the edge of their range," she said. She took her tricorne off and leaned out, letting her eye slide past the corner of the building. Her fingers tightened on the hat.

"What are they doing?" asked Eli.

"They're splitting up." She inched back and turned to him. "Neither of them is coming this way, but now they're spreading their certainty, blocking off that whole side of town. We won't be able to get around them."

He thought about leaning out to look for himself, decided against it. "So what do we do?"

Harry wrung her hat in both hands, then pushed it back on her head. "We keep moving," she said.

"Where?"

"I don't know yet," she snapped.

They headed back the way they came, the snow squeezing into mud beneath their feet. Two men stood talking in front of another building and didn't seem to notice the chill. Eli could feel the cold seeping back into his bones, although the saloon had given him a nice respite. At the next intersection, Eli took a cautious step forward.

And froze.

The smaller faceless man stood in the middle of the street, a mere forty or fifty yards away. His mask swung to the left, to the right, and back as he studied the buildings on the far side of the street. Eli could see the thin elastic and the gleam of translucent plastic on the side of the man's head as it tilted in their direction.

Eli held out his arm to block Harry. She caught her breath, stopped her leg in midstride. She shifted her balance and stepped back. Eli followed her.

"How close?" she asked.

"Really close."

She half turned and took a few quick steps, trying to keep her eyes on the corner as they retreated. "Close enough to be certain?"

It took Eli a moment to process the question. "I . . . I thought so. He didn't seem to notice me, though."

Harry guided them between buildings. They passed piles of trash, a small stable, and then they were back out on another street, glancing over their shoulders as they went. She went half a dozen steps and changed direction, dragging him to a nearby building. Eli looked for a sign, but the window and the door were both bare. "What's this?"

"Hopefully a chance to save our lives."

A chiming bell and warm air welcomed them into the office. A counter split the room in two. Their side had nothing but the door, a small stove, and a neat pile of gray, gnarled wood accented by a few white pieces. Across the counter stood two sets of shelves. Small jars and bags filled one, all tagged and spaced out. Sheaves of paper and rolled-up maps spilled across the opposing shelves. A few of the longer rolls of paper leaned in the corner between the shelf and the wall.

Someone, Eli decided, needed to invent the file cabinet soon.

Harry took a step to the side and revealed the set of scales on the counter. Its brass arms caught every flicker of light in the room. A tray of weights sat next to the scales. Each of the lead blocks had been arranged by size, largest to smallest.

She cleared her throat. "Good afternoon," she said, keeping her voice calm.

In the back of the room, a thin man closed a safe with a heavy clang and spun the dial. He had round spectacles with frames so thin they could've been actual wire. His collar stood up straight, and his necktie looked like a silk handkerchief tied around his throat. His thick mustache would've fit well in any '70s movie. "Good afternoon," he said, setting his palms flat on the counter. With his slumped shoulders, the man's pose made Eli think of a Muppet.

"I'm wondering if you could help us," Harry said.

The clerk's gaze drifted up to the tricorne, then back to her face. "I can try."

"You know the town well?"

The man gave them a polite smile and gestured at the map on the wall. "Every square mile and measured acre."

"Where's the nearest train track?"

He shook his head. "Afraid the railroad's not quite here, ma'am. Hopefully by next year."

"But surely they've set down some track?"

"Station's just south of town." He pointed at the left-hand wall without hesitation. "About half an hour's walk. Nothing more than a platform right now, and not even a mile of track."

"Is there anything closer?"

The clerk smiled again. "Just the one station, ma'am."

"I didn't ask about the station, sir. I asked about tracks. Is there anything closer? An abandoned line, maybe?"

"If it's abandoned, it's not going to do you any good, is it?"

"It's a bet," interrupted Eli, pulling his gaze from the window. "A wager. I told her there wasn't anything closer and she didn't believe me."

"Please," Harry told the clerk, not missing a beat, "I've got a half dime riding on this."

"Well, I am very sorry, young lady," he said, "but there's nothing closer than the station, and nothing running closer than Kansas City."

She sighed.

"See," Eli said, "I told you."

The clerk gave her a pitying look. "Hopefully this will be a lesson to you about the evils of gambling."

"It will," said Harry, bowing her head. "Oh, one more thing. The post office?"

"One street over, two streets down." His finger pointed out at the road and swung to the left.

"Thank you," she said, pushing Eli back outside. The little bell over the door rang again as they left.

Her boots thumped down the wooden sidewalk, dragging Eli behind her.

"Post office?" he asked. He heard a sound and wrenched his neck around, expecting to see the faceless men a few doors down.

"Believe it or not," said Harry, "I'm still trying to save our lives."

They dashed across the snow-and-mud-swirled street, peered cautiously around the next intersection, and then headed down along the wooden walkway. They passed more people. Another coach rumbled by them, this one dragged by a pair of enthusiastic horses.

It took a few minutes to reach the post office, a small cabin with delusions of grandeur. A wooden sign hung out front with meticulous letters and a picture of a man on horseback. They stepped onto the porch and pushed the door open.

Inside, another counter divided another single-room structure, although this one gave far more space to the area behind. Mismatched stones made up a chimney, and three different shades of crumbling mortar bound them together. Another pile of wood sat by the fireplace, and a single bench, not much bigger than Eleanor's rumble seat, sat under the front window.

The man behind the counter kept his head down, his nose mere inches from the book on the counter. Eli could see a lot of scalp through the man's hair. An array of at least fifty cubbyholes flanked him on one side, three hanging sacks on the other.

Harry tapped her fingernails on the counter. The man sighed, set a string across the page, and closed the book. He looked up at them with watery eyes. His back stayed hunched over. "Yes?"

"I need to mail a letter," said Harry.

"Mail won't go out till tomorrow afternoon," the postmaster drawled.

"I'd still like to mail the letter." Her fingertips tapped on the countertop again, four quick strikes.

Eli looked out the window at the snow and mud. Every figure that strolled into his field of view made his stomach churn. A pair of linked memories tickled his mind—being chased through town by Zeke as a kid, and the gut-churning anticipation of getting caught.

The hunchbacked postmaster let out a wheezing, attention-demanding sigh. He stepped back, reached below the counter, and came back with a jagged sheet of brick-red stamps and a small pot of glue. "Your letter?"

"I also need an envelope," she said. "And paper."

The man's watery glare shifted to Eli. "Is your wife familiar with the procedure of mailing a letter?"

"I am," Harry said, "and I'm standing right here."

"Sir," said Eli, "it's been a really stressful afternoon for us. If you have pen and paper we could use, it'd be appreciated."

The postmaster wheezed again. Then he shook his head, muttered something to himself, and ducked below the counter again. He returned with a sheet of rough paper and a square envelope. "That'll be ten cents for the stamp, the paper, and the envelope."

She nodded.

He turned to another table behind him and returned with a small black pot and a carved wand of ivory or bone. One end held a brass nib. "This is my good pen," the postmaster said. "Don't dip it deep or you'll stain it."

"Of course," said Harry. "Thank you."

The man shuffled a polite step or two away while Harry scratched out a message on the paper. Eli stood next to her and read as she wrote. She made no attempt to hide the words.

URGENT! Calling in my second favor. Independence, Missouri. November 19th, 1853. I require passage for myself and my partner. We shall be on the train platform at

She looked up and her eyes found the postmaster. "Do you have the time?"

"Time?"

"Yes. What time is it right now?"

He let out another wheezing sigh. "The mail won't go out until tomorrow."

She nodded impatiently. "Yes, but the time at the moment is . . . ?"

The man rolled his watery eyes and pulled a silver pocket watch from his vest. "Five past four."

"Thank you. Again."

at 4:15 in the afternoon. Please be there.

Harry signed the letter with a flourish and blew on the page. She scratched out the initials *JH* on the envelope and an address in Kansas City. She blew on that as well, then folded the letter in half, and in half again.

Her hand vanished into her pocket and Eli heard a muffled set of clicks. She drew out a handful of round tokens. Most had red, blue, and black edges, although he glimpsed a yellow one too. Each one had a set of lines and curves scratched and inked across the face.

Harry used a finger to swipe through the tokens and selected a blue-edged one. She held it between her fingers as if she were examining a gemstone. The lines across the wood surface formed a glyph, and just as she flipped it back into her palm, Eli recognized it as stylized initials. The back of the *J* and the side of the *H* shared a common line.

Harry slid the token between the folds of the letter and pulled the coin purse from her other pocket. She shook some coins into her palm, plucked two small ones, and pushed the dull pieces across the countertop to the hunchbacked postmaster. "Acceptable?"

He held the coins close to his eyes, and for a moment Eli was convinced the man was going to set them on his own eyelids like a corpse. "These are old," he said. Accusation didn't drip from the words, but it brimmed up and trembled at their edges.

Harry fastened the purse and dropped it back into her coat pocket. "Still acceptable, though, yes?"

The postmaster studied the coins, then wheezed out another breath and set them down on the counter. "They are," he conceded. He folded the sheet of stamps back and forth until two came loose in his hand. He wiggled the cap off the glue and smeared a small blob on the corner of the envelope. "It'll go out tomorrow on the afternoon coach."

"Please make sure it does."

He waved a hand, dismissing them as he pressed the stamp into position.

The two of them stepped outside. Eli scanned the town, dread rumbling in his gut. Snow still drifted down, maybe a little heavier than before. Fewer people seemed to be out and about.

Harry checked the streets. "Come on," she said.

"Where?"

"The train station." She quick-stepped across the street.

Eli caught up with her. "Didn't the other guy say the trains aren't running yet?"

" 'Yet' being the important word." At the next corner she looked, decided, and pointed them on their way. They strode side by side, checking every doorway and intersection. Now and then one of them wove around a pile of droppings or a thick patch of near-frozen mud. Eli kicked a stone hidden by the thin coat of snow and the tremor echoed in his shoe.

"So what was that thing?"

"That?" Harry glanced at the road behind them. "Mule droppings, I believe."

"The thing you put in the envelope with the letter."

"Ahhh." She froze as a tall, dark-suited man walked across the street in front of them. He turned to reveal bright eyes and thick muttonchops. "It was a favor," she told Eli.

"A what?"

"A favor." Harry led them back up onto the wooden walkway and down the street. "When you're in someone's debt—I mean, really and truly owe them—you give them a favor. They can call it in at any time, and you can't say no when they do. Refuse to honor a favor, word will get around, and then no one will honor one you try to call in. So it's no small thing to give one, and you don't use them lightly."

"Seems like an odd way to keep track of things."

"Not when you travel through history," said Harry. She paused at the next intersection to glance around the corner, then they hurried across, sticking close to the buildings. "It's not often you meet people in the same order they're meeting you," she continued. "So we all have our own marks, something we'll recognize even if we haven't made that particular arrangement yet."

Eli glanced back, reassuring himself they weren't being followed. "Couldn't somebody just fake one if they needed it? They're just wood and paint, right?"

Harry shook her head. "No one would risk it. Creating a false favor would be worse than failing to honor a real one. Once people found out, the counterfeiter'd be ostracized. They probably wouldn't even be allowed in the iteration or the paradox."

"What's that?"

"What are they," she corrected him. "If we can stay alive long enough, Mr. Teague, you may get to find out."

The homes and shops began to spread themselves thinner. The wooden sidewalk came to an end. A carriage passed them going the other way. Harry took four stomping steps. The clinging snow lost its grip and tumbled from her boots. "We're running out of cover. I'd hoped the station would be closer to town."

Eli looked up ahead. A half mile or so down the road—not much more than a broad trail at this point—stood a wide platform with a small cabin on it. "About that," he said.

"Yes?"

"If there's only a mile of track, how's a—"

"Hello," called out a voice behind them. "Mrs. Pritchard. Mr. Teague."

Harry launched into a sprint, her cloak flapping out behind her. Eli threw himself after her. After a dozen strides, his shoe slipped on a muddy rock and he clawed at the air to keep his balance. He slid, caught it, ran again.

A pair of cracks echoed behind them and the ground ahead of Eli spat up two little tufts of snow.

The clearing opened in front of them and Harry veered to the right. The field behind the platform was gouged with dozens of wagon tracks that showed through the light snow cover. The path itself curved toward a set of stairs that mounted the platform.

A man in a long charcoal coat and stubby round hat stepped from the shack up on the platform, a long cane tucked under his arm. He waved and called out a few words Eli couldn't hear. Then his gaze settled on something behind them.

Eli glanced back.

The two faceless men marched down the path, side by side, arms and legs moving in perfect sync. They each had a pistol out, aimed at the runners. "Please, Mr. Teague," shouted the larger one, "let's not make this unpleasant."

They were too close, he realized as he turned back to the train station. Less than two hundred feet away. Close enough to be certain.

"Keep running," snapped Harry.

"Where?" he gasped.

She pulled ahead in response, her boots pounding the dirt and snow. Another crack echoed from behind them and a spiky flower burst open on one of the platform's wooden legs, right by the point of Harry's hat. She flinched away and kept running, right past the stairs and along the tracks.

Eli slipped in the snow again but kept after her, putting a few trees between him and the faceless men.

The man on the platform, the station guard, swung his long cane up and braced it against his shoulder. He didn't have it aimed at them. He shouted something that might've been *Hold it right there*, but the wind and exertion took his words away from Eli's ears.

They kept running. The man passed from view. Eli heard a series of gunshots and a wail of pain. He looked at the sloping ground ahead of him, alongside the tracks, and risked a glance back.

The station guard stood at the top of the stairs clutching his shoulder, his body twitching. The two faceless men had almost reached the platform. Just over a hundred feet at most. They had a clear shot again, but the larger one was turning his head the other way.

Beyond them, a hundred or so yards down the track, the gleaming cylinder of a steam engine chugged toward the platform. Eli could hear the pulsing hiss of steam and oiled pistons. Smoke billowed up from its stacks, black against the falling flakes of white.

The train pulled alongside them as they ran, a massive bullet of steel studded with lines of rivets. The brakes hissed and squealed, a scream of metal on metal, but sheer momentum kept the engine moving past them. Eli counted four more cars that rolled by even as he and Harry kept sprinting. It felt like a football stadium sliding past him, yard by yard.

Then the shrieking stopped. The brakes gave a final, coughing hiss and fell silent. The train rolled on, slower but still moving at a good ten or fifteen miles per hour.

A few yards ahead, a figure reached down from the engine, grabbed Harry's upraised hand, and pulled her aboard. Eli heaved, threw his legs forward, and a bullet rang off the train next to him. Another one tugged at his sleeve. He staggered, lost his pace, and heard a third shriek through the air near his head.

Harry leaned out from the engine cab, a pistol in each hand. "Come on, Mr. Teague!" The Colts fired off three-four-five-six rounds at whatever was running up behind Eli. Then the pistols spun down into their holsters and she stretched her fingers out to him. "Run!"

Eli ran. He threw himself forward, kicked at the ground, tried not to think of the huge steel wheels grinding on the track next to him. The cold air scraped his throat, ripped at his lungs.

Harry gripped a long handle with one hand and leaned out to him. A bullet sparked against the side of the engine near her. She winced but didn't flinch away.

Eli stretched, reached, brushed her fingers. Harry grabbed at his wrist. He felt her grip drag him forward, toward the wheels. He panicked, almost fought her, and then Harry gritted her teeth and pulled.

Eli got his other arm up on the edge of the engine's platform. Together they heaved him up high enough for him to get a foot on the metal platform. "He's on!" she shouted over her shoulder.

Steam hissed around the wheels as the train lurched forward again. Eli kicked at the side of the engine as Harry hauled him up onto the trembling deck. By the time he was on board, their speed had almost doubled. He risked a cautious peek back, but the station and the faceless men had vanished beyond a curve.

Harry took a few deep, panting breaths and turned to the open door behind her, a heavy sliding plate at the back of the engine. "Come along, Mr. Teague," she said, leading him inside.

The engine's cab bordered on hot, even with the door open to the outside. The steel circle of the train's boiler dominated the front of the small room. Hoses and pipes draped across it like thick strands of hair framing a face, each one dotted with a brightly painted lever or twist handle. Needles trembled on a double handful of brass gauges and dials that sat scattered across the boiler's surface. Orange-yellow light flickered around an iron hatch at floor level.

A tall slab of a man stood in the corner and leaned into a long lever arm that stretched across the cab. A shirt and vest pulled tight across the lean V of his body. The cuffs of his shirt sat folded above the elbows, revealing lean, powerful arms that flexed on the lever. He could've been a statue come to life, carved from a block of dark stone to represent work and industry.

Despite the man's large presence, his eyes met Eli's on an even level when he turned. Creases surrounded his dark eyes, and his black hair and beard were cut close to his head. Just enough gray peppered his chin and scalp to give him character without making him look old.

The top button of his collar hung open. Rather than a scarf or bow, the man wore a long twentieth-century necktie, the knot pulled loose and the end tucked into his vest. Small stars dotted the blue-black silk, along with an odd white shape that repeated across the tie. Three parallel lines and an oval, all threaded with finer details.

"We're away," he boomed over the rumble of the engine, eyeing Eli but directing his words to Harry. "I heard bullets hitting my train, woman. I felt it."

"Don't be melodramatic," said Harry, pitching her own voice over the noise. "You're making an awful first impression."

His face split into a broad smile. "Come here and say hello." He scooped Harry into his arms, and she wrapped herself around his torso. "When are we now? How long's it been?"

"About seven years, for me," she said, squeezing him harder. "Right after the funeral."

He patted her back with a large, scarred hand. "I'm so sorry," he said. "I still miss him."

"So do I."

"And I'll never forgive him for proposing to you before I could."

She pushed herself away and slapped his arm. "You're still a daft fool."

"So every woman tells me." He set his knuckles against his waist and turned his gaze on Eli. "And who's this, then? Picking up strays now, Harry?"

"In a manner of speaking," she said. "John, this is my new partner, Mr. Eli Teague. Mr. Teague, may I present my dear friend, Mr. John Henry."

21

John took Eli's hand in his own. He had powerful fingers. Eli had never thought of fingers as muscular until the other man's grip surrounded his hand.

"John Henry," echoed Eli, taking his hand back.

The other man put his arm across his waist and gave a slight bow. "In the flesh."

"*The* John Henry?"

"I would assume over the centuries there have been a few," he said, "but I think I can safely say, yes, I am that John Henry."

Eli glanced at Harry and waited for her to laugh.

John chuckled and turned back to the engine. He adjusted the overhead lever and reached out to twist one of the round handles half a turn to the left. The floor rattled beneath their feet, then settled back to a low vibration. "So, you led the faceless men right to the *Bucephalus*," he said over his shoulder. "Sloppy, Harriet. Very sloppy."

"If they hadn't been there," she said, "I wouldn't have called in the favor."

"If you hadn't gotten sloppy," said John, "they wouldn't have tracked you there."

"I wasn't sloppy."

He tapped a gauge and snorted.

Harry scowled at him. "I wasn't."

"Lord only knows how much damage they did to the exterior," muttered John. "It's a miracle we got away."

Eli looked around the train's cab. His eyes focused on the piece of glass above the boiler. The top of the boiler showed in it, along with a few hundred feet of track in front of the engine, rolling toward them like a conveyor belt. It reminded him of the big television at the bar he'd visited with his friends on the night he'd seen Harry again. His gaze drifted to the side of the screen and he saw bolts, brackets, and the edge of another piece of mirrored glass.

"So where's that beautiful automobile of yours?" John finished adjusting the lever and turned back to Harry. "You haven't lost her, have you?"

"Never," said Harry. "If you've got room in your storage car and can swing around, I was hoping we could bring her on board."

"'Swing around'?" He turned to stare at her from beneath a furrowed brow. "Harriet, my dearest, do you know how much work it takes to turn a train around? Even one as magnificent as the *Steel Bucephalus*? As it is, it's going to take me a week to hide her from them again"

"You're honoring your favor, aren't you?"

"Of course I am." He straightened up and glared at her. "How dare you suggest otherwise!"

"Then you need to turn around anyway," Harry told him. "You're heading west and you need to take us south to New Orleans."

"I'm doing no such thing."

"I called in my favor. You're here, we're on board, you're taking us to New Orleans."

"I just saved you from the faceless men," said John. "We're even."

"I didn't ask you to save us. I asked for passage. To and from. Rescuing us was just a fortunate benefit of your timely arrival."

John opened his mouth, then shook his head and sighed. His annoyance fell away, and a wry smile blossomed in its place. "You should've been a lawyer."

"Excuse me," said Eli. "I don't mean to sound rude but . . . well . . ."

John shifted his attention. "Yes?"

Eli carefully selected a few words. "Aren't you . . . made up?"

Harry sighed.

John straightened up. "Regarding my existence, Mr. Teague, if I may use the phrase Samuel stole from me after an otherwise pleasant breakfast, the report of my death was an exaggeration."

Harry coughed. "John, before you launch into your speech about how history has wronged you—"

"Is it so wrong for a man to want his accomplishments—"

"—and it is a wonderful speech, please don't misunderstand me, but I was wondering if you could confirm we'll be picking up my car."

John sighed again. Loudly. Theatrically. "There's a good wye in Kansas City, 1995, that I was already prepared to use. We can be back to pick up your automobile"—he checked four of the gauges and tapped one of them a few times until the needle settled—"an hour before I found you?"

"That should be fine," Harry said with a nod.

"Excellent," said John. He reached up and nudged the long handle. "We're about twenty minutes out from the turnaround. I made up the guest rooms for you, if you'd like to refresh yourselves."

"You," said Harry, "are the most wonderful of hosts."

"Yes," he mused, "I really am."

The shapes on John's tie resolved themselves in Eli's eyes. The starship *Enterprise*, the classic one. Another repetition of the pattern was half-hidden by his waistcoat.

He looked back and forth between Harry and John, still half-convinced a punch line lurked somewhere just beyond his sight.

John chuckled again. "I think we may have stunned your companion with my very existence."

Harry reached out and squeezed Eli's hand again. "Mr. Teague," she said. "You're fine, aren't you?"

Eli looked at her and saw the concern in her eyes. "Yeah," he said. "Yeah, I'm fine. It's just . . . this is a bit much."

"If you'll pardon me for a moment, then," she said, "I shall leave you to John's hospitality and stories while I go freshen up."

"Okay."

She vanished through the heavy sliding door.

John gestured up at the rectangle of glass. "Clever, yes?" he said. "One of the big problems with steam trains is that the bulk of the boiler sits between the engineer and the tracks ahead. This is, at heart, a simple, broad-view periscope like the ones Mr. Lake used on his submarines. It gives me a full view of the tracks without exposing myself or extensively modifying the cab of the *Steel Bucephalus*."

"The *Steel Bucephalus*," echoed Eli. His eyes wandered around the engine's cab. Three long steps would carry him from corner to corner.

A trio of hooks held a single long coat between them. Dark wood and brass fittings made up the rest of the room.

"One moment," said John. He stepped through the rear door and returned a few moments later with an armful of split logs. The toe of his boot caught the low door on the boiler and swung it open. Crackling flames and heat rolled out, but John ignored them as he fed the logs into the firebox. He kicked the door shut and brushed a few splinters from his sleeves.

Eli cleared his throat, feeling a desperate need to say something. "I thought all these old trains were coal powered?"

"Many of them were," agreed John, "until diesel became the standard. I designed the *Bucephalus* as a wood burner because whenever I go, there's always fuel to be had."

Eli looked around the cab again, then back at John. "You designed the train?"

"I did."

"All of it?"

"Modesty forbids me from taking too much credit, Mr. Teague. The boiler is a stock model from 1871, as are the wheels. Many of the fixtures, fittings, and pistons were acquired in the 1930s, just after the stock market crash. The gearing itself is my own design, an enclosed variable-gauge system for the assorted tracks I encounter as I travel through history."

"The train travels through time?"

"Through history."

"Right. Still getting used to that."

"And yes, she does."

"A time . . . history-traveling steam train." Eli felt a smile blossom on his face.

"Yes," John said, one corner of his own mouth curling up, "I know. I've been told several times. And seen the film twice."

Eli shook his head. "But you built all of this."

"I hired some laborers now and then, but mostly me, yes. Over the course of about nine months. A good time period to give birth to a creation."

"I just . . ."

"Yes?"

"Well, if you're John Henry—"

"I am."

"—all the stories make you out to be . . . well, just a guy with a hammer. Who isn't too fond of machines."

John sighed and shook his head. "Mr. Teague," he said, "as I started to say earlier, I have been the victim of one of the most determined smear campaigns in history."

"You can just call me Eli."

John studied his face, then smiled. "A confident man, willing to go right to a first-name basis. I admire that, Eli. Please call me John."

"Thanks."

"As I was saying, Eli, the stories and songs have cast me as some brute Luddite who hates all progress and machinery. This couldn't be further from the truth." He stretched out an arm to take in the gauges and hoses covering the wall of the boiler. "I love machinery, technology, gidgets, all of it."

"Gadgets."

"Yes, thank you. The point is, I believe in machinery—with people behind it. A better drilling machine. A faster loom. A stronger engine. But these things don't get rid of the need for people, and they can't work without them.

"I'd worked on the railway for fourteen years. Half of my life. First as a digger, then as a steel driver in West Virginia. I knew the ground, the rocks, where to plant the charges to do the most work." He looked at Eli. "Do you know what my original wager was?"

"The one to race a drill machine, right? To dig the tunnel?"

"Not precisely. It was a steam hammer. A large but portable machine. They were trying to sell it to the railroad managers in 1871. Three drops of the weight, four tops, and it could plant a charge anywhere you wanted it.

"We all gathered around to watch a few demonstrations, and it was true. The rig could drive steel three times as fast as any man. It made them sloppy, though. They could place a hole anywhere, and they did. The stone and shale and clay didn't matter anymore, so they assumed the other aspects of the job also didn't matter. They were working faster, but not smarter."

John turned his head to check a few of the gauges. He pulled a dangling rag from one of the hoses and gave a dial a quick polish. Then his attention returned to Eli.

"So I told the salesman if he let me run his portable steam hammer, I could dig the tunnels three times faster than his crew. He wouldn't hear it, naturally. The machine made everyone a master driver, you see, and it certainly wasn't going to work better with a black man running it. Mind you, at that point in history, he was a bit more explicit when referring to my skin.

"So I made him a bet. The one you've heard stories about. I bet him I could beat his machine. First crew to dig one hundred yards of tunnel wins."

"And you won," said Eli.

"I did," said John. "So you can imagine my surprise when, over the next few years, word reached my ears I'd fallen over dead trying to beat the steam hammer. As it turned out, he was using our contest as a sales pitch."

"With a different ending."

John leveled a finger at him. "Precisely. I hunted the man down, found him in Alabama, and challenged him again. Right in front of an audience of buyers. He hemmed and hawed, but in the end it was race me or lose all his potential sales."

"And you beat him again."

The other man sighed. "I did, and it didn't make a difference. He made his sales. They twisted the story. Said I died. Again." He reached out and set one of his well-used hands against the wall of the cab. "About a year after that, I first heard about the dream. Two years later, I started work on the *Steel Bucephalus*."

"So, how do you travel through . . . history with it?"

John's brow went up. "Harry hasn't explained the basics to you?"

"No, she has, sort of," Eli said. "Not really. I just don't understand how you do it with a train. It's kind of . . . limiting, isn't it?"

"Before 1830, tracks are spotty," agreed John. "Almost nonexistent before 1826. Fortunately, there isn't much history before 1826 either. Fifty years. Barely a seventh."

"But I thought . . ." Eli looked at the boiler and then out at the trees passing by them. The train had been in motion for over ten minutes, at least, and they hadn't reached the end of the brief span of track around

Independence station. "I thought you needed to use these, the slick spots, to move back and forth in history."

"Indeed you do," said John. "And what better enduring symbol of the United States is there than the railroad? Trains, Eli, are the symbol of America's reach across this continent. That's what these tracks represent. There's not a man, woman, or child from 1826 to 2046 who doesn't look at a set of train tracks and remember that era. There are so many spots along every set of tracks where the dream became focused. Towns and cities and bridges where the railroad meant things were getting better, that things were amazing. The Golden Spike. The Great Change in 1886."

"Must confuse the hell out of people sometimes. A train appearing on old tracks."

"The *Steel Bucephalus* is the source of at least seven 'ghost train' stories I know of," said John, the edges of his lips turning up. He turned his smile to the boiler. "She can go almost anywhere and anywhen in America. And much faster than any of the other searchers in their little automobiles. No offense, my dear."

"None taken." Eli turned to see Harry standing in the door. Her cloak, coat, and hat had vanished, leaving her in the shirt and vest he first remembered her in. She looked relaxed, probably owing to her scrubbed face and damp brow. "At least, none while I'm riding your cumbersome beast of an engine."

"John's been telling me his history," said Eli.

"'John,' is it?" she asked. "Thick as thieves in just a few minutes. Should I be worried, Mr. Teague?"

"Worried?"

"You're not going to leave me for the soft life of a train, are you?"

"What?" Eli shook his head. "No."

"Of course he isn't," said John. "What man would? But I'm being a poor host—dominating the conversation and talking about nothing but myself. Truth be told, I'm intrigued to hear how the two of you became partners."

"We kept running into each other," Eli said. "And then a faceless man came looking for her and found me instead. After he left, I went looking for Harry to warn her."

The other man frowned and glanced at Harry.

"Mr. Teague," she said, "is from Sanders, Maine."

"Oh?" said John. "Oh! Is he? Well, then, that explains it."

Eli blinked. "Explains what?"

"Never made it up to Sanders, myself," continued John. "There are some wonderful tracks running through York around 1907. A beautiful stretch across the Cape Neddick River, as I recall."

Eli looked at Harry, then at John. "Explains what?" he asked again.

John paused. "I was wondering how you kept running into each other," he said. "It's so unlike Harry to visit the same place twice if she doesn't need to."

"But she did," Eli said. "A few times. That's how we met."

"Of course it is," he said. "If you're from Sanders, it makes perfect sense."

Harry made a quick side-to-side movement with her head. John caught himself in mid-gesture, one hand rising up. His eyes darted from her to Eli, back to her, back to Eli. "Oh," he said again. "I just assumed . . ." His voice trailed off and two of the boiler's gauges grabbed his attention. He studied one with intense focus.

"What?" asked Eli. Images of his mother flashed through his mind, of Robin and Corey at the Emporium, of Jackson's, the Pizza Pub, and of his small apartment. "What's wrong with Sanders?"

"Nothing's wrong with it," Harry said. "Not in the way you think."

"What's that supposed to mean?"

"I'm so sorry," said John. "You're traveling together, so I assumed he knew."

"I hadn't explained it to him," Harry said. "Not in so many words."

"What?" demanded Eli.

She sighed. "Mr. Teague," she said, "do you remember what I told you about the slick spots? The places that slide loose from history?"

He nodded. "Like the town on the Nevada border," he said. "The one stuck in the '60s."

"Yes," said Harry. She pitched her voice soft and gentle. "Precisely. And these are the places we use to travel. Each one is an entrance to a different point in history."

"Yeah," he said, "I remember. What about Sanders?"

And even as he said it, the world crashed down on him. The Emporium video store. The radio stations. The lack of internet and cell phone towers and cable television.

She reached out for his hand. He let her take it. "We're talking about Sanders, Mr. Teague. You're from one of the slick spots."

22

N o, I'm not," Eli said.

Harry nodded. "I'm afraid so." She shot a look at John. "I had hoped to introduce the idea with a bit more subtlety."

"My apologies," said the engineer. "I merely thought—"

"Don't try to take the blame. It's my own fault."

"It's nobody's fault," Eli said, "because it isn't true."

John opened his mouth to speak, but closed it at a glare from Harry. He turned and decided to study the gauges and the view through his mirror. "The wye should be coming up soon," he said to the boiler. He began to hum a song Eli found familiar, but couldn't place.

"Eli," she said, "I know you think we first met in the 1980s, but think carefully. When did we meet the second time? What year was it that night on the side of the road?"

He shook his head. "I'm not from a slick spot."

"Eli, I've used Sanders at least five times to travel through history," Harry said. "Every building, car, and piece of technology in your town tops out at 1988."

"Maybe it's a . . . a former slick spot."

John shook his head, but kept humming.

"Look," Eli said, "you told me slick spots form when a lot of people think everything's perfect. The dream works on them wanting things to stay the same, right?"

"Correct," said Harry.

"Believe me, nobody thinks that in Sanders. It's not stuck at a high point; it's at a low one. The town sucks. I mean, it's my hometown and I love it and I . . . I want to get home. But it's sucked since I was a little kid. There aren't enough jobs. The roads need a ton of work. I think everybody wants it to change and get caught up with the times."

Harry frowned. "That doesn't make sense," she said.

He shrugged.

Outside the windows of the train engine, the trees and snowy clearings had been replaced by warehouses and pavement. The city had risen like bread to its high point and then settled back enough to form a hard crust, one charred on the edges. In the mirror above the boiler, weeds and broken bottles decorated the oncoming tracks.

John's humming picked up as he reached the chorus of his song. Eli recognized it as an old Peter, Paul, and Mary song. Something his mom used to hum and sing years ago.

Harry turned to him again. "You said you worked with computers, yes?"

"Yeah," said Eli. "At a bank in Dover."

"And you just drive in and out?"

"Yeah."

"With what kind of car?"

"An old, patched-together Taurus, a . . ." He sighed. "An '88."

She looked at John. "Could that be it? If he's slipping out and spending a lot of time outside of the town limits?"

"I'm not slipping out."

She ignored him. "Could it be affecting his perceptions?"

John stopped his humming with a cough. "Possibly. I have heard stories of anomalies, people who sensed something wrong about their town."

"There's nothing wrong with my town," said Eli.

Harry started to say something else, but he waved her off and stared out at the city.

Turning the *Steel Bucephalus* ended up being a somewhat monotonous procedure. John braked, adjusted levers, and then spent fifteen minutes backing the train up. Then he moved forward again and Eli recognized some of the landmarks, now on the opposite side of the track.

Twenty minutes later, the *Bucephalus* slowed to a halt. The three of them climbed down from the engine and into the snow. Harry tugged her cloak tight around herself. "I'll take care of Eleanor," she told Eli. Caution colored her voice. "You can help John."

Eli glanced at the forest, still red with the early sun. The second time he'd seen the same sunrise. "Are you sure?"

"I survived many years without you at my side, Mr. Teague. I'll be fine." Then, to reassure him, she swept her cloak and coat back to reveal the holsters hanging against the back of her thighs. She winked, adjusted her tricorne, and marched off into the forest, snow crunching under her boots.

"Come on, then," said John. He'd pulled on the hanging coat from the cab and then a thick black overcoat over that. A gleaming top hat rode on his head. "Let's get the ramps down before I catch a chill and regret stopping for the two of you."

They marched to the far end of the train. Eli counted five cars along the way. One, right behind the engine, was stacked high with an immense pile of split logs. The next four looked like passenger cars with dozens of small windows, although all the drapes were pulled on the last two. The final car looked like a boxcar. John pulled on the wide door's latch to drag it open, and he and Eli hauled themselves up.

Shelves lined the inside of the boxcar, and stacks of cardboard boxes covered most of the floor. Two long metal plates stretched across the floor, each one almost two feet wide and over ten feet long, with book-sized teeth jutting down at one end. They reminded Eli of huge car ramps, and then John started to move one and he realized that was exactly what they were. He grabbed the other end, heaved it up, and they walked it to the door.

"You give a lot of people rides, I guess?" Eli asked, dipping his chin at the ramps.

"Enough to make them worthwhile," said John.

Eli climbed down and walked the ramps away from the boxcar as John fitted the teeth at the end into a slot on the floor. They finished the second ramp just as the sounds of Eleanor's engine echoed through the woods. The car's wheels spun as it lurched and lunged through the snow.

Harry lined the Model A up with the twin ramps and John guided her with small movements of his hand. The tires slid once on the steep slope, but Harry recovered and Eleanor crawled up and into the boxcar. A few quick maneuvers lined the car up between the doors, facing the back of the train. John and Harry used a half dozen bright-orange ratchet straps to secure the car while Eli watched from below, poking at the ragged tear the faceless man's bullet had left in his coat sleeve.

They returned to the warmth of the engine's cab. John hung both of his coats and began to adjust levers and valves across the boiler's face. "If the two of you could grab a few logs," he said, "I think we can be on our way."

Harry led Eli out across the connector to the next car, and they each gathered three or four chunks of wood. John waved at the open door beneath the boiler, and they tossed the logs into the flames. One fell short and Eli gave it a kick with the side of his shoe. John pushed the door shut with his boot and watched one of the gauges for a few seconds. "Excellent," he said. He pulled on the whistle cord two times, eased back the brake, and the *Steel Bucephalus* rolled forward down the tracks.

"Wait a minute," Eli said. "This already happened."

Harry and John looked at him. "I beg your pardon,?" she asked.

He waved his hand at the window, toward Independence. "Right now," he said, "we're walking through town. The earlier us. I didn't think about it then. We heard the train whistle. Two times, just before we went in the saloon."

"I would guess so, yes," John agreed.

Eli looked back and forth between them.

"I think our Mr. Teague is getting his first real taste of what it means to travel in history," Harry said.

John reached up and inched the overhead throttle back a few inches. "There's a lot of good straightaways in this part of the country," he said. "Especially if I cut over into the 1930s. We should be able to make it through most of Arkansas by nightfall, and then I can have you in early 1850s New Orleans by a little after lunch tomorrow.

"Eighteen fifty," said Harry. "It needs to be late March of 1850."

He rubbed his chin through his beard. "A little tricky. New Orleans wasn't really interested in train lines in that era—too much river traffic." His hand dropped from his chin down to his hip. "If memory serves, there's a few miles of the New Orleans and Nashville tracks the *Bucephalus* can reach. Work on the line's stalled by the mid-1840s, and it's practically abandoned by 1850."

"Thank you."

"No need to thank me. You called in a favor."

"And as always," she said, "you've gone above and beyond."

"Nonsense," John said. "There's favors, and then there's just being a good host. Speaking of which—" His eyes went from her to Eli and back. "When was the last time you two had a decent meal?"

THE DINING ROOM took up the back half of the Pullman car with the guest quarters. It could've been a hotel suite. Nice carpet, a few plush chairs, a high-backed couch, a small stove, even a bookshelf and a small boom box. John had furnished his train with random items that had caught his eye throughout history.

Half the cans for dinner looked like World War I rations. The other half had pull tops and brand names Eli didn't recognize. John warmed it all on a stove in the tiny kitchen and served it on fine plates and bowls. It tasted wonderful after two days of biscuits and jerky. The three travelers shared a bottle of wine, which John insisted had been given to him by Franklin Delano Roosevelt. Harry had rolled her eyes and snorted, and while John smiled at his own statement, he wouldn't back down from it.

Then Harry and John had some private matters to discuss, so Eli had retired to his guest room. It had a small desk with a chair, a standing wardrobe, and a high twin bed with what looked like a very modern mattress, although Eli didn't know what counted as "modern" anymore. Thick drapes hung on either side of the window, and for a brief while he watched the dark countryside roll by outside.

After a few sniffs of his collar, Eli pulled off his shirt and tossed it on the chair. He'd been wearing the same clothes for almost two weeks now, since Boston. They needed to be washed, or at least rinsed. He wondered if John had a washing machine somewhere on the train.

He pried off his shoes, then peeled off his wool socks and the cotton ones underneath. The skin of his feet prickled at the touch of air, and the carpet's texture felt wonderful. He tried clenching his feet, making fists with his toes like in that movie, but it didn't loosen his feet much or make him feel like an action star.

He spread his arms and flopped face-first onto the bed. The wool blanket scratched at his chest, but he welcomed any sensation not tied to his shirt. He rolled over and stared up at the ceiling. A basketball-sized globe of frosted glass stared back at him, its gaze bright enough to make him close his eyes.

He lay there and thought about Sanders. The town that never got cable or cell phones or a single computerized cash register. Where comic books still came on a spinning wire rack. Where a VHS rental store had survived his grade-school years. And high-school years. And college years.

Could Harry be right?

He mulled it over. Then his thoughts wandered to Harry, and going out to bars with his friends, and Nicole down at the theater, and not having a job when he got home. The thoughts blurred together into a series of warm images and soft sounds and faint raps . . .

He blinked his eyes open. A light chill had crept across his arms and chest. It was still night outside his window, but the train didn't seem to be moving.

Two more knocks echoed through the room's door. "Mr. Teague?" Harry stage-whispered outside. "Are you up?"

He tugged his shirt back on, pushed a few buttons through their holes, and opened the door. Harry stood in the narrow hall between their rooms, her knuckles raised to knock again. Her free hand held the lapels of a thick white robe together. The kind of robe people expected at a hotel or a spa.

"What's up?"

"Did I wake you?"

He shook his head. "Is there a problem?"

"No, I just . . . I needed to talk to you about something." She waited in the hall. Eli realized what she was waiting on and got out of the way.

Harry stepped into his room. She glanced at the bed for a moment, then shifted her attention to the small chair and sat down. The robe fell away to reveal faded red leggings with frayed cuffs. When she reached down to sweep the edge of the robe over herself, Eli glimpsed the same color between her lapels.

"Are you wearing red long johns?" he asked.

"A gentleman does not question a lady about her undergarments."

"He might when she shows up at his room in the middle of the night."

She scowled at him, then her face softened. "Please, Mr. Teague," she said, "this is a serious matter."

"Sorry. Okay, what's up?"

Her fingers flexed on the robe's lapels. "I know the past few days have been difficult for you. Not just the events, but also some of the things you've learned. I wanted you to know I'm very impressed with how well you're dealing with things. So is John."

"Well," said Eli, "for the record, I'm still not sure I believe all of it."

"I know," she said. "I don't think the wine came from Roosevelt either."

He chuckled.

"I've mentioned, I believe, that it can be difficult to keep track of the passage of time when one travels through history."

"Yeah."

"One of the great challenges is to keep track of how long the search has been ongoing. This is difficult, since the search itself exists outside of history. It limits the ways we can record things."

Eli nodded. "Like with the favors."

"Precisely. We want to honor those who came before us, so we do it the only way we can. By word of mouth." She met his eyes, held his gaze. "Christopher Pritchard. Phoebe Fitzgerald. Abraham Porter. Alice Ramsey. Roscoe Montgomery."

He blinked. "What?"

"This is the Chain," she said, putting emphasis on the word. "Our Chain. Every searcher has one. It's our links back to Roscoe, who first found out how to travel with the slick spots and taught others."

"How did he figure it out?"

She shook her head. "I don't know."

"Seems like a weird thing to just stumble across."

"I know he drove a delivery truck in the 1930s, I believe between New Jersey and New York. He ended up on the road sometime just before America entered World War Two." She shrugged. "I wish I had more to tell you. So much of this has been passed down from person to person."

"Okay."

"Christopher Pritchard," she said again. "Phoebe Fitzgerald. Abraham Porter. Alice Ramsey. Roscoe Montgomery."

"Alice Ramsey?"

"One of the few who left the search. Maybe the only one. She was on the road for about ten years, I believe, and then decided to go back to her old life. Slipped in almost right where she left off."

"I thought everyone was in this until they die? That's the only way out?"

"It always is. Except for Alice. The faceless men never went after her for some reason."

"Well, maybe I could go home the same way."

Harry shook her head. "I'm afraid not. Others have tried. They were killed." She sighed. "That's just the way of the search. Sooner or later, almost all of us catch a bullet in the head, like they did to Theo. It's how Roscoe died. And Phoebe." Her eyes slid to the floor.

"And Christopher," added Eli.

"Yes," she said. "And Christopher."

She settled back in the chair and stared out the window.

Eli took it as the perfect moment to say nothing.

Harry cleared her throat. "Christopher found me when I was nineteen. He came into town in Eleanor, scared several horses and two mules, and began to draw water from one of the town's public wells."

"Two mules?"

"My family used the mules for everything. I'd ridden into town on one for groceries, led the other one to use as a beast of burden."

"I can't picture you riding a mule."

"In a dress," she added. "I had to ride sidesaddle. Or I would've if we'd had more than a blanket."

Eli smiled.

"Now please stop interrupting while I unburden myself, Mr. Teague. This is difficult enough."

"Sorry."

"He was amazing," she said. "In my whole life, I'd maybe met a dozen people who weren't from our town, and they all looked the same. Closer to poor than to rich. At least a week of dirt on them. Tired. Everyone was lean and wiry back then. Even the women.

"And there he was. So different. And handsome. Six foot tall, half that across the shoulders. And he just looked so . . . safe. So relaxed and confident, like nothing could hurt him. He stood there and pumped water like he'd done it as a career, even though he was plainly rich." She glanced at Eli. "I'd heard of automobiles, of course, but no one I knew had ever seen one before. They were a thing for wealthy men. And here was one right in front of me. I stood there, staring at him, for a good five minutes before he noticed me." The corners of her mouth quivered. "I'd never seen a man over the age of twenty without a mustache.

"He said hello and asked if I needed to use the well. To this day I can't remember what I said. He'd never tell me. I think he liked teasing me with it. But I ended up standing next to him and filling an old canteen that had been hanging dry on my mule's pack for a year or so, just for an excuse to talk to him.

"He had on a brilliant red undershirt. I'd never seen such vibrant colors, or such fine-woven cloth. Almost like silk. And there was a face painted on it in dabs of black ink. I remember at the time I thought it was an image of the Lord Jesus. He was one of the few people I'd seen paintings of at the time." She glanced at Eli. "I learned later it was Ernesto 'Che' Guevara. He was a freedom fighter in the late—"

"I know who he is," said Eli. "Mrs. Pritchard."

She smirked. "We talked for an hour. About Eleanor. About the world outside. He'd already traveled most of the country at that point. And most of history, as well, although he was very clever about not letting on."

"And then you ran off with him?"

"No," snapped Harry, although her eyes brightened. "What kind of woman do you take me for?"

"The kind who'd show up at someone's door in her underwear at one in the morning."

She raised a threatening fist. "Christopher was a gentleman, unlike some people. He left—alone—but promised to return. And he did, just a week later. I remember thinking his beard had grown very fast."

Eli nodded.

"He kept coming back. Sometimes to refill the main tank. Sometimes the reserve. By the seventh or eighth visit it was plain he wasn't coming for the water. And our town well was awful. In retrospect, he must have been cleaning Eleanor's filters and carburetor out every night.

"The twelfth time he came and stayed for four days. He'd told me a little about the search, but I still didn't understand what a risk he was taking, staying in one place for so long. He bought some good clothes, went to see my pa, and asked permission to court me."

Eli pursed his lips. "This was . . . 1902?"

"By that point, 1904."

"They were still doing that then? Asking permission to court someone?"

"No, as a matter of fact, they were not. It wasn't unheard-of, but it was a bit old-fashioned. Pa had heard about the mysterious stranger seen with his daughter. This made him seem more eccentric than respectable. He asked Christopher to leave and forbade me from ever speaking to him again."

"Ahhh."

"It was two months before I saw him again. At the well, filling Eleanor's tanks. Looking for me. It was a week before Christmas." She glanced at Eli, and the edges of her mouth twitched again. "That's when I ran off with him." She sighed, a slow, happy sound that warmed the small guest room.

"We searched together for six months before he formally proposed. Three weeks later we were married in the city of Las Vegas. Entertainment capital of the world. Elvis Presley himself performed the wedding."

"When was this?"

"2006."

"Okay," said Eli, "just to be clear, because of all this time-travel stuff—"

"History travel."

"Right. When you say Elvis Presley performed the ceremony, do you mean *the* Elvis, or . . ."

"I didn't think to ask."

"Ahhh."

"We were together for three glorious years. Three years, three months, three weeks, five days. Three, three, three, five."

"And then . . . ?"

The light in her eyes dimmed. "And then we weren't."

A few possible responses went back and forth in his mind, and Eli picked the one he hoped would be best received. He reached out and set his hand on hers. Harry tensed, relaxed, then turned her hand over so their palms slid together.

Her hand was very warm. She squeezed his once—a good, solid grip—and then released it. "Thank you, Eli."

He took his hand back.

She sat up, squared her shoulders, and raised her eyes to his. "Christopher Pritchard. Phoebe Fitzgerald. Abraham Porter. Alice Ramsey. Roscoe Montgomery."

He nodded. "Christopher Prit—"

"No," she said. "My fault. You need to start with me. Harriet Pritchard, then Christopher Pritchard, Phoebe, and so on."

He nodded. "The next link in the Chain."

"Precisely."

"And you want me to learn this so . . . ?"

She snorted. "For a clever man, you can be quite daft at times."

"I . . . Thank you?"

"I'm teaching you because you're my partner, Eli. Because someday you may have to teach it to someone else. You're the next link."

"Oh. Thank you."

"You've earned it. So . . ." She shifted in her chair. "Harriet Pritchard. Christopher Pritchard. Phoebe Fitzgerald. Abraham Porter. Alice Ramsey. Roscoe Montgomery."

"Harry Pritchard," echoed Eli. "Christopher Pritchard. Phoebe Fitzgerald. Abraham . . . Porter?"

She nodded.

"Abraham Porter. Alice . . . Ramses?"

"Alice Ramsey," she said. "Then Roscoe Montgomery. Say it again."

"Harry Pritchard. Christopher Pritchard. Phoebe—"

"You should use my proper name."

"But I know you as Harry."

"This is for posterity. I'd prefer it if people remember me as a woman."

"But not a lady." He gestured at her knee. The robe had fallen open again to reveal red flannel.

"Don't be an ass," Harry said, but the edges of her lips twitched as she did. "Say the Chain again. Properly this time."

"Harriet Pritchard," he recited. "Christopher Pritchard. Phoebe Fitzgerald. Abraham Porter . . ."

23

Eli stepped from his guest room. Harry had left him an hour ago, after they'd recited the Chain back and forth a hundred or so times. Then he'd stretched back out on his bed and . . .

Stared at the ceiling.

He flexed his toes on the carpet of the narrow hall. Bare feet still seemed luxurious. Even having an untucked, half-unbuttoned shirt felt refreshing.

He hooked his thumbs into his pockets and wandered back to the dining room. The lights had been dimmed. He hadn't seen John Henry since dinner. The train seemed huge and sprawling for one person, and Eli wondered what kind of hours their host kept when he had the train to himself.

"Can't sleep?"

Eli jumped and looked over his shoulder.

The man himself sat in one of the chairs in the corner. He'd removed his coat and loosened his tie again. A book sat in his lap where he'd lowered it.

"You scared the hell out of me," said Eli.

John bowed his head. "Apologies, my friend." He kept his voice pitched low and quiet. "Is there something wrong with your room?"

Eli shook his head. "No, it's wonderful. This whole train's amazing. And not just because I've been sleeping on dirt and blankets for a couple of days."

"I'm pleased to hear it."

"What about you? Keeping an eye on us?"

John shook his head. "Harry's one of the few people I completely trust with the *Steel Bucephalus*. And she trusts you."

"How do you know?"

"Because you're traveling with her. That woman doesn't let anyone into Eleanor for a second longer than they have to be there."

Eli shrugged.

"So," John said, gesturing at the chair across from him, "what brings you out and about at such a late hour, Eli Teague?"

He sat down. "Every time I start to nod off," he said, "I remember where I am. And when I am. Or when I could be, I guess?"

"We're in the summer of 2033," said John. "This particular branch of track has been abandoned for a while at this point. It's a nice seven-year stretch of history where I can park the *Bucephalus* at night."

Eli bit his lip. "Can I ask you a question?"

"Of course. You're a guest."

Eli patted out a quick drum solo on the arm of the chair.

"I'm not a genie, Eli, and I don't have much of a temper. You don't have to worry about how you phrase it."

"You and Harry, you've both traveled back and forth a lot."

"Tens of thousands of miles, each of us."

"The length of American history?"

John nodded. "Slightly more for her. As I've said, I'm limited by the tracks."

"Why only three hundred years?"

John raised his bushy eyebrows. His pleasant smile dimmed just enough to notice.

"I get that you want simpler machines," said Eli. "Things you can fix yourself with local resources. That makes sense. But nobody has a . . . an antimatter battery or a Mr. Fusion or something. And both of you talk about history as, well, a set block of years. That you can only go so far forward. And everybody she's mentioned to me, all the searchers . . . it seems like they're almost all from the past or the present. Well, my past."

John nodded. "You're very observant, my friend. It took me months of traveling to discover something you noticed in just a few days."

"So what is it? Is there a war? Does the United States . . . disband or something? Fall apart?"

"Things get . . . tricky once you pass 2050."

"Tricky how?"

John closed his book and set it on a side table. "People get lost up there, in the far future," he said. "Most of them never come back. Some do, maybe a quarter of them, but they've never seen the same thing. Everyone who returns tells a different story."

"Like what?"

"Some say it's a paradise. The dream's been restored, the country progresses and prospers in harmony. Others say things have collapsed into anarchy. Warring city-states, like the Dark Ages of Europe." He sighed. "And yes, a few say it's just a wasteland from the atomic wars. Some see survivors. Some don't. One old-timer even said he saw—"

John stopped and smiled.

"What? What did he see?"

"He claimed he went way up there, to 2063, and everything was gone. Everything. No cities, no water, very little life. Just miles and miles of sand . . . and huge monsters up in the sky, eating anything that was left."

Eli raised an eyebrow.

"He barely got away, as he tells it."

"As he tells it," Eli echoed.

John shrugged. "He'd only tell the story if you got a few drinks into him."

"So what's that mean? That we can't travel far ahead?"

"Everyone has ideas, of course. Personally, I think it means we're running out of time."

"Is that a clever play on words or . . . ?"

"I think," said John, "when the dream was stolen, the future began to unravel. Maybe there was a set future for the United States at one point, a grand destiny, but it began to fray and come apart, to spread itself in different directions. And I think it's going to continue to unravel, all the way back to the beginning."

"You mean, back to when the dream was made."

John nodded. "Our whole country undone." He gestured out the window, at the blackness. "What will the world be like," he wondered, "if there never was a United States of America? The world wars? The space race? All the many inventions and innovations and entertainments born here?"

A few heartbeats passed. Eli became aware of a faint, distant wheezing with a coarse, rasping edge to it. He imagined old pistons and gnashing gears, and then remembered being woken up when he and Harry slept under the stars.

John glanced over his shoulder at Harry's room. "Forgive me," he said, his attention returning to Eli. "I don't mean to make it sound like the end is nigh. I just think there's much more at stake here than individual goals."

Eli nodded. "Harry's kind of said the same thing."

"More of us should be working together. Myself included." He sighed. "You'll have to forgive me. I tend to get a bit maudlin sometimes when I sit up at night like this."

"Doesn't everyone?"

"Depends on what we're drinking, I suppose."

"Do you stop every night?"

"The *Bucephalus*?" John shook his head. "Depends on where I'm going. When I need to be there. I never slept much when I was a younger man. It's a trait I'm glad has followed me into middle age. Lets me cover more ground."

"So you just travel all the time? Back and forth across America."

"Back and forth," he agreed. "Forward and backward. If there are tracks somewhere and somewhen in the United States, odds are I've ridden them."

"Must be a lot of work. Keeping all this up and running. And clean."

John chuckled. "I have some people on retainer. I just don't like the idea of servants, forced to live here in their master's home." He swung his hand to take in the room.

"Why do you need all this, then?"

"The guest rooms?"

"No," said Eli. "Well, yes. Even going with the idea that you've chosen a train as your . . . your mode of transport, why do you need all this space?"

John set his fingertips together.

"I mean, it seems like Harry and everyone she talks about gets by with cars. You could've done a mobile home or something, but you went with a mobile apartment building. A mobile mansion."

"I suppose I did, didn't I?"

"So why do it if you're just going to be alone?"

John stared over his fingertips at Eli. "Let me show you something." He stood up and gestured for Eli to follow him. They walked back through the train car to the rear door, outside onto the car's small deck, and across the connector into John's private car. Simple carpet lined the floor. Three chairs formed a loose triangle. Another stove, this one not quite as polished and elegant. Two wardrobes stood face-to-face halfway down the modified Pullman car. They moved past them, revealing a simple bed, a desk, and another bookshelf. Eli had expected something more lush and not quite so . . . functional. It reminded him of a few loft apartments he'd seen.

John walked straight through to the door in the back, pulled a key ring from his coat, and unlocked it. They stepped outside, and the cold platform chilled Eli's feet. He stepped across to the next car, one of the ones with the shades drawn. He thumbed through the brass keys and unlocked that door as well.

"This," said John, stepping aside, "is my search."

Summer camp art projects popped into Eli's mind, with bright yarn twisted around Popsicle sticks to form colorful shapes. Then the patterns separated and refined in his eyes, and the room looked more like one of the museum exhibits he'd always tried to find interesting in college.

The Pullman car was filled with standing panels, not unlike the cubicle dividers Eli knew so well from his local Stahlbank branch. These, at least, matched the aesthetic of the train, with deep-red fabric panels framed in dark hardwood. They stretched the length of the car, breaking it up into three long aisles.

Each panel had a poster-sized picture on it. Heavy threads of yellow, orange, and red crisscrossed each image. The threads led to hundreds of bright plastic pushpins, each one marking a specific point on . . .

Eli looked again. Not pictures. Maps.

A few of the colorful threads ran between maps. Some stretched over panels and across aisles. Manila tags hung on those.

Eli stepped in close to study one in the center aisle. A typed index card at the top of the panel declared it to be January 4–October 23,

1838. The United States reached the Pacific coast up by Washington, but lacked a big square swath that included most of the southwest, including a whole stretch of coastline. There were nine pushpins in the map, five along the northeast coast, one on the other side of Florida toward the Gulf of Mexico, and three scattered out across the Midwest. It was hard to be sure where without state lines.

He followed a line across two panels to another map, June 12, 1840–April 1, 1841. A spiderweb of threads sprawled across this one too. Thirteen pins, all in different places. The strings were different colors and different lengths. He spun to look behind him, at August 7, 1892–December 31, 1892.

"Is this . . ." Eli turned to John. "Is this all the places you've been?"

The other man shook his head. "To be honest, I've traveled to less than half of them."

Eli stepped into the next aisle and looked at the map against the train's inner wall. February 15, 1940–November 8, 1940. "It's the other searchers," he said. "You're keeping tabs on them."

"No, although many of them are up there in one way or another."

"Then I have no idea," said Eli. "I'm still not even sure what questions to ask half the time."

"Astronomy is another fascination of mine," said John. "Celestial mechanics. As I said, I've always slept very little, so as a boy I'd watch the stars. I've sat in on several lectures from Neil deGrasse Tyson and Carl Sagan."

"Carl Sagan is the *Cosmos* guy, right?"

John nodded. "In astronomy there's a method of searching that's best called mathematical prediction. It's a way of looking for things which can't be seen by tracing the effect they have on other things. This means looking for minor alterations in orbits, radiation levels, and light refraction. For example, the existence and location of Neptune was predicted by studying the orbit of Uranus.

"For me"—he gestured at the panels—"it means watching for examples of the dream influencing people's lives."

Eli looked at the aisles of maps, the miles of string. "So all this is . . . it's the same sort of thing Harry's following?"

"In a way." He stretched out a finger and set it on a pushpin. "These are all people who've been touched by the dream."

"There's thousands of them."

"Tens of thousands," agreed John. "Almost four hundred maps of the United States, stretching across almost three hundred years. The diagramming continues in the next car. And I'm always refining my data."

"How?"

"Sometimes it's easy. The son of a wealthy, successful businessman becomes a wealthy, successful businessman? That isn't the dream's influence, just plain old nepotism. Other folks just claw their way up through good, honest work. There's nothing special or unique there." He reached out and touched the Pullman's doorframe, then sighed. "And a number of them are false positives. They're people who were affected by the dream before it went missing. They're part of its original path through history. The only ones I can use are from after it vanished."

"How do you tell them apart?"

"With a great deal of difficulty."

"This is why you have a train," said Eli. "You need the space."

"Precisely."

"What are you going to do with it?"

"The *Bucephalus*? I can't ever imagine leaving her, even when the search is over. I'll probably stay with her until—"

"The dream," said Eli. "What will you do with the dream if you find it?"

"Ahhh." John reached out, set a finger against an orange thread, and traced it back across the country, across history. "If I were to find the dream," he said, "if the stories are true that the finder could have an effect on the country . . . I'd like children to grow up in an America where the color of a person's skin doesn't matter. Where we all have the same rights and the same protections under the law. Where people can simply be free."

Eli managed a weak chuckle. "You know that sort of happens anyway, right? Back in the '60s. Or forward, for you, I guess. I mean, there are still a ton of problems and issues because some people just won't let go of things, but there was the Civil Rights Movement with Martin Luther King and—"

John held up his hand and returned the smile. "I'm well aware of

Reverend King's work, my friend, and what he accomplished. And what still needs to be done. There's just one small point that fascinates me."

"What's that?"

John lifted his finger off the thread, then tapped the map with it twice. "Reverend King, as people so often quote, had a dream. Something inspired him."

Eli felt his eyelids stretch wide. "You think he . . . is he a searcher?"

"No, no." John shook his head. "Or if he is, I've never seen him or heard of it. No, Eli, my point is, what if King is inspired because I'm the one who finds the dream? Suppose the dream needs to be taken somewhere, and in moving it through history, my will effects change in the decades before he's born."

"So are you saying . . . you have to be the one to find it?"

"Not at all. I have no idea. But it's a possibility, isn't it?"

"I . . ." Eli juggled cause and effect in his head for a moment. "Maybe?"

"I believe in fiction it's referred to as a predestination paradox," John said. "Our effect on the past has always been part of the past. Whatever happens is what always happened. Personally, I like to think of it as the transparent aluminum defense."

The reference sounded familiar, but Eli couldn't place it. "So that's what you're going to do with it?"

John nodded. "That's all any of us tries to do, isn't it? Make a better future?"

24

Gregson Russk sat in his room above the saloon in 1866 and studied the piece of paper. As rooms went, he'd been in far worse and couldn't remember many better. He still drank in the two-bit saloon across town, but sleeping on a feather mattress felt damned good after two years of his lumpy camp bed.

Or it had. Now he couldn't wait to get out of the room. Out of the damned town.

He studied the slip of paper. Letters and words had never been his strength. He wasn't one of those men who could guzzle down whole pages the way some men guzzled booze. But he could force his way through, digging through the alphabet like he dug into the side of a hill. He knew his own name, and important words like "gold" and "California" and "Buchanan."

The woman who'd given him the scrap of paper was either a fool or a saint. Maybe his guardian angel. He would've signed the whole claim over to her for this information. At one point, he'd done far more drastic things for far smaller leads.

The morning coach would take him to Kansas City, and from there to Memphis. He thought of sending a letter ahead, or even a telegraph, but in the end decided it would be better to just see Edmunds one last time in person before shooting him.

He set the scrap of paper carefully between the pages of *Aesop's Fables*, right where "The Farmer and his Sons" ended. He closed the book, then wrapped it in the sheet of heavy vellum that had protected it out to California and back. The volume went onto the wooden slats under the mattress, right next to the small bundle of papers that was his claim on the gold mine. He tugged the blankets this way and that until the bed looked undisturbed.

His treasures hidden away, he pulled on his coat, dusted off his hat, and snuffed out the lamp with a puff of air that whistled across his jagged tooth. Supper awaited. And tomorrow, on his way to find Louisa.

He pulled open the door to his room.

Two men stood in the dim hall. Each wore a small-brimmed hat, like some kind of mashed-up derby. They had short-cut coats and odd, wide neckties. The taller man had his hand raised to knock. His eyes were closed, as if he'd been listening at the door.

"Hello," said both men in unison.

Russk fumbled for words, but they'd never been his strength.

The tall man pulled a small book from his pocket and swung it open like a bored preacher opening his Bible for the ten thousandth time. "Are you," the man asked, "Gregson Edgar Russk?"

"I am."

Both men gave a single nod. The tall, square-jawed man held up a leather billfold. He flipped it open to reveal a multipointed silver star—maybe a sheriff's badge, or a US Marshal's—and then flipped it shut just as quick. "We'd like to ask you a few questions about a pair of fugitives we believe may have been in the area."

"A . . . what?"

"Criminals," said the other man. He packed a lot into the word. The coarse edge reminded Russk of someone lowborn trying to put on airs. He'd seen a few men strike gold and act this way. He'd done it himself. The thought gave him a brief smile.

"Is something funny?" asked the shorter man. He had a trim waistcoat on beneath his jacket.

"No. Pardon. You're looking for . . . what, some kind of robbers?"

"In a manner of speaking," said the tall man. He stepped into the room, forcing Russk back. "We believe they're trying to acquire stolen property."

The smaller man followed him in and closed the door behind them.

Twice during his years in California, men had wandered into Russk's small camp and made him itch. The first had been a lone Mexican. The second time, eight months later, were two men who sounded like limeys. They'd all eyed his equipment, asked if he'd been lucky, and eventually gone for their guns when they thought his attention was elsewhere. He'd given them all Christian burials, even if they didn't deserve it.

These two men gave him the same itch.

"The two fugitives are a man and a woman," the tall man told him. "They'd most likely be wearing unusual clothes, and may have been riding a horseless carriage."

Russk thought of his guardian angel and her skinny companion. Thieves or not, they'd done right by him. "Lots of men and women in Independence," he said. "Can't right remember any that stood out like that."

"He's lying," said the smaller man. "He's seen them. Recently."

The tall man stepped forward.

Russk brushed his coat back, exposing his holster, and screamed in pain as the bones in his hand shattered.

The smaller man stood next to him, having crossed the room in a blink. He squeezed again. Russk felt two more snaps that made his whole body shudder.

"Stop that," said the tall man. "It's unnecessary."

"He was reaching for his weapon."

"Then disarm him. We're here to talk."

"He'll talk now," the smaller man said. He made an odd noise, something between a cough and a laugh, as if his mouth were covered with a heavy bandanna.

The night beyond the room's window brightened. There'd been some clouds, and now the moonlight hit every snow-covered roof in town. Russk's room brightened enough for him to get a better look at his two attackers.

The light from outside gleamed across their faces. Each man wore a mask of thinnest glass, almost a glaze. Lips, wide eyebrows, and flushed cheeks had been painted onto the fragile forms. The smaller man's mask had a swooping mustache and a narrow beard as well.

Beneath the glass, through the tiny holes in the glass face, Russk could see the square-jawed man's eyes still sat mostly closed. Entirely closed, in fact. Both men could've been asleep beneath their masks. Then he focused his eyes a little better in the dim light. He turned his attention to the smaller man. The smooth skin beneath the glass mask flexed and wrinkled, but . . .

Gregson Edgar Russk, who had killed five men, two Chinamen, and a pair of mountain lions without more than a flinch, sucked in air to scream.

The smaller man punched him in the gut. Russk's breath blasted out and something in his stomach flared with hot agony. His knees gave out and he tried to fall, but the man still held his hand. His wrist twisted as he slipped to the floor, something popped, and the pain almost distracted him from his gut.

He glanced over his shoulder at the bed. He needed to survive. Louisa needed him to survive, even if she didn't know it.

"He's talked to them," said the smaller man, staring over Russk's shoulder at the bed. "She gave him something. It's hidden under the bed."

"I know. It isn't important."

"It might tell us where he's going."

"He," said the tall man, "isn't important."

Russk threw his left arm across his body, grabbing at his holster. He fumbled his side iron out. His finger hadn't even touched the trigger guard before the smaller man lifted the weapon away and tossed it onto the bed.

The broken hand shifted into new painful shapes as it settled against Russk's body. He stared at the faceless men. "What'n hell are you?" he spat through gritted teeth.

"You may refer to me as Fifteen," said the tall man. The empty eyes of his mask stayed aimed at Russk's face. "It's important we find the man and woman you spoke with before they escape justice. Any help you can give us would be greatly appreciated."

"Don't know where they went," he said. "They left the saloon a good half hour before I did. I swear on my mama's grave."

"Did you see anything unusual outside before or after you left? An unusual carriage, perhaps? Some kind of odd vehicle?"

Russk shook his head.

"What did you talk with them about?"

Another shake of the prospector's head. "Nothin'. They didn't want nothin'."

"We didn't ask what they wanted," said the smaller man. "We asked what you talked about."

Russk thought back over the odd conversation he'd had with his guardian angel, trying to think of anything the two men would want to know. "Nothin', I swear. I offered to tell 'em where my claim was and they weren't interested. They just . . ."

"Yes?"

"It . . . it weren't anything special. They just wanted to know why I went out to California."

"And why did you?" asked Fifteen.

"I just . . . I met a fella back in N'Orleans. He told me about his trip out west and I thought, 'I could do that.'"

"His name?"

"Hawkins. Frank Hawkins."

"When was this?"

"'Bout three years ago."

Fifteen settled back on his heels. "And you told this to the fugitives? All of it?"

Russk nodded.

"New Orleans, 1850," said the smaller man. "We can track them. Railroad log books. Unexpected trains on the track."

"It's an odd period for a train," said Fifteen. "Records will be spotty at best. John Henry will either be easy to find or next to impossible."

"Cross-reference with Hawkins?"

"Agreed."

Russk looked back and forth between them, understanding none of it. His hand swelled. The ring finger and pinkie stuck out a little too straight, as if they'd cramped. They tingled, but the sensation didn't seem connected to the rest of the hand.

Fifteen reached up and adjusted the knot of his necktie. "We may return with further questions, Mr. Russk," he said. "It would be best if you remained here. Do not attempt to leave town."

The prospector coughed. "My sister," he said before the torn thing in his gut flinched, and he coughed again. Drops of blood landed on the back of his damaged hand.

The faceless man turned the sockets of his mask toward the bed, then back at Russk. "The information came to you through illegal means," he said, "but poses no security risk to the country or its history. I'm willing to overlook it this once, in view of your current and continued cooperation."

The shorter man stepped forward. "What?"

"We're done here."

The smaller man's left hand opened and shut, clenching into a quick fist three times. "We're not done. He's a collaborator."

A shiver ran across Russk's shoulder blades and slipped down his backbone. He'd heard those words before, with just that fire beneath them. Justice dealt out by locals who didn't want to wait for the law, or didn't like the way it had ruled. The smaller man had a bad case of badge fever, all excited by his own authority.

"We're done here," repeated Fifteen. He directed it at his partner this time. "Thank you for your cooperation, Mr. Russk." The faceless man reached up, touched the brim of his hat, and walked out into the hall.

The smaller man pointed his blank face at Russk for a few moments. His hand twitched open and closed. Open and closed. Open and closed.

Then he followed his partner into the hall, pulling the door shut behind him.

25

The *Steel Bucephalus* came to a halt in the morning sunshine. Its wheels shuddered on the rails with the fading squeal of the brakes. A last puff of steam erupted into the air as the train settled on the tracks.

Harry leaped down from the platform. Weeds had forced their way up through the gravel that lined the track, but not enough to muffle the crunch of her boots on stone. "You sure it won't be a problem?" she called back at the engine as Eli landed next to her.

John appeared on the platform and crouched low. "None at all," he said. "Getting her unloaded is always easier than getting her stowed away."

"Are you sure?"

He nodded and pointed at some large buildings half a mile away. "I'll leave her over in the Uptown warehouse district, just west of the docks. Lots of searchers use it for parking." He handed her a square of paper with an address scribbled on it.

Harry took the paper and glanced over at the buildings. "Anyone there right now?"

"No one I know of."

Eli walked to the edge of the gravel, lifted one foot, and rotated his ankles as he looked around. His shoes felt restrictive after hours without them. He'd rinsed out his clothes, but they still had the matted feel and faint odor that too many days of wear brought. John had, thankfully, offered him a clean shirt with a stiff collar.

The *Bucephalus* had halted on a long stretch of track that looked abandoned. Lots of weeds. Some rust. Eli looked around at the half dozen or so shacks and small houses on this side of the train, but nobody seemed interested in the train steaming a few hundred yards from their homes. Maybe everyone had left for work for the day. Or maybe trains were already so commonplace that people ignored them.

John held one of the platform's gleaming handles and swung himself down to the ground. "We've politely not discussed what you're doing here."

"Yes," said Harry, "it's been wonderful."

"There are only three notable people you could be looking for in New Orleans, 1850," said John. "If you're coming from an 1853 town on the California trail, it isn't Etienne Barbier or Sarah Welles."

"Maybe we found someone new."

"Then you wouldn't've called in a favor. You would've paid for your passage with information like most searchers." He studied her face. "You have a solid lead, don't you? One you're not willing to share."

Harry said nothing. She dusted off her tricorne and pushed it up onto her head.

John shook his head. "Eli?" he called out.

"Yeah?"

"It was good talking with you last night."

"You too. Thanks for the ride."

"It's been a pleasure traveling with you, John," said Harry, "as always."

He took her hand and kissed the knuckles. "As always, the pleasure is mine." He turned, reached for the rail, and pulled himself back up into the cab. "I'm fond of both of you now. Take care of each other out there on the road."

ELI WATCHED THE dockside hotel and tugged at his collar. He'd expected the hat to bother him more—he'd never been a hat person, even in the dead of New England winters—but the collar could've been a shackle on his neck. A tight, thin shackle of linen that had been starched into steel.

In the belly of the hotel sat a tavern. Not so high up the sea captains, their officers, and the occasional dock foreman didn't feel welcome to spend their money there. Not so low in the gut that the hotel couldn't attract a higher level of guest just before or after their voyage. Eli knew its type. Bars and restaurants in the resort towns of southern Maine often made the choice between catering to locals or to tourists. A few careful ones managed both.

He'd been prepared to go inside and strike up a casual conversation with their target when Harry came out, her rumpled frock coat flapping behind her, gesturing him away from the door.

"Right behind me," she whispered as she walked past him.

A few moments later, a tall man appeared in the hotel entrance. Even if Harry hadn't warned Eli, the man would've been easy to pick out. He wore a thick, shaggy cloak that looked like it belonged in a sword-and-sorcery movie.

Frank Hawkins had a face for movies. A black-and-white, *Creature Double Feature* face, either ready to bring someone back from the dead, or maybe freshly back itself. It was long and thin, but not malnourished. The man's jawline and thick eyebrows reminded Eli of Abraham Lincoln—the younger, beardless Lincoln who sometimes appeared in older photographs. If someone had introduced the man as Lincoln's older, more intense brother, it wouldn't have been hard to believe.

Hawkins exchanged a few familiar-sounding words with a sleepy-looking doorman and headed down the street in the opposite direction.

Eli glanced over his shoulder at Harry. She waved him into action before darting down a side street. Eli looked back and scampered after Hawkins.

Keeping track of the man turned out to be easy. He took long strides, but the crowd parted around him. Most people along the waterfront kept a cautious distance from the buffalo-cloaked figure. He also wore a bowler—a deep, earthy brown one with a wider brim than Eli's. Years of weather had faded and aged it beyond its time.

Eli kept a casual pace and closed the distance between them in just three blocks.

He eased back, keeping a nonthreatening gap between them, and raised his voice. "Excuse me? Sir?"

Hawkins paused on his relentless march, then took three more steps.

"Sir?" Eli took another step forward, cutting the distance between them to a few yards at most.

Hawkins turned. Eli imagined it was a lot like when buffalo turned to stare down the thing they were about to trample. The man took in a breath and it steamed out through his nose.

Eli stepped back and cleared his throat. "Sorry to bother you," he said.

"Hrrrrr."

They stared at each other. It struck Eli that he didn't know what to say. He'd rehearsed some openings for the bar, but not for a "random encounter" on the street.

"I was heading this way myself," he spat out, "to meet up with my partner."

Hawkins stared at him. "Best get moving, then. Don't want to miss him."

"Her," said Eli, and then he knew why the man's words had seemed familiar. "I . . . I'm sorry. I heard your voice back at the hotel. Are you from Maine, by chance?"

Hawkins blinked. "Ayuh," he said. "You know Maine?"

"I'm from there myself."

"Y'don't have an accent."

"Yeah," said Eli. "I'm from the south."

"Whereabouts?"

"Sanders."

Hawkins stared at him again. "Went through there once," he said, "just before my first trip out west." He looked at Eli again, then gestured to the spot next to him. He pulled out a silver flask. "Have a drink for the home state?"

Eli felt a little knot loosen between his shoulder blades. "Thanks."

"Whiskey?"

"Great." He stuck out his hand. "Eli Teague."

"Frank Hawkins." He squeezed the hand and yanked it once up and down.

"Pleased to meet you, Mr. Hawkins."

Hawkins grunted as they continued along the wharf. He tilted the flask back, let it drop, and his tongue darted out to clean his lips. He held out the container.

Eli huffed out some air, as if blowing out a candle, and downed his own mouthful. It was harsh stuff, higher proof than anything he'd ever done shots of while out with his friends. He puffed out the fumes before they could settle in his throat.

"Helps kill the burn," he explained when he noticed Frank's look.

"The burn's why you drink it."

"It's an old college trick," said Eli. "Lets you fit in a lot more drinking on the weekend."

"Weekend?"

"Never mind," said Eli, handing the flask back. "Not important."

Frank grunted again. A wet black rat hauled itself up over the edge of the wharf and scurried across the cobblestones toward them. The big man slammed his foot down and the rodent fled off toward the warehouses.

Up close, Eli could see the weathering that sun and cold had performed on the man's skin, much as it had on his hat. Hawkins wasn't much older than Eli. Maybe even three or four years younger.

What kind of life had this guy led?

Eli gestured toward the docks. "Coming or going?"

"Eh?"

"Did you just arrive or are you getting ready to go?"

"Go. We leave for California tomorrow by way of Panama."

"Right," said Eli. "Through the canal."

"Canal?"

"The Panama . . . never mind." He coughed into his hand. "Look, can I ask you a question?"

Hawkins frowned at him. "You don't talk like you're from Maine."

Eli shrugged. "Southern Maine."

"Hrrrrr."

"So. California. Hoping to find gold?"

"Found it already," said Hawkins. "Going back to find some more."

"What sent you out there?"

"Eh?"

"To California."

The lean man stared at him. "Gold," he said again, as if speaking to an idiot.

"Right," Eli said with a cough. "Gold's great. But I was wondering . . . what actually made you do it? Leave Maine and travel three thousand miles out to California. I mean . . ."

He stopped walking. He thought of Dover apartments and nights out with his friends. "Why risk it? Why leave? Wouldn't it be better to just be poor with your friends and family than to move and end up . . . who knows where? Why risk things by leaving?"

The leather around Hawkins's eyes softened. "You left, didn't you? You're here."

"Yeah, but not on purpose. I got . . . I thought I was helping someone and I just made a mistake. And now I can't go home."

"Why not?"

"It's . . . complicated."

"Hrrrrr."

"I just . . . how did you do it? Why did you do it? All I can think about is getting home, and you're heading out for a second time."

Something scratched and swelled in the other man's throat. A laugh. A short, grim, Clint Eastwood–worthy laugh. "Life's not something you tuck away and wait to use. Life runs out. Every day, every minute, whether you use it or not."

"But . . . what if something happened?"

Hawkins looked up at a steamer as they passed it. The crew's heads bobbed back and forth up on deck. He passed Eli the flask again. "I was seventeen the first time I saw a man die," he said. "Been on the trail for a month and Munso got sick. Influenza. Tried to keep him warm. but the fever took him. Lucky it didn't take me. Two years later, saw my second death. Chinagirl stabbed a man twice in the throat with her hair needles. He'd hired out her little sister, roughed her up. Big sister didn't take kindly to it."

Eli blew more whiskey fumes from his throat. "You're not making it sound much better."

He coughed out his short laugh again. "Can't tell you what to do with your life. It's yours to use or waste. Just know we're all going to die someday. I'd rather die out there, takin' a risk or two and doing something other than sittin' at home doing nothing."

Eli glanced down the wharf. A few blocks ahead, Harry leaned against a gaslight post. She made a point of not looking at them, but Hawkins followed Eli's gaze.

"She in your stable?" he asked. His voice regained its coarse edge without accusing Eli of anything. "That what this is?"

"What? No."

"Your wife?"

"Business partner, actually."

"Said she wasn't in your stable."

"It's a different business," said Eli, hearing an edge in his own voice.

Hawkins grunted. "She's dressed like a man."

"Yes, she is."

"Hrrrrr."

They approached Harry. She beamed sweetly, but made no move to join them. Hawkins kept an eye on her, glancing back as they walked past.

Eli tried to focus again on his mission. "Nothing inspired you? There wasn't a moment you realized this was it, your chance to . . ."

"What kind of nonsense is that?"

"Not nonsense," Eli tried to assure him. "I'm looking for something myself. My friend and I." He tipped his head back over his shoulder, in Harry's direction.

Frank stopped walking and squared his shoulders. "Look, friend, I don't know and don't care what you're peddling."

"I'm not peddling anything."

"You're a bad liar. Don't try to make a living at it."

"I just . . . I need to know if something drove you to California. It's important."

"You want to know what sent me west?"

"Yeah. I really do."

"I went because I was too young and dumb to know any better," Hawkins said. "I had nothing to lose, and I thought if I died out there on some great adventure, at least people'd think I did something with my life. It was dumb luck I survived and made the trip worth my while, and then I had the experience to do it again without suffering half as much."

"You just . . . you just did it all through hard work."

Hawkins grunted and flexed a callused hand. "No 'just' about it," he said. "I spent three years either in the saddle or with a pickax in my hand. Earned every damned cent I have." He poked a hard finger into Eli's chest. "And I resent anyone who implies otherwise."

He turned and marched away.

Eli's shoulders dropped. He sorted through his emotions and memories, trying to figure out if his response was more dejection or relief. He felt comfortable saying it was both.

Harry caught up to him. "Well?" she asked to Hawkins's retreating back.

Eli shook his head. "Nothing."

She frowned. "Are you sure?"

"Yeah, pretty sure. The guy doesn't think he was inspired, he thinks he was stupid and lucky."

Harry looked after the man, now just a broad-shouldered mass of buffalo hide striding along the wharfs. "Maybe you misunderstood."

"I don't think so," said Eli.

A quartet of dockworkers spilled out of an alley and Hawkins vanished behind them. Harry glared at the group. "I was sure," she said. "I was so sure he was it."

"Is it a normal thing? Do people always know when they've been inspired by the dream?"

She shook her head. "Very few realize the dream's helping their choices, but they almost always pin it on something. A person, a random coincidence, a moment when they realize they could make their dreams become reality."

Eli let his gaze wander across the wharf, the ships, the scattered men unloading crates and barrels. "Maybe he's still the guy we're looking for."

"How so?"

A pair of rats dashed across the street in front of them. The two rodents leaped onto a coil of rope and scrambled up toward the attached freighter. One slipped and hung from the hemp line for a moment. It swung back and forth, and Eli almost went to go help it before it clawed its way back onto the rope and scurried up after its partner.

"Well," he continued, "you're saying most people find something to credit with their inspiration."

"Not all, but most, yes."

He stuck his hands in his pockets and tried to line up his thoughts. "Inspiration's a weird thing. Like you were saying, it can be almost anything."

She gestured for him to go on.

"Kind of odd that he's so convinced nothing inspired him, isn't it? One hundred-percent sure it didn't happen."

"How do you mean?"

"Well, I mean, I don't deal with a lot of people at the bank. Mostly other employees with computer problems. But I've noticed that a good chunk of the time if you're trying to figure out how something happened, and you ask somebody, 'Did you do X?' if they're absolutely, positively, no-question sure they didn't do it . . ."

"It's because they did it," finished Harry. "You're not half bad at this, Eli."

He gestured down the street. "There might be nothing to it. He might just be a surly guy. But maybe come up with a better way to ask him . . . he might say something."

"Perhaps."

"Do we want to go after him?"

"In a manner of speaking. Do you know when his ship leaves?"

"Tomorrow."

Harry nodded. "It might take a bit of driving, but we can probably reach tomorrow morning in about two or three hours. Perhaps we can try again."

They wandered back down the street. Eli counted seven more rats that crossed in front of them, although he saw a few more bouncing alongside warehouses to vanish through gaps in the walls. He and Harry passed the hotel and a few small shops, and then cut across into the warehouses. Dirt replaced the cobblestones, and the center of the street became a well-pounded, orangey-brown mash spotted with grass. It ripened the air.

They paused at a street corner while a team of mules dragged a huge wagon up the street. Eli glanced around at the drab buildings. "I always thought New Orleans would look more . . ."

"More what?"

"French, I guess? Especially back . . . well, now."

She smirked. "The French Quarter's back that way," she said. "If you really want, once we've got Mr. Hawkins squared away, we can go for a quick walk-through."

"Really?"

Harry shrugged. "I'm sure we can spare a few hours, perhaps duck into Lafitte's. I don't think anyone else is following this lead, and history's not going to collapse in the next few—Pissbucket!"

"What's wrong?" He looked for another rat somewhere in the street, although Harry hadn't reacted to any of them yet.

"As if the day couldn't get any worse," she muttered.

The mule team dragged the wagon out of the way to reveal the anachronism half-hidden in the alley across the street. The automobile glared at them with four headlights. Its peaked grille reminded Eli of the *Steel Bucephalus*, but instead of brushed steel the car was a deep, rich red.

A wave of déjà vu hit Eli in the face. Seeing the car out of context threw him, and it took him precious seconds to reconcile the car with its surroundings. "Oh, Christ," he muttered. "It can't be."

"What?" Harry glanced over at him. His expression cracked hers for a moment.

Calling the gleaming car red was technically wrong. The 1940 Cadillac Sixty Special didn't come in red. It came in oxblood maroon.

A bulky figure with fire-red hair and a long, heavy coat climbed out of the driver's seat and stood by the rear passenger door. She stared at Eli for a moment with the same look of mild confusion, and then swung the door open. The figure inside crawled out and stood up as straight as he could.

"Hrrruuhhh," he said. He looked at Harry and gave a short bow that wasn't much more than a nod. "Mrs. Pritchard," he croaked.

Harry snorted in response.

The hunched figure of Archibald Truss turned his attention to Eli. "You work for me, don't you? Teak, isn't it?"

26

Mrs. Pritchard," said Truss. He walked to the front of his Cadillac. "I thought I might run into you here in New Orleans. Word on the road is, you've finally stumbled across something valuable."

"News to me," said Harry.

"No need for false modesty. How many of us have been searching all these years? Since the first rumors decades ago?"

"And again," she said, "I'm afraid I have no idea what you're talking about."

"You're part of this?" Eli spat out. His head had stopped spinning long enough to let him form words.

The old man raised a shaggy eyebrow. "I could ask the same thing about you, Teak."

Harry turned to stare at Eli. "You know each other?"

"He owns the bank I work for. He's . . . my boss. Sort of."

"Your boss?!"

Truss snorted. "If I'd realized you were a man of the road, Teak, you'd've been doing more than minding computers in some pissant backwater New England hole. You'd probably be running most of the Northeast for me right now."

"I . . . I kind of find that hard to believe," Eli said.

Another mule cart trudged between them, and Harry used the moment to turn on Eli. "You work for him?" she growled. "That weasel is your employer?"

"I didn't know I worked for him," said Eli. "I mean, I knew I worked for Truss, yeah, I just didn't know he was a searcher."

"He's not a searcher, he's a weasel! A greedy, self-centered—Have you been working for him all along?"

"No!" Eli shook his head as the big cart moved on. "I took a couple of personal days when I came looking for you. And I'm pretty sure they fired me when I didn't show up for work last week. Then. Whenever it was."

Across the street, Truss held up a hand. "Don't worry about that," he called out. "We'll talk about it later."

"No, we won't," Eli said.

Harry's glare shifted back and forth between the two men, and even settled on Svetlana. Eli could see a cruel smile spreading across Truss's face. The grin of a little boy who's stirred the anthills and knows what happens next.

"Let's stop wasting time, Mrs. Pritchard," said the old man. He raised his head and widened his smile. "After all this time, I feel like we know each other. Can I just call you Harriet?"

"No."

The smile shrunk. "We both know what you have and what it's worth. I'm offering to buy it."

Harry shook her head. "It's not for sale."

"In my experience, 'it's not for sale' is the first step in a negotiation."

She smiled her sweet, fake smile. "I've heard experience is what you get when you don't get what you want."

"To be clear," Truss said, "when I'm saying I'll buy it, I'll offer a very fair price."

A noise—a very sharp, deliberate noise—came from behind them. Harry spun around, one of her pistols whipping out as she did. Eli flinched back and turned to look.

Helena scraped her heel against the corner of a warehouse a few feet away. Her modern clothes had been ditched for a dark dress and corset with a tight coat over it. She settled against the building and crossed her arms. She and Harry shot daggers at each other for a moment before Harry's pistol drifted back down.

"You can't buy us off," Eli said to Truss. He glanced at Harry. "Money's useless, right?"

"A fair point," she said, her gaze sliding back to the old man. "Money's no good on the road, and your favors aren't worth the wood they're scribbled on. So what could you even offer us?"

Truss's sneer shifted again, back into something closer to a smile. "But that's what I'm offering you. Both of you. A way to get off the road."

Harry laughed. "There's no way off the road. You drive until someone finds the dream or you die."

"Or until you find a way off," said Truss. "Like Alice Ramsey did."

The mocking smile vanished from Harry's face.

The old man's grin widened, showing off too-white veneers. "Want to know something fascinating about the faceless men? As a show of my goodwill, I'll tell you their greatest weakness."

"Lots of long-range gunfire, last I checked."

"Paperwork."

Eli and Harry both blinked. "I beg your pardon?" she asked.

"Paperwork," repeated the old man. "Bureaucracy. The faceless men find us through the ripples we leave in history. Government records, business records, banking, newspapers. That's how they find things beyond their certainty."

"Hasn't really seemed like a weakness, in my experience," Harry said.

Truss snorted again. "Oh, but it is. The faceless men can't find anything when there's no record of it, no paper trail. Eliminate that and the odds of them finding something—or someone—drop like a rock." He turned his beady gaze on Eli. "And what's the best way for someone to get rid of their paper trail, Teak?"

Harry glanced at Eli. "Do you have any idea what he's talking about?"

Some of the stories and jokes about Truss rolled to the front of Eli's mind. "You become someone else," he said, staring at his boss. "You set up a fake identity with all the paperwork and ID to back it up."

Truss extended a bony finger and stabbed it emphatically toward Eli. "Why do you think the faceless men have never come after me," said the old man, "even though I have a seventy-year business sitting in plain sight, right under their noses? I switch identities depending on when I am. Like the old song says, I am my own grandpa. And my great-grandpa. The faceless men see a well-documented family line, but don't realize it's all just one person." His face twisted into another skeletal grin. "Truss isn't even the name I was born with. They keep looking for Edward Longcarriage."

Harry gaped at him. "And we're supposed to believe that fools them?"

Truss made a showy, exaggerated shrug. "It's like hiding money. Or a mistress. They might know you're doing it, but if they can't make the connections, can't actually catch you at it . . ." He put up his hands in a what-can-you-do pose.

Helena let out a wispy laugh behind them.

Eli glanced over his shoulder, then back to Truss. "So you're offering to . . . what? Give us new identities?"

"If that's what you want," Truss said. "Pick somewhere to settle down and I'll make it worth your while. New identity, passport, perfect credit history. I can even get you a high school yearbook if you want it. I think I own four or five private schools."

Svetlana held up four fingers.

"Four, then. Still easy to get a full history for the two of you. Or just rewrite the one you had. Hell, Teak, we could drop you back in history right where you left. Nothing new to get used to except the fact you'll be filthy rich. How much do you want? A hundred million?" He tossed the number out with the ease of a man standing behind a bar and offering a bowl of pretzels.

"Not interested," Harry said. "Some of us aren't in this search for personal gain."

Eli pictured a hundred million dollars breaking down across banking spreadsheets, and briefly considered just how much personal gain they were talking about.

Truss spread his hands again. "Your choice, of course. All I can do is dangle the carrot. You still have to take it."

"I know you, Truss," said Harry. "Everyone knows you. You're not to be believed or trusted."

"You can trust I'll pay handsomely to get what I want. But at some point . . . I'm going to stop offering."

Harry flicked her coat back. Her hands settled by the holsters. "I'm hoping that wasn't a threat."

Helena walked past them, stretching her arms out and straining her corset. She rolled her head as she crossed the street. Her neck popped as she settled next to her employer, across from Svetlana. If the two women noticed Harry's weapons, it didn't show on their faces. Or in their body language.

Truss looked at them. The thin lines of pleasantness vanished. "You've got two days to think about it. I'll be in touch."

Svetlana escorted the old man toward the Cadillac's rear door and closed it after him. The two women slipped into the Sixty Special's front seats. The engine grumbled to life, the headlights flared, and Eli flinched as the car rolled forward. It swung around and headed up the street. The horn sounded twice as it vanished around a corner.

Harry dropped into a crouch, like an exhausted runner. "Consarn it."

Eli took a few steps past her, looking up the street and listening. "He's gone," he announced after a moment. "I can't hear their engine."

Harry pushed herself back to her feet. The fingers of her right hand rolled themselves into a fist.

"I said he's go—"

She slammed the fist into his shoulder, right where it flowed into his chest. A solid, bruise-leaving punch. "YOU WORK FOR HIM?!" The second blow hit hard before the pain from the first one had fully registered.

Eli saw the next one coming for his face and got his hands up. Her knuckles cracked against the side of his wrist, sparing his nose. "I didn't know who he was!"

Her fists trembled in the air.

"I told you, he owns the bank. There was about a hundred levels of bureaucracy between him and me. I'd only seen him three times in six years. I'd only ever spoken to him once."

Harry's fist dropped a few inches. "I trusted you."

"You still can. You saw his face. He was surprised to see me here."

"That weasel's ability to lie is legendary on the road."

"He doesn't even know my name."

"As I *just* said," she snapped.

"He's a liar," said Eli. "Not me. Have I ever lied to you?"

She stared at him. "I don't know. A few hours ago I would've said no."

"And you'd be right."

"I wish I could believe you, Mr. Teague." She emphasized the formal name. "But there's just too much at stake."

27

They drove for six hours.

From the sun and the occasional road sign, they seemed to be heading west again. They traveled along Route 66. For an hour or so, the road became hard-packed dirt under the Model A's wheels.

At one point, in the distance, a few skeletal buildings flickered and became a small town for a few moments. He guessed it to be somewhen around the Great Depression, but mostly because the town looked damned depressing, even at its peak. Then the moments passed and the buildings fell back into history.

Eli tried to engage Harry a few times. He asked questions about where and when they were, others about her past. Twice he asked about the faceless men. He wondered, out loud, why Truss was so eager to get what little information they had about Frank Hawkins. Harry glanced at him a few times during these questions, then shook her head and returned her attention to the road. His questions gave way to random statements about things they passed. Big trucks. Odd rocks. Fields of different grains.

After a while, Harry made a point of shifting the Model A's gears whenever he tried to talk. Eleanor's transmission whined. The noise moved conversation from challenging to almost impossible.

Eli took the hint. The past three hours had been silent. He shifted on the rumble seat and watched history roll by outside the car.

Two hours after sundown, they stopped for the night somewhere in Oklahoma. She didn't offer him food, and dumped out the blankets. Eli grabbed himself one of the greasy biscuits—only one left after this— took his blanket, and walked a few feet away.

Harry folded her own blanket, swung it out, and folded the top few inches over to make a thin pillow.

"Good night, Harry."

A long minute passed. "I'm sorry," she said. Her voice barely carried through the night.

"What?"

He heard her move, saw her outline shift on her own blanket. She cleared her throat. "I said I'm sorry."

"The crickets are really loud tonight, could you—"

"Don't be an ass, Mr. Teague."

"Sorry."

"Please forgive me for being so . . . closed off today. Truss generally puts me on edge, more so when he has me at a disadvantage. And then adding in the revelation of your past with him—"

"I don't have a past with him."

"Your relationship, then."

"I definitely don't have a relationship with him," said Eli.

She snorted. "Let's just say your tenuous connection to him didn't present itself at the most opportune moment in our fledgling partnership. I'm reasonably certain you have no loyalty to the weasel, and I'm sorry I reacted as I did. I ask your forgiveness."

He looked over at her. "Reasonably?"

"I'm only human."

"Well, in that case, of course I forgive you."

"Thank you."

Eli rolled onto his back and stared up at the night sky. "At least it's still a partnership."

"I suppose it is."

"I spent a few hours today wondering if you were going to leave me stranded somewhere."

"Oh, I still might," she said, readjusting her body on the blanket, "but you can rest assured it'll have nothing to do with this."

"I'll remember that as I'm dying alone somewhere."

Harry chuckled. A soft, light sound that faded into the night. "Plus, you'd probably make a mess of history," she added. "Make my job even more difficult."

Eli stared up at the stars and yawned. The sky seemed bigger than it did back in Sanders. He'd read about it before, some kind of perception thing, but he'd never thought it would seem so . . . true. He swung his head left to right in lazy arcs, trying to find the edge of the night.

"So," he yawned, "are we going to head back tomorrow and try to catch up with Hawkins before Truss does?"

She was quiet for a long time. Eli felt a twinge of worry that he'd somehow offended her again, and then realized she'd just beat him to sleep. He waited to hear her snore, but then sleep caught him too.

THE NEXT MORNING, they drove for another three hours without conversation, but it was a gentler silence. Eli used the time to watch the country roll by outside the Model A. He'd heard of the Great Plains in school, but never imagined such a vast stretch of . . . flat. Being able to see for miles and miles in every direction was overwhelming and hypnotic all at once.

Somewhere near the edge of the Texas panhandle, the road vanished altogether. They drove for an hour across a dry valley while the wind hurled sand and dust at them like rain in a downpour. Eleanor slowed as Harry pulled up her scarf and leaned over the wheel to get her face close to the windshield.

At one point, through the dust, Eli glimpsed a covered wagon being pulled by two bulky cows, or maybe oxen. A man and a small boy sat at the wagon's front, their faces wrapped in scarves and bandannas. The boy pointed at the Model A, gesturing wildly to the man with his other hand.

Then the air cleared again, and Eli saw the road stretching out a quarter mile to their left.

Harry sighed. "Route 66 is a pain."

They pulled onto Interstate 40 and drove for another hour before a sign alerted them to food, gas, and lodging a few miles ahead. Harry glanced at the fuel gauge, hovering on the lower side of 1/4. She tapped her fingers on the steering wheel.

Eli coughed some dust from his throat. "You want to stop for water? For Eleanor?"

"She needs it, and a cleaning." Harry pulled into the right-hand lane. "We all need it after that dust storm."

Fifteen minutes later they swung onto the exit. Eli had half expected a pair of bathrooms and some vending machines, but the rest area seemed to be closer to an oversized truck stop. At least a dozen gas pumps out front, a car wash, signs for two restaurants and a store. A nearby motel didn't seem to be connected to the complex, but certainly took advantage of it.

A pole stood in front of the main building, and it flew one of the largest American flags Eli'd ever seen, the kind of thing that would be displayed on battleships or maybe at the White House. Its edge stretched at least a third of the way down the flagpole. Two more flags hung from the large roof over the gas pumps. Red, white, and blue bunting draped every restaurant window. Another flag had been mounted above the main door of the store, and when the doors whisked open, Eli glimpsed a mannequin dressed like Uncle Sam. The pageantry looked much newer than everything else. "Must be the Fourth of July," he said to Harry as they circled the complex.

Eleanor settled into a space next to a small bank of air and water pumps. Eli climbed out, stretched his arms up over his head, and brushed some of the dust storm from his shirt and pants. Harry slid out across from him, pulled off her tricorne, and rolled her head in slow circles until her neck gave a loud pop.

"Feel better?"

"A bit. Get the tools from the trunk, please."

"What's wrong?"

"Nothing yet. Time for you to start earning your keep."

"I thought I did that already with Hawkins."

"Tools," she repeated, pointing at the back of the car. She batted a cloud of dust from the hat.

Eli got the toolbox from the trunk. When he returned, she'd opened up the hood and exposed the engine. "Crescent wrenches," she said before blowing some more sand away.

"You need help?"

"I don't believe so, but thank you."

Eli handed her tools and watched while she removed the carburetor.

A little more work popped it open and revealed the dull plates inside. She held it up for him to see. "They release here," she said, pointing, "and then slide out like this." The first plate popped out into her fingers. She handed it to Eli, then gave him the rest of the carburetor.

"Ummmm . . ."

"There's a toothbrush in the toolbox. Clean all of them. Both sides. It should take about an hour."

He looked at the array of plates, then down at the bag. "Really?"

She slid her coat off and shook it by the shoulders. More dust and grit rained down on the pavement. "Basic maintenance. Once you're familiar with it, you'll probably be able to get that time down to forty minutes." She pointed at the toolbox. "Clean."

"Yes, ma'am," he said. "And you?"

Harry walked off toward the main building. "Cleaning up. I have dust in too many places it shouldn't be."

"Okay, then," he called after her. "I'll just sit out here in the sun."

She waved at him without looking back. "You'll get your turn."

Eli sat on the small curb with the carburetor in his lap and tried to get the most shade he could from the water pumps. He scrubbed at the first plate for ten minutes with the hard bristles until it gleamed in the sunlight. The next one didn't pop out quite as easily as it had for Harry, but it came loose and he set the brush to it. The third one came loose with less effort.

He had the fourth plate in his hands when a rumbling engine made his skin tremble. He looked up in time to see a blue 1969 Mustang roll by behind Eleanor. Its shadow swung around beneath the Model A as it pulled up in the next slot on the driver's side. A door opened, shoes hit the pavement, and the door slammed shut.

"Harry?" A man's voice drifted over the car.

Eli set the carburetor down and stood up with all four plates in his hands.

"Oh," said the stranger. He wore a brown leather coat with wide lapels, something that would've been popular with '60s musicians, but wouldn't've looked too out of place back in either New Orleans or Independence. Under it were old jeans and a gym-gray linen shirt. "Sorry, man. I thought you were somebody else."

"No problem."

He gave Eli a once-over, then looked at the car again. "This is Eleanor, yes?"

"Yeah." Eli held up the plate and brush. "I'm just cleaning the carburetor out."

The man gave Eli a grin, revealing teeth yellowed by age and tobacco. Eli guessed him to be in his mid-fifties and a few inches under six feet. Short, brown-blond hair streaked with gray topped a creased face that had probably looked boyish for far too long, even dominated by thick salt-and-pepper eyebrows. He had a narrow mouth and a strong chin, but neither so much as to be distracting.

"Did mine last week," he said, jerking his thumb back at the Mustang. He cleared his throat. "So, how'd you end up with Eleanor, Mister . . . ?"

"Teague. Eli Teague. And I don't own her, I'm just a partner."

The man's brows furrowed. "Really? So who owns her?"

Eli studied the man's eyes for a moment. "I didn't catch your name."

The man's mouth moved toward a scowl, then relaxed. "Sorry," he said. "Not trying to pull anything. I'm—"

"James!" Harry trotted across the parking lot. She took two quick steps around the Mustang and wrapped her arms around the man.

He returned the hug, lifting her feet off the ground. "I was worried for a minute," he said, gesturing at Eli.

She shook her head. "He's harmless. James, Mr. Eli Teague. Mr. Teague, James."

"We've met," said James. He held out a hand. "How you doin', Eli?"

He shifted the plates into one hand, reached out with the other. "I'm good."

"Sorry if I caught you off guard just then."

"No, it's okay," said Eli. "I get it."

"New to the road?"

"Yeah, sort of."

James nodded. "I know that look. My first month on the road, my only two moods were amazed and terrified. You'll get used to it."

Harry cleared her throat. "Mr. Teague is my new partner."

The older man's face jammed for a moment, unsure what expression to take on, and settled for cautious approval. "Congratulations."

"He looked a little too close at some things and now I'm stuck with him."

"Hey," said Eli. He held up the carburetor parts. "I'm carrying my weight."

James nodded slowly. "So, where you headed?"

The corners of Harry's mouth twitched. "Where are *you* headed?"

He chuckled. "Okay," he said, "tell you what. Here's one on the house for you. You know Theo Knickerbocker?"

"Of course," she said, her expression neutral. Eli followed her lead and nodded.

"Caught up with him in 1984. He's working the oil fields in North Dakota. He sold me a tip on a Chicago mobster. Turned out to be a bust, though."

"Tough luck," said Eli.

"Yeah," said James. "Least I didn't spend too long on it. And I think it might've led me to something else."

Harry smiled. It didn't quite reach her eyes, but it got closer than most of her smiles did. "Don't suppose you'd like to share?"

James smiled back and winked at her. "Don't suppose you would? I heard a rumor from John a few months back that you'd found a hot new lead in New Orleans."

Eli paused in mid-brushstroke to frown. "Was that anoth—"

Harry silenced him with a quick slash of her hand. "Maybe," she said to James.

The older man smiled again. He had, Eli admitted, a damned good smile. "Okay, then," said James. "When's the next time you'll be in hourglass?"

Harry glanced at Eli. "I think we may be heading there now."

"Really?"

She nodded. "I need to get off the road for a few days and plan."

"So you'll be at . . . ?"

"The second iteration."

James nodded. "How long has it been since the first time around?"

"Almost nine years. Since the wedding."

"Been a while then."

"I didn't want to go for a long time. It was too much of a reminder."

"Yeah," said James. "Never good when two big things end up on the same day. Get married on Christmas, then when your marriage goes bad the day's ruined forever."

"Something like that, yes."

"Ah, hell," he said. "Didn't mean it like that."

"I know."

An awkward silence hung between them, and Eli decided to kill it. "I'm sorry for asking but . . . do I know you?"

James shook his head. "Not yet. I've been on the road for almost thirty years now, and this is the first time I've laid eyes on you."

"You just look kind of familiar to me."

The other man shrugged. "Since I've got you here, you want to cover for me while I fill up?"

"Of course," said Harry.

James dragged one of the water hoses over, glanced around, and stuck it in the Mustang's fuel tank. Harry put herself between the hose and the rest of the parking lot. She and James talked quietly on the other side of the Mustang while Eli finished the last of the carburetor's plates. Other cars pulling in and out of the rest stop, plus the sound of the scouring toothbrush, obscured their distant words.

Eli finished his chore, snapped the plates one by one back into their slots, and then fitted the top of the case over them. He stood up, hefting the carburetor in both hands, just as James pulled the hose from the Mustang's side and let it retract into the pump.

"Good meeting you, Eli," the older man said. His handshake was solid and sincere.

"You too."

"Maybe I'll see you at the second iteration."

"Ummm . . . sure?"

James kissed Harry's cheek and climbed back into his Mustang. He gave Eli a final two-fingered wave before pulling out and heading for the eastbound freeway ramp. The engine roar faded away.

"Come on, Mr. Teague," Harry said. She pulled the carburetor bolts from her pocket. "Let's get that back in so you can wash up and buy us lunch."

He held it out. "Why am I buying lunch?"

"It's 2002," she said. "I don't have any money they'll take here. So either you pay or we don't eat until sometime tomorrow."

THE RESTAURANT REMINDED Eli of a Friendly's or Denny's, just with many more flags. A woman in a star-spangled cowboy shirt waved at them from across the room. "Just sit anywhere, folks!"

They claimed a booth with a view of the parking lot. Harry set her tricorne on the table, pulled menus from a holder behind the napkins, and handed one across to Eli. Pictures filled the list of meal options. He set his own hat on the seat next to him while his attention drifted through the oversized, laminated pages. Several items had been tagged with American flag stickers.

Two glasses of water clunked onto the Formica. Another woman in a red-white-and-blue shirt stood at the head of the table. A glossy flag the size of a playing card covered her belt buckle, or maybe it was the buckle. "You folks ready to order?"

Harry blinked innocently at Eli. "Sure," he said, still torn between the cheeseburger and the club sandwich. "You can go first."

"I would like to try," said Harry, looking between the waitress and the menu, "your all-American cheeseburger, cooked medium-rare if it could be, with . . . freedom fries. Those are similar to french fries, yes?"

The waitress barked out a laugh, then gave a quick nod and scribbled on her pad. "You want a drink?"

"Coffee, please."

"I love your costume, by the way. Very patriotic."

"Thank you so much," said Harry. "I love yours too."

The waitress beamed and tugged at her shirt. She turned her attention to Eli. "What about you, hon?"

"I guess I'll have the club sandwich."

"Fries for you too?"

He reached his finger out, touched another selection on the menu, and then closed the vinyl sleeve. "Sure," he said.

"Drink?"

"I'm good with water."

"So, one cheeseburger, medium-rare, one club sandwich, both with freedom fries, and a coffee."

Harry beamed at the woman until she walked away, then the smile vanished. She stuck her menu back in the wire holder and stared out the window at the Model A.

Eli cleared his throat.

"Yes?"

He gestured out at the freeway. "Who is he, anyhow?"

"James? Another searcher." She noticed something on the tabletop. Her finger poked at a streak and rubbed it into oblivion.

"How'd he end up on the road?"

She shrugged. "He was a racer in the 1950s. Heard bits about the search from other drivers, decided he wanted to be part of it. He faked his death and got on the road."

"Faked his death?"

"It's not common," said Harry, "but some people try for a clean break. They don't want things to reflect back on their earlier life."

Eli mulled over that. "Was he a professional racer?"

"Wanted to be, but it wasn't his paying job, at the time. He worked on a few movies, I think. Then he started searching for the dream."

"Anything I would've heard of?"

Another shrug. "I was never one for the pictures. Besides, his driving abilities are what matter now."

"Do you know what he's looking for?"

She studied the edges of her tricorne. "Same as everyone else, I suppose. Happiness. Peace of mind. Freedom to live how you like without having to hide who you are." She took the hat in her fingertips and rotated it on the tabletop.

Eli looked out at Eleanor. A group of college students on their way in had stopped to look at the car. One of them pulled a silver camera from her purse and took two or three quick pictures. Another craned his neck to look inside, toward the dashboard, then looked around awkwardly.

"Y'know," Eli said, "you've never said what you'd do with it."

She glanced up from the hat. "Hmmmmm?"

"The dream. If you found it and got to make a wish or shape destiny or however it goes. What would you do?"

The waitress reappeared, this time with a tray of food. Harry slid her hat out of the way and accepted her plate. Eli took his. The waitress spun away while Harry dusted her fries with pepper and salt.

Eli pulled a tiny sword of red plastic out of one of the club sandwich quarters. A toothpick flag decorated one of the other sections and he plucked that out as well. "These people take Fourth of July a little too seriously."

Harry used a butter knife to saw through her burger. "I believe it's early May."

He looked around at the garish display. "So what's all this? Memorial Day?"

"Desperate patriotism," said Harry. She raised the burger half to her mouth and took a bite.

Eli pushed a trio of fries into his mouth. "So what would you do?"

She held up the remains of the piece with two crescents chomped out of it. "What is it that makes a cheeseburger so satisfying? Everyone eats them. Even vegetarians find ways to make cheeseburgers."

Eli bit off a mouthful of sandwich. A perfect balance of dry turkey and mayo. They hadn't skimped on the bacon either. When his mouth was empty, he asked, "So you want the dream so everyone can have cheeseburgers?"

Harry had another mouthful of burger and followed it up with some more fries. "I want to find the dream," she said, "so the search will be over."

"But what would you do with it?"

"I'd get it back to where it's supposed to be," she said. "That's all." She picked up a french fry and poked the cheeseburger with it. "I love driving, I love seeing the country, but I'm just so tired of the search. Of seeing people compete against each other when there's centuries of America to see. Of hearing about friends who spent their lives searching for the dream and had nothing to show for it when the faceless men killed them."

She poked at her food two more times, then flipped the fry around and bit it in half.

"Christopher had big plans for the dream," she said, "and for a while I wanted to carry them out. Honor him. But after all these years . . . I'd just like this to be over so my friends will stop being killed."

Eli tried to think of something to say, and while he did Harry took another bite of her cheeseburger. He ate some of his sandwich while he tried to think of a clever segue. And by then he realized they were just going to eat in silence.

"How's everything?" asked the waitress, appearing from over Eli's shoulder.

"Just fine," he said. "Could we get the check?"

She slid a pair of receipts from her apron and put one facedown on the table. "Whenever you're ready," she said. "You just take your time. You want a refill on that coffee?"

Harry gulped down the last of the cup. "Please."

When she left, Eli looked at the bill and did some more mental math. "Well," he said, "I'm officially broke."

Harry peered at the upside-down check. "Can you leave a tip?"

"If I give her everything I have left. I think it's sixteen percent. Maybe seventeen."

Harry nodded. "We'll be good for now. Thank you for lunch."

"You're welcome." He picked up another quarter sandwich. "So . . . now what?"

"Eat up. The road beckons."

28

Eleanor shuddered and bounced over the uneven ground. The rumble seat slammed up against Eli's butt again and again. Every third or fourth bounce, it caught his tailbone and jarred his whole spine.

The headlights brushed against something shiny in the night, and a car loomed out of the darkness. A red 1975 Dodge Dart Sport. Harry swerved away from it and Eli glimpsed what looked like an old open-topped touring car, maybe a Maxwell, parked just beyond the Dodge, and then they both vanished into the darkness.

"What are those doing out here?"

She ignored his question and swung Eleanor around a World War II–era jeep with a white star on its side.

The headlights lit up car after car. There were dozens, maybe hundreds of them. Eli saw Chevys and Tuckers and Dodges. He saw another Model A that could've been Eleanor's twin by a skeletal tree, and right next to it a '69 Mustang that was either deep blue or black. An old Indian motorcycle leaned on its kickstand in front of the Mustang.

Eleanor rolled past all of them and slowed to a stop. Harry flipped a few switches, and the engine sputtered twice before stopping. She sat with her hands on the wheel and took in a slow breath.

Maybe a mile or two away, a faint glow outlined a cluster of buildings.

"So," asked Eli. "Where are we? Or when?"

"California. The second week of March 1886. The town's called Hourglass."

"Never heard of it."

"You wouldn't have." She flexed her fingers twice on the wheel. "It's a little boomtown, one of the last. Six months old now, all but abandoned in another seven."

"Gold?"

Her hat settled back on her head. "History travelers."

"What?"

She slid out of the car and tugged her coat closed around her. "This is where we all meet," she said. "The second week of March 1886, in Hourglass. It was a boomtown because at one point hundreds of people poured through the town. Some of them more than once."

He stepped out of the car. As his eyes adjusted, he recognized the shapes of over a hundred cars around them. Probably closer to two hundred. They were parked in loose, uneven rows and clusters.

Harry walked past them all, headed for Hourglass. Eli took a few steps to catch up and fell in beside her. "So the whole town is searchers?"

"Not the whole town," she said. "There are almost two hundred residents, actual citizens of 1886. I think some of them are a bit confused by things they glimpse or overhear this week, but for the moment all they really see is cash on the barrelhead. And by the time they start to think about it, the week's over and we'll all be gone."

"Never to return?"

"Of course we return. It's not much of a clubhouse if you can only visit it once."

"But you said it's just for one week."

"Correct. And when you come back, you come back on Monday. Or Sunday night."

The low moon cast a dim half-light across the desert, enough to see the basic landscape and the loose path Harry followed toward the town. Eli could make out tracks from boots, shoes, and even a few pairs of sneakers. He saw branches and stones that he stepped past, but the stark moonlight shadows could easily hide rocks, holes, or who knew what. Plenty of things to trip on and break an ankle.

"Have you been here before?"

Harry stuck her hands deep into her coat pockets. "Yes," she said. "Nine years ago. This was our wedding reception and our honeymoon. A party with all our friends that lasted five whole days."

He looked at the town. They'd cut almost a third of the distance already. "All of history and you had your honeymoon here?"

"Mind your tongue, Mr. Teague. You're speaking of the happiest days of my life."

"Sorry."

She leaned her head back and looked up at the stars. "Truth be told, I don't remember much of it. I drank too much, slept too little, and spent far too much time . . ." She paused, gazed ahead at the buildings, and tugged the point of her hat down to shadow her face in the moonlight.

"Yes?"

"It was my honeymoon, Mr. Teague. Don't be an ass."

He chuckled. So did she.

"To answer your question, though, we had it here for the same reason we're here now. It's safe."

"Safe?"

"The faceless men won't come here. It's the one place and time in American history we don't need to worry about them."

"Because of the, what'd you call it, the iteration?"

"What?"

"This is where the second iteration is?"

She nodded. "The first time around, the second iteration, and the last paradox."

"Are they . . . wormholes or something?"

"I beg your pardon?"

"These things, are they wormholes or some kind of space-time event or—"

"They're saloons, Eli."

"What?"

Harry stepped around a large patch of dry grass that reached up close to her thigh. "Hourglass has three saloons. Well, two saloons—the First Time Around and the Last Paradox. The Second Iteration is more of a public house, really."

"Three saloons with time-related names, all in the same town" said Eli. "That's a lucky find."

"Not really. Abraham Porter created the whole town."

"Porter from the Chain?"

"The very same."

"How'd he manage that?"

"He cheated a bit. Set up some long-term trusts and investments, pushed for certain trade routes, hired a dozen different people over about a decade."

"That must've been a lot of work."

"Not when you can use the road. Took him about two days, altogether. And three tanks of water."

"And it doesn't strike anyone as a little . . . I don't know, weird that a town of two hundred people has three bars that all have related names?" He shook his head. "Hell, has the word *paradox* even been invented yet?"

Harry raised an eyebrow. "Is that meant to be a joke?"

"Seriously, doesn't anyone else notice how weird it is? The town, the bar names, all that. I mean, if not now, some historian must've stumbled across it in books or old journals or something."

"Lots of strange-named things out here in the desert."

"Like what?"

Harry pointed off toward the horizon while they walked. "The town I was born in is about eighty-five, maybe ninety miles that way."

"Yeah?"

"Shame."

"The town is called Shame?"

She nodded. Her arms stretched out at her sides. Her frock coat lifted up, flapping like a set of awkward wings. "I'm seven months old right now. Almost exactly."

"Ever tempted to drive over and see yourself?"

Harry shook her head and let the coat settle around her. "I'm not there. Mother and Pa left right after I was born. Some trouble in the town or something. They never talked about it." She jerked her thumb back toward the parked cars. "I think they're on a train pulling into Indianapolis right about now."

Eli nodded and kicked at a rock. It skittered through the dirt ahead of them and vanished into the shadows. "So, 1886. I think right now my family is in . . . Sanders."

"What was their trade?"

"No idea," he said, "but I don't think they were any good at it."

"Why do you say that?"

"Because if they'd made any money, they would've left."

The loose path widened out. Hoofprints and wheel ruts appeared. Eli pictured people coming into town on foot, on horseback, in wagons pulled by oxen or mules, and all being funneled onto the same trail.

An old, unlit shed appeared first, distinguishing itself from the shadowed and silhouetted buildings. A few more steps and a large, two-story barn loomed behind it. Even from here, the building smelled of smoke and hot metal. A rusted anvil sat out front.

The trail became a dirt road, which Harry led them down. They entered Hourglass with what looked like a blacksmith's shop on one side of them and a simple church on the other. A wooden cross had been nailed above the door, and on top of the small steeple a metal one gleamed and glinted in the moonlight. They passed a few houses that ranged from bare, weather-beaten shacks to quaint homes with curtains in the windows.

Harry paused at an intersection. A quiet saloon stood on one corner, its doors pointed out toward the main street. Eli saw people walk by the entrance inside and heard the murmur of several voices. A striped circle of red, yellow, and black decorated the window, the colors made bolder by the dark curtains behind them.

Eli looked again. Not a circle—a snake. Swallowing its own tail.

"The Last Paradox," Harry said.

"Are we going in?"

She shook her head. "Not our time."

"What's that mean?"

"This," she said, "is where everyone ends up. Everyone who makes it."

"Makes it . . . ?"

"To the end. Once you know the search is over, you come to Hourglass one final time and go to the Last Paradox."

"Why?"

"Because that's the goal Abraham gave us," she sighed. "To make it till the end."

Harry moved on. She crossed the street and continued down the main road. Eli followed. "So the people in there have found the dream?"

"Perhaps. Or it's just a few locals enjoying the only saloon not packed with strangers."

"Couldn't we just go in now? Find out where the dream's hidden? What's going to happen?"

She glanced back. "Of course not."

"Why not?"

"Because what would you think if we went in and you weren't already in there?"

"Why wouldn't I be in . . . oh."

She nodded once and continued on without saying more.

The next block had a few more residences, a general store, and what looked like a town hall, or maybe a courthouse. A barbershop squatted next door, almost identical to the one in Independence, although the red-and-white post on this one made Eli think of old painted tin toys. It had a wide base, and he wondered if wind-up mechanisms were a common thing yet.

Hourglass was bigger than Eli had first thought, but not by much. Looking ahead, he guessed fifty or sixty buildings made up the whole town. Most of them had wooden walls, but he saw some mortared stone here and there, and even a few brick chimneys. Three roads altogether— one east to west, two north to south, like a two-barred cross.

"Where are the horses?" he asked.

"In barns and stables, I'd imagine."

"Shouldn't there be some tied up in front of the saloons?"

"Why?"

"In case someone needs one."

"Then they'd go out to the stables and get it. Besides," she waved a hand at the street, "you've seen what it can be like with horses passing through. Why would someone want to keep them in front of their business?"

A man in a long leather duster walked by on the far side of the street. A rifle balanced on his shoulder. He watched Eli and Harry as they approached. His free hand reached up to touch the brim of his hat. "Gentlemen," he said. "Evening." As his hand came down, they saw the star-in-circle badge on his lapel.

Eli nodded, then reached up to mimic the man's gesture. On a whim, he lifted his derby a few inches off his head. "Good evening."

The man grunted in reply. He gave Harry a second glance, but that was all. Her coat hid the shape of her body and the broad point of her hat hid her face with shadows. He walked past them and headed off toward the Last Paradox.

"That's Blinovitch," Harry said. "Keeps everyone in line if we get too rowdy. Thursday night is going to be very rough on him, if memory serves."

After a few minutes of strolling they came to the town's other intersection. On the far corner stood the tallest building Eli'd seen in Hourglass, a good three stories high. It had swinging doors set into the corner of the building, just like a classic western saloon. Music and voices and laughter spilled out into the street through those doors.

Across from it, going off the two wooden stars flanking the door, sat a squat police station. More likely a sheriff's office, Eli corrected himself. Were police even a thing at this point in history?

Diagonally across from the sheriff's office, to Eli's left, the stone-and-mortar block of a bank stared over at the saloon with barred windows. To his right, facing the bank, sat another square, two-story building. A carved sign hung from the upper balcony, two identical bottles, side by side.

Harry paused to look over at the saloon, then stepped toward the blocky tavern. "Come on," she said. "I'll buy you a drink."

Eli looked at the sign. "The Second Iteration?"

"Yes."

He glanced at the saloon. "And that's the First Time Around."

"Very good, Mr. Teague."

"Sounds like they're having a real party over there."

"They are. I told you it lasted most of the week."

Eli furrowed his brow. His eyes leaped from Harry to the corner doors of the saloon. "That's your wedding reception."

"Yes."

"Going on right now."

"It started yesterday," she said. She tipped her chin back over her shoulder, back down the street, back toward the dozens and dozens of parked cars. "I brought us in on Tuesday night."

There had been another Model A parked amongst the cars. Another 1929 business coupe. Same year, same model.

Same car.

Eli pointed across the street. "You're over there right now? Younger you."

"Yes," said Harry. "Me and Christopher. John. Alice. James. I think maybe even Truss. Pretty much everyone who traveled the road is over there drinking and eating and confusing the hell out of the piano player with song requests." She blushed. "Please pardon my vulgarity."

"I'll live. Somehow." He looked over at the First Time Around. "Am I over there?"

Harry gave him an odd look. Head to toes and back. "Do you remember being there?"

"No, but I figured maybe I . . . I end up there. Later."

She shook her head. "That's not how it goes. Usually."

"Why?"

"Come inside," she said, gesturing at the door into the Second Iteration. "I'll explain what I can, and I'm sure somebody here can explain anything I can't."

29

The Second Iteration looked almost luxurious after the patched-together saloon back in Independence. Two chandeliers filled with ivory candles lit the room, and small oil lamps sat on every table. Rugs covered most of the wooden floor, but where they didn't, Eli saw well-fitted planks.

At least three dozen people filled the room. Maybe as many as fifty. Enough that he couldn't get a good sense of the tavern's size. Dozens of conversations filled the air, none shouting but each still straining to be heard over all the others.

A man at one of the nearby tables grinned and stood up. "Harry," he said. "Eli. I was worried you two'd never get here."

"We're just a day late," she said. "No cause for alarm."

"A day you'll never get back," said James. His face wrinkled with a smile as he hugged her. "At my age, you start counting them." There was more gray in his hair than there had been yesterday, and a few strands of white, as well, but his grin didn't seem a day older.

"We're going to grab some drinks," she said. "We'll catch up?"

"'Course," he grabbed Eli's hand in a solid grip. "Good to see you both again."

"He's awfully friendly," said Eli as they worked their way through the crowd. "Yesterday I thought he was going to clobber me for a few seconds."

"Yesterday for us," she said. "Looks like three or four years for him. He might know you better by now."

"What?"

She glanced back at him over her shoulder. "I told you before, we don't always meet each other in the same order."

"Even here?"

"Especially here."

"That must get really confusing."

She shrugged. "Sometimes you just have to play dumb. Or be cryptic."

They reached the bar and she waved down the man behind it. The bartender looked at them over a set of rectangular lenses wrapped with a wire frame. The left-hand lens had a crack running from top to bottom. "Evening, sir. Ma'am." His eyes flitted from their faces to their clothes and back. "You folks . . . part of this?"

"Absolutely," Harry said. She pulled her coin purse out, fished through it, and spun a handful of coins onto the bar. Then she took two of them back, plucked out three different ones, and added them to the collection. "This is for me and my partner here," she said, jerking her thumb at Eli. "You'll let me know when it runs out. If it doesn't, keep whatever's left."

The bartender eyed the coins for a moment. "You sure about this, ma'am?"

She rapped her knuckles on the bar. "Two bourbons."

The bartender studied her face, shook his head, and swept the coins off the bar with his hand.

"Eli," she said, "why don't you find us a table while I wait for the drinks?"

He waded through the crowd. Men and women. More skin colors than he'd ever seen in his small Maine town, even during summer tourist season. One or two older than James, two or three looking barely into their teens. Most of them shared drinks and quiet conversations while a few laughed with groups and others sat alone.

He saw two more tricorne hats in the crowd, and—proving Harry right—a fair number of derbies. One man wore a cowboy hat and the woman across from him had one of the thin, flat caps Eli always pictured newsboys wearing.

A quartet of searchers played poker. Three chips landed in the pot with the click-clack sound of wood on wood. A tray of them sat off to the side. Eli leaned in to peer at it, then realized it looked like an attempt to read cards over someone's shoulder. Two of the players, a man and woman, glanced up at him. The man next to him, a broad-shouldered, lumberjack-looking fellow, twisted around and looked up. "Oh," he said, his scowl melting. "Hey, Eli. Good to see you."

"I . . ." He stared back at the man, at the other players, and remembered Harry's advice. "Thanks. You too."

The lumberjack reached up to grab Eli's hand and squeezed it tight.

The woman chuckled. Her dark hair was cut short with sweeping bangs, and a black fedora sat near her elbow. She wore a charcoal suit with an ivory shirt and a wine-colored tie. The ensemble made her look like a detective in an old noir movie.

The lumberjack's eyes went from Eli to the tray of poker chips. "D'you need a favor?"

"No," said Eli. "No, I'm good, thanks."

"Don't be a dork," the detective said to the lumberjack. "You're just confusing him."

"What?"

"He doesn't know us yet," she said, waving her free hand at Eli. "This is his first trip to Hourglass, remember?"

The lumberjack blinked and looked up at Eli again. "Christ," he said. "Sorry about that."

Eli put up a hand. "No," he said. "It's okay. I should've expected a little . . . weirdness."

The detective chuckled again. She winked at Eli. "Take a green one," she said, nodding at the tray. "It's a good color for you."

"Now who's messing with him?" asked the fourth player, his eyes still on his cards. He hadn't looked up once.

On a guess, looking from table to tray, it looked like about a third of the poker chips were missing from the set. Eli reached out, ran his finger along the poker chips, and pulled out one of the ones with flaking green paint on the edge. Old nicks and scratches covered it. If the town was only a few months old, the tray of chips had passed through several owners before ending up at the Second Iteration.

"Wait a minute," he murmured. He flipped the poker chip over in his palm. His gaze dropped down to the columns of wooden tokens.

"Mr. Teague," Harry shouted across the room. "I do not see a table to put these drinks on!"

"Christ on a crutch," said the lumberjack. "She's still calling him 'Mr. Teague.' Is this their first week together?"

The detective smirked and turned her attention back to the game. "Catch you on the rebound, Eli," she said, her eyes on her cards.

Eli stepped away from the card game and the tray of poker chips. He glanced down at the green one in his hand. "Do I need a favor?" he murmured.

He looked up from the token and spotted a table with a flickering lantern. He found Harry in the throng with drinks held high, pointed, and saw her follow his gesture. They met at the table. Eli dropped his derby on the table as Harry sat. He fumbled with the lamp until the wick was a little higher.

Harry placed her own hat on the table, then pushed one of the glasses across to him. "To your health," she said, raising her glass.

He mirrored her. *"Kampai."*

"What?"

"It's Japanese."

Her brows went up. "You speak Japanese?"

"No. But my junior-year roommate studied it in college. He toasted with *kampai* all the time, thought it made him look like a sophisticated world traveler. I picked it up after a few dozen times."

"Sounds like a bit of a fool."

"He was. But he was a nice guy too."

"What's it mean?"

"To your health, I think."

She pursed her lips, nodded, and tipped her drink back.

Eli pushed out a breath and swallowed a mouthful of bourbon. It was warm and smooth, and he felt the soft prickle it left along his tongue. He blew out again. And a third time.

"Good, isn't it?"

"Hah. I should not be doing this on an empty stomach."

"Truer words," she said, raising her own glass again.

He dropped the wooden token on the table. "The favors are old poker chips."

She nodded. "Yes, they are. What of it?"

"I thought they were . . . I don't know. Custom-made or something."

Harry snorted. "No, people just grabbed what they needed. This is where a good number of favors get swapped, after all." She gestured at the poker chip on the table. "Is green going to be your color?"

"It looks like it, yeah." He gestured around them. "So. Explain."

She sipped her bourbon and studied his face.

"You're across the street and you're here," he said. "And you don't try to cheat history by going to warn yourself about anything. You could warn—"

Eli stopped before he said the name. He looked at the table for a few moments, a fine piece of furniture made from dark lacquered wood. Then he took another drink and checked out the chandelier.

Harry's gaze didn't falter. "Outside, you asked why we had our wedding reception here."

He nodded, but kept his eyes from hers. "Yeah. I know you said it's safe, but it just seems . . . risky. Especially if you all keep coming back here. Isn't this a, what do they say? A target-rich environment for them?"

She took another sip. "The faceless men won't come here. Ever. This one week, in this one town, is the one place searchers are safe from them."

Eli looked around the bar. Searchers lounged in chairs and leaned against the bar. A woman in what looked like a gray Civil War jacket rested her boots on a table next to a plate decorated with crumbs and streaks of gravy. A felt top hat balanced on her forehead, shading her eyes. On the far side of the room, an older man with a curling white mustache and an eye patch told a quiet story to three interested listeners and one distracted man while they all drank.

"Okay," he said, "so they're relentless zealots who respect town boundaries."

She barked out a laugh.

"Why?"

Harry swallowed another mouthful of bourbon. "This is going to be one of those explanations that's been passed down the Chain," she said. "Are you going to get upset and interrupt?"

He snorted and tossed back a shot's worth of his own drink.

"Abraham Porter designed Hourglass to be our safe harbor. We all come here. Once, twice, hopefully three times during our life as searchers. So many of us overlapping at once creates a situation which could have repercussions throughout history were it to be disrupted.

"For example," she continued, "my wedding party is going on right now across the street. It sets off ripples as the people there interact with each other and with the town's residents. The piano player. The bartender. The cook. The serving girls. The other townsfolk out for a drink, or perhaps kept up by our revelry. The sheriff and the deputy who check in on us. Do you follow so far?"

He nodded and raised his glass again.

"Those people interact with their families, bunkmates, what-have-you. The thing is, many of them also interact with us over here." She gestured across the bar with her glass. "James is here, and Irene is trying to devour him with her eyes. But he's also over at the First Time Around right now, almost twenty years younger and flirting with one of the Huang sisters and also with the young boy who plays piano. Two or three of these people might meet up tomorrow and whisper about their nights, not realizing they're all talking about the same man."

Eli nodded again. "Okay. That makes sense."

"And that's why the faceless men stay away. As long as we all follow the rules, this town is a Gordian knot in the lines of history. It's having hundreds, maybe thousands of effects, and all of these effects loop and twist and tie back to here and now." She waved her hand at the door. "Out there, they can pick us off one or two at a time and neaten up whatever problems it causes in history. But here, during this week, it would be catastrophic. One extreme action here would affect thousands of different threads at once." She swallowed another mouthful of bourbon. "Melodramatic as it may sound, attacking this town could destroy America."

Eli sipped his own drink. "And you're sure it's safe?"

"We know it's safe because we've all seen it. I've already been here this week, remember?" She waved her free hand at the crowd. "So has everyone else in this room. And some of us maybe down the street at the Paradox too. The faceless men never set foot in Hourglass."

"So why don't you just stay here? Take some time off. Not . . ." He glanced around the crowded room. "Not be part of the search?"

"Stay here for a week? That's the plan."

"What?"

"It's only one week," she said. "If we all tried to come back again and again, we'd start tripping over ourselves, and upset the system Porter created. That's why no one goes back and forth between the saloons. Hourglass is perfectly safe as long as we all follow the rules."

"Ahhh."

She looked around the room, had another sip, then leaned in closer to Eli. "We're on the right track with Hawkins."

"Are you sure?"

"I am. Ask me how."

Someone bumped Eli and jostled his drink. He glanced up, then back at Harry. "Ummm . . . how?"

She moved her glass side to side in front of her, gesturing at the room. "I know everyone here."

"Okay."

Harry watched his face for a moment. "Think, Eli," she said. "How can I know everyone here?"

"Well . . ." He glanced around the room and caught glimpses of the detective, James, the lumberjack, an Asian woman in a red dress, the man with the eye patch, the top-hat woman. "Are they all part of the Chain?"

"Some of them. Others are friends and acquaintances from different Chains. But I know them all. How?"

He picked up the green-edged poker chip and flipped it back and forth between his fingers. "If you know them," he said, "it means they came before you."

"Yes."

Eli looked around again. "There's nobody"—he lowered his voice—"there's nobody here who comes after you? After us?"

She shook her head. "Not a one. The searchers end with us. With our generation. There are no more links." She picked up her glass. "Hawkins is it."

Eli nodded once. "Or maybe the faceless men wipe us all out."

"Oh, you're a cheerful drunk." She threw back the last of her bourbon. The empty glass came down hard on the table. "I need another," she said. "You?"

"Good for now, thanks."

She stood up and strode back across the tavern.

Someone shuffled by in the crowd, patted Eli's shoulder, and said, "Greetings, programs," with a laugh. The stranger vanished into the crowd before Eli got a look at him. Instead, he found himself eye to eye with a Latina in a rumpled white tuxedo. She raised her brows and stared back at Eli over her spectacles until he looked away.

He caught a glimpse of the card game as people parted for a moment, and locked eyes with the noir detective. She blew him a kiss, tossed three chips into the pot, and then the shifting bodies hid her table again. A moan of despair from the lumberjack rose over the crowd, followed by laughter.

Harry returned with three glasses and clunked them on the table. "Good to see you haven't wandered off," she said.

"That's why there's three saloons," he said. "First, second, and last. Whenever you come back to the town again, you go to the next one so you don't run into yourself. And you're running into everyone else in more or less the right order."

She bowed her head. "Very good, Eli. Took me a while to catch that one when it was first explained to me."

"What happens if someone tries to come more than three times?"

"To the best of my knowledge, no one's ever made it that far."

"And nobody goes back and forth between the bars?"

Harry froze, then shook her head. "No," she said. "Not yet." She selected a glass, saluted him with it, and took a sip.

Eli sighed and had another sip of his bourbon. "Who are the other drinks for?"

"One for me," she said, raising her glass again, "and I got you another one anyway. I didn't want to go back to the bar again in a few minutes."

"Who's the third one for?"

"Also for me. I just told you I didn't want to go back to the bar. Please keep up."

"I'm trying my best."

"Normally, I prefer not to imbibe on such a scale. It's not good for driving, and accidents on the road are bad enough when one isn't traveling through history. But we're not on the road at the moment, and . . ."

She gazed down at her drink, then took a sip.

"And?"

Harry looked at him with hard eyes. "And I'm about to do something I find unpleasant. So the bourbon helps."

"Hopefully it doesn't involve plans for me," Eli said.

Another sip. "I'm afraid it does, Eli."

His own glass paused halfway between the table and his mouth.

"Nothing sinister, I assure you," she said. "Well, not to the best of my knowledge. Just unpleasant." She stared down into her glass again. "More for me than you."

The woman with the top hat started awake and grabbed for her hip, where an olive-green, nylon holster protruded from inside her Civil War jacket. Her hat tumbled to the table, rolled, and fell to the floor. A man in a camel-colored overcoat bent to scoop it up before the crowd trampled it. She relaxed and thanked him.

Harry cleared her throat. "I need you to go across the way. To the First Time Around."

"What?"

"Just go over there. Buy a drink for yourself. Two if you like." She reached into her coat pocket and dropped two quarters on the table. The two coins she'd set aside before.

"You just said the whole point of the saloons is that people don't go between them."

"Usually." She set a finger on each coin and slid them across the table to him.

"Are you trying to get me in trouble or something?"

"You won't get in trouble."

"But I thought people aren't supposed to meet themselves."

"You won't meet yourself," she said. "You're not over there. Not yet, anyway."

He picked up the two quarters. "Are you trying to get rid of me?"

"No, Eli. I don't think so anyway."

"You don't think so?"

"I don't know all the details. I just know you have to go over there."

"How?"

"How which? I presume by walking."

"How do you know I have to go over there?"

She picked up her drink again. Studied it. Swallowed a mouthful of it. "Because I saw you over there."

He blinked. "What?"

She sighed. "On the second night of our party—the Tuesday night—Christopher wandered off to the bar and ended up talking with someone I didn't know. A man I'd never seen before, with a short wool coat, a derby, and a few days' worth of whiskers."

Eli glanced at the derby on the table and let his gaze continue down to his pea coat.

"Whatever they were talking about," she went on, "I could see Christopher became very serious. I asked him about it later and he wouldn't tell me anything, said it wasn't important. I'd forgotten about it altogether until we were standing outside, looking over at the First Time Around. I remembered what night it was. And I realized how you were dressed."

He rubbed the coins together between his fingers. "That was nine years ago."

"Nine years ago," she said, "is right across the road."

He took a sip of his own drink. "And you think it was me?"

She shrugged and didn't meet his eyes. "I guess we'll find out, won't we?"

30

The night had eaten up a little more of the day's heat. Eli tugged his jacket closer around himself. Cold enough for a chill, but not enough to warrant buttoning up.

Across the dirt-road intersection, the First Time Around tossed out flickers of light and sound. He heard voices. Laughter. Notes from a piano. Enough to overwhelm any other noise in the small town.

He walked across the street.

The First Time Around had cleaner paint and glass than many of the older buildings Eli'd seen in Hourglass. The planks and posts of the boardwalk in front of it were straight and sharp. No scrapes or gouges or nicks, just two or three small scuffs by the stairs. Barely a year into the life of Hourglass and someone had decided to invest in a real, three-story saloon.

Someone, apparently, being Abraham Porter.

The swinging doors at the building's corner were bright blue, not sun-faded in the least. Someone had written POLICE BOX in white chalk across the twin doors. A handprint had smudged the B.

Over the tops of the doors he could see people. Dozens and dozens of people. The sound and life and energy of the party spilled out and washed over him.

He glanced back over his shoulder, half expecting to see Harry watching him from the Second Iteration. The tavern's door was empty, though. The night watchman made his way back up the street, his rifle still on his shoulder.

Eli pushed the blue doors open and stepped inside.

The chandeliers in the First Time Around had twice as many candles, enough to make Eli think "fire hazard" before anything else. The white ceiling reflected the light back down at the patrons. Mirrors on the walls added to the brilliance and magnified the size of the crowd.

Eli stared at the seething mass of people. Harry had called it her wedding reception, but it seemed like at least three different celebrations were in full swing. Smaller groups orbited the bigger clusters, and there were still dozens of people in trios or pairs or standing alone. The heat of them warmed the big room.

He stood by the door for a moment, overwhelmed. A man and a woman walked past him, and the man thumped him twice on the shoulder with a smile. The woman glanced back to wave at Eli as they moved on.

Eli reached up, tugged his derby down a little tighter on his head—a gesture that already felt comfortable and familiar—and waded into the saloon.

According to Harry, he needed to be by the bar. He could get a drink, watch the room, and try to blend in.

Of course, nobody was blending into the crowd. He could see clothes from at least a dozen different points in history, sometimes mixed on the same person. His eyes panned the crowd, wondering if he'd see young Harry before she saw him.

He had no idea what Christopher looked like. Eli tried to remember any distinguishing feature Harry'd mentioned and couldn't come up with one past "big." Hopefully, at their reception, he'd be the man spending the most time with Harry.

Eli passed the woman in the top hat and the lumberjack at a table together with a bottle of what looked like red wine. Each of them grinned as they looked from each other to a map of the United States that didn't seem to extend past Texas. As he watched, the man slid the woman a red-edged poker chip decorated with a blue spiral.

A man with twin anchor tattoos and a sweat-stained tank top left the bar, and Eli squeezed in next to a thin man wearing a dark suit and a black hat. The bartender appeared, an older woman with brittle blond hair, and Eli asked for a bourbon. It seemed to be a good default drink in almost every era they'd visited.

The bartender waited, stared, and after a moment Eli took the hint. One of his coins slid onto the bar. The woman swept it up and replaced it with a glass, then did a slow pour until he signaled her to stop at three fingers. She walked off without a word.

He sniffed the bourbon. It didn't burn his nose as much as the stuff across the street. Next time they were in the late twentieth century, he'd make a point of getting some vodka.

He turned and leaned back against the bar, bumping the man in the suit as he did. Alcohol splashed on the bar. "Sorry."

"No, it's my fault," said a soft voice. She slid her own drink away and tilted the black fedora back to look at him.

"Did you follow . . ." The question dissolved on his tongue.

An ounce or two of baby fat made the detective's face a little rounder and fuller. Twenty, maybe twenty-one years old at the most. Her youthful, smooth skin gleamed in the candlelight. She smiled at him. "Did I follow . . . who?"

"Sorry," he said. "I thought you were somebody else."

"It's the hat."

"Probably."

He tried to look casual as he studied the crowd. She leaned back against the bar, mimicking his pose. Her coat fell open to reveal a loosely knotted tie and a black satin vest that matched her hat. She raised her own glass toward him. "To the dream?"

"To the dream," he agreed. They drank. "Eli."

"Monica."

"Good to meet you, Monica."

"And you, Eli. So, we don't know each other yet?"

"I . . . no, I guess not."

"Such a shame," she said. "You weren't here last night."

"No, I . . . I got in late. Just a few hours ago." He looked at her again. Her clothes were loose at the shoulders and waist, tight across the chest and hips. A man's outfit, not tailored for her frame at all.

"Like what you see?"

"I . . . sorry," he said, his eyes snapping back to hers. "I wasn't . . . I'm still new at this. All the outfits and clothes are still kind of—"

She waved him off. "We're all new at this," she said. "And I grew up in the '70s, Eli." She smiled and clarified, "Nineteen-seventies."

"Still sorry."

"Like the woman says, I will survive." Monica downed the last of her own drink and twisted to put the empty glass on the bar. As she turned back, she reached out and ran a finger across his chin. "If you can't find who you're looking for, come find me. You might get lucky."

She sauntered off into the crowd before he could respond. Then his eyes flitted away and he almost dropped his bourbon.

John Henry stood at the far end of the bar, younger and broader. His big hands gestured as he spoke with a man about Eli's age and two Asian women in contrasting red and black robes. The man looked familiar. Eli added ten years to him, then twenty, and at thirty he recognized Theo Knickerbocker.

John would be part of the wedding party. He'd more or less said so back on his train. He and Harry had known each other for years.

Eli began to scan the crowd in John's area. James stood by the piano with a cigarette in his hand, at least two decades younger than he'd been across the street. Eli caught his breath when he recognized the man.

Then a squeal of laughter echoed over the voices, and Harry rose up out of the crowd.

Like with Monica, the years made a subtle difference. Harry's hair stretched longer. The curves sat smoother on the planes of her face. Her eyes were bright and wide, the lids not weighed down by those extra years.

Her teeth gleamed in the candlelight. A smile stretched across her face and up to her eyes. Happiness beamed out of her like light from the chandeliers.

The man whose shoulders she straddled had to be Christopher. He looked like a large man who'd been wrapped onto an average-sized frame. Big shoulders, big arms, big chest, all squeezed into a black jacket, but still somehow an average-sized man and not a heavy one. His eyes were bright, his golden hair just long enough to be shaggy. He had the same happy aura as Harry. One hand rested on Harry's thigh, balancing her, while the other held a half-empty glass mug.

Eli's attention turned back to Harry. Her vest was a white, satiny thing, and a cluster of snowy ruffles tumbled down the front of her shirt. The wedding gown of a history traveler, Eli mused.

His eyes dropped away. He'd been staring too long at the bride.

Someone was bound to notice, and Eli didn't think he should attract any more attention than necessary. Although he wasn't sure how much that would be either.

He scanned the crowd again. One of the Asian women who'd been speaking with John, the one in black, had wandered over to share James's cigarette. James spoke to her in an offhand way, still focused on the piano player.

Eli looked up at Harry again. She had a drink in her hand, and some of it rained on Christopher as Eli watched. "John," she shouted across the room. "Come toast our happy day with us!"

John's laugh boomed across the crowd. "That was two days ago."

Laughter from the crowd now.

"Then come toast today with us," she cackled.

Eli smiled and turned to watch the room again. Young Theo had wandered across the room to lean over the lumberjack's shoulder. A woman with a long black braid and a battered motorcycle jacket led the other Asian woman, the one in red, upstairs, but kept gazing back at Harry with a wistful smile.

The crowd spat up a woman in front of him. Eli guessed her to be maybe ten or fifteen years older than him, with just enough silver hair for it to stand out. He recognized the woman's leather bonnet, but this close he could see that what he'd mistaken for a brass button back in Pasadena was actually some kind of large coin, or maybe a medal, pinned to the hat. Her trench coat was folded open to reveal a long red scarf and khaki cargo pants. "Begging your pardon," she half-shouted at him, "can you wave down Siobhan?" She pointed past him to the bartender.

He turned and tried to get the woman's attention. How did people get a bartender's attention before there were paper bills or credit cards to flash? Did they wave a quarter back and forth? Shout? The bartender turned and he straightened up, catching her eye. She wandered down and money changed hands.

Eli studied the bonnet. It didn't look much newer than it had in Pasadena. Neither did she. That afternoon couldn't be more than a year or two in her future.

"You're staring," said the woman. "Do we know each other?"

He shook his head.

She gave him a sly smile, showing a set of wide teeth with a narrow gap. "Do we know each other eventually?"

He shook his head again. "No," he said. "I think I saw you at a distance once. You were . . . across the road."

"Oh, that's cryptic," she said. "I like that." She studied his face for a moment and gave a single nod, but said nothing else. Siobhan the bartender brought her a thin bottle and the bonneted woman winked at Eli before vanishing back into the crowd.

Eli turned to look for Harry and Christopher again. She'd dropped back into the crowd. John had waded over to her and their conversation now included young Theo. The man did get around.

The crowd parted and Eli glimpsed a large man in army green sitting at a table across the room. The crowd shifted again and he got another look. The man's mouth and brow formed two flat, parallel lines above and below his eyes. They made the stern face look even more like a block. Something about it seemed familiar.

The face or the expression.

Five years ago—or a hundred and thirty years from now—Eli'd been the best man at Corey and Robin's wedding. Not the youngest couple he'd seen get married, but still pretty young even with a little hindsight. A few times at the reception, Eli had happened to glimpse Robin's father watching all the barely-out-of-college kids drinking and dancing and celebrating, and more than a few of them making out right there on the dance floor.

Robin's father had smiled proudly for photos and whenever his daughter and new son-in-law looked at him. But his overall expression, his mood, had been disappointment. At the wedding. At the behavior. At the public displays of affection.

The man on the far side of the First Time Around was proud of all this, but on some level the party disappointed him.

Just as Eli realized who the man had to be, Abraham Porter's eyes shifted and locked onto Eli's. He gave a faint, polite nod of acknowledgment, maybe even a hair of approval. Then the crowd shifted again and Porter vanished.

Eli lifted his drink and let his eyes slide over the crowd. Where had Christopher gone? Had he ducked into a bathroom—or run to an outhouse? Had he—

Something slammed into his back and shook his teeth. A hand like a baseball mitt. "Siobhan," bellowed a voice. "Another round of the good stuff for the party. And one for my new friend here."

Christopher dropped against the bar. His brilliant blue eyes swept up and down Eli even as he brushed his scruffy hair back across his scalp. "Do I know you?"

Eli shook his head.

The other man studied his face and grinned. "Am I going to know you?"

"I don't think so."

The bartender set down two glasses, each brimming with at least a triple of something that smelled of Halloween candy and wood fire smoke.

"I only ask," said Christopher, "because you seem to have such a keen interest in me and my lovely new bride."

Eli glanced back at Harry again. He reached for one of the glasses and Christopher set a hand on his arm. It was a gentle touch, but Eli felt the strength lurking behind it.

"It's my wedding," said the broad-shouldered man. "I want it to be a happy, peaceful celebration without any trouble. But if trouble comes looking for me and the folks I love, well . . . I'll still do what needs to be done."

"Nothing needs to be done," Eli said. "Honest."

"Excellent." Christopher moved his hand. He picked up one of the glasses and nudged the other toward Eli. "To the happy couple," he said with a grin.

"To the happy couple," echoed Eli.

They drank. Eli gasped. Christopher chuckled and slapped him on the arm. A few drops of liquor flew from Eli's glass to the floor.

"It's a bit strong," said Christopher. "Puts hair on your chest. And a few other places too." He raised his glass again and Eli tried to keep up.

"Thank you," said Eli. "For the drink."

"The groom pays for everything. That's what my da taught me." He looked at Eli's clothes again. "Nineteen . . . seventies?"

"Eighties," Eli said. "Sort of. I think."

"Oh, swell times," said Christopher. "I spent more than a few nights then before my Harry made an honest man out of me."

"It's a nice place," said Eli. "Or time, I guess."

"From the 1920s myself," said Christopher. "Used to be a banker, believe it or not."

"Really?"

He nodded sagely. "Worst of the worst. Just a grubby step or two above being a loan shark."

"What happened?"

"The crash," he said. "Invested poorly, lost everything. Wealthy as Midas one morning, poor as a priest the next night. I was trying to throw myself off the Brooklyn Bridge when a woman grabbed me."

"Phoebe Fitzgerald?"

Christopher's brow shifted. "You know Phoebe?"

"Reputation only."

He mulled over the phrase and nodded in approval. "She's a good woman." He gazed across the room. "I owe her a lot."

Eli followed his gaze. "Is she here? I thought she was . . ." His tongue tripped over the words. "I mean, for me she's . . ." This time he made no attempt to recover and let his tongue face-plant between his teeth.

"Still a bit wet behind the ears, aren't you?" Christopher raised his glass again. "No insult meant. Took me months to wrap my noggin' around it all. Harry, she's brilliant and it took her two or three weeks. It's a strange life we've chosen, and it can be a lot to take in."

Eli nodded in agreement.

"How long have you been on the road?"

"Ummmm . . . about a week now, I think, actively. Maybe six days."

"Six days. Christ on a crutch. And you're already in Hourglass. Took me almost a year just to hear about this place." Christopher finished off his drink and waved to the bartender. "Shut me off after this next one, Siobhan," he said, "or I won't be able to perform my duties tonight."

The bartender laughed as she poured another two fingers into the glass.

"So," Christopher said, raising his fresh drink, "you know of

Phoebe, but you don't know me, and you were staring at me and my lovely bride. Which makes me wonder if you were just staring at her."

Eli sipped his own glass. The liquor steamed in his throat. He'd barely finished half his first drink.

Christopher gulped another mouthful. "Can't fault you for that. She's a fine-looking woman. Couldn't take my eyes off her from the first time I saw her." He looked at Eli. "That's not why you're staring, though, is it? You know her."

Eli mimed taking a long drink of his own, but let most of it wash into his mouth and back out into the glass. The vapors numbed his tongue. He glanced at the door. There were almost a dozen people between him and the swinging panels. If he understood the rules, the other man wouldn't follow him into the other bar.

"Nineteen-eighties means you're not from her past," Christopher said, tapping his finger against his tumbler. "I'm guessing we meet up sometime in the future? And you decided to come back and invite yourself to the wedding reception."

"She brought me," Eli said, and regretted it.

"Ahhh," said Christopher, his smile growing. "You're traveling with us. You snuck over here from the Second Iteration, didn't you? You cheeky bastard. Porter'll slap you silly if he finds out." He took another big mouthful of his drink.

"I don't think I'm supposed to say anything. Rules and all." Eli looked over at the crowd of people around the bride. "You should be getting back to the party, shouldn't you?"

Christopher paused. "She brought you," he echoed. "She brought you, but you don't know me."

Eli watched the man's face soften. Christopher's eyes shifted to the distant bride.

"Ahhh." He set his glass down on the bar. "Them? The faceless men?"

Eli thought about cryptic answers, then direct ones, and ended up studying the half inch of liquid at the bottom of his glass. An answer in itself.

Christopher's lips tightened. "Do you know when?"

"I . . . I really don't think I'm supposed to talk about it."

"I won't tell anyone if you don't," he said. "Call it a wedding gift."

Eli's gaze shifted from the bourbon to the polished surface of the bar. He didn't know much about woodwork, but he guessed the dark planks of the bar hadn't been cheap. They made the chalky rings from past glasses stand out.

Christopher closed his eyes. "Nah," he said. "You're right. Better if I don't know. Just . . ." He looked out across the room at the young Harry. "They don't hurt her, do they? Tell me that at least."

"No." Eli shook his head. "No, she's fine. I mean, she's fine now, so if she was hurt then it wasn't bad. Not physically hurt," he added. "She's still . . ."

"Yes?"

"She doesn't talk about it much."

"Still recent?"

"No. I mean, not today. Or, not when I know her. She's not going to meet me for another nine years, I think. At that point, for her, it's been almost . . ."

Eli stopped and looked over at Harry. She'd paused in her celebrating and now stared across the room at the bar. At her husband talking with the man in the short wool coat and the derby.

Eli studied his drink again. Christopher studied his.

"You want to know an ugly truth?" He waved his glass at the crowd without waiting for an answer. "This party isn't for me and Harry. Part of it is, sure. But the reason everyone is so happy is because they don't have to accept the future yet."

"What do you mean?"

Christopher looked at him. "I saw you talking with Alice a few minutes ago. Phoebe's here too. So's Abraham." He glanced across the room and took a slow breath. "More than half the people in this room are dead, from my point of view. Most of them were killed. Murdered. Everyone who makes it over to the Second Iteration either knows how they're going to die or how someone they care about is going to die, if they haven't already. Traveling through history, like we do . . . it's all about meeting ghosts. And eventually realizing we're all somebody's ghost."

They leaned against the bar for a moment, not talking or drinking.

"I should get back to Harry," said Christopher. He smiled at Eli. "Thank you."

"For what?"

The broad man lifted his glass and downed the last of his drink with two deep swallows. "You've told me I get to spend the rest of my life with the person I love most in this world. What more could anyone ask for?"

Christopher gave Eli one last pat on the back, set his glass on the bar, and pushed back into the crowd. He waded through to Harry, who glanced from her husband to Eli and back. Then Christopher swept her into his arms and she smiled and the searchers around them laughed at something he said.

People surrounded them again and they vanished from sight.

Eli took another look around the bar. Part of him wanted to finish his drink, and maybe spend his other quarter to get one more bourbon. Maybe flirt with Monica again. It seemed like a waste to leave before he had to, considering he could never come back again.

But he couldn't stay. Harry hadn't mentioned the man in the derby hanging around.

He took a last sip of his drink and left it sitting on the bar with a half inch still in the bottom of the glass.

Eli paused at the door to glance over his shoulder, the crowd parted one more time, and the last face he saw in the First Time Around ended up being Abraham Porter, still leaning back in his booth, although the woman with the leather bonnet had joined him. Something about the large man still set off little twinges of déjà vu.

Eli pushed the blue doors apart and stepped out into the dark night of Hourglass. They closed behind him with a faint creak, just loud enough to be heard over the music and voices.

The night watchman had vanished again. Down one side street or another. Or maybe he just went home after a certain point. The dark form of another figure wandered up the main road, a woman from the sway of the hips.

And then something hit the back of Eli's head and sent a tremor echoing forward through his skull. The world spun, his legs collapsed, and everything went black before the tremor even reached his eyes.

31

The first pain, the one in his head, dragged Eli back to consciousness. He tried to lift his chin, and the pain in his neck and shoulders made him aware of his body. He tried to take a breath and a constricting pain tightened around his chest.

"I think he's awake."

Someone poked him twice in the breastbone. Thick fingers grabbed his chin and wrenched his head left and right. He tried to slap the hands away, but his own hands . . .

Coarse rope held his hands up over his head and pressed them tight together. He tugged and felt it bite at his wrists. The muscles of his arms ached.

He flexed his ankles and found nothing beneath his feet. He stretched his toes down. Still nothing, but now his body rocked with the movement.

Eli opened his eyes, blinked away the last dark cobwebs, and looked around.

A fire pit burned at the center of the room. It and two lanterns threw flickering shadows in every direction. Patches of straw covered the dirt floor, which sat a good six inches farther away than he was used to seeing floors. A few posts of bare wood broke up the space and stretched up into the exposed rafters. The closest post—or would it be a beam?—had a pair of black-iron horseshoes nailed to it, the prongs pointed up into the darkness. A coil of rope hung alongside the horseshoes, either on a hook or a bent nail. He looked around, tried to spot a door, but the space was just big enough that the flickering firelight couldn't reach to illuminate the walls.

"Finally," muttered a familiar voice. "Was starting to think you'd need a goddamned bucket of water thrown in your face."

A strong hand settled on Eli's shoulder and pushed. He glanced back, caught a glimpse of fire-red hair, and felt a taut rope bounce against the back of his skull. It hit a tender spot and electric pain flared behind his eyes.

Svetlana shoved him, turned him more.

Truss sat on a crate. A blanket had been spread beneath him so his expensive clothes didn't touch the bare wood. He peered at Eli over his square glasses. "You've probably got a few things you want to spit out. Might as well get that over with."

"What the hell is this? What do you think you're doing?" A chill ran through Eli's arms. He didn't know where his coat had gone. "What the hell do you want from me?"

Truss examined his fingernails.

Eli kicked and pulled and swung back and forth. He thrashed and felt the cord under his arms cut and bite at the soft skin there. The coarse rope scraped his wrists raw and plucked at the hairs on the back of his head. It hit the lump where he'd been knocked out and sparks flashed behind his eyelids again.

Exhaustion waited for an opening, lunged in, and dragged his legs back down. He took a few deep breaths and struggled against the double-loop of rope over his chest. He tried to slump and his shoulders and neck and wrists ached.

Truss yawned. "You're thinking of me as some sort of criminal, Teak, am I right? I'm sure Pritchard and her—"

"Teague."

The old man raised a shaggy brow.

"My name isn't Teak. It's Teague."

Truss glanced at Svetlana. The big woman gave a single nod. He shrugged. "Still got some backbone," he said. "That's good."

Eli glared at him.

"I'm sure Pritchard and her friends have filled your head with all sorts of stories. But you know me. You've known me for . . . five years?"

Svetlana held up both hands, six fingers.

"Six years. I think you know me better than they do. You've worked for me. You know I'm a businessman. I don't have anything personal against you or them."

"That'd sound a lot better if I wasn't strung up in a barn."

The old man's face split in a grin. "Truth be told, it isn't personal. I don't care about any of you. Not in the slightest. You're assets, to be used and discarded. Assuming you're even worth the effort of discarding."

Eli glared at the old man. His wrists ached. Something trickled from his armpits that could've been sweat or blood. Maybe both.

"And I know you too," said Truss. "At least, I know your type."

"A minute ago," Eli muttered, "you didn't even know my name."

The old man's too-white grin widened. "You ended up on the road by accident, didn't you? Lured into a car by Pritchard's charms? Or did you just see something you shouldn't have?" He pointed a bony finger at Eli. "You don't want to be on the road. I've seen it dozens of times. You just want to go home to your nice, safe, normal life. And I can make that happen.

"One question, Mr. Teague. Answer it honestly. This is your only chance to walk out of here. Your last chance to get the carrot. Lie to me, try to string me along, and it won't go well for you. Understand?"

Eli nodded. The movement made his head throb again. Memories of Sanders, his mother, his friends his life—they all flitted across his mind. Regular meals, regular showers, a real bed. He imagined going home with even a fraction of the money Truss had promised them in New Orleans, and all the things he could do with it.

Truss adjusted his glasses on his nose. "So?"

"Even if I knew anything," Eli grunted, "I wouldn't tell you."

The old man shook his head and sighed. "Fine, then."

Something scraped in the dirt behind him. He heard a short muffled screech, then a longer one. The dragging sounds stopped for a moment, then came closer to Eli. He twisted his head around and set his body swaying again.

Svetlana came into sight and grunted. Her broad shoulders flexed and she pulled her burden alongside Eli. Another heave brought it between Eli and Truss. She made a final small adjustment and then walked off behind Eli again.

Two wide planks made up the top of the workbench. Cuts and gouges and small holes covered the surface. The legs looked the same, but with less wear and tear.

A thick wooden dowel, almost a broomstick, pinned two big blocks of wood to the side of the workbench closest to Eli's legs. Threads ran the length of the dowel, like a huge wooden screw, with a heavy crossbar at the far end. Together, the two blocks could've filled a shoebox.

Eli realized what the contraption was just as Svetlana came back and dropped a hammer on the workbench. It had a long handle and the head of a small sledge, just a rough block of steel with a little bit of shaping on the edges. It looked like the kind of thing a blacksmith would pound an anvil with.

Truss pushed himself up off the crate. He stepped forward and put himself on the opposite side of the workbench. His fingers danced on the planks like a man playing piano. "Now, let's be clear about something, Teague. I'm going to have my woman here break both of your knees."

Eli tried to kick off the bench, to put some distance between himself and it, but Svetlana set a strong hand against his back and kept him hanging in place. He tried to swing his legs back, to shove the woman away. Knuckles rapped against the lump on his head again.

"It's going to happen," Truss continued. "Three things you can take as absolute fact—you're going to pay taxes, you're going to die someday, and tonight both your knees will be smashed into gravel. The only question, the one uncertainty you're facing, is how it's going to happen. And that's entirely up to you."

Eli looked down at the workbench.

"Tell me what I want to know, when I ask, and it'll be quick. Two blows with the hammer. Badda-bing, badda-boom. You'll scream a lot, believe me, I've seen her do it many times before. But—it'll be over in seconds. You'll pass out and by the time you wake up your body will have already reset your nerves to make it less painful.

"String me along or refuse to answer, and I'll have her put your knees in the vise. One at a time." Truss spread his fingers at the wooden blocks, a geriatric spokesmodel displaying the latest in torture equipment. "We'll take three hours to turn the crank for each one. Three hours of pressure for each kneecap before they break and pop and get crushed down into shards and powder. Six hours altogether. Maybe more.

"If, somehow, you're still not talking—I've seen this dozens of times and it's never failed to get me an answer, but I'm willing to give you the benefit of the doubt—if you're still not willing to talk after the knees, we'll move on to your elbows. Do you understand?"

"Yes," said Eli. "Yeah, I understand."

"And you believe me?"

Eli stared into the old man's cold eyes. "Yeah. I do."

"Then let's begin." Truss moved back to his crate and sat down. It struck Eli that what he'd mistaken for a blanket was his own coat. "Has she found it yet?"

"What?"

"Your girlfriend. Mrs. Pritchard. Has she actually found it? Does she know where it is?"

"Look," said Eli, "I don't know anything. I've barely been part of this for a week. Anybody—everybody in this town knows more than me. I still don't even know how—"

"Shut him up."

Svetlana rapped Eli on the back of the head. Right on the lump. Eli's head pulsed and his vision faded to gray for a moment.

"Loyal to a fault," muttered the old man. "Put his leg in it."

Svetlana grabbed Eli's foot and swung his legs forward. Eli tried to fight, tried to jerk his leg away, but the woman's grip was like iron. Eli's right knee bumped against the side of the vise once, twice, and then slipped between the two blocks.

He threw his weight back and tried to pull free. Svetlana snapped a fist out and caught Eli in the gut. The backhand made his muscles spasm, and for a moment or three he gasped, drowning in the air. By the time he found his breath, she'd spun the crossbar and tightened the vise on Eli's kneecap.

The pressure felt like kneeling on a hard floor. It came from each side, though. The vise had a firm grip, just enough to worry Eli that thrashing or pulling might wreck his knee faster than the vise could.

"You were a good employee, Teague, as I recall. Brave enough to stand up to the old man, yes? I'll give you one more chance. The maul instead of the vise." He leaned forward and stared over his square lenses at Eli. "Does she have it?"

Eli set his jaw and gazed past Truss. He focused on the horseshoes. He could deal with the discomfort of the vise for an hour or so. Long enough for Harry to find him. She couldn't be far.

Truss shook his head and gestured at Svetlana.

A gasp slipped off Eli's tongue before he could stop it. In one second the mild discomfort jumped to actual pain. Senior year of college, he'd dabbled with Buddhism for a month to impress a redhead whose name he couldn't even remember. Two hours of kneeling on the student center's threadbare carpet convinced him that nothing the poli-sci major could offer him would be worth putting his knees through that again.

The pressure on each side of his knee was worse than two hours of kneeling on carpet-covered concrete.

"That's half a turn," said Truss. "At this width, there's about twenty-two threads between the sides of the vise. That means we can tighten it by the same amount forty-three more times."

He glanced at Svetlana, and the big woman wrenched the crossbar around again.

Eli screamed. Light flashed behind his eyes as nails of pain squeezed into his knee. He thrashed against his ropes but the vise had him. Flailing just made his leg twist around the unmoving knee. He sucked in three sharp breaths and heard a moan rattle behind his teeth.

Truss left him like that for a minute. A full, seconds-ticking-away minute. A few deep breaths helped Eli focus past the pain and get his heartbeat under control.

The old man kicked his toes against the bench. The tremors echoed up through the vise. "You can feel free to scream more, if you like," he said. "No one will hear you. We're almost a mile outside of town. North side, away from where everyone parks. No one comes out this way."

Eli managed to bite back a moan.

Truss studied his nails again. "Has she found it already?"

Eli tried to clear his head. Harry'd mentioned how valuable information could be on the road. Theo had made a living selling clues and factoids. She'd mentioned how important having the advantage could be.

He hoped she'd forgive him.

"I don't know," he said, shaking his head. "Maybe. There's a guy in New Orleans. We were going to double back and question him again, but she got worried when you showed up."

The old man's lined face twisted into a snarl. "What guy in New Orleans?"

"Hawkins. Frank Hawkins. He's a miner, a prospector, whatever you'd call him. We backtracked to him, and he acted like he wasn't inspired by the dream, but we think he was hiding something."

"The dream?" spat Truss. He shot a look past Eli to Svetlana. "I don't care about the damned dream. Has she found the *favor*?"

Eli blinked. "The . . . what?"

The old man's snarl turned to a look of disgust. "I thought you were smarter than this." He glanced at Svetlana. "Give him a full turn."

32

on't," said a voice behind him. One word, calm and cold.

Truss and Svetlana both looked past Eli. Svetlana pushed her hand into her coat, but a bark from the newcomer stopped her. Eli tried to swing himself around, but it only made his trapped knee ignite again.

The old man glanced at the wall, at the outside.

"No," said Harry's voice. "She won't be waking up anytime soon, and when she does, she's going to have a nasty scar."

"Didn't kill her, then?"

"Saving all the bullets for you," she said sweetly. "Can you walk, Eli?"

"Maybe," he grunted.

"Release him," she said.

"I'm glad you're here," said Truss. "Better to have this talk face-to-face."

"We have nothing to talk about," said Harry. Her voice sounded sharper, closer. "Release Eli. Now."

"Well, well, well," the old man said. "We find ourselves negotiating after all. I'm holding something you want. You're holding something I want."

"I'm holding a .45 pointed at your head. I'd be careful about saying what you want right now."

"You have it, don't you?" His smile was half awe, half greed. "You've got the favor."

"I don't know what you're—"

"Don't play the fool with me," snapped Truss. "You've got Porter's favor! The only one he ever gave out."

Silence crashed down on the barn, broken by the sound of wind stretching tight across the building's corners.

"A simple trade," the old man said. "Give me the favor, I give you Teague. Everyone's happy."

"Seeing as I still have this gun pointed at your head," said Harry, "my counteroffer is that you cut him down and I'll make an honest effort not to shoot you."

Truss leered at her. "You're very impressive, Pritchard, but I think you're still not seeing the big picture." He tipped his head toward Eli and Svetlana. "From where I'm sitting, I can see the knife my woman's holding to Teague's leg. That's the . . . the femoral artery?"

Svetlana grunted.

"Eli?" asked Harry.

"Yeah," he called into his armpit, "still here."

"The knife?"

Eli glanced down. The matte-black blade looked like plastic, or maybe some kind of ceramic. Both sides had an edge and a curve, giving it a leaflike shape. The point pressed hard enough against Eli's jeans that he couldn't see the tip. "Very real."

Truss's leer spread. "Stalemate. Back to negotiations."

"What guarantee do I have you'll let him go?"

The old man snorted. "As I was just telling our mutual friend here, I couldn't care less about the two of you. I just want the favor."

A new sound rumbled beneath the gusts of wind. A distant engine, growing closer. Truss's eyes flitted back and forth behind his lenses.

"Sounds like Helena's back on her feet and behind the wheel. She'll be here soon, and then our negotiations will be at an end. Three to one."

"Three to two," said Harry.

"I don't think Teague is in a position to help, but if you want to pass him one of your pistols, you're welcome to." Truss glanced up at Eli's bound hands. "Assuming you can reach."

The engine's rumble grew louder. Eli couldn't be sure in the quiet of 1886, but he guessed the car to be maybe two, maybe three miles away and closing.

"Take the knife away and we'll talk," Harry said.

"Give me the favor and I'll have her take the knife away."

"I don't have it on me," said Harry.

The old man shook his head. "That's a shame. Make Teague bleed a little."

"I said I didn't have it on me," she repeated. "I didn't say it wasn't here."

Truss scowled, then understanding lifted his brows. He looked up at Eli. "You've been holding out on me."

"No," said Eli. "No, I haven't."

"He doesn't know," Harry said. "I slipped it into his jacket pocket."

The old man's eyes went wide behind the square lenses. He twisted to look at the wool coat spread across the crate. He took a step toward it.

"Ah-ahh," said Harry. "Not another inch until Eli's down."

Truss stepped anyway and stretched out greedy fingers.

Harry shot the coat. The crate bucked as the blast rang out between the barn's planks. Truss shouted out some creative swears. Eli cringed, Svetlana flinched, and the tip of the knife pricked Eli's thigh.

"Eli comes down," Harry repeated.

As the sound of the gunshot faded, the engine sound returned. It was louder than the wind now. Eli recognized it.

"Now," he said, trying to twist his head back. He forced his voice to stay calm. "Get me down now."

Truss reached back, never taking his eyes off the wool coat, and waved at Svetlana. The big woman looked up at Eli and shook her head. She pulled the knife away and spun the crossbar on the vise.

The pressure vanished so fast Eli gasped from the sudden lack of pain. Then he swung away from the bench and began to creak back and forth. He turned on the rope and Harry came into view. Her tricorne was mashed down on her head. The Colts stretched out before her, one aimed at each of Eli's captors.

Svetlana did something and he dropped a few inches. The dirt floor slapped up against his soles. His knee flared and static roared through his brain. He wobbled, lashed out, and grabbed a sleeve. He pulled, tried to lift his leg and get his balance at the same time. His spine felt long and loose.

The sleeve belonged to Svetlana. The big woman made no effort to brush Eli off, but also none to steady him further. She just stared at Eli like someone who'd found an odd-colored stain on her arm.

Harry stepped forward. "Come to me, Eli."

He pushed off the big woman and staggered over to Harry. Staples and thumbtacks filled the space around his knee, biting with every step. She flung her arm around his back, and he threw one across her shoulders. The pistol under his arm settled back on Svetlana.

"It's okay," she said. "I've got you."

Eli saw his hat on a lopsided chair. He snatched it up, pressed it down on his head, and leaned close to Harry. "We have to go," he whispered. "Now."

"I can hold them off."

"It's not them I'm worried about."

Their eyes met. She stared at him, trying to read his expression. Then her mouth wavered and she swallowed. Eli gave the smallest nod he could.

"But they can't come to Hourglass," she murmured under her breath.

"We're not in Hourglass," Eli whispered back.

"If you're sure your boy-toy's unharmed . . . ?" Truss said. His fingers stretched and clawed at the air.

Harry kept the gun on Svetlana, gestured with the one covering the old man.

Truss scurried to the coat. His fingers searched across the wool and worked their way into one of the pockets. Then they slid over, plunged into the second pocket, and flailed inside. His gasp sounded like old-man sex. He withdrew from the pocket, his fist tight. He scuttled to one of the lamps.

Harry glanced at Eli's knee. "Can you walk?"

"I can manage."

Truss held the small disk up to the light. His ecstatic look faded to a scowl. "This isn't it," he snarled. "This isn't even a goddamned favor. It's not marked." He flipped the green-edged poker chip between his fingers, then flung it at the fire pit.

"Buyer beware," Harry called across the room.

Outside the barn, the car engine roared like a monster come to life.

The Hudson Hornet smashed through the plank wall, a battering ram of black steel and chrome. Splinters and nails darted in every direction. Truss made a loud squawking noise like a frightened bird. One of the lanterns flew across the room, just missing Svetlana and exploding against a beam. Oil splashed across wood and straw before igniting.

The Hornet's doors swung open like spreading wings. The tall faceless man from Boston stepped out of the driver's side. The shorter one from Independence emerged across from him.

"Hello," they said in unison.

Flames from the lamp already covered a quarter of the barn. Svetlana moved to put herself between Truss and the faceless men, even though it pushed her employer closer to the flames. Harry elbowed Eli back toward the door while trying to keep all their enemies at gunpoint.

The smaller faceless man drew his pistol, a huge semiautomatic, and aimed it at Eli. His shoulders tensed. "Eli Teague," he said. His free hand twitched and flexed at his side, clenching into a fist. Open, closed. Open, closed.

Eli limped backward and stared at the smaller faceless man. His eyes stretched wide in the fire-dry air. "Zeke?"

The name staggered the faceless man. The arrogance flowed out of his stance. His fingers twitched open and trembled.

"Zeke, what did they—"

"Zero!" snapped the tall faceless man. "Stay on mission."

Zeke—Zero—clenched his fist one last time.

He shot Eli.

Pain thrust into Eli's aching shoulder and exploded into hot knives.

Svetlana raised her pistol and fired, squeezing the trigger again and again. A bullet sparked off the Hornet's door. The tall faceless man jerked once, twice, and then his head snapped to the side.

"Fifteen!" snarled Zero. His pistol swung around and shot Svetlana. The round plowed through the top of her scalp and sent part of it spraying back into the flames. A river of blood washed down over her eyes as she tumbled back.

Truss shrieked again.

Eli wobbled, his shoulder a mass of burning, grinding shards that blotted out the pain in his knee. Harry grabbed him by the waist before he could fall over. She dragged him away from the fire and toward the door. His head lolled back and he locked eyes with Truss through the smoke. The old man scurried after them, then backtracked to go around a pile of burning hay.

The tall faceless man, Fifteen, straightened up. He rolled his head twice and his neck gave out a loud pop. The thin plastic of his mask was cracked and curled along one cheek. "Archibald Truss," he said, his voice booming over the fire. "Also known as Reginald Truss, Aristotle Truss and Edward Longcarriage."

"Please understand," said the old man, "I'm no threat to you. I'm not even interested in the dream. Never looked for it once. I just want to conduct my business—"

Fifteen reached into his coat and slid his own pistol from its hidden holster.

Harry swung Eli around, and flames replaced his view. The temperature in the barn had to be close to a hundred degrees, and rising fast. The flames crawled across the rafters and inched down the beams. Clouds of smoke billowed near the barn's ceiling, but crept downward.

"Pritchard!" shrieked the old man from across the room. "Call in the favor! I'll give you whatev—"

Another gunshot echoed behind them. Truss stopped pleading.

"Eli Teague," shouted Zero. Whatever other comments he had vanished beneath the sound of his pistol.

Harry kicked the door open and dragged Eli through.

The outside hit him like he'd been pushed into a pool of ice water. It seemed ink-black after the eye-squinting brightness of the burning barn. Harry kept pulling on his waist and Eli staggered after her. His feet kicked stones he couldn't see and stumbled on the uneven ground. The razors of hot pain in his knee and shoulder stabbed at every nerve.

"Come on," Harry gasped. "Eleanor's this way."

The cold air gnawed at his face and hands, but sweat drenched his torso inside his shirt. He could feel it dripping down his back and chest. He tried to catch his breath and Harry yanked him forward again.

Eli blinked once, twice, thrice and the world rose up out of the darkness. He could see a few scraggly bushes and patches of grass. Orange light played off a boulder to his left. Touches of it flickered across the landscape. It stood out against the pale moonlight blanketing everything else.

His eyes adjusted and the dark-blue blur next to him became Harry.

She stepped over a pale log. He tried to follow her, caught his toe, and almost fell. He turned it into a low-hanging stagger and pushed himself back up with his next few steps. It made his knee scream and his shoulder howl.

A few more steps and a shape in the distance resolved into the familiar lines of Eleanor. Maybe another hundred feet. Eli felt dizzy and cold, but he could make another hundred feet. He wished he still had his coat. He'd have to grab one of the blankets once they were away.

He blinked again. He could feel the sweat drenching his body and his clothes, but shivers ran through his limbs. His fingers bordered on painfully cold.

Only one side of his body was sweating.

He reached up and touched his shoulder. Raw pain cut into his flesh and he yanked his hand back. The warm sweat on his fingers was dark in the moonlight.

Dark and sticky.

Harry glanced over at him. "Not far now." Then the relief on her face shifted to worry. She staggered to a halt. "Eli?"

He leaned into her, then looked down at his bloodstained shirt. It gleamed wet and dark. "We," he said, "we should get to the car."

Then the world whirled around him and became ink-black again.

33

First, he became aware of background noises and voices. They had the tones and echoes of a big room. Then the world behind his eyelids brightened. He felt the crisp sheets on his chest and a spongy, crinkling mattress against his back. The smells of laundry and latex and linen and antiseptic all tickled his nostrils.

At which point, Eli had to admit he was awake and opened his eyes.

He blinked at the bright lights set into a white ceiling. He turned to the side, felt a twinge in his shoulder, and tried to focus on the bank of instruments. He saw a trio of bouncing lines and shifting numbers and some smaller numbers and a few other things he didn't understand.

He turned the other way, blinked a few more times, and found Harry watching him from her chair. Her face looked pale, and her sleeves and collar glared white in the harsh lights. Her vest hung loose, and her coat draped over the chair behind her. A medical-green curtain stretched around them.

"It's small comfort, I'm sure," she said, "but you've convinced me you're not working for Mr. Truss."

Eli coughed out a weak laugh that scraped in his throat. "I hate you so much right now."

"That's the spirit." She reached out and squeezed his arm. Her hand stayed there, just above his wrist. "I spent two days searching the town for you, and when I remembered the fire at the old barn I circled back to look there."

"You . . . you used your third time in Hourglass?"

"Sort of," she said. "I never went to the Last Paradox, so I don't think it counts."

He swallowed and tried to wet his throat. She seemed to understand, reached behind her, and came back with a squared-off bottle of water. She set it in his hands and helped guide it to his mouth. The water was delicious. The plastic felt thready. He glanced at it and frowned.

"Cellulose bottle," she said. "They're all the rage right now."

He furrowed his brow. "Where are we? When?"

Harry leaned in closer. "It's a public clinic in Reno. 2031."

"We're in the future?"

She squeezed his arm again, sharper this time. "Keep your voice down. We've attracted too much attention as it is. Don't need anyone hauling you off to the madhouse."

He looked around the curtained-off area. The movement tugged at the base of his neck and he felt another dull ache. Bandages wrapped his shoulder in a blinding-white cocoon. His mind pulled out some fuzzy memories and wiped the dust from them. "He shot me?"

"The faceless man," she said with a nod. "Shattered your shoulder blade, tore up several muscles, although some of that may have been Truss stringing you up in the air. You lost a lot of blood." She paused. "A *lot* of blood. I got us away from Hourglass, plastered you up as best I could, and brought you here."

"All the way to Reno?"

"It wasn't that far, relatively speaking. Easy to get to, lots of ways to get out. In a big city, a nonlethal shooting doesn't stand out as much as it would in a small town."

He looked at the bandages again. "What did they do?"

"Cleaned you up. Infused you with several pints of blood. Glued you back together and wrapped your shoulder blade in a protein sheath. Your kneecap, as well. You're going to have scars, but you should be fine."

He tried to raise the water bottle, got it halfway to his mouth. "But . . . ?"

Harry lifted his arm the rest of the way. "But," she said, "we still showed up at a public clinic in the middle of the night with a bullet wound. Plus, your driver's license is over ten years expired, and I don't have one, so they're fairly sure we're giving false identification." She glanced over her shoulder again. "I overheard one of the nurses saying the police should be here in half an hour, and that was ten minutes ago. I don't know that the faceless men have traced us here, but just in case . . ."

He nodded. "We should leave."

"Yes, we should."

Another memory floated up into his consciousness and shook the cobwebs from itself. "Zeke," he said. "The other faceless man, the one he called Zero. That was Zeke Miller."

Harry's face dropped. "You know him?"

"Most of my life, yeah. We're not friends or anything. He's been a jerk pretty much since I met him in kindergarten. A bully."

"Was he the one who hit you with the rock?"

Eli blinked, frowned, and then a few more memories drifted into view. "Yeah, that was him," he said. "What did they do to him?"

She looked away. "They made him into one of them."

"Why? Why him?"

"I don't know."

"It can't be coincidence, right? I find you and they take him."

She shook her head. "We're fortunate. He must still be getting used to seeing the world the way they do."

"What makes you say that?"

She shrugged. "Because they don't miss, and he hit you in the shoulder instead of in the head."

Eli snorted and tried to sit up. Harry stood up and helped pull him forward. "That probably wasn't an accident," he said. "Zeke's pretty much a sadistic bastard. Not really a surprise he'd go for hurting someone over killing them."

"It's doubtful there's very much of him left."

He swung his feet over the side of the bed and paused to gather his strength. His head felt empty. Wobbly. Harry ducked down and pulled his shoes from beneath the hospital bed just as he realized he only had socks on. She forced the left shoe over his toes, pulled it onto his heel, and tied a fast knot in the laces.

Eli looked at his arm and bare chest, at the wires and tubes running off them. A little thing like a plastic clothespin surrounded one fingertip. He reached to pull one of the pads off his chest, but Harry held out a hand to stop him. "They'll see if the readings stop," she explained. "Wait until we're ready to go." She picked up the other shoe.

He peeled off the tape holding his IV in place. In the movies, people yanked tubes from their arms without hesitation, but he felt pretty sure there'd be blood everywhere if he tried it. He pinched the needle between his thumb and forefinger, pulled, and watched the sliver of white plastic slide out of his arm.

Harry got his second shoe on and helped him to his feet. The wires connecting him to the machines pulled tight, so he turned to create some slack. "Shirt?"

"Cut off you when we arrived, and too bloody to wear, regardless. Arms back."

He flicked the clip off his finger, obeyed Harry, and watched the three bouncing lines on one screen go flat. She worked something over his hands and wrists. He shrugged the sleeves up his arms and marveled at how little his shoulder and knee hurt. The future had some fantastic painkillers.

The sleeves tightened on his arms as the jacket came up over his shoulders. Harry's frock coat. It couldn't close in the front.

"Not perfect," she said, stepping to his side, "but it'll have to do." She reached up and pulled the wires loose from his chest. "Let's go."

She put one arm around his waist and used the other to pull the green curtains open. A dozen other curtains made semicircles around the room, small tents to give the low-budget illusion of privacy. Harry guided Eli past them all to a wide door. Her hand reached out and snatched something off a cart—a white paper bag, folded over and stapled shut. "Hey," someone called out. An older woman's voice. Harry ignored it.

They pushed the door open. She held the bag in front of them, flipping it around so she held it up from underneath. A lean man in scrubs glanced at them, then went back to typing on a keypad.

Eli's head and neck felt very light and loose. His knees wobbled. Harry swung his good arm over her shoulder. "There we go," she said in her loud and bright voice.

The orderly didn't look up again.

Another set of doors led them into a waiting room. Bright-orange chairs stood in back-to-back rows. Dozens of men, women, and children sat and waited. Some had visible cuts or bruises, others just looked bored. A television up near the ceiling showed two women in waitress uniforms while a laugh track blared from a crackling speaker.

Across the room, a pair of policemen wandered in through the main door. One of them looked young-trying-to-appear-tough, the other had the gray brows of a tired veteran. They scanned the room in a practiced way. The older one's gaze settled on Harry and Eli.

Harry didn't break stride. She pulled Eli past the chairs and right up to the older officer. "Excuse me," she said, her voice just a hair too sharp. "I'm trying to get him outside before he throws up again." She waved the bag at the officer, trusting the medication would make her point.

Eli tried to mime a heaving stomach, but set off another bout of lightheadedness. His head swung forward. He reached out to find something to steady himself, and his fingertips brushed the older man.

"Jesus," muttered the officer, even as he stepped aside. "I hate coming over here."

Harry gave a half bow of her head and guided Eli to the door. "Come on," she said, "I'm not cleaning up after you again."

He managed to look apologetic and ashamed before Harry dragged him outside.

Warm air rushed over him and took away the hospital's antiseptic chill. They stepped around a time-dulled black-and-white police car Eli recognized as a Dodge. Old muscle cars and beaters filled the parking lot outside the clinic, dotted with an occasional gleaming vehicle made of plastic and primary colors. Eleanor didn't look that out of place, all things considered. Eli almost laughed at the thought that the hospital lot didn't look that different from the parking area outside Hourglass.

Harry helped him into the passenger seat and tossed the paper bag in his lap. "Might be something useful," she said as she jogged around the car to the driver's side.

"Like what?"

"It's an emergency clinic," she said as the Model A started up. "I'd guess the vast majority of what they hand out is antibiotics or painkillers. Either'd be good for you right now."

Eleanor backed up, around, and lunged forward. Harry rushed them through the parking lot and out onto the main street. Brakes screeched and horns honked behind them as she took the first corner, then the second in the opposite direction. She went another two blocks before she slowed down.

The cars around them made very little noise. Half of them were almost silent. Snippets of music and phone conversations leaked from open windows.

Eli tore open the paper bag. It took him a few moments to read the label, partly because of the car's constant vibrations, partly because he couldn't get his eyes to focus quite right. The pills had a long, multipart name, so he looked at the instructions "Take one for pain every twelve hours," he said. "May cause drowsiness."

Harry nodded. "You need the rest." She reached one hand over the bench and pulled her tricorne out from between the back of the seat and her duffel bag. Then she dropped the hat on her lap and grabbed the wheel with both hands as an oversized pickup truck swerved to cut them off.

"Where are we headed?" Eli wrestled with the bottle's cap and shook one of the pills into his hand.

"East. Across town." She pushed the tricorne onto her head. "If they do end up searching for us, they'll assume we'll take the shortest route out of town and go the other way. It should buy us some time."

He dry-swallowed the pill. It caught in his throat for a moment before dropping into his stomach. "And then?"

She glanced at him. "We'll get you a new shirt and coat somewhere. Probably a rest stop in the '90s will have something simple we can afford." She gestured into the back with her elbow. "Your derby's there."

He reached back and his clumsy fingers slapped her shoulder. "Sorry."

"All's forgiven."

Eli felt around until his fingers found the dome of his hat. They slid down to the brim and lifted it up, around, and set it on his head. The familiarity of the hatband pressing against his scalp soothed him. "What I meant," he said, "is where are we headed in the bigger sense?"

"Keep heading east, I suppose, for the moment. At some point we need to figure out how we're going to get to Hawkins again."

She steered them around a white, rounded car that hummed like a spaceship. Eli stared at it as they went by and realized the man at the wheel was reading a newspaper while the car drove itself. The man glanced up, noticed the Model A, and gave them a small smile.

"Why does someone do that to themselves?"

"I beg your pardon?"

"The faceless men. How can they do that to themselves?"

"I believe it's done to them." She sighed. "I have to believe that."

Eli forced his eyelids up. Either the drug took effect very fast or their rapid exit from the clinic had exhausted him. "It's him, isn't it?"

Harry kept her eyes on the road. "Beg your pardon?"

"Him. The big one who calls himself Fifteen."

"I don't know what you're talking about."

Eli yawned. "That's why Truss wanted the favor so bad. And you too, right? You're both hoping he'll still honor it."

She said nothing.

He forced his eyes open again. "It's Abraham Porter."

Harry's face fell. She stared at the road.

"He's the one I met back at the bank. The one who's been chasing you. Chasing us. He's Fifteen."

34

W e're in Utah," Harry told him when he woke up. "Perhaps half an hour from the Colorado border and Artesia."

Eli pawed his way out of the blanket, stretched, and adjusted his butt on the rumble seat. Eleanor trembled beneath him. He looked at the scruffy plants stretching out from the highway, and the distant hills. Not what he'd expected from Utah. He'd pictured it as the kind of red-orange landscape coyotes might chase roadrunners across. "Artesia? Don't think I've heard of it."

"I took a shortcut," she said. "We're in 1961, or thereabouts. In your time, I think the town's called Dinosaur."

"Dinosaur?"

She nodded. "A nod to the local tourist trade."

"Ahhh. Still haven't heard of it." He wadded up the blanket and pushed it behind the bench. He stretched again, and the stiff collar of his new work shirt pressed against the underside of his chin. The hard creases scratched at his skin. They still hadn't fallen out after almost eight hours of wear. Granted, he'd been asleep for most of that time.

"How do you feel?"

"Better." He rolled his shoulder, then stretched his arm out the Model A's side. Wind slapped at his palm and he turned his hand flat to sail alongside the car. He lifted his leg and flexed the knee up to his chest. "Good," he decided, "considering I was shot and tortured yesterday."

"Almost two days ago, now," said Harry. "You've slept through a lot of it."

"Are you still good to drive?"

"I should be fine for another five or six hours. Enough to get us across Colorado. Maybe even into Kansas, I think."

For a few minutes they rode in silence. A sign announcing the upcoming state border approached and passed them. Some of the hills dropped away to become stark, chalky cliffs. Someone had told him once that Utah was beautiful. He couldn't remember who, but they'd been absolutely right.

"Hungry?" she asked.

"Starving."

"There's some food back there for you." She waved to the back again. "I pulled into a truck stop a while ago. You didn't even budge."

He looked, moved the blanket, and found the brown paper bag. "Thank you."

"It's another club sandwich. I hope that's acceptable."

"It's great," he said. The sandwich was wrapped in wax paper with a pair of toothpicks pinning it shut. No flags this time. Next to it in the bag sat a paper sleeve of cold french fries. Eli pulled one free and enjoyed the salt. He held the sleeve out, and Harry helped herself.

"So," he said after munching a few more fries. "Abraham Porter is one of the faceless men."

Harry swallowed her own fries and stared at the road. "Yes," she said. "Yes, he is."

"Did anyone see this coming?"

She shook her head. "Not at all. Abraham was a good man, overall. Honest. Fair. Some might say fair to a fault. He did so many good things, but he also burned more than a few bridges doing what was 'right' in his mind. He was very much a 'doing what needed to be done' sort of man."

"I've known a few people like that."

"Haven't we all," she said.

"I saw him in Hourglass. Abraham Porter, I mean, not Fifteen."

"At the First Time Around?"

He nodded.

"Sourpuss, isn't he?"

"He reminded me of a disapproving dad."

The corners of Harry's mouth trembled. "That may be the best description of him I've ever heard. You know, on the last day of our wedding celebration in Hourglass, he took me aside to tell me he thought it presented a very poor image, that I wore pants and also that I didn't wear a brassiere."

Eli snorted out a laugh without much amusement behind it. "I recognized him. The shape of his face and jaw. It just didn't click until they showed up at the barn."

The almost-smile on Harry's face collapsed.

"How did they get him? Or, I don't know, recruit him?"

"I don't know. Phoebe never spoke about it to Christopher. We figured it out on our own, after the wedding, much like you did." She glanced at Eli. "I recognized his voice."

"Does everyone know? All the other searchers?"

She shook her head. "John knows. Truss did, clearly. I believe a few suspect." Her fingers drummed on the wheel. "You must understand, Eli, the faceless men have killed dozens of searchers. Hundreds, perhaps. They were always dangerous, but Abraham made them ruthless. Enough of him survived the . . . the process, I suppose, that they all took on his black-and-white view of things. That's when they stopped looking for the dream and started hunting searchers. There's a reason the crowd at the Second Iteration is so much smaller than at the First Time Around."

Eli let a few miles go by beneath the tires. "So you think you can stop him if he'll still honor the favor?"

"He'll honor it," said Harry. "As I told you, he was fair to a fault."

"*Was* fair to a fault," echoed Eli. "That was then. He's one of them now, right? One of the guardian zealots."

"I believe there's enough of him left in that thing," said Harry. "Truss believed it too. If he and I can agree on something, it must be true."

"Or extremely wishful thinking."

She scowled at him.

"So," Eli said, "he honors the favor and you think you can prevent him from killing anyone else?"

"No," she said. "A favor won't work on that scale. At best it would serve as a . . . are you familiar with a game called Monopoly?"

"Everyone on Earth has heard of Monopoly."

"Then you know about the Get Out of Jail Free card."

Eli nodded.

"That's what the favor would be. One instance of being caught or cornered by the faceless men. The holder could call it in and safely walk away."

"Which is why Truss was screaming for you to use it in the barn."

Harry glanced at him. "The man's whole fortune was built from tiny nudges and adjustments throughout history. Imagine if he could've given something one big, hard shove without the worry of being caught. With no restrictions whatsoever."

Eli took in a breath to reply, but instead he just blew it out between his lips.

"For the moment, though, it's a moot point." She tapped her fingers on the steering wheel. "I don't know how long Truss waited for us in New Orleans, and once Mr. Hawkins sets sail we can't reach him until he lands in California—wherever and whenever that happens."

Eli shook his head and pulled the toothpicks from his sandwich. "Keep going east. Boston."

"Why?"

He unwrapped the wax paper. The sandwich had been cut in half and slumped to the side over time. "We have a new lead."

"We do?"

He nodded and the stiff collar jabbed at his neck again. "Yeah. When I saw Zeke—Zero—well, I think a few things fell into place in my head."

"And?"

"And . . . I think I know where the dream is."

Harry laughed. Her hands twitched on the wheel and Eleanor wobbled for a moment. "I beg your pardon?"

"The dream," Eli repeated. "I'm pretty sure I know where it is."

"Do you, now?"

"Yeah." He rewrapped the wax paper so it made a rough holder for the sandwich.

"Not so much a lead then as an actual location? A specific place?"

"Not super specific," he said, "but I think within a mile or two, yeah."

"I've been searching for nine years. John's been at it for almost twenty. But here you are, with just a handful of days on the road and you've figured it out. Down to within a mile or two."

He shrugged. "I think so."

She laughed again. "Everyone has crazy theories now and then, Eli. Especially when they're starting out. They're sure they've spotted something everyone else missed. I did. I was convinced the dream had to be in Florida, in a swamp near Disney—"

"This isn't a crazy theory," he said.

She shook her head.

He took a hungry bite out of the sandwich. Toasted bread made damp from the tomatoes and mayo. Dry turkey. Limp lettuce. Stringy bacon. It might have been the most delicious thing he'd ever tasted.

He swallowed a second mouthful, wiped his mouth on the back of his hand, and turned to Harry. "I'm serious."

"I'm sure you are," she replied. "I'm also quite sure you're medicated."

He repositioned his fingers on the sandwich. "Head for Boston."

"Why?"

"You want to find the dream, right?"

"Yes. Which is why I'm asking you why you think it's in Boston."

"I don't."

"Now you're just being tiresome."

"I said we should head for Boston. It's the nearest big city." He bit off another mouthful of sandwich, chewed, and swallowed. "I think the dream is in Sanders."

She snorted. "Your hometown?"

"Yeah."

She raised an eyebrow. "Please, Eli, you must explain how I and almost every other searcher has passed through your town again and again without ever noticing a single clue."

He wrapped up the second half of the sandwich. "You noticed," he said. "You just didn't realize what you were noticing."

Her faint smirk faltered. "What?"

"You and John tried to tell me Sanders was a slick spot."

"Yes," she said. "I'd used it half a dozen times myself before I even met the younger you."

"No, it isn't. It can't be."

"Eli," she sighed, "history has lost its grip there. It's a slick spot."

Eli shook his head. "No, it's not. Because if it was, I wouldn't know about the internet or cell phones or computers. I'd be living somewhere history slipped past, like the people in the '60s town, or in Independence."

She turned her eyes back to the road. "The night we met by the side of the road," she said, "what year was that?"

Eli held out the sleeve of french fries to her. "It was 2017," he said. "My friends could tell you that too. They were married in 2012, right there in town."

Harry took another pair of fries. "This doesn't make any sense."

He wiggled on the rumble seat. "You told me time slowed down around the dream, right?"

She nodded. "It's part of the reason the faceless men live so long."

"And that's what's been happening in Sanders. Time flows differently there. It flows slower."

Harry took in a breath. Held it. Thought about it. "And the road?"

"I think Sanders has lots of slick spots where you can get on the road, yeah, but only because the dream's there." He let a few ideas spin in his head. "Maybe because people in town are so much closer to it, it's making spots off individual wants and dreams, rather than, y'know, the whole town's: Here's the place great-grandpa proposed. Here's where you found your lost dog. Here's the sign that . . ." He stumbled on the words for a moment. "Here's the sign that tells us we're home."

Her jaw shifted back and forth as she chewed on the words.

"And one more thing," Eli said.

"Yes?"

"Hawkins? He's from Maine too."

She nodded. "I recognized his accent."

Eli bit two french fries in half. "He told me he passed through Sanders once. Just before he decided to go to California."

Harry took in another slow breath. Her fingers danced on the steering wheel. "As far as leads go," she said, "it's more compelling than some I've followed. Do you have any idea where in your town the dream might be?"

He sighed. "Well, no. It just makes sense that's where it ended up. It all fits."

She took another slow breath.

Eli let her think about it for a few minutes. "How long do you think it'll take us to get there?"

Harry bobbed her head side to side as she calculated the miles. "Kansas tonight," she said. "If we go nonstop tomorrow, we could possibly make Washington by tomorrow night. Or"—she glanced at a road sign as it whizzed past them—"we could start heading north after Denver, go for Cleveland."

She murmured directions to herself for another mile and a half. Eli toyed with unwrapping the other half of his sandwich and taking one more bite. Instead, he twisted the bag shut and set it on the floor between his legs.

"I can't see us getting there in less than two days," she said.

"Even with a shortcut through history?"

"We can take all the shortcuts you like, Eli, we're still over twenty-two hundred miles away."

"Right. Sorry."

Another mile rolled by beneath Eleanor's tires.

Eli cleared his throat. "What about John Henry? Could the *Bucephalus* get us there any faster?"

"Possibly," she said, "but if you're sure that's where the dream is, I'm not sure I want to be calling another searcher into the area with us."

Eli smirked. "Worried there's not enough wishes to go around?"

"Worried I'll call in a favor and look like a daft fool for following my drugged-up partner's suggestions."

"Okay, then."

"We'll get there soon enough, don't worry."

Eleanor whizzed past a small brick marker with some kind of plaque, and then a wooden sign welcomed them to colorful Colorado.

35

A little under two days later, they drove past the snow-dusted sign welcoming them into Sanders.

Eleanor roared down the road toward the center of town. Eli took in a breath to warn Harry about Zeke's standard speed trap. Then he realized the trap probably hadn't been set that afternoon.

Or had it? He couldn't be sure when the faceless men had recruited Zeke. Maybe they hadn't yet.

"I brought us back a few weeks after our last encounter," Harry said. Her words came out in a cloud of steam.

"A few?"

She shrugged. "Six or seven. I didn't think we needed to be exact."

Eli flipped up the lapels of his tweed blazer. A Goodwill store in 1970s Des Moines had provided the coat and the faded blue sweatshirt under it. Not perfect for a New England winter, but all they'd been able to afford.

"Maybe slow down a bit," he suggested.

"I'm fine."

"Just to be safe."

She rolled her eyes at him. But the Model A slowed down. "Satisfied?"

"You realize drivers like you were the reason my mom never wanted me walking in the street when I was a little kid."

"If only she'd known that one day you'd be tempted away by such a reckless driver."

"Let's hold off telling her for now."

They rolled down a snowbank-lined Main Street, past the Silver Arrow restaurant and Jackson's. He glanced in the small bookstore's window. Two of the three wire racks had vanished over the years, but as they drove by he glimpsed the survivor past the soap-drawn snowflakes on the glass.

Harry looked at him. "Where am I going?"

"I'm not sure," said Eli. He looked through the windshield and saw the Pizza Pub coming up on their left. They had their gaudy silver Christmas tree in the window. "I guess it has to be somewhere people wouldn't notice it."

"Possibly," she said. "I suppose it depends on who took it. Perhaps someone has it in plain sight out in their living room."

Eli bit off a laugh. "I hadn't really thought about that," he said. "Do you think someone from Sanders stole the dream? Or did they just hide it here?"

"I have no idea," she said. "I always tended to wonder more about the why and the how, myself." She gestured toward the road ahead. "Which way?"

"Keep following the road, I guess. Bear to the left."

She guided Eleanor around the bend and onto Cross Street. On the dashboard, the red-orange light by the gas gauge flickered twice. "We'll need to fill up soon," she said, patting the console next to the steering wheel.

"I think there's still two or three gallons in the reserve."

She nodded and studied the houses along the street.

On their right stood the old Protestant church. A snowbank blocked the parking lot where he'd talked to Harry all those years ago. He swung his head, glanced past the Catholic church, and caught a glimpse of the baseball field. Brown tufts of dead grass stretched up through the snow around the wooden bleachers and across the outfield. In the distance, beyond the field, he could see the back of . . .

"Oh, Christ," he said.

"What?"

"Turn left up here," he said as they passed the two churches.

"Won't that circle us back around into town?"

"Yeah."

The road curved around, past another line of dirt-streaked snowbanks, and revealed the sprawling structure that, without knowing it, he'd brought them to see.

The Founders House.

"Pull over there," he said, gesturing at the lot across the street.

Eleanor slid between twin mounds of snow into the parking lot. Harry steered the car around until they faced the building dead-on. Eli stared at it through the windshield.

She followed his eyeline as the engine stopped. "I remember that place," she said. "It's been closed for years, yes?"

"Yeah. I'm not even sure when it was open." He let his eyes run over the rambling structure. Clapboard walls painted that blue-gray colonial white. Dozens of big windows framed by dark shutters. At least three brick chimneys he could see from where Eleanor was parked. A wide, wooden staircase led up the hill, past two landings to the main entrance. "I've lived here my whole life," he said, "and never really looked at this place, y'know?"

"I suppose."

"I know a bunch of kids growing up who used to throw rocks at the windows. My mom told me once they did it when she was a kid too."

Harry let her own gaze drift across the building. "What are you looking for?"

"Broken windows."

Her head turned sided to side. "I don't see any."

"Neither do I."

"Is it significant somehow?"

"Maybe. Like I said, I've lived here my whole life. Probably gone past this place two or three times a week, every week. And you know what?"

She raised a questioning eyebrow.

"I've never seen anyone working here. Not fixing windows. Not painting it. Not mowing the lawn or raking leaves or shoveling the steps." He cast his gaze back and forth over the building again. "I think I never really looked at this place—none of us ever looked—because it never attracted attention. It went out of its way not to attract attention."

Harry took in a slow breath. "And you think the dream's in there."

"Yeah."

She drummed her fingers on the steering wheel.

He shrugged. "I'm open to a better idea."

"No," she said. "No, I think . . . you're right."

Eli and Harry slipped out of the car and walked to the edge of the parking lot. They took a few clumsy steps over the snowbank and set their feet down on the road. Eli glanced both ways, suddenly aware he had no idea what day of the week it was in Sanders. He hadn't noticed many cars in either church parking lot, so not Sunday. He looked over at the back of the Silver Arrow and saw a few cars and two pickups. A usual weekday lunch crowd for the restaurant, even in the winter.

They reached the base of the broad wooden staircase that stretched up to the Founders House. Sixty-six steps, split by two large landings. A childhood memory flashed in his mind—racing up and down the staircase with his friends.

They stood at the base of the stairs and looked up at the mass of clapboards and windows and old shutters.

Harry crossed her arms and took three deep breaths, pushing each one out between her lips as a cloud of steam.

"Are you okay?"

"I'm a little overwhelmed," she said. "This . . . this is it. We've done it. The dream's in there. I can almost feel it."

Eli took in a breath of his own. The cold air prickled at his skin. Or maybe it wasn't the air. He looked at the broad wooden staircase leading up to the Founders House.

"I know what you mean," he said. "It's kind of bizarre. All those years I was looking for you, and the thing you were looking for was sitting here the whole time, right under my nose . . ."

She glanced at him. He stared up at the building, lost in thought. "Eli?"

"Sorry. It's just . . ." He blinked and looked at her. "I just had a bit of déjà vu. Didn't Truss say something like that? Being right under their noses?"

"I believe so," she said. "But he was talking about hiding from the faceless men."

"Right." The conversation floated up to the top of Eli's memories. "He said he was so well hidden he'd set up a business right under their nose."

"And then they shot him dead."

Eli nodded slowly and looked at the staircase again. He remembered being a kid, riding bikes past those steps with Josh and Corey, making little-kid bets, daring each other to run up to the stairs. But none of them ever made it to the second big landing.

None of them got *that* close to the Founders House. Not even Zeke or his idiot friends. Nobody.

He remembered something sprawled in the dust. The bad house in a 1960s desert town. Cobwebs draping back and forth across it like threads.

Stretching back and forth like strings.

"Oh, no," he murmured.

"What?"

Eli took her arm and stepped back into the street. "We have to go," he said. "I think . . . I think I've made a mistake. A really, really bad mistake."

"What?"

He took another step back, pulling her with him, his gaze still focused on the Founders House. Nothing stirred in the building. The windows stayed shut, the drapes hung still. It loomed silently over them.

"Eli, what is it? Is this the wrong place?"

"This is very much the wrong place," he said. "We need to get back to Eleanor."

"Why?"

"Right under their noses," he said. "John told me about false positives when you search. Finding people who were influenced by the dream before it vanished rather than after."

The sounds of traffic grew in the distance.

"All the strange time effects in Sanders," Eli said, "they're a false positive. This isn't where the dream is. It's where the dream *was*."

They reached the far sidewalk and Harry shook her head as they reached the snowbank. "No," she said. "It can't be. Before it vanished, it was still being guarded by the—"

She took in a sharp breath. Her wide eyes stared up at the house the founders had built. "Pissbucket," she hissed.

They were in the parking lot now, less than a hundred feet from Eleanor, backing away from the sprawling old structure. The sound of engines filled the air. A distant growl.

Eli looked back up at the Founders House, pictured the town in his head, tried to imagine the path the sound would take between all the buildings. "Run," he said.

They reached Eleanor just as the Hudson Hornet blasted around the corner of the Silver Arrow, shoving air out of its way and creating a wall of pressure that rattled the restaurant's windows. It rushed up Front Street and skidded to a stop across the entrance to the parking lot, spraying a wave of slush into the air.

Then another Hornet came around the corner. And another. Eli glanced back as he ran around Eleanor's engine. A fourth slick black shape roared down the hill. Its engine screamed as the driver down-shifted.

He threw himself onto the bench as Harry landed behind the wheel. Eleanor's engine revved. The Model A's tires squealed on the pavement as the car shot forward. Harry slalomed through the snowy grove of parking meter posts.

Behind them engines growled. Eli heard the synchronized thunk of four cars shifting gears. Tires shrieked on the pavement as they spun up to full speed.

The swarm of Hornets launched themselves after Eleanor.

The Last
Paradox

36

The Model A shot into the narrow passage between Sanders Craft & Fabrics and the old storage center. Eleanor's running boards grazed one wall and spit out white sparks. "Go left," shouted Eli as Eleanor burst out of the alley across from the cinema.

Harry spun the wheel hard. She downshifted, slammed her foot on the gas, and the tires grabbed the street. The Model A threw itself forward, and Harry jerked the wheel just before sideswiping a parked car.

Engines growled around them. Cars blocked the far end of the alley. Tires squealed on pavement. Sounds echoed back around the Silver Arrow.

"Through town," Eli said.

They raced down the same streets they'd traveled just half an hour ago. Harry's gaze flitted to the mirrors. "Where to next?"

"I don't know."

"It's your town! How do we get away from them?"

Someone on the sidewalk shouted at them to slow down. Instead, Harry cut the corner by the pizza restaurant, making another car screech on its brakes and skid in the snow-covered street. The Model A flew past the fire station and . . .

They heard the growls, closing fast. Before they reached the end of the block, Eli looked back and saw the first of the Hudson Hornets roar around the corner, barely two hundred feet behind them. The black car fishtailed, its tires spraying slush across the storefronts.

A hand came out of the driver's side with a pistol and fired two quick shots in their direction. Something whizzed past Harry's window and yanked at her hair. She shrieked.

"They're close," Eli said

"Not close enough, thankfully. Right or left?"

Eli saw a dozen yards between the Model A and the T-intersection. They were going in circles. Right or left? Right took them away from the Founders House, left took them toward—

"Left!" he spat out. "Churches. Loaded with history."

Harry took the corner, swinging around a little silver import. Eleanor leaned to the side, close to tipping, but leveled out as they raced forward.

At the far end of Church Street, a black shadow swung into view and roared toward them.

"Hang on," said Harry. She leaned into the steering wheel as Eleanor rushed forward. Eli braced his feet.

The Hornet filled the road. The growl of its engine shook the air. The driver—a faceless man in some kind of clear animal mask— reached an arm out the window and fired four quick shots at the Model A, one after another. The cap of the gas tank sparked. The windshield spiderwebbed out a high corner.

Eli braced for impact.

Right between the churches, Eleanor hit a thin patch of history spread across the road. The tires spun on the pavement. The snowbanks vanished. Harry steered into the skid and let the car slip back ten, twenty, thirty years, at least. Then she hit the gas, the tires caught, and they rushed forward.

She let her foot off the accelerator. The Model A bounced twice before getting a good grip on the dirt road. A stone bounced up to hit the undercarriage as the car squished through a dark patch of half-dried mud.

"Where . . . when are we?" asked Eli.

Only three other cars in sight, one of them parked just off the road. She glanced back and saw a fourth car parked in front of the solitary brown church. Most of them looked closely related to Eleanor.

"Mid-'30s," Harry guessed. "Maybe '40s, the way this town is. I was just trying to get away from them."

She turned right at the end of the road, away from the Founders House and into a residential area. Lots of small houses, not much more than three-room bungalows. Two of them had picket fences out front. A pair of large Victorians bookended the street.

Eli looked back. "Did we lose them?"

"Maybe one or two of them. For a few minutes. They know where we slid, so there's only so many whens to check before they can be certain."

"I don't recognize any of these houses," he said.

"Perhaps we slipped back further than I realized."

A roar echoed up over the buildings. The mechanized growl of an angry beast appearing on the road at speed. One, maybe two of them. Eli heard a distant scream and the growl of acceleration.

"Pissbucket," muttered Harry. She stepped on the accelerator. Eleanor lunged forward again.

"I think the state line's up ahead," said Eli.

"Town and state line? That's good. Lots of history there."

She drove past the line and into New Hampshire. Then she pulled hard on Eleanor's wheel, made a bumpy turn across the dirt road, and raced back the way she'd come.

"Never go in straight lines?"

Harry nodded. "If the faceless men track us again, they'll be going the wrong way. We'll be a mile or three ahead before they get turned around."

Eleanor bore back down on the line. Stones and grit sprayed from beneath the Model A's tires. The gears whined and the engine—

Coughed. One sputter. But it hit just as they reached the town line, and without the momentum she'd planned on, their skid through history became a gentle glide.

Eleanor fell short.

"What happened?"

"I'm not sure." Harry looked at cars, license plates, trying to find something, anything, that would tell her when they'd ended up.

"Left up here," he said. "Farther from the Founders House."

She turned onto an even less-developed street with spaced-out little houses sitting far up from the road. As she did, the engine coughed again. It kept hacking as Eleanor began to lurch. "Oh, no," said Harry. "No, no, no . . ."

"What?!"

The red-orange light flared on the dashboard, a tiny warning beacon. The needle of the fuel gauge rested below the E. A flat line. Completely dry.

"No, no, NO!" She smacked her hands against the steering wheel. "Come on, Eleanor. Just a little more, girl. We just need you to give us a little—"

The engine sputtered twice and the car lurched forward again past a small house. It gave a final, wet cough and died.

37

P issbucket!"

Harry worked the steering wheel back and forth, coaxing another twenty feet out of the car, getting a little more momentum from the slight slope of the road. The Model A rolled along the road for another thirty yards. Then, finally, she guided it onto the shoulder. The tires crunched on the gravel and dirt.

Harry and Eli lunged up and out of the car before it settled. She reached across to the gas cap; he ran for the spare tank. "It took another hit," he shouted from the back. "It's almost empty."

"Consarn it!" Harry growled. She leaned across the hood, twisting to keep her coat between her chest and the hot cowling, her arms trembling as her hands gripped the gas cap. She twisted, but it refused to budge. Her fingers felt a gouge along the back edge. Half gouge, half dent.

Eli leaned around the back of the car. "Maybe having a bright-red target on the back of the—"

"Get the tools," she snapped. "That hit jammed the cap."

She heard the trunk open, and a moment later Eli ran forward with the toolbox. She snatched it out of his hands, and he took her place, reaching across the hood to try prying the cap open.

"Leave this to me," she said, flinging the toolbox open. "Go find us some water."

"Where?"

"Anywhere!" she snapped. "It's your town. Go!"

He dashed back, grabbed the tank, and ran for one of the houses.

Harry pushed a few items aside and pulled out the big pipe wrench.

Her thumb spun the wrench wider and wider as she stepped up onto the running board and stretched over the hood. She fit it around the gas cap and pulled.

The cap didn't budge.

She pressed her knees against Eleanor's side and heaved. She leaned her shoulders back and levered all her weight against the car. "Turn, you useless thing," she snarled.

The cap didn't budge.

Harry tightened her grip on the wrench and threw herself back. Her shoulders throbbed with each yank. Her fingers ached.

On the fourth yank, the cap shifted.

"Yes!" She swung the pipe wrench, tightened it again, and this time it turned easier. Still stiff and rough, but it moved.

As she did the faint rattle of sprockets and chain came from the Model A's rear, followed by the light crunch of something biting into the dirt and rocks. Too small to be a car. To be one of them.

"Hey," said a high-pitched voice. "Whatcha doing?"

Jesus, Mary, and Joseph, thought Harry. She shot a quick look at the back of the car.

A little towheaded boy with a bicycle stood near Eleanor's rear bumper. He had the mop of uncut hair common to children from a dozen eras. Seven or eight years old, tops, dressed in faded jeans and a striped T-shirt. Maybe the 1970s or '80s? An oversized backpack hung off his shoulders. He'd probably grow into it in another year or two.

Assuming the faceless men didn't kill him as a witness. Or worse.

She tossed the wrench aside, grabbed the cap in her hands, and twisted it loose.

She had to stay focused. The child had to go. Quickly, quietly, without causing a fuss.

Harry stepped down off the sideboard, the cap clenched in her hand. "Kind of busy here," she said. "You should head on home."

"Is something wrong with your car?"

Harry nodded. "Just out of fuel," she said. She reached over and gave Eleanor's hood a few awkward pats. "We'll be on our way soon, hopefully."

The little boy spun to point back the way they'd both come from.

The backpack swung on his shoulders as he did. "There's a gas station in town," he said. "They can help."

Harry shook her head. "No, thank you," she said. "I've only got a few minutes to get back on the road."

The boy seemed to ponder this, then came up with a new idea. "I could go get some gas for you," he said, waving an arm at the bike. "I'm really fast."

"I don't need gas," said Harry. "My partner's off taking care of things." She looked over her shoulder and tried to figure out which one of the houses Eli had gotten off to. Then she looked back, and her gaze drifted past the boy to the road. No sign of the Hudson Hornets yet, but they had to be close. She flexed her fingers around the gas cap. "You should get out of here, child."

"I live right over there," the boy said, pointing past the car. "It's okay."

"It isn't," Harry told him. "You should head home. Bad things are coming."

The boy followed her stare to look down the road, but lost interest. "What's your name?"

"I'm Harry." Had that been a growl in the distance? No, just a motorcycle. Maybe an old dirt bike. Loud, but without the power of the Hudson Hornet's engine. "Now, go home."

The boy kept talking, but she ignored him. It had been at least eight minutes now since Eleanor had stalled. The faceless men couldn't be that far behind. She passed the gas cap back and forth between her hands and wondered what was taking Eli so . . .

Wait.

She stared down at the little blond boy. Her voice caught. "You're . . . Eli?"

The little boy leaned back. "Yeah?"

Harry dropped to her knees and grabbed his small shoulder. She could see it all at this level. The eyes. The chin. The cheekbones hiding under a thin layer of baby fat. "Oh my God," she said. "Look at you! You . . . you're so cute."

Little Eli's face wrinkled up.

"I'm so sorry," she told the little boy. "This is just . . . this is a complication. Or it could be. It's a good thing you're not here right now."

She looked over his shoulder to the road. "You really need to go," she said. "Go now. Run home and don't talk to anyone. Don't even look at anyone. Especially if they're carrying a big water tank."

Little Eli cleared his throat. "I have water."

Harry froze. Her grip tightened on Eli's shoulders and she looked him in the eye. "You what?"

"Water," the boy said. "I've got some if you're thirsty." His shoulders wiggled under Harry's hands, and when she let go the backpack slid to the ground. He slid out a small thermos decorated with the worn-down image of a red-and-blue mechanical man.

Harry grabbed it. She twisted off the cup, then the lid. She pushed her nose into the opening and smelled the crisp scent of pure water.

She threw herself at the Model A's front. Not quite a quart, going off the weight, but at least seven or eight ounces. "It's better than nothing," she muttered.

Little Eli ran after her, struggling with his pack. "What are you doing?"

Harry stretched her arms across Eleanor's hood and oh-so-gently tilted the thermos. The water poured in, and after a few seconds she was rewarded with the sound of water splashing into water. Just enough.

She shook out the last few drops and sealed the fuel tank with a quick twist of her wrist. It could only turn twice. She tossed the thermos to Little Eli and ran around the front of the car. His footsteps padded behind her as she reached in to flip the switches for the ignition sequence.

Eleanor shivered once, twice, and then sprung to life. The needle on the gas gauge trembled and went up a fraction of an inch.

"Hey! You said you were out of gas."

"I said I was out of fuel," Harry told him. "And you gave me close to a pint."

"I just gave you water."

"Yes," she said. "You're a lifesaver, if I haven't mentioned that yet."

"Hey!" shouted another voice. Eli—her Eli—ran up the road, the spare tank swinging at the end of one arm. "How'd you get it running?"

"Quiet!" she yelled. She ran to meet him in front of the car.

"I couldn't get anything, the faucet was rusted solid." He looked at Little Eli. "Who's the—"

"Quiet," she snapped again. She slapped the tank out of his hands. "Get in the car. Eyes front. Look at nothing, say nothing, do nothing."

Eli's jaw sank, pulling his mouth open and stretching his eyes wide. Harry watched his eyes flit back and forth between Little Eli and the bicycle. Awareness sparked in Eli's eyes.

Harry whacked his arm. "Now!"

Then they both heard it. A distant tickle at the edge of hearing.

The growl of a big engine.

Eli got into the car.

Harry ran around Eleanor and slid behind the wheel. She grabbed her tricorne from Eli's hand, slammed it back on her head, then glanced over at Little Eli. He'd followed her around to the driver's side. Confusion and amazement filled his eyes in equal measure.

"Hey," she said, snapping her fingers. She pointed at his little feet. "Your mother doesn't want you in the street, yes?"

In the passenger seat, Eli trembled.

In the street, Little Eli looked down, then back up, his eyes bigger than ever.

"Get off the road and stay there," she said. "In fact, stay there for a few minutes after we go, just to be safe."

Little Eli nodded and glanced at his bike. Then his gaze and expression shifted.

Harry glanced in the rearview mirror and saw something small and dark far down the road, growing larger and louder by the second.

"Time to go," she said. "See you in a couple of years, Eli."

"What?"

Eleanor's tires clawed at the dirt, pushing the car onto the pavement. Harry hit the gas. The wheels squealed on the road and threw the Model A forward, knocking Harry back in her seat. She spared a quick glance in her window and saw Little Eli on the very edge of the road, waving his hands at a cloud of dust. Or maybe at them.

And only a hundred yards past him . . . a Hudson Hornet.

"Looks like only one of them," she said. "If you have any thoughts on where we might shake him off, they'd be appreciated."

Next to her, Eli let out a mouthful of air. "That was me," he said.

"Yes." She slid into the other lane, went wide, and took the corner at speed.

"All this time, that was me. I was him."

"Yes," she said, "and I think we avoided making a huge mess of history right then."

He shook his head, then turned it into a nod. "Yeah, that was it. I remember all of it."

The next turn put them in unfamiliar territory, but a dozen yards under the wheels and a slight bend in the road brought them within sight of the post office. "You remember that?"

"That was when we met."

"No," she said, "we met at the church when you were a young man." They swung around another corner.

"Believe me, I remember that whole day. I must've gone over it in my head a thousand times. I spent the morning biking around town, had lunch in the baseball field, spent an hour afterwards throwing rocks . . ." His voice trailed off.

She glanced at him. "What?"

"I think—"

A bullet punched through the rear window and spun Harry's tricorne off her head. She screamed, almost blotting out the echo of the gunshot. The hat bounced against her arm and into Eli's lap.

"Are you okay?"

"Ears are ringing," she said

She spun the wheel as a second shot reached their ears. Eleanor made a tight turn, the rear wheels almost sliding across the pavement, and Harry saw a scattering of the local landmarks. The baseball field. The fire station. The Founders House loomed behind them.

One more shot rang over the sound of the engine. Eleanor wobbled, and Harry felt the wheel twitch beneath her hands. She risked a glance out the side and back, glimpsed the rippling black around the spoked wheel. "Dammit," she yelled. "They got the tire."

Eli looked back at the cracked rear window. "How fast can we go?"

"I think this is as fast as we can go. Hang on." They passed another building, she spotted a slick spot in the road, and they skidded back into history.

Eli braced his legs against the floorboards. The wind outside the car was a good ten degrees colder. "How far?"

"As far as she could take us." They came out of the skid and the tires caught dirt. "At least a hundred years back," she said.

Eleanor lumbered across the dirt road. Most of the buildings had vanished, and Harry noticed just one church standing alone in the distance. The baseball field had reverted back to just . . . a field, filled with waist-high grass and surrounded by a split-rail fence. The apartment building and firehouse off to the left were gone, replaced with a large structure that might have been a barn once and found new purpose. A red carriage with a large brass water tank sat out front.

Harry glanced over her left shoulder at the back end of the car. "We're shredding the tire," she said. "It's not going to last long, and we won't make it far without it."

"We don't need to. Turn us around."

"What?"

"Trust me."

The Model A's engine whined as Harry spun the wheel. Eleanor fought her, but grudgingly made a wide turn in front of the old firehouse, heading back the way they'd come. The car slid for a moment, and then the tires caught the ground. A house appeared over by the church. The grass in the field grew another inch.

Eleanor lurched again and Harry felt something slap the underside of the floorboards. A deafening rattle sprang up in the back that shook the whole car. Eli looked back through the cracked window. "I think we just lost a—"

"Tire," Harry agreed without looking back. She gritted her teeth as the engine coughed. "We're done."

And in the distance, they heard the growl of the Hudson Hornet.

38

Eleanor coughed two more times. The second one sputtered off into a gargling sound. The term "death rattle" popped up in Eli's mind.

He reached over and pushed, twisting the steering wheel hard to the left. Harry smacked his hand away, but the wounded Model A clattered off the dirt road. One of the headlights burst as Eleanor cracked through the sun-dried rails of the fence. The car rolled over the broken wood, pushed a few feet into the tall grass, and died with a gasp.

Eli pushed Harry's hat at her and forced his door open before the engine went silent. "Come on."

She glanced back toward the road, toward the approaching engine roar. "Do you think we can—"

"Now! Come on!"

She shoved her door open, followed him, caught up to him. They waded through the grass, cutting across the field in a beeline toward the church.

Running through the tall grass felt like wading through water. Near the top, the light, bobbing tufts rippled away from the slightest touch. Down beneath, though, the thick, heavy stalks resisted each movement. They pushed back.

Eli glanced back and, over the top of the grass, saw the Hudson Hornet spin out onto the road behind them. Its tires sprayed dirt as it lined up on Eleanor.

"Don't look," he told Harry.

They raised their knees and slogged through the grass. It slowed every step, shortened every stride. Eli guessed they'd gone a hundred feet at most.

The heavy, hollow sound of two cars crashing together echoed over the field. Harry winced and glanced back. Her pace faltered. Eli saw her eyes and lips and could guess what had happened to Eleanor. "Come on," he said. "We can't stop."

The Hornet's engine revved. Its tires spun. Another wooden crack echoed across the field. A new sound muffled the growl of the engine. A rustling *whisk-whisk-whisk-whisk-whisk*.

Grass pushed under a bumper.

"Move!" Eli yelled.

In his mind's eye, he tried to plot out the Little League field. The field he'd been in hundreds of times growing up. They'd passed the eventual baselines and had to be closing on his old position. He glanced over at the back of the Founders House, half a block away, and tried to remember how it looked from left field.

The Hornet roared past them, flattening a wide swath of grass behind it. It plowed through what would one day be third base and swung a wide turn that would've leveled the bleachers. The engine revved again and again.

"This way," said Eli. He pointed and tugged on her sleeve. They loped through the field.

"Where are we going?"

"Trust me!"

The shape appeared through the tall grass, snaking across the field like a jagged slate line. The old stone wall, not quite as old at the moment, and much more solid. Eli didn't remember its stones being quite so dark, but maybe another century of New England weather would lighten them.

The Hornet's growl grew behind them, along with the *whisk-whisk-whisk* of grass falling beneath the car.

Harry swung her legs over the wall without missing a beat. Eli leaped and dove over it, trying his best to make it look like a stumble that had flipped his feet into the air. The grass on the other side cushioned his landing and he rolled onto his side next to Harry. She dragged him to his feet and they glanced back as they ran.

The faceless man hit the brakes just in time. The Hornet slid into the wall, but had shed enough momentum that the impact made a clunk rather than a crash. The wall let out a series of heavy clicks as its slabs of rock shifted. One slid off with a long, dry scrape and thudded into the ground like an ax into a tree stump.

Zero's mustached mask glared at them over the steering wheel. His arm stretched out the window.

Harry tackled Eli into the grass and bullets whipped through the air above them. A few angled down to whisk through the grass. She rolled over, he pointed, and they crawled away as more bullets whipped around them.

The gunfire stopped. The Hudson Hornet's engine rumbled again as it backed away through the grass. Eli raised his head. "Of course it's Zeke," he muttered.

"You know him," Harry said. "Will he come after us on foot or go around?"

Eli shook his head. "There's an opening in the wall about thirty feet farther down. His car'll fit through with no problem."

"Does he know that?"

"He knows this place as well as I do. Maybe even better now that he's . . . Zero. But we can hope."

Ahead of them stood a wide grove of saplings with a few full trees scattered among them, including two big pines. Some of them looked almost as thick as Eli's thigh, but most of them had trunks the size of Harry's wrists. Very few of them looked big enough to slow the Hornet if Zero chose to go straight through them.

They ran for the trees.

Eli tried to recall the lay of the land. The steep drop behind the Catholic church—where the church would be someday—had a narrow path up its slope, which always made a good landmark. Would it still be there? Would he have time to find the square rock?

As if to make the point, the Hornet let out an angry growl from its engine. "Run, Eli Teague," Zero bellowed. "Run while you can."

The grass thinned and they could move easier. Harry and Eli pulled themselves around the thin trees, swinging from left to right and back. They could almost run now.

Another fifty or sixty feet separated them from the base of the slope. Eli couldn't see any sign of the path through the twiggy branches and patches of leaves. If he couldn't find the right spot, what other options did they have?

Harry staggered to a halt against a tree and sucked in a breath. "There's no way out, is there?" she panted. "We can't get away from him."

"We're not going to get away."

Her eyes opened wide.

Behind them, the Hornet wailed out four triumphant blasts of its horn. The growl of its engine rolled across the field and through the gap in the wall. A crack echoed behind them as the big car plowed over a sapling and snapped it in half, crushing the small tree beneath it.

"Jesus," muttered Eli.

They lurched back into motion, weaving between the trees. They just ran. He ran away from Zeke. Like he always did.

Another crack echoed through the trees, and one more right after it. Zero slalomed the Hudson Hornet back and forth through the grove, smashing through the path of least resistance. Eli felt sure there was a cat-and-mouse aspect to it as well.

"I always knew one of them would get me," Harry panted.

"We're not going to die," Eli said.

"You just said—"

"I said we weren't getting away from him. Come on!"

"What?"

Eli cut left and raced through the trees, and Harry raced after him.

He hadn't come out here since he was ten or eleven, a couple of years after he'd first met Harry. He searched the ground ahead of them for the big, squarish rock he'd hung out on sometimes when Zeke and his buddies had claimed the bleachers. The rock that sat just a few yards from—

"There!" said Eli, pointing at the stone. A few tufts of grass had disguised its shape. Which meant . . . "Here!"

"What?"

He led Harry between two narrow trees about six feet apart. He eyeballed each one and put them at maybe an inch thicker than the wooden fence posts. A few twiggy branches spread between them, and a few more as thick as his thumb.

He stopped between the trees, then turned toward the approaching car. It plowed over another sapling. "We'll be safe here."

"What? No, we won't!"

"Trust me."

Harry looked at the Hornet. It paused just over thirty yards away, engine growling, pointed right at them. She could see nothing of it but grille and windshield. "He's got a clear shot at us," she said. "In every way."

The idea dove deep into his mind. After all he'd seen and done over the past few weeks, there'd be an awful, bitter poetry to dying in his hometown a hundred years before his birth. To being killed by Zeke after all the fights and abuse and harassment. What if he'd been standing on his own crushed remains all the times he'd wandered out among the trees to . . .

He reached over and grabbed her hand. "I know what I'm doing." As he said it he glanced at the ground and pulled her back a few more steps.

The Hudson Hornet revved its engine once, twice, and charged, crunching another tree beneath its wheels. Fifteen, twenty, thirty miles an hour.

Harry's fingers crushed his.

The big car filled their vision.

Harry threw herself back and—

Time paused once more for Eli.

The two trees framed the glossy black Hornet in his vision. He could see the red HUDSON crest set into the grille and pick out all six letters, along with the small ships and chess pieces on either side of the center triangle. The fender had seven scrapes and one deep gouge from the stone wall, and the left headlight was cracked but still held together.

Eli could see Zero's mask glaring at him through the glass, with its straight-line beard, wide brows, and Snidely Whiplash mustache. Even from this distance and through the plastic mask, he could see the individual wrinkles on the faceless man's brow, the blank skin twisted into the closest it could get to a scowl but starting to flatten out. At the very last instant, Zero had recognized the spot Eli'd led him to.

Then time got back up to speed, and the Hornet hit the trees.

The front end slipped between the two trunks. It bounced between them. The Hornet gouged forward a few more feet and the big car went from forty miles an hour to a dead stop in one second.

The Hudson Hornet had a big steering wheel. Zero's body folded up and over it to slam into the windshield. The glass collapsed out of its frame. A few loose pieces went skittering across the hood. The faceless man wasn't flung from the car like some human missile, but he had enough momentum to slide down the hood to the front of the vehicle.

Zero tried to push himself up, slipped, and fell to the ground with a thump.

The Hornet's growl faded to a whine, and the engine died.

Eli stood eight feet from the front of the car. His body shuddered, urging him to run or attack while acknowledging it was too exhausted for either. Cold sweat soaked his shirt and pants.

He hoped it was sweat soaking his pants.

A few feet to the side, still clutching his hand in a death grip, Harry gasped out a breath. She'd thrown up her free hand to protect herself. The hand insisted on staying up. "How . . . how did you do that?"

He took in a deep breath of his own. The smell of hot metal filled the air, and he could taste oil and gas in it. He turned and took two uneasy steps toward her. "History."

"What?"

He waved a hand back at the trapped Hornet. "When we saw . . . me, I remembered, back when I was a kid, a bunch of us would come out here and throw rocks at an old rust bucket stuck between these two trees. It'd been there for about a hundred years."

She stared at him, then at the Hornet.

Eli shrugged, but wasn't sure his fatigued muscles actually followed through with the movement. "It just hit me a few minutes ago. I think it's one of those . . . what did John call them? A transparent paradox?"

Harry snorted a breath through her nose. "His transparent aluminum defense. A predestination paradox."

"We're lucky this is such a boring town," Eli said. "If there was anything else to do, I wouldn't've been out here throwing rocks so often."

She barked out a laugh. "You poor thing," she said. "In my day the kids only snuck out to the woods for a bit of bread and butter."

The term meant nothing, but her naughty smirk made him laugh anyway.

A stick snapped behind him.

"Stop laughing at me," growled Zero.

39

The mask hung around Zero's neck. A dozen nicks and punctures covered the smooth flesh of his face, each one trailing blood. A red gash stretched across the space where his left eye should've been.

He took a step toward them. His trip over the steering wheel had broken his arm in at least two places. Possibly a few ribs too, the way his chest sagged on one side.

"You've been laughing at me my whole life," muttered Zero, taking another step. "Making my life hell. Not anymore."

"Zeke," said Eli, "we need to get you to a doctor. You've been—"

"Not anymore!" roared Zero. The skin around his jaw stretched tight and shook like a drum. His working arm swung up to grab at Eli.

Eli smacked the arm away, but numbed his hand in the process. It felt like stopping the casual swing of a baseball bat—yet another sensation he knew thanks to Zeke. He took a few steps back.

Zero limped after him. With his swinging, twisted arm it gave him the gait of a B-movie zombie.

"Turned everyone against me in school," snarled the faceless man. "Then in the whole town. This is all your fault! They turned me into this because of you! To help them find YOU!"

His fingers stretched out, flexed, and Eli had no doubt they could crush bone.

He ducked and slammed into Zero. He drove his shoulder into the faceless man's gut and kicked at the ground. Zero slid back and crashed against the Hornet's wide fenders.

The faceless man brought his arm down hard. Eli's back shuddered and the muscles on one side spasmed. The impact shook his spine and forced his eyes so wide they watered. He tried to keep Zero pinned against the car, but the pain crumpled his body and he slid to his knees.

Zero's head twitched, just a moment before a rock hit him in the side of his jaw. He growled, more annoyed than hurt.

Harry bent down, grabbed another egg-sized stone, and flung it. Zero reached out and caught it. His head never moved. He flicked the rock back at her, and it struck just under her chin. Harry dropped, wheezing, to her knees and grabbed at her throat.

Eli gritted his teeth and straightened his back so he could stare at Zero's blank face. Blood soaked the sleeve of the faceless man's broken arm from biceps to wrist and dripped from his fingertips. Across one cheek, a purple bruise worked its way up from beneath the skin.

"No more," Zero whispered to Eli. "My whole life's messed up because of you."

Eli's hands dropped, and his knuckles scraped something hard. His fingers explored and found its shape. Harry's first stone. Eli wrapped his fingers around it.

Zero grabbed the front of Eli's shirt and dragged him to his feet. The motion took next to no effort, as if he were hefting a gym bag. The forest whirled and Eli slammed against the car. The Hornet's front end wrenched his back and set off another spasm. His hands flailed and he almost dropped the stone. His fingers pulled it close to his palm and tightened his grip.

"I'm the hero now," said Zero. "I'm going to take care of you, and then your damned searcher girlfriend, and then—"

Harry's pistol came whipping into Eli's line of sight. Zero grabbed for it, but Eli's shirt held his fingers. The fabric tore, half a second too late, and the steel barrel caught the faceless man in the side of the head. Certainty let him dodge the pain, but not the actual attack.

"Fucking bitch!" he roared. He shook the scraps of cotton twill from his hand and reached for Harry.

Eli brought the rock up, ignoring the pain in his back as he twisted around. The stone smashed into Zero's temple, right across from where Harry's pistol had struck. Right where a walnut-sized chunk of gravel had hit Eli almost sixteen years ago. He felt bone shift under the blow.

Zero made a muffled, bubbling sound deep in his throat. His hand came back around, fingers wide, but the movement threw him off balance. He teetered for a moment.

Harry pistol-whipped him again, cracking it across his temple.

Zero made another gargling noise. His knees folded and he collapsed to the ground, stretching out like a line between them. He twitched two more times and grew still.

Eli glanced at her. "Is he dead?"

"Maybe?" She coughed twice, rubbed her throat, and watched the body. "He's not breathing."

"Do they normally breathe?"

"I don't think so. No?"

Eli bent his knees as slow as he could, but when he dropped it still jarred his back. He fell to all fours and took a moment. Three deep breaths helped him calm the pain.

Harry crouched next to him. "Are you okay?"

"I think so," he said. "In the long run. Nothing a long hot bath and a dozen aspirin won't fix. Or a bottle of whiskey."

"If we make it out of this, I'll see what I can arrange."

"How about you?"

She coughed again. It had a raspy edge. "I've been better," she said, "but I'll be fine."

He reached out a cautious hand and pressed the fingers against Zero's neck. It took three tries to find a pulse. "Still alive. His pulse seems . . . good, I guess? Steady, at least."

"I can take care of that," said Harry. The pistol spun in her hand. The grip came to rest against her palm and her finger settled on the trigger.

"Whoa! We can't kill him."

"Why not?"

"He's a victim. They did this to him." He replayed Zero's rant in his head. "They did this to him because of me."

"Eli," she said, "I think it's wonderful that you care so much about your childhood bully, but he's one of them now. He's a faceless man, and that means he's the enemy."

"So we kill him and then what?" He waved his arm across the field to where the Model A sat. "Do we have time to fix Eleanor's tire?"

"Doubtful, since we left the toolbox back with little you."

"Dammit," he muttered, "that's right."

She looked at the Hornet. "Do you think we can get it free of the trees?"

Eli frowned. "I don't think it's moving any sooner than Eleanor."

"We . . . we'll have to steal a car."

He looked around. "I'm not sure there are any cars here. Yet."

A low growl rose up in the distance.

"Excellent timing, Mr. Teague." She sighed. She looked down at Zero, shook her head, and holstered the pistol.

"Okay," he said. "We can't get away through history. We can't get away on foot. Can we hide?"

She shook her head. "Certainty. They'd know where we were as soon as they got close. No hiding, no disguising, we just can't be near—"

"Yeah?"

She stared over at the Founders House, just visible through the thin trees. "We're near them," she said. "We're sometime around 1900. Right under their noses."

"What?"

She rolled Zero over and reached into his coat.

Eli watched her frisk the faceless man. "You looking for his pistol?"

"No," she said, moving on to another pocket. She pulled out a notepad, tossed it aside, continued her search. "New plan. We're not going to look for the dream."

Harry held up her prize. Zero's badge.

"We're going to go in there," she said, "right now, and we're going to steal it."

40

They ran across the field, away from the growling engine, through the gravel, and around the Founders House. Spikes of pain jarred Eli's back with every step, but after a few minutes they'd calmed enough for him to run without help from Harry.

The sprawling structure had two back entrances and a side entrance. Each was chained and locked. In his gut, Eli already knew the only way in was through the front door.

At the base of the broad stairs, Harry pushed the badge into his hand. "You hold it," she said.

"Why?"

She shrugged. "Faceless men, not faceless women."

"D'you really think it matters?"

"Do you really think it doesn't?"

He wrapped his fingers around the badge and they headed up the steps.

At the first landing, the dread hit. The childhood nervousness and confusion in the pit of his stomach. The feeling of being watched. He stumbled to a halt. Harry took another step and did the same. She glanced at him with worried eyes. "You too?"

He nodded.

The growl of the big engine echoed across the town.

They ran up to the next landing, stumbled again, then hit the top of the staircase, almost fifty feet above the road. Eli looked for a Hudson Hornet and was stunned for a moment by the view he had of Sanders. He could see the roof of the Silver Arrow, the fabric store just past it, the movie theater . . .

Harry shook the door. One of the small glass panels rattled. She brought her boot up and slammed her heel beneath the knob. On the third kick the wood splintered. It tore free on the fourth, and glass shattered as the door slammed back against the inside wall.

She grabbed Eli's arm and dragged them inside.

A few sheet-covered chairs slouched around the first room of the Founders House. An impressive fireplace stood at the far end, swept clean of all signs of an actual fire. A long, barren counter stretched off to the left, and an American flag stood next to it. Eli had seen many rooms like this as a teen, closed down for the winter until what little tourist trade Sanders had came back.

"Here," said Harry. She'd found a set of double doors leading away from the lobby. They were half glass, and Eli could see color and light beyond them. They each grabbed a handle and swung the doors open.

They speed-walked down a long hallway with patterned carpet and waist-high molding. A chill hung in the hall, like an overpowered air conditioner. Wall sconces provided light, and between them hung small portraits of men in colonial clothes like Harry's. Eli saw Benjamin Franklin, George Washington, and someone who might've been Thomas Jefferson, but he didn't recognize most of the ones he got a good look at.

He glanced back over his shoulder and saw the distant patch of sunlight that marked the lobby. "How long do you think this hallway is?"

Harry looked back, then ahead. "Fifty, maybe sixty yards? Why?"

Eli shook his head. He fumbled with the badge. On television, police and FBI agents made flicking it open look so casual. He couldn't figure out how to brace his fingers across the leather panels to expose the oval disc of silver and gold. Words stretched across it, but in the uneven light of the sconces they either made sense or looked like a jumble of Latin. In the dimmest parts of the hall, they could've been Egyptian pictographs. "Do you know how this thing works?"

"It makes people see what the holder—"

"Yeah, but how? Do I just hold it or is there a code word or a spell or something?"

She frowned. "I don't know."

They passed a double door with big steel push-plates and large windows honeycombed with wire. It would've looked more at home in a school or hospital. Through it, Eli glimpsed a long, tiled hallway.

The main hallway came to an end at a set of wooden doors carved with intricate reliefs and scrollwork. Eli couldn't focus on any one element through all the thick detail. Above the doors, a Latin phrase had been carved with just as much skill and precision.

AB INITIO

Harry grabbed his free hand. Her grip made the bones of his palm ache. "Ready?"

Eli nodded, took a deep breath, and held up the badge.

They pushed open the ornate doors and marched into the cathedral chamber on the other side.

Desks sat in endless rows, as did wooden and metal file cabinets, the ultimate open-plan office. Standing maps, much like John Henry's, appeared here and there. Eli's gaze followed the maps up and found chandeliers the size of swimming pools, and a spiderweb of clear pipes suspended above it all. As he stared, something whizzed through one of the pneumatic tubes and vanished into the distance.

Harry squeezed his hand and they stepped away from the doors, deeper into the room. Eli's gaze drifted back to ground level in time to pass a broad table covered with a huge map. The people around the table moved small models and tokens with long sticks.

Not people, he realized.

Faceless men.

They sat at desks and stood by maps and gathered in small clusters with file folders and loose papers. Some wore shirtsleeves and suspenders. Others had suit coats and vests. Eli saw short, wide ties and long, narrow ones. He saw a few wearing tall boots and long dark frocks like Harry's.

None of them had masks. Just blank ovals of flesh. Not even the weak illusion of identity here.

He'd expected a few dozen faceless men. A platoon or squadron or something. Not hundreds.

Maybe thousands.

Could there be a faceless man for every searcher? Did Harry have it backward? How many others, supposedly dead, had been converted into faceless men? Ones from Chains that didn't involve her or Porter?

Harry's hand tightened around his. Eli's fingers stiffened around the badge. He lifted it, placing it between them and the room.

A faceless man in a long coat and top hat walked by them without reacting. Another one stepped around them, barely registering them as he did. Two walked by, side by side, and didn't acknowledge them at all.

"It works," he murmured.

"Stating the obvious," she whispered back.

They walked forward blindly, farther into the throng, hands tight and shoulders pressed together. Faceless men passed in front of them, walked alongside them, watched them go by. Harry's fingers tightened around his.

"Hey, nimrod," someone shouted.

Eli's neck stiffened, and the edges of the leather badge case bit his fingers as they clenched around it. His pace stumbled, and Harry dragged him along. "What?" she whispered, studying his face.

He turned his head. "I think they found us."

A clearing formed in the swarm of faceless men, an open space they all walked around and avoided. Eli and Harry meandered along the edge of it. A few yards away stood a pair of faceless men flanking a wheelchair. Strapped into the wheelchair was a man—a normal man—in a Sanders police uniform.

"Zeke," murmured Eli.

"Abraham," muttered Harry.

"That was me," said a faceless man on the other side of the clearing. Eli recognized that voice too. He fought the urge to turn and look.

"Damn straight it was, moron," snarled Zeke. "Hittin' a guy in a wheelchair?! What the fuck's wrong with you? Watch where you're going!"

Harry tightened her grip and pulled. He glanced at the knot of faceless men once more and then let her lead him back into the crowd. He stepped up to her side and held the badge out in front of them. A faceless man at a desk turned his head to them as they walked past, then returned his attention to his paperwork.

Eli looked back as they passed a long cabinet of pigeonholes stuffed with envelopes. The far wall had almost vanished in the dim light. It had to be close to half a mile away. "Wait," he said.

Harry took another two steps before she stopped. "What?"

He looked back again, then leaned in close to her. "We've been walking pretty much in a straight line from the lobby."

She nodded.

"That first hallway, the main hall, was about fifty yards. And this room got to be almost a thousand feet across. Maybe more."

She glanced around them. "Yes?"

Eli looked at the room. "The Founders House isn't that big," he said. "If we've walked a quarter-mile, we should be out the back door and somewhere in the baseball field. We might even be past the first-base line."

"I don't mean to sound shallow," she murmured, "but at the moment my greater concern is being noticed and shot in the head."

"Okay. Yeah." He glanced around the huge room. "Where should we be going?"

"What?"

"Where's the dream supposed to be? Normally?"

Harry blinked. "Why are you asking me?"

"I thought you knew where we're going."

"I don't know. I've been following you."

"What?"

A faceless man turned his blank skull to them as he walked by. Eli held the badge a little higher and the agent continued on without pausing. Other faceless men stepped out of the way without hesitation, never turning or even registering them. A few turned their heads as Harry and Eli passed, but overall he sensed they had more important things to do.

Harry tugged on his hand and got them moving again. She muttered in his ear as they passed under a chandelier. "Why would you think I'd know?"

"I thought there'd be some stories or something," said Eli. "You've got a story for everything about this."

"Nobody's ever been in here before," she said. "At least nobody who ever came out."

"Okay," he said. "Okay, let's think this through. Where would it be? Where do you put the most valuable thing in the country to protect it?"

"In a safe? A vault?"

"Maybe? But where?"

A gaunt faceless man looked up as they walked past his desk. He followed them with his blank features. Eli shot a quick glance back over his shoulder. The figure was still focused on them.

"You're holding the badge too high," whispered Harry. "It's attracting attention."

"We'll attract more attention if I put it down."

"You don't know that."

"Fifteen always held it up high," said Eli. "I don't think he did it to look cool."

They walked past file cabinets and rows of desks and more faceless men. "Perhaps we should head back to the edge of the room," murmured Harry. "There might be a sign or a map. And we wouldn't be at the center of things."

Eli's fingers tingled. He tried to flex them and a spasm slid up his ring finger, stiffening it. The badge almost slipped away and he twisted his hand around to catch it.

"Careful," muttered Harry.

He felt another pinprick. Not from his fingers. Eli turned the leather case to look at the badge. The letters shimmered across the gold and silver surface. It felt like static electricity racing across his hand. "I think we're running out of time," he said.

"What?"

"The badge. It's . . . I think it's rejecting me or something."

Harry scowled. "The ones chasing us must've found Zero."

Eli looked at the dozens of faceless men around them. "How long do we have?"

"I don't know."

"How long did it take when they shut Porter's off?"

"I don't know," she snapped. "I thought we'd have more time, closer to the dream, that they wouldn't think we'd . . ."

Her eyes got wide.

"What?"

"Look around," she said. "Look as far as you can see, at the distant ones."

"What am I looking for?"

"The dream affects time," she said. "It flows differently as we get closer to it."

He nodded. "Right."

She studied the crowd. "Look for the faceless men who are moving slower."

Eli felt his own eyes go wide.

He looked down the rows of desks and cabinets, the aisles created by corkboards and pneumatic tubes. There were hundreds of faceless men, all in suits, all in motion. Filing, processing, marching from place to place. Trying to pick one out, to look for a particular detail, was like a childhood puzzle. Find the difference between these two—

A few hundred yards away, off to his left, a faceless man closed a file folder and moved it to a bin on the corner of his desk. His arm swung in a graceful, steady arc. He released the folder and it drifted down into the bin. Eli's heart beat twice while the file dropped.

"There," he said. "That way."

"Are you sure?"

The badge prickled his fingers again. "Sure enough."

They headed down the row. Eli pushed the badge across his body, keeping it close to Harry. Three faceless men passed by, each holding a clear mask in their hands. One was a clown's face. Another looked like some kind of animal, maybe a fox or wolf. The third turned his head to study Eli and Harry.

A wall loomed up ahead. The far side of the room. Eli could see some kind of arch or doorway there.

"Hello, Mr. Teague," a voice called out behind them. "Mrs. Pritchard. That is you, yes?"

Every faceless man around them straightened up from desks, reports, and conversations, their heads turning to focus on the two searchers. Harry's fingers tightened on Eli's and pulled him into a run. Blank skulls swung to follow them. They dodged between suited figures and grasping hands and reached the far wall.

Molding wrapped the archway there, and heavy curtains hung behind it like a small stage. They'd been tied off to each side, revealing a staircase of white marble. It would've fit very well in a big courthouse or capitol building.

A shot rang out and one of the curtains rippled.

They ran up the stairs blind, their shoes hitting each step with a *whap*. Harry raced ahead. Eli struggled to keep up, and took some small relief in seeing the top of the stairs only thirty or forty feet above.

Another gunshot echoed in the marble stairway. Harry shouted and grabbed at her leg. She stumbled off the top step and into the room by the landing. Eli ran to join her.

The room at the top of the stairs had marble floors and walls. A massive set of doors dominated one side of it. Eli didn't see any other furniture or decoration. Or light sources, even though midday brilliance filled the room.

Harry sprawled a few feet from the stairs. Her pants were bloody, but not so much that it leaked down to the floor. "Just grazed me," she said through clenched teeth.

"Can you walk?"

"Possibly?"

Footsteps echoed up the stairwell. Lots of them, in perfect sync. Harry let go of her leg and grabbed for her pistols.

"No, give them to me," said Eli, shoving the badge into his jeans. "You can barely stand."

The Colts spun in her palms and stopped with the grips to him. "Have you ever even fired a gun before?"

"Nope." He aimed at the stairwell and squeezed both triggers at once. The pistols bucked in his hands and he heard a crack of metal on stone over the echo of the gunshots.

The footsteps stopped.

He squeezed off two more rounds with each pistol. The noise echoed in the room. One of the rounds sparked in the stairwell and left a black mark on the wall.

"Hello, Mr. Teague," said a voice. Fifteen. "I see you have weapons now."

Eli answered with a few more shots. The footsteps retreated. Quickly. Unevenly.

"What's going on?" whispered Harry.

He leaned back to her. "I don't know," he murmured back. "You keep saying they can dodge, they can't miss, but they haven't been able to shoot us."

"They *just* shot me," she whispered through clenched teeth. "You were just in the hospital four days ago."

"But they didn't kill us."

She rolled her eyes and pushed herself up the wall to her feet.

Eli studied the doors on the far side of the room. They had to be close to ten feet tall, and each one wider than he was tall. The clean, elegant panels held a round disk of brass which stretched between the two doors, and a simple, old-fashioned keyhole sat at the center, right on the hairline seam between the doors. At the top and bottom, four brass sliders locked the doors in position.

He peered a little closer. The doors didn't seem to be made of wood, but they also didn't look like metal. After a few moments of staring, it almost seemed like the door was painted on the wall, like an elaborate Wile E. Coyote work of art. The longer he looked, the less sure he felt about the material.

A sound came from the stairwell. He turned and squeezed the triggers two or three times each. The faceless man standing there flung himself back. The noise of shuffling, sliding, falling bodies echoed up to them.

"Mr. Teague," called Fifteen. His voice echoed up the steps. "What do you think this will gain you? There's no way out of the rotunda except past us."

"We don't have a lot of time," said Harry.

Eli studied the doors. "I know."

"Or a lot of ammunition."

"Surrender now," Fifteen said, "and I promise your execution will be swift and painless."

Eli looked at the lock. "Any ideas?"

She shrugged. "If I had my toolbox, there's a lockpick set in it, but I have a feeling they wouldn't work."

He reached out, brushed the lock, and felt a hum of power travel through his arm and down to the floor. His fingers jumped back, then reached out again. It reminded him of a low-level electric shock, conducted down to the . . .

Not to the floor.

He handed one of the pistols back to Harry and felt the square badge case buzzing against his thigh. He fumbled it out, flipped it open.

A gold and silver key sat in the leather case. One end was a heavy disc covered with more shifting letters and symbols. Its long neck ended in three simple teeth, the kind of thing used to open a cartoon jail cell.

Harry fired off four precise shots at the stairwell, one after another. On the fourth the slide of her Colt locked back. She released it, dropped the weapon into its holster, and plucked the other pistol from Eli's hands. "Whatever you plan on doing," she said, "now would be an excellent time for it."

"Hey, this heist was all your idea."

Eli pulled the key from the case and slid it into the lock. It twitched between his fingers and then grew rigid, as if something had clamped down on it. "I think it's—"

The key lunged an inch deeper into the lock, spun around twice, and then sank in up to its disk. It rotated one more time, then vanished into the lock.

Harry pulled the trigger twice, then twice again. She holstered the pistol. "We just need to get to the dream," she said. "We know whoever stole the dream got away without a trace."

"Fingers cross," said Eli.

The brass sliders at the top and bottom of each door retracted, vanishing into the doorframe. The seam between the two doors darkened and widened. The keyhole swelled with it and came apart, just an odd ripple on the edge of either door. Eli looked for some sort of lock mechanism as the doors opened wider, but saw nothing other than smooth whatever-the-doors-were-made-of.

The gap stretched to a foot wide, then two. Harry put a hand on Eli's shoulder and pushed him forward. She limped after him.

The air in the circular chamber smelled of dust and old paper and wood. Museum smells. Soft light illuminated a large stone table, almost a plinth, at the center of the room.

Dozens of flags hung in the chamber. The one on Eli's left had the stripes of an American flag, but a squat British flag sat in place of the blue field of stars. The one next to it had a familiar array of thirteen stars and stripes, and the one past that had the stars arranged in a circle. Eli followed them around the room, watching the pattern of stars change from grids to circles to uneven arrays and back.

His eyes returned to the first one and counted. Forty-seven American flags. Despite the smell in the air, all of them looked new. The last one had a dense grid—six rows of nine stars each.

Definitely a plinth, not a table, at the center of the room. A rounded slab of . . . granite? Limestone? It had to be five feet across and two feet tall. It looked old. Ancient old.

It also looked very empty.

41

Harry took a few limping steps forward. "Where is it?"

Eli approached the plinth, then gazed around the chamber. "It's . . . it's not here."

"Yes, I can see that."

He studied the flags, the vaulted ceiling, the backs of the doors. "We must not be early enough. It must've vanished sooner than everyone thought."

She shook her head. "It vanished in the '60s."

"Yeah, but how does anyone know that?"

"It's what came down the Chai—"

"But how do they know?!"

"I don't know!" she snapped. "It should be here!"

Eli heard the rustle of clothes and shoes in the marble room behind them. He shuffled around to face the door.

Fifteen strode into the chamber. He wore his transparent mask, the one Eli had first seen weeks ago and one town over. His suit looked sharp, as if he'd had it cleaned and pressed just for this encounter. Half a dozen immaculate faceless men flanked him on either side.

"Being in this room," he said, "is an act of treason against the United States, punishable by immediate execution." His pistol came up. The other faceless man mirrored him.

Harry reached past Eli, holding something up. For an instant, he thought it was one of her pistols, that he was going to be her human shield in a last stand against the faceless men.

But she held a small object between her thumb and finger. A poker chip. She raised it slowly, as unthreateningly as possible, to put it between them and Fifteen.

The faceless man's chin went up and his head tilted back. Just a little. As if the wooden token had caught his attention.

Eli studied the chip himself. Dark-red paint, an eerily exact match for blood, ran along the edge and up onto the face at points. Some of it had chipped away or rubbed off over time. Where the bare wood showed, it had the dark, smooth look left by years of handling.

The marks on the poker chip's face looked like an elongated loop and skinny triangle, both stretching across the circle. Then, where they intersected, his focus shifted just a little. Just enough. He saw the stylized "AP," the sides of the two letters pressed together to form a single line.

Harry swiveled her wrist, turning the token back and forth. "You know what this is?"

"It's a dislocated item," said Fifteen. "A poker chip from one of the saloons of Hourglass, California, 1886. You fugitives use them as representative tokens."

"It's a favor," said Harry. She limped up next to Eli, keeping the wooden token in front of them. "Your favor."

Fifteen pulled the slide back on his pistol. It slammed into place with a hard *clack* that echoed across the second landing, and then the weapon dropped to point at Eli's chest.

"Whatever information you may have about the location of the dream can be just as easily cut out of you as long as your head's intact."

Eli swallowed.

"Except," Harry said, "I'm calling in the favor." She thrust the poker chip forward like a horror-movie nun warding off vampires with her cross.

Fifteen paused, a faceless statue. "You're what?"

"This is the only favor Abraham Porter ever gave out." She locked her eyes on the empty sockets of the mask, on the smooth skin beneath the transparent plastic. "That *you* gave out, before you became one of the faceless men. This is your favor. I'm calling it in and asking you to honor it."

Fifteen's chin came down, then tilted ever so slightly up again.

"I ask for safe passage," she said. "Eli and I walk out of here, un-

harmed, un . . . unchanged. No pursuit. We're simply allowed to leave."
She looked at the empty plinth. "To leave all of this."

A moment of silence stretched out in the tabernacle of the dream.

Fifteen took a step forward. Then another. He was twelve feet away.
Ten feet. Eight. The pistol stayed level with Eli's chest.

Eli and Harry stood their ground.

The faceless man reached out with his free hand and plucked the
favor from Harry's grip. The pistol never wavered. His fingers moved
up and down, pushing the wooden token onto its edge and over onto the
other side. He flipped it again and again.

Harry's wounded leg gave out. She fell against Eli with a grunt, her
empty hand still held out in front of them.

"Tell me, Mrs. Pritchard, Mr. Teague . . . why did you, or any of
the searchers, think that a faceless man would be bound by some vague
contract made by a dead man?"

Her hand dropped. "He isn't dead."

"Abraham Porter no longer exists."

"But he isn't dead," Eli insisted. "You're him."

"I had no existence before the faceless men."

"Then you're a liar," said Harry.

The poker chip made a crisp, sharp sound as it snapped in half. Eli's
stomach dropped. The pistol jabbed into his sternum to catch it.

"I," said Fifteen, "would mind your tongue. The faceless men are
the true heroes of America."

"Heroes who don't honor their debts," said Harry.

"Abraham Porter is—"

"Was a good man," interrupted Eli, trying hard to ignore the pistol.
"An honorable man. Honorable to a fault, the way Harry tells it. She
couldn't imagine a situation where he wouldn't honor a favor when it
was called in."

Fifteen closed his fist around the two pieces of the poker chip and
squeezed.

"It seems I was wrong," said Harry, pushing her chin up.

Eli's gut swirled again and carried up memories of talking over
Truss, back when the old man was just his boss at a small branch of a
bank. Of knowing he was either saving his job or ending it. Of being
almost sick with fear and confident at the same time.

"Are the two of you," asked Fifteen, "familiar with the concept of the filibuster?"

Eli glanced at Harry. She met his gaze, then looked at the faceless man. "The . . . what?"

"The filibuster is a delaying tactic used in the United States Senate, to prevent a bill from being brought to the floor for a vote."

"Okay." Eli glanced down at the pistol.

"The senator must keep talking," explained Fifteen. "They cannot sit down. They may not take breaks. They cannot eat. They cannot drink anything except water or milk."

"Milk?"

"If any of these rules are violated," said the faceless man, ignoring him, "or if the Senate invokes cloture, the filibuster is at an end and the business of government proceeds. Do you understand?"

Eli swallowed. "I . . . no, I'm not sure I do." He glanced at Harry, and she shook her head.

Fifteen opened his fist and let the broken splinters of the favor fall to the stone floor. "I am honoring Abraham Porter's favor in a manner that matches the rules of our government. We are delaying your execution. You may speak for as long as you wish, without moving, without a break, without nourishment. And when you're finished, unless you've somehow convinced me of a reason to let you go, I will shoot each of you in the head."

Harry straightened up. "What?"

The faceless man took a step back. The hand holding the pistol settled down to his waist, pointing it between them. "Your time has begun, Mrs. Pritchard, Mr. Teague."

42

Eli stood by the plinth and tried not to focus on the enormous pistol aimed in his general direction. It had to be close to a foot long. The angular barrel had squared-off ridges along the top, like the teeth of a gear.

Harry leaned against him to keep weight off her leg.

Fifteen's trigger finger tensed. "I'll consider twenty seconds of silence the end of your delaying tactic, which is in six, five, four, thr—"

"Wait," said Eli. "So we're just supposed to talk and make a case for you not to shoot us?"

"Yes," said the faceless man.

"That wasn't what I asked for," said Harry. "I requested safe passage."

"Which you will have," Fifteen said, "if certain conditions are met."

She glared at him. "This is not how favors work."

"Mrs. Pritchard, I am only even considering this to honor the memory of Abraham Porter, a fine American and a veteran. If you prefer, we can skip directly to the execution."

"Okay," Eli blurted out, "you've got us. We came here to steal the dream."

As one, the faceless men tensed.

Harry shot him a look.

Eli took a breath and tried to organize his thoughts. "We used Zeke's badge—"

"Zero," said Fifteen.

"We used Zero's badge to . . . to gain access to your secure headquarters. We thought if we could get the dream, if we turned out to be the ones who stole it, then we could also return it. We could end all of this. We had good intentions.

"But the dream was already gone," he continued, waving his hand at the empty plinth. "So we couldn't steal it. We didn't do anything wrong."

"Regardless of the dream's location," said Fifteen, "your intent was theft. You have entered the rotunda. The punishment is execution."

"Yeah, but why isn't . . ." Eli counted off a few seconds. "Are we allowed to ask questions during this . . . this thing?"

"You are," Fifteen said. "I'm under no obligation to answer them."

"Okay, then," Eli sighed. "If the dream isn't here, why do you have to kill us?"

"Because only the faceless men are allowed in the rotunda," said the fox-masked faceless man, "in order to keep the dream secure."

"But it isn't here."

"Irrelevant," said Fifteen

"More to the point," said Harry, "why isn't it here? It's the early twentieth century. The dream didn't vanish until the '60s."

"In fact, Mrs. Pritchard, it was 1898 when you and Mr. Teague entered the Founders House."

"Then where's the dream. It should be—"

"The main office exists outside the normal flow of time. It is always now here."

"Which now?" Eli asked.

"All of them."

Harry glanced at Eli. "Is that why Sanders is different?"

"Because of its proximity to the dream," said Fifteen with a nod, "the town of Sanders exists outside the normal flow of history. As such, the town and its citizens are anomalies for us. They represent uncertainty."

"Citizens," said Eli. "You mean . . . me?"

"That's correct. Like all citizens of Sanders, you are an anomaly."

"It isn't that there's something weird about me? It's the whole town?"

"Sanders is, from a temporal point of view, the most important town in the country. Possibly in the entire world, if you consider the role of the United States on a global scale."

Eli's shoulder twinged where he'd been shot. Memories of the Boston bus station and fleeing the fork in the road swirled behind his eyes. Harry commenting how lucky—

Fifteen made a tiny gesture with his pistol. "Five seconds. Four. Three."

"That's how I got away at the bus station," Eli said. "That's how Harry and I kept getting away." He looked down at himself, over at her. "That's why Zeke . . . Zero didn't kill me. That's why you're all right up close to us now. You're uncertain. You can *miss* me!"

The empty sockets of Fifteen's mask stared at him.

"If Zero was also an anomaly," said Harry, "why did you take him?"

"Our recruitment criteria are not for public knowledge."

"It was because of me," said Eli. He looked at Harry. "I was traveling with you, so you were uncertain too. They were trying to even the odds. Cancel out our advantage.

"But it didn't work, did it?" Eli spat out the ideas as fast as they formed. "Zeke just became an . . . an uncertain faceless man. He was just as unpredictable to you as I was."

"Very perceptive, Mr. Teague."

"He's hurt," Eli said. "Back in, what did you say, 1898? He was in a crash."

"We are aware. The faceless men take care of our own."

Eli nodded and ran the paradox through his head again.

Harry's gaze drifted to the empty plinth. "Is it possible that someone from Sanders took the dream?"

"No. We have searched the town extensively."

"When?"

Fifteen said nothing.

"Oh, Christ," said Eli.

Harry glanced at him. "What?"

He looked at her. At the plinth. At Fifteen. "I think . . . I know where the dream is. Right where it is."

The faceless men tensed.

The empty sockets of Fifteen's mask bored into him. The huge pistol rose up and settled a few inches from Eli's chest. "Where is it?"

Eli closed his eyes for a moment, studying the thin line of thoughts that had fallen together in his mind. He worked through the line—

through the chain—of events to make sure he hadn't doomed Harry and himself.

"It's . . . complicated."

"Mr. Teague, if this is an attempt to delay your filibuster—"

"No, no," he waved his hands. "John Henry mentioned an idea to me, that he thought we were running out of history because the dream was gone. That things were unraveling. Getting eaten up. It's what first got me thinking. In programming, sometimes you have something called a recursive function. It's a function that calls itself, and it'll keep doing it again and again until it gets the answer it wants. But if the function isn't written right, it'll just keep calling itself forever. And it eventually eats up all the system memory and causes a stack overflow. The computer crashes."

Fifteen's head shifted to the left. "You believe the dream has created some kind of loop?"

"I think it's made a lot of them." He looked at Harry. "Like how we stopped Zero. I knew the trees would stop his car because I'd already seen the car stopped when I was a kid. But it was only there to see because I'd already done it."

"The predestination paradox," said Harry.

"Right." He looked at the faceless men again. "As I understand it, the founding fathers created the dream—or had it created—in the 1770s. And it existed for the next two hundred years or so as America grew and expanded."

"Until it was stolen in 1963," Fifteen said.

"We'll get to that," Eli said, waving away the interruption. "The real point is, something else was going on in the United States for those two hundred years too."

Beneath the clear mask, Fifteen's flesh rippled.

"We were." Eli looked at her "Me and Harry. Harry and Christopher. John Henry. Alice Ramsey and Abraham Porter and Phoebe Fitzgerald. James and Monica and Theo. Everyone at Hourglass. All of the searchers. And all the faceless men. We were there, traveling back and forth, looking for the dream."

"Because it had vanished," said Fifteen.

He nodded. "Right. But, from a chronological point of view, we were there first."

"That's the nature of traveling in history," said Harry. "Effect sometimes comes before cause. Like hearing the train whistle in Independence."

"Right," said Eli. "Exactly. So, for two hundred-plus years, hundreds of searchers were looking for the dream." He turned his attention back to Fifteen. "Plus all of your . . . your people looking to get it back too. Maybe thousands of us, from a certain point of view, when you consider people overlapping as they travel to different periods. And, based off what Harry's told me, what happens when a community of thousands of people want the same thing? When they all believe the same thing? What's the dream do?"

The faceless man didn't move. Eli counted off fourteen seconds before the masked head moved side to side.

"No," Harry said.

"No," echoed Fifteen. "That's wrong."

"I don't think so," said Eli. "It all makes sense."

"No, it doesn't," Harry said.

"It does," said Eli. "Thousands of searchers looking for it. Hundreds of faceless men trying to get it back. For hundreds of years. Overlapping again and again and again. So, finally, the dream makes what they want possible." His gaze fell on the empty slab of stone. "It vanishes. It has to. So we can all search for it."

Fifteen shook his head again. "Our sworn duty is to find it. It's the searchers' goal as well. If this was a mechanism of the dream, as you suggest, then it would've been found by now."

"I don't think so," said Eli. "Because the searchers all individually want to find it themselves. Each of them has their own ideas on how the search should end and which of them should find it."

"The faceless men don't. Our one goal—"

"According to Harry, since you became one of the faceless men, your goal has been to wipe out the searchers."

Fifteen said nothing.

Eli took a breath and organized his remaining thoughts. "Nobody knows how the dream was stolen, right? How somebody found your base, made it past all of you, and then back out with the dream?"

"We are investigating several possibilities."

"I'm an anomaly," said Eli. "And we had one of your badges. We didn't even get to the stairs before you spotted us." He gestured past Fifteen at the line of faceless men. "We never would've made it back out."

"Agreed."

"So how did someone else do it? If we couldn't do it with those advantages, how did someone get all the way in here and back out without any of you seeing them?"

Harry looked at the plinth. At the doors. At the faceless men. "It would be impossible."

"It would be," Eli agreed. "Nobody could've made it past all of the faceless men. It couldn't happen. Unless the dream stole itself."

"No," said Fifteen.

Eli shook his head. "If someone else had it, shouldn't we all see their influence somewhere else in the country? Shouldn't there be another slow town out there, one that's lagging behind history?"

Fifteen didn't respond.

"If the dream vanished thirty years before I was born, why are we still seeing all of its effects here in Sanders?"

Eli's gut churned. A bead of sweat ran down his back. The awful sense of a moment of truth loomed over him again.

"There's only one place the dream can be," he told Fifteen. "It hid itself in the last place anyone would look."

He reached his hand out over the empty plinth. He couldn't quite reach the center without leaning, but he got pretty close. Two feet of empty space stretched between his palm and the limestone plinth. Harry shuffled her feet to stay leaning against him.

"You said it's always 'now' here, right?"

Fifteen didn't move. The blank skin behind his mask didn't flinch.

"So that either means the dream was never here, or . . ."

Eli lowered his hand.

And set it on top of the dream.

43

Harry gasped. Eli turned his head and, as it had for him a few times in the past, time slowed to a halt.

Growing up in Sanders had been boring most of the time, and he and his friends had all declared various plans to escape their town. Eli would be an archeologist and dig up old battlefields around the world. Robin wanted to draw comic books. Josh had plotted out a path to the Supreme Court.

For almost three years, Corey had been obsessed with movie special effects. He'd rent sci-fi movies from the Emporium and watch them again and again, studying how things had been done. None of them could go a week without at least one intense lecture about Ray Harryhausen or Stan Winston or Phil Tippett.

The idea of forced perspective had come up a lot. Tricks to make small things look big or big things look small. According to Corey, it usually involved models, special sets, and camera lenses that worked like bifocal glasses. Done right, the effects looked amazing. Done wrong, they looked like . . . models and sets.

All the objects Eli could see around the dream—the plinth, the flags, the lid of the wooden case, even his own outstretched hand—gave off the subtle, unconscious cues that told him he was seeing the thing inside the case in forced perspective. That he wasn't seeing its true size. That he *couldn't* see its full size.

It looked like a model of an atom, its swirling rings etched with symbols. Then it turned and looked like a mechanical snake twisting around to swallow its own tail. Another twist and it looked like an old-fashioned astronomical model, with planets and moons whirling on concentric rings.

The surfaces of the dream gleamed with gold and brass, dark wood and ivory, glass and iron. Dense, intricate detail covered some parts—were those *hieroglyphs* around the image of the eagle?—while others had been polished smooth. He looked at himself in its mirrored surfaces and couldn't shake the feeling it looked back at him.

Then the moment ended. The gentle pressure of his hand landing on the lid pushed it shut. The box closed with a low thump, hiding the dream from his view just seconds after he'd found it. His palm rested on the wooden case.

The thump echoed back to him and he looked up.

The faceless men had all dropped to one knee. Even Fifteen, right in front of them. Their heads were bowed, their hats in their hands. It struck Eli that their pose made them look like a group of knights waiting for a blessing.

Or for orders.

"What . . . what's going on?"

"Mr. Teague," said Fifteen, not raising his head, "you have custody of the American Dream."

Harry shuffled closer. "It's yours," she whispered. "You did it. You found the dream."

"I did?"

"You have custody of the dream," Fifteen repeated. "The country is now yours to shape and guide."

Eli looked down at the faceless man. "Could you stand up, please. It's kind of . . . weird talking to you like this."

Fifteen rose to his full height. His pistol vanished into his coat, but his hat stayed in his hands and his chin stayed down. "Is this better, Mr. Teague?"

"I guess. Why are you all . . ." He looked at the other faceless men. "Why are you doing this?"

"The faceless men serve the dream," said Fifteen, "and the dream now serves you."

"Consarn it," murmured Harry.

Eli looked at her, at the wooden case. "How does this work?"

"No one knows," she said. "Until now, this had just been part of the story."

"How do the other parts of the story go? What do I do? Do I have to phrase my wish in the form of a question or something?"

Fifteen raised his chin a half inch. "If I may?"

"Yeah, sure."

"The dream affects beliefs. It strengthens them, but it can also shape them. As the custodian of the dream, you may decide which direction the country will take."

"You mean . . . I can control what people think?"

"More, *how* they think. Their leanings and preferences."

"As of when?"

"Whenever you want. We are outside of history here. You may begin where and when you like." The faceless man's muffled words carried a terrible weight. The weight of failure.

"How long do I have to decide what I want to do?"

"Consider it," said the faceless man, "like chess. Your move isn't complete until you remove your hand."

Harry took his other hand. Squeezed it once. Let go.

Eli looked down at the case. It was almost two foot square. He was no expert, but he thought the wood was oak. Plain, but well made. He'd probably never give it a second look at a yard sale or antique store.

He could feel the warmth of it, the power, seeping up into his fingertips. He imagined it making him strong and powerful, like the comic-book superheroes he'd read about as a kid. This could be his origin story. The point when his life finally started to mean something. The moment that he . . .

"This shouldn't be about me," he said.

Fifteen's chin went up another half inch.

"I mean it." Eli shook his head. "Even if the dream was supposed to belong to one person, I shouldn't be the guy shaping the country, no matter how much it might need it. Before these past few weeks, I'd barely met anyone who didn't live within thirty miles of me. I hadn't seen any of the country. Hell, I barely ever left Sanders.

"The whole idea was that everyone would have a chance to live the life they wanted, right? It was never intended to let somebody force their dream on everyone else." He patted the wooden case with his fingertips. "The founding fathers were right to keep this locked away. To leave it with you."

Fifteen bowed his head. "Thank you, Mr. Teague. So what will you do with it?"

He looked at the box. At Harry. "I thought I wanted to go home, but really I was just scared. Truth is, all I ever wanted was to get out. To see everything else. And I can do that now."

"Then you release the dream back into our custody?"

The muscles shifted in Eli's arm. His palm lifted off the wooden case, dragging his fingers behind it. He opened his mouth to speak and—

Harry pushed his hand back down onto the box. "Wait! Will we be safe?"

Fifteen turned the blank gaze of his mask on her. "Safe?"

Eli took in a breath and pressed his hand against the case. "Yeah, safe," he echoed. "I'm not going to move my hand and then you kill both of us?"

The faceless man said nothing.

"Being in here is punishable by execution, right? So here's my one wish or order or . . . whatever. Harry and I leave here without being killed." He looked at her and thought of Christopher Pritchard, of Phoebe Fitzgerald, of Theo Knickerbocker. "Nobody else gets killed."

Fifteen bowed his head. "It will be as you say, Mr. Teague."

Eli looked at Harry. Her chin dipped once, her eyes stayed on his. "Okay, then," he said. "I'm releasing it."

"Back into our custody?"

"Yes." He cleared his throat and raised his voice. "I release the American Dream back into the custody of the faceless men."

He raised his hand. Static electricity crackled under his fingertips like the screen of an old television set. He stretched his fingers wide and lifted them away from the lid.

The wood box sat on the stone plinth. Unmoving. Unconcerned.

The faceless men rose to their feet as one. Hats slid back above masks. Pistols vanished into coats. Fifteen reached up and set his fedora on his blank skull. "Thank you, again, Mr. Teague."

"You're welcome."

Fifteen extended one finger to point at Eli's chest. "Remove them. Now."

The faceless men leaped forward.

44

The faceless men slammed into Eli. The clown and the gaunt one grabbed his arms and yanked him away from the sandstone plinth. Eli struggled, but it was like fighting statues. The chamber spun, a whirlwind of marble and flags. He caught a glimpse of two other faceless men lifting Harry as she kicked and fought. His feet stumbled as they dragged him away.

The brightness of the marble antechamber made him squint. The doors of the rotunda swung shut and closed. A click echoed from the restored keyhole.

They hauled him back, and Eli's stomach lurched as he began to drop. They'd thrown him out onto the staircase, he realized, to break countless bones as he tumbled and crashed down forty feet worth of marble steps. He wondered if the fall would kill him.

But they held on, dragging him backward as they charged down the stairs with an eerie, metronomic speed and precision. The marble room rushed away, and the heavy curtains closed across the staircase. They held him facing the archway, but the sounds of motion and typing and muffled conversations reached his ears.

The two faceless men released Eli's arms and stepped away. After the whirlwind trip away from the dream and down the stairs, the lack of support left him swaying. He shuffled his feet into better positions and looked around.

Harry stood a few yards away, favoring her bad leg, flanked by her own pair of faceless men. She brushed her hair out of her face and shook her coat back into position. Her eyes met Eli's and mirrored his own confusion.

The clown dipped his head and held out Eli's derby. A faceless man with an expressionless mask presented Harry's tricorne.

Fifteen stood before the curtain. He strode forward, between Eli and Harry. The sounds of business and work faded to silence.

"The dream has been restored," he boomed to the chamber.

His voice echoed across the massive room. Applause broke out. Some of the faceless men cheered, the sounds muffled by flesh and distance. It reminded Eli of old newsreels, of polite, contained expressions of joy.

The noise level settled back to normal, although the chamber seemed brighter. More energetic. Unburdened.

"All remaining agents in the field should be recalled," said the gaunt faceless man with the fox mask.

"Agreed," said Fifteen. "At this point all efforts should be put toward relocation."

Eli glanced at Harry. "Relocation?"

Fifteen's blank face turned to aim at Eli. "The security of the dream has been compromised."

Harry shook her head. "No," she said, "it hasn't. Eli's correct. It's never left your care."

"Security has been compromised," said Fifteen, extending a finger, "by the two of you."

Something rolled over in Eli's gut. Harry's hands settled low at her sides. Right by the holsters holding her empty pistols. Her eyes flicked from side to side, watching the faceless men around them.

"The dream will be moved," the faceless man continued, "because its location and the location of the office have been confirmed by outside parties. This action follows all existing protocols."

Eli blinked. "What's that mean?"

"The founding fathers were very thorough," said Fifteen. "Contingencies exist for almost every situation, including a compromised location." His blank face swung back and forth, pointing at each of them. "The dream will be moved, and the office of the faceless men with it. This time tomorrow, the Founders House will just be an abandoned hotel near the center of Sanders. This will have some effects on your hometown, Mr. Teague, most noticeably—"

"What happens to *us*?" said Harry. Her fingers flexed reflexively by the holsters.

For a man with no face, Eli thought Fifteen did an amazing job of looking confused. "What do you mean?"

"You said we've compromised the security of the dream."

"You did," agreed Fifteen. The empty sockets of his mask turned to Eli. "You've seen the dream. Touched it, even. You both now know where it's located within our base of operations, and where our base is. This is why we need to relocate."

Eli and Harry waited. "And?" she asked.

"And nothing," said Fifteen. "Per Mr. Teague's request, there will be no punishment."

Eli counted three heartbeats. "So . . . you're just letting us go?"

"Correct," said Fifteen. He gestured down an aisle of desks and file cabinets. "This way, please."

Fifteen marched forward. Eli and Harry followed, her arm draped across his shoulders. Two faceless men fell into step on either side of them, with two more shoulder to shoulder behind them. It felt like a Secret Service kind of formation, the way a president would be guided through a crowd.

Harry cleared her throat. "What about Eleanor?"

Fifteen turned his head to her without slowing. "Who?"

"The car," Eli said. "Our car."

"The 1929 Model A business coupe," said Fifteen with a nod. "It's currently a dislocated object in 1898. It will be retrieved and restored to any appropriate era you wish."

"Thank you," said Harry.

Their group moved smoothly through the swarm of faceless men, passing maps and desks and card catalogs. They turned once beneath one of the massive chandeliers, marched down a second aisle, and came to a wide set of double doors. The formation shifted around Eli and Harry as a faceless man on either side stepped forward to hold them open so Fifteen never broke pace.

The hallway beyond looked like a hospital basement, with pale green floors and stripes on the walls. Their footsteps echoed against the concrete. It reminded Eli of his recent injuries.

"What about Zeke and his Hornet?" he asked. "What'll happen to them?"

"As you've no doubt realized, Mr. Teague," said Fifteen, half turning his head to his shoulder, "the Hudson Hornet will remain where it crashed. It is dislocated, but the nature of Sanders should prevent it from causing any damage to the timeline."

"And Zeke?"

"Zero will be repaired and go through rehabilitation. It's my own fault for rushing him into the field. Adjusting to the nature of being a faceless man is overwhelming for some people. More so if they are an anomaly. We'll repair his wounds and his mind. The faceless men have always taken care of our own."

"Will it work?" Eli asked. "Will you really be able to help him?"

"It took several years," said the clown, walking at Eli's shoulder, "but eventually I was able to resume my duties and responsibilities. Thank you for your concern."

Eli stared at the sockets above the plastic smile, at the shape of the skull behind the mask. "Zeke?"

"I am currently known as Thirty-Three, Mr. Teague."

"Are you . . . are you okay?"

"I have health, certainty, and purpose. I am one of the faceless men, and always have been."

"That's . . . good?"

Thirty-Three gave a polite nod.

They came to a single door with a large glass window. Sunlight fell through it to make a bright square on the concrete floor. Fifteen stopped with his toes just on the edge of the light.

In the distance, Eli could see buildings, an open space, and what looked like some kind of snow-covered scaffolding. Then the images lined up in his mind and he realized he was seeing the baseball field bleachers from behind. They were looking out one of the back doors of the Founders House.

"You're free to go," said Fifteen. "You may also continue using the dream's effects to travel through our country's history."

Harry's brows went up. "Really?"

"It's a natural consequence of the dream's existence. It isn't our place to restrict it. We will, however, continue to monitor for disruptions to the timeline of the United States. Any serious incidents will be dealt with. Harshly."

"I understand," she said.

"Excellent," said the faceless man. "Please pass word of this along to your fellow searchers."

Thirty-Three stepped around his superior and opened the door. The sunlight shifted angles. Cold air rolled into the hall. Off in the distance, a car engine chugged away. A very modern engine, to Eli's ear.

Eli turned to Harry. A few loose strands of blond hair swung free from her tricorne and caught the sun. "Shall we?" he said.

"Yes," she said. "Yes, I think we shall."

Fifteen reached out and set a hand on Harry's shoulder. "Not you, Mrs. Pritchard."

Her arm stiffened across Eli's shoulders. His tightened on her waist. "Why not?"

"You told us we were free to leave," she said.

"And you are," said Fifteen. "You were promised freedom, but not freedom together. Mr. Teague must be returned. He'll be the only one leaving this way."

Eli and Harry looked at each other. "Returned . . . where?"

"To Sanders," the faceless man said, gesturing at the door. "Your town is an anomaly. You are part of the town. It needs to be as complete as possible when it catches up with the rest of the country."

"What?"

"Your town will be freed of the dream's influence. Its progress will no longer be slowed. I'd expect the first few weeks to be . . . startling. You can also be an active agent there, helping to smooth over any confusion or suspicion that may arise."

"He's my partner," said Harry.

Fifteen nodded. "And most likely will be again. Eventually."

Eli frowned. "How long is that?"

"As long as it takes for new connections to establish between Sanders and history. Weeks. Months, perhaps. No more than a few years."

"A few *years*?" they both said at once.

"I wish I could be more exact. Nothing like this has ever happened before, or will ever happen again. It's a unique moment in American history. As I said before, Sanders is one of the most important places in the country."

Eli and Harry looked at each other. Her grip on his shoulders loosened "What if—" Eli began.

"There's no way around it," Fifteen told them. "Once you leave, Mr. Teague, relocation will cut off the town. There will be no more of the slick spots, as you like to call them. Not here, at least. The only way to travel in and out of Sanders will be the same way everyone else does."

He gestured at the door.

"I . . ." Eli looked at Harry, the door, back to Harry. "Thanks, I guess."

"Thanks?"

"For saving my life half a dozen times. And not dumping me on the side of the road somewhere. Thanks for convincing me to finally get out of my town."

"You did that on your own," she said. "Even if it was for very stupid reasons."

He chuckled. "Yeah, I guess they were."

She wrapped her arms around him and squeezed. She was a good height to hug. They fit well in each other's arms. "Thank you for . . . everything."

"I guess I'll see you . . . sometime, maybe?"

She glanced at Fifteen. "Eventually," she said. She took a few limping steps back. "I'll find you again. I promise."

"I'll be waiting."

45

He stepped out of the Founders House into a patch of snow and heard the door shut behind him. He looked over his shoulder and saw an empty hallway through smudged glass. He wondered if Harry and Fifteen and Thirty-Three stood there watching him, hidden from sight, or if the dream had already moved them along to somewhere else. He looked up at the sprawling structure, hoping to see any sign of life, and saw none.

He shuffled through the ankle-deep snow across the back lot, down the gravel side road, and out onto the slush-covered street. No Hudson Hornets. No Model A. Nothing.

He walked through the slush toward the Silver Arrow.

Within half an hour, he learned he'd been gone for over three months. He'd missed Christmas and New Year's. People had given up hope. His mother had gone past hysterics to mourning. The fact that Eli's apartment had been found vandalized with the door kicked in, and that Zeke Miller vanished a few days later, had led to numerous whispered theories. Small towns might not run on gossip, but it tended to be a standard alternative fuel source. People talked a bit louder about Zeke's temper, his stalker-ish behavior toward some women, his long history with Eli. Sealed school records became points of coffee shop discussion. Depending on who was asked, Eli had been run out of town, kidnapped, or possibly even murdered.

Eli shook his head at all of it. As he explained to many people, with complete honesty, he hadn't seen Zeke's face in months. When asked where he'd been, he shrugged and managed to look embarrassed. He'd been struck with wanderlust, taken a few days off, and just kept going.

The impulsive after-college road trip, many years late. There may have been a woman involved.

People sighed and smiled. Dependable Eli Teague could be just as irresponsible as the rest of them sometimes. It fit well into the history they all liked to believe.

Over the next few days, he went back to the station to give statements about his absence to Captain Deacon, to the state police out of Alfred, and to a bored-looking FBI agent out of Portland who'd been called in when Eli's car was found in Boston. A missing persons case had been opened, and procedures had to be followed before it could be closed. No, he hadn't been kidnapped. No, he hadn't been threatened. No, he hadn't seen Officer Miller during that time. Eli sat in the chair and answered all their questions with a straight face.

"Are you a steampunk fan?"

Eli blinked. "What?"

"Steampunk." The FBI agent pointed his pen at the hat sitting on Deacon's desk. "I've got a friend who is. She has a bowler too."

"It's a derby," corrected Eli.

"What's the difference?"

"I'm not really sure," he said, "but I'm pretty sure there is one."

"Not into steampunk, though?"

Eli shook his head.

"Strange choice for a hat, then."

Eli shrugged. "Used to be the most popular hat in the country."

The FBI agent smirked as he packed up his paperwork, his first real expression in their five-minute discussion. "Yeah, well, what was it Obama said about horses and bayonets?"

Eli's car had been towed from the Boston parking structure and impounded. He owed thirteen weeks of storage fees—a frightening sum—if he wanted it back. Much to his surprise, his apartment was still his. Captain Deacon had labeled it a crime scene after Zeke's disappearance. The lock on the door had been fixed, but the rest of the small space had been left as they'd found it. Eli cleaned up a few things and threw away many more. His bed felt too soft, so he dragged the blankets onto the floor, cracked the windows open, and slept soundly in the cold, fresh air.

He'd been equally surprised to find out he still had a job. Bill had hired a new systems person—a woman with spiky hair, dark eyes, and a much more impressive résumé than Eli—but after his absence and reported disappearance, no one had gone through the actual motions of firing him. Bill told him they'd sort things out, either getting him a position at another branch or at least some back pay so he'd have a cushion while he looked for something new.

Eli spent his free time checking in with his friends. Jack in the Box, the fast-food franchise, had slipped into Sanders and made a quiet offer for the Emporium building. Corey and Robin had considered it for all of two days, and accepted with a little encouraging nudge from Eli. The tidy sum, more than they'd make in a decade of video rentals, would let Robin go back to art school and Corey launch a Twitch show with a sizeable budget.

When the gossip mill became too much, Nicole had packed up and moved a few towns over into New Hampshire. A manager position had opened up at one of the big multiplex cinemas in Newington. Eli stopped by to visit and found her planning her film festival. They both smiled and spoke warmly, but the recent events had stomped out whatever spark the two of them might've once had. Nicole kissed him on the cheek as they hugged goodbye, and Eli felt sure he'd never see her again.

Even his mom had good news, despite all her worry about her son. It turned out the family home sat in a geographically perfect spot for a cell phone tower. The day after he talked with the FBI agent, a company approached her about building on her small patch of land, deep on the back of the property line. The lease was double what she made as a librarian.

It seemed as if the American Dream had finally caught up with Sanders.

And then, right on cue, Eli got fired.

Bill asked him if he could swing by the bank. When Eli arrived, his boss—his ex boss, he already suspected—looked close to a panic attack. "She's been waiting to talk to you," said Bill. "She wouldn't leave. Said she wanted to explain things to you personally."

Helena stood at the back of the bank, next to one of the spare desks.

Eli glanced out through the blinds. He didn't see the Cadillac Sixty Special anywhere in the parking lot, but he couldn't see the whole lot from where he was. Was this another case of timelines not lining up? Could this be an earlier visit, from her point of view?

He walked closer, away from Bill and the others. Helena stared at him like a bug. A thin scar, at least a year old, ran along the side of her forehead. The kind of thing you'd end up with, he guessed, if someone pistol-whipped you.

Truss was still dead. Or dead already. Dead to both of them?

Which meant what to Helena?

The woman reached into her jacket. Eli tensed, prepared to leap behind the flimsy barrier of the cubicle partition. It wouldn't offer much in the way of protection, but it would keep him out of line of sight for . . .

Helena pulled out an envelope.

"Mr. Elias Teague," she said. Her voice had a soft edge, almost a lisp. She had impressive projection, but the air itself blunted her words. "The situation with your employment has come to the attention of Mr. Truss. I'm sure it comes as no surprise that, under the terms outlined in your contract, you've been terminated. Effective immediately."

Eli said nothing. He'd expected as much.

"However," she continued in the same lisping tenor, "Mr. Truss has offered you a token severance payment, in recognition of your years of service."

She held out the envelope.

Eli stared at the woman. Leaned in a little closer. "Mr. Truss," he murmured, "is dead. Arguably, he's been dead for a hundred and thirty years."

Helena said nothing.

"What is this? Some kind of final revenge? Hate mail from beyond the grave? Did he buy out my mom's mortgage or get my citizenship revoked or something?"

The woman held the envelope out like a blade raised to slash down.

Everyone in the bank had their eyes on the exchange, even if they couldn't hear the quieter parts of it.

Eli took the envelope. Tore it open. When a cloud of poison dust didn't poof out, he opened it all the way.

Inside sat a check. A large one. Eli counted nine digits before the decimal point, then counted again to make sure.

"What's this supposed to be?"

"Mr. Truss may have passed on," said Helena, now in a much lower tone, "but he's left an impressive corporate structure behind. One which won't notice his absence for months. Maybe even years."

"So you're in charge now?"

"Mr. Truss is in charge," she said, blinking too-innocently, "just as he's always been. And I'll deliver his messages to all the various executives and district managers, just as I always have."

Eli held up the envelope. "So this is . . . a bribe?"

"An incentive," lisped Helena. "I don't want any hard feelings between us. Go out, live the life you always wanted. There are people keeping tabs on you these days. People who would listen to you. As I see it, if you're busy and happy, you won't feel inclined to talk to any of them about me. Which means things here can continue as they are."

"So it's a bribe."

Helena smirked. "If it makes you happy to call it that. Either way . . . you're fired. What happens next is up to you."

Eli folded the envelope and the check and stuffed them in his back pocket. "And what if I decide it's not enough?"

She shrugged and reached into her jacket. She pulled something out and pressed it into Eli's palm. She had very warm fingers.

A wooden poker chip, with golden yellow edges and a pair of marked signs, cents and dollars, each one with two vertical lines running through it.

"I owe you one," Helena said. "Good enough?"

Eli flipped the favor back and forth between his fingers. "Yeah," he said. "Yeah, it is."

"Then our business is concluded, Mr. Teague," she said at regular volume. She gave a short bow, walked past Eli, and gestured for Bill to join her at another desk.

Eli walked over to the other spare cubicle. His belongings waited in a box there. He tried to think of anything in the box worth taking home, but decided it would be rude to just leave it behind for Bill or someone else to deal with.

The new systems tech—he realized he'd never learned her name—stood up inside her cubicle. "Axed you?"

"Yeah."

"Sucks."

"It's okay."

"Better than a couple of years ago," she agreed.

"Yeah."

"Any tips on keeping everything up and running?" she asked. It had the distinct air of a polite, rhetorical question.

"Nope. Actually, yes. There's a buggy line in the transfer code. I think I flagged it just before I left, but it never got fixed."

She glanced down at her computer. "Seriously?"

"Yeah. Sorry."

"You think you flagged it?"

He tried to shrug, but the box interfered. Instead he gestured back at Helena. "Mr. Truss showed up in person. Messed up the whole day."

"Ahhh," she said, this time in a tone that implied she'd already heard stories about Archibald Truss.

Eli nodded. "Good luck."

"See you around."

Another week passed. He checked in with his mom every day. He went out with his friends on Tuesday night. They smiled at his derby. Robin still wanted to know about the woman who'd given it to him, refusing to believe there wasn't a story with a woman behind the small-brimmed hat.

He used his banking skills to set up a few different accounts. His big check went into one, then spread out into the others. He could be rich now or comfortable for the rest of his life. He went with comfortable.

More weeks passed by. Eli spent his days walking around town. He visited Jackson's and looked through the last wire comic rack. He stopped by the Emporium during its big closeout sale. He stood outside the theater, which still had last month's playbill taped in the box-office window. He bought a nice lunch at the Silver Arrow one day and two oily slices at Pizza Pub on another.

Had the buildings in Sanders always been so close together?

He tried three different stores in the area, searching for a new coat. He found a thigh-length overcoat he liked in the York thrift store. Simple lines, strong stitches, wooden buttons.

One day in early March he circled the Founders House a dozen times. Nothing moved in the windows or curled from the chimneys. On his thirteenth circuit, Corey appeared. "Hey," he called out.

"Hey," Eli replied. "I thought you guys were still packing."

Corey nodded his head back toward the Emporium, its top floor just peeking out between two other buildings. "We are. Robin saw you walking around over here. Recognized the hat."

Eli touched the brim and smiled. "Guess it does make me stand out a bit."

"Pretty sure it's the only one in town." Corey lifted his chin and studied the old building. "Remember when we were kids and we'd run up the front steps here?"

"Yeah."

"I gotta be honest," Corey said. "Place used to scare the shit out of me when we were little. Even just now, when Robin asked me to come see what you were up to, I got a little case of the heebies."

"It's just an old building," said Eli.

"Oh, yeah, I know that. Now. But back when we were little . . . I'm pretty sure monsters lived in it then."

Eli smiled again. "Truer words."

They started walking again, heading toward the front steps.

"So," Corey said, shoving his hands in his pockets. "What're you doing?"

He waved a hand up at the Founders House. "Just looking."

"Okay."

Eli took off his hat and rubbed the back of his head. "Sorry. Had a lot on my mind."

"Figured." Corey glanced up at the building again. "I've gotta be honest. I'm kinda half tempted to chuck a rock at a window."

"I won't tell anybody."

"Nah. Just my luck, Barney'd see me do it too."

"Goddamned perfect Barney," said Eli.

"Yeah, tell me about it. I mean, he's making every other guy in town look bad. Can't he just gain a couple pounds or get a zit or something?"

They both chuckled, then walked the rest of the way to the big staircase in silence.

"So, what are you doing, Eli?"

"Nothing. Like I said, just looking."

"No, I mean . . ." Corey paused, arranged his thoughts. "Y'know when you first vanished, before all the Zeke stuff started, you know what we all thought?"

"What?"

"'Finally!' Me and Robin and Josh, even Nicole. We all figured you just finally decided it was time to leave, to go do something with your life."

Eli raised an eyebrow at him.

"Look . . . you know I love you. Me and Robin both. But . . . the bank fired you last week, right?"

"Yeah. Almost ten days ago now."

"And you've picked up the check the last three times we've gone out, so I know you got a ton of back pay or severance or something."

"Severance," said Eli. "They were generous."

Corey shrugged. "So what are you waiting for? You're a smart guy. You could do anything. Anywhere." He turned away from the Founders House and looked out across the town. "It's time to move on, buddy."

46

The classified ad caught his eye. A mint-green 1967 Chevy Impala, as-is. Some work needed. He called the owner and they talked for a few minutes. The man gave Eli an address in Kittery and said he could stop by that evening.

Eli borrowed his mother's car and went to check it out.

"Had a couple calls about it," said the owner, who introduced himself as Bear. His heavy frame spoke of youthful muscles gone soft after years of being bathed in beer. "Mostly college kids. They want to know if they can get it painted black like that *Supernatural* car."

Eli didn't understand the reference. The only two supernatural cars he could think of were a red '58 Plymouth Fury and a customized '71 Lincoln Continental Mark III. Nobody would ever mistake a '67 Impala for either of them.

Bear took him over to the garage, walked past it, and pulled a tarp off the vehicle there. As Eli had suspected, the Impala was mountain green, not mint. The paint was faded in places, worn away down to metal in others. Rust coated the undercarriage. Salt corrosion had eaten a few tiny holes in the floorboards, and one the size of a half-dollar behind the driver's seat. All four tires were smoother than an old pair of sneakers.

It had been a long time since the car had a roof over its head. Not the best thing in New England. The engine looked good, though, and the battery was new.

Bear repeated the Impala's need for some work, then asked for a large sum, "it being a classic and all." Eli countered with two-thirds as much, pointing out how much repairs would cost. They batted prices back and forth for a few minutes before settling on an amount Eli said he could pay in cash.

He caught a ride from Corey the next day and drove home with his new car. He stopped for new tires first. Second, a general tune-up of the engine, transmission, brakes, and alignment. New headlights, as well. Saturday, when he had the car inspected, he slipped the mechanic an extra fifty. The woman set a few metal plates along the Impala's floor to cover the holes and deemed the car road-worthy.

He didn't bother to touch up the weather-beaten green paint. Automotive camouflage. People rarely broke into a car that looked like crap.

The night after he screwed his own license plates on the Impala, he took his mother out to dinner and told her his plans. More or less. The following night he met up with his friends at the bar in Dover, bought them a few rounds of drinks and nachos, and explained what he was doing. Josh shook his head and laughed. Robin smiled and looked at the derby. Corey nodded approvingly.

The following morning—two months, two weeks, and two days after his return—Eli Teague kissed his mother goodbye, climbed into his beat-up Impala, and left Sanders.

He took the southern route, driving down Interstate 95 and eventually cutting across 85 to 40 West. The Impala's radio didn't work, and while that would've driven him nuts at one point in his life, he found the sounds of the road soothing enough. When he got tired, he pulled into rest-stop parking lots and slept in his car with his derby tipped down over his eyes. He changed clothes twice in the passenger seat, ate most of his meals behind the wheel.

As he passed through Memphis, he considered diverting south to New Orleans. He wondered how it had changed in the hundred and sixty years since he'd last been there. The exit for southbound 55 came and went. He didn't look back.

Eli drove through Amarillo, Albuquerque, and Flagstaff before entering California. He allowed himself one detour and took the Impala down through Los Angeles to cut back and drive up the coast. The Pacific Ocean was beautiful, but as a lifelong New Englander, he couldn't shake the surreal feeling that the water stretched out the wrong way, especially when the sun went down.

He spent a night in a San Luis Obispo hotel, where he took a long shower and slept until the maid woke him up the next morning. He ate a late breakfast at a diner near the beach, filled up the Impala's gas tank, and got back on the road.

Noon passed before he reached Sacramento. He drove through and continued northeast, into the mountains. He reached over and dragged the legal pad off the passenger seat. A few glances confirmed the directions he'd spent hours searching for online and in library books.

He reached the small ranger station a little after four o'clock, but the park ranger had already left. Eli glanced through the window at the one-room office and wondered how often he or she came by to check on things. A gate stretched across the dirt road, chained at the middle, so Eli drove the Impala around the building and back onto the southbound road.

He passed a few weathered, charred beams reaching up from the ground. A wooden sign stood near them. He guessed it described the site as the remains of a barn.

Another three minutes of driving brought him to Hourglass.

Half the buildings had vanished altogether, half of what remained had become wooden skeletons. According to the few snippets of history he'd been able to find, the First Time Around had caught fire on May 31, 1886, killing nine people as it burned to the ground. The chandeliers had been a huge fire hazard, after all. The bank had closed in July, taking the post office, the sheriff's station, the Second Iteration, and most of the citizens with it. The remaining families and businesses struggled on for a few months, but—as Harry had said—the town had been abandoned before the end of the year.

He killed the Impala's engine, left the keys in the ignition. The sun hung above the horizon, but the air had cooled already. He punched his derby down on his head and slung his coat over his shoulder.

It took him a few moments to orient himself, even though he'd been there just three months ago. The few black-tipped stubs to his left were the remains of the First Time Around. The bank's foundation still looked solid, as did two of the walls. A few steps past the bank gave him a view of the Second Iteration's stripped and sun-bleached husk. The wooden sidewalk's frame still stood, but all its planks had long since vanished.

Eli wandered down Main Street, toward the vast plain where hundreds of cars had parked for one brief week over a century ago. He counted foundations where the houses had been stripped away by nature or scavengers.

He reached the next intersection and smiled.

Somehow, in the odd way of such things, the Last Paradox remained mostly whole. Only a dozen or so shingles sat up on the roof. The front railing had split at some point. One of the swinging doors had been claimed by history but its twin still hung by rusted hinges. While the left-hand window had broken and been cleaned away at some point, the right-hand one sat with just a single crack to show the passage of time. The painted snake, its tail clutched in its mouth, had barely faded or flaked at all.

He stared at the old saloon for almost ten minutes.

Eli reached out and set a hand on the dry railing. "I suppose it's my last visit," he said to nobody in particular.

He went inside.

Much like the outside, the interior of the Last Paradox had fared better than most. It was the ghost-town saloon that television had prepared him for. Three tables still stood, and twice as many chairs, but many of their brothers and sisters still lay where they'd fallen. A spiderweb of cracks stretched across the bar's mirror, and a few squares and triangles of glass had fallen free. He counted half a dozen bottles still shelved behind the bar. Dusty cobwebs draped the rafters and the metal loop that would've passed for a chandelier.

He'd heard of spots like this, which had somehow escaped the worst of history and humanity. Abandoned for decades, but never looted or repurposed. Shelves still stocked, woodpiles intact, coal buckets full. A pot sat on the battered stove in the corner. Plates, glasses, and bottles were scattered on the tables.

He went back outside and walked the rest of Main Street. The road had been picked and kicked clean over the years. Old tire tracks from park vehicles decorated most of it. No nails or broken glass or other immediate hazards.

Eli lined up the Impala. The engine rumbled between the old buildings. He watched the road for a ripple, a swirl in the dust, anything that stood out.

The air sparkled and he hit the gas. The Impala roared down Main

Street and through a patch of sunlit dust. Eli muttered, took the car down to the edge of town, and turned around. He crawled back into Hourglass, his eyes glued to the road.

A faint shimmer danced in the air, and the muscle car leaped forward again. The new tires gripped the dirt every inch of the way, never losing traction for a second as he blasted through the heat haze. He sighed and circled around at the big intersection, swerving past the remains of the First Time Around and the bank.

The third time he drove the Impala at what turned out to be a swarm of gnats as they looped and spun and twisted across the road.

The fourth time was another patch of dust.

The fifth time the setting sun hit a smear of gnat juice on the windshield and created a glow.

Eli brought the Impala around again. He was running out of sunlight. Four, maybe five more runs, unless he wanted to keep trying in the dark.

Something in the corner of his eye caught his attention. He slapped his foot down on the brakes. A heartbeat later he killed the engine.

Harry sat on the steps outside the Last Paradox. Her frock coat sprawled open to show off a red vest and a baggy shirt, while her tricorne balanced on one knee. A brown bag sat next to her, along with a small drift of what looked like peanut shells. Her lips were pressed tightly together, but the corners of her mouth and eyes fluttered.

"Harry?"

"Please," she said, waving him on, "don't mind me. Just continue making an ass of yourself." She shook two nuts out of the shell and pushed them into her mouth, stifling a laugh.

Eli got out of the Impala, dragging his coat after him, and walked over to her. "How long have you been sitting there?"

"How long have I been sitting here watching you drive up and down the road like a fool? Long enough that you'll be regretting it for some time to come." She pulled another peanut from the bag and tore it open. Then she giggled and dropped it back in the bag.

"I waited for weeks and you didn't show up."

"Well, I've been looking for you for months," she said, pushing herself up off the steps. "I showed up in Sanders and everyone told me about how you'd bought a car and driven off into the sunset."

"Once I realized I was going in and out of town with no problem, I figured it was safe for me to leave and come looking for you." He crossed his arms. "Besides, how can you be late when you can travel through history?"

"Not there," she said. "Not anymore. The closest slick spot to Sanders is down in Boston now, and it's almost a year off."

"That far?"

She nodded. "The best I could find was about four months after they let you go. Almost a third of them are gone. James thinks there may be a dozen or so new ones, but nobody's quite figured out where they are yet. And Eleanor was a wreck. I worked on her for a month, and that was with John's help."

They stood there for a moment. Harry knocked some dust from her tricorne. She examined the hat to make sure she hadn't missed any spots.

"So," said Eli. He looked past her to the tavern. "We made it to the Last Paradox."

"We did," said Harry. She pushed the hat up onto her head. "Thanks to you."

"I just got lucky, put a few things together. You did all the work."

"We did it together, then."

"Yeah."

They looked at each other.

"So," he said. "Now what? There's no search. No dream to be had. What do we do now?"

Harry's lips formed a soft, nervous smile. "There's always a dream to be had."

"Yeah?"

"Yes."

He felt his own lips pull into the same awkward smile and felt a sudden need to check his boots for dust or dirt.

Harry cleared her throat. "As I see it, there are two options in our immediate future."

"Okay."

"One," she said, jerking her thumb behind her, "is there's a celebration going on here back in 1886."

"Right here?"

She nodded. "Everyone who made it. About three dozen of us. James is there. John's there chatting with Monica. Did you meet her?"

"Dark hair, wears a business suit?"

"That's her. Danny Cooper's with her. Alice Ramsey's come back for the end—and she's so old now! Maisie Huang was just heading in when I left."

"When you left?"

"I had to go looking for my partner," she said. "Who, I might note, is not smart enough to just stay at home where I can find him."

"Sorry."

"You should be. Dumb luck I found you here."

"I think I found you."

"Don't nitpick, Mr. Teague." She overemphasized his name.

"So option one is a party."

Harry nodded. "And they're all waiting for you."

"Me?"

"Us, technically. We are the ones who found the dream."

"Ahhh. What's option two?"

She looked at her own boots. "I've been driving around America for a while now. I was thinking it was time to try somewhere new. Maybe Canada. Or Cuba."

"There aren't any roads to Cuba."

Harry looked up at him. "Not yet," she said. "But I happen to know a shortcut if you don't feel like waiting."

She blinked twice and met his gaze again.

"Well," said Eli, "is there any reason we can't do both?"

"None at all." She reached out, then pulled her hands back. "Eleanor's just around the corner. Do you have everything?"

Eli looked down at the coat hooked on his fingers. He felt the brim of his hat against his head. He glanced back at the Impala and imagined a park ranger finding the muscle car in the center of town in a few days, still with half a tank of gas and the keys in the ignition.

"Yeah," he said. "I've got everything I need."

The corners of her mouth twitched, and her lips stretched a little wider across her face. She leaned forward, brought her face close to his, and then settled back on her heels. "Okay, then. Let's go."

They stepped off the stairs of the Last Paradox together.

"Oh," she added, "one thing."

"Yeah?"

"If this is going to be a permanent arrangement, I'm going to need you to chip in for fuel."

"I'm sure we'll work out something," Eli said.

"I'm sure we will."

Afterword

This is the longest I've ever spent on a book.

Okay, that's kind of a lie. Not a great way to start this. It's the longest I've ever spent on a published book. My actual "first novel" (never before seen—with good reason) took me almost nine years to finish, depending on how you want to count it. And then another three years to edit.

Since I've started doing this full time, though . . . yeah, this has been the longest.

It's also been very odd writing a book about the United States and the American dream as all of 2016 and the first few months of 2017 have rolled by. Things I worried were a bit too dark now feel almost cartoonishly simple. Things that started out feeling a bit optimistic have come to feel almost hopelessly naive.

Then again, nobody seems to be getting tired of watching movies about Captain America . . .

As always, I'm both thrilled and stunned some of you decided to pick up my latest tome. Even more surprised you've made it all the way to the back and are reading the afterword, hoping to glean some more fun facts about the people and things and situations I made up this time.

Of course, this time I didn't make all of it up.

For example . . .

James Dean was an American film icon, nominated for two post-humous Academy Awards, who absolutely loved automobiles. In fact, he considered giving up Hollywood to devote more time to racing. His death in an automobile accident was far too well-documented to be a hoax . . . but it's nice to dream.

Alice Ramsey was the first woman to drive across the United States in 1909, and the third person to ever do it. At age twenty-two she took three friends from New York City to San Francisco in a brand new Maxwell touring car, setting a new cross-country record in the process. She repeated the trip numerous times during her very long life and would often be away on the road for weeks at a time.

Henry "Frank" Hawkins was one of the original miner 49ers, rushing out to California from Maine at the age of fourteen! He made several successful trips out west, trying different routes, and finally settled in New Orleans (although he still visited Maine from time to time). It's probably also worth mentioning that he's my great-great-grandfather.

Many of the cross-country oddities mentioned in this book—the town of Dinosaur, the wrong soldier statue in York, Maine, Pasadena's fork in the road, Lafitte's Blacksmith Shop Bar in New Orleans—are real and you can visit all of them.

But, yeah . . . I did make up some of it. The town of Hourglass, alas, is pure fiction. So is Harry's hometown of Shame, but we may still need to visit it someday, just to find out exactly why her parents left. Sanders, Maine, is also fiction, but the Founders House is loosely inspired by the old Ocean House Hotel, which stood on a hill in York Beach for almost 130 years before being torn down in 1985.

I also tweaked history a bit. There were a few times and places where I needed things to happen. Or to have happened, as is the way with time travel. If you didn't notice them, don't worry. If you did, I meant to do that. Really.

And, of course, there are a lot of folks who helped me with this in one way or another and deserve a bunch of thanks.

First off, all of you following me on Twitter or Facebook who put up with my constant vague hints and refusal to tell you anything useful. I have to assume you're sticking around for all the geeky nonsense.

Ed and Alex educated me on the fine differences between bourbon and rye whiskey.

Ray and Bo both offered helpful tips and insights about classic cars.

Dennis, my dad, helped me with some railroad history.

Mary talked to me about wounds and injuries, plus some cutting-edge medical stuff that might be boringly common in a decade or so.

CD, David, and John all read early versions of this book, caught many problems, and offered many suggestions. CD and Kristi went through a later version of it too.

David, my agent, championed this book when it wasn't much more than three pages of notes and something we'd talked about over drinks at San Diego Comic-Con.

Julian, my editor, continued to believe in it even after the completely crazy, everything-but-the-kitchen-sink-it-got-away-from-me-yeah draft I first handed him.

And, as always, so many thanks to my lovely lady, Colleen, who puts up with so many random, rambling discussions and segues about train tracks, 1850s coinage, time paradoxes, plus all the usual moaning and self-doubt. I'm still not sure why she puts up with it, but I think it's good for all of us that she does.

P.C.

Los Angeles, March 2017

READ ON FOR AN EXCERPT FROM
PETER CLINES'S NOVEL

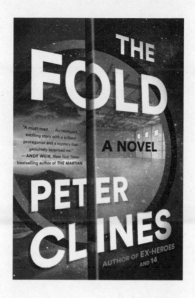

"A must-read for anyone who likes a good science-fiction thriller . . . an intelligent, exciting story with a brilliant protagonist and a mystery that genuinely surprised me."

—Andy Weir, *New York Times* bestselling author
of *The Martian* and *Artemis*

"Part techno-thriller, part supernatural mystery, all awesome."

—*SF Signal*

"I just don't think it's that good," said Denise. "It doesn't do anything for me."

Becky bit back a smile, even though Denise couldn't see it over the phone. They'd had this conversation every other week for two months now. It still made for a good distraction, though, and helped fill up the time until Ben got home.

It always worried her a bit when Ben was away. Ben was in charge of high-security projects. Mostly weapons. Often in high-risk areas.

Granted, this had been one of the lowest-risk work trips he'd ever taken. Just four days in San Diego. And on a non-weapons project.

"I mean, Marty really likes it," Denise continued, "but it just seems like nothing but boobs and snow and blood. And the frozen zombie things. I just don't get them. It feels like not a lot ever actually happens, y'know? Five years and they're still talking about winter."

Becky gathered up some socks, underwear, two T-shirts, a skirt, and a bra that had been scattered across the bedroom floor. She was a horrible slob whenever she had the house to herself. Worse than she'd been in college, for some reason she couldn't figure out. "So why do you keep watching it?"

"Ehh. Marty really likes it. He won't admit it, but I just think he likes all the boobs. Are you guys still watching?"

She walked to the bathroom, and shoved the armload of clothes into the hamper. The bathroom was a mess, too. Her yoga clothes and more underwear. How had she gone through so much underwear in four days? "We're a couple episodes behind, but yeah," she said. "I think he likes the boobs, too. And the dragons."

Becky put her foot in the trash can and mashed down the small pile of bathroom trash, just enough so it didn't look like it was overflowing. "We were talking about doing a DVR marathon this weekend. Something to relax a bit after his trip."

"When's he get back?"

"His plane landed a little while ago," she said. "He sent me a text saying he had to stop at the office and give a quick report to his boss. Probably be home any minute now."

"Cleaning up your mess?"

She laughed. "You know me too well."

"I should let you go, then."

"Yeah, probably."

"Give me a call next week," Denise said. "Maybe we can all do dinner at that new Japanese place."

"Okay."

She hung up and tossed the phone on the bed. She looked around and tried to spot anything else he could tease her for leaving out. There was a wineglass on her nightstand, and a plate with a few cheesecake crumbs. And another wineglass on her dresser. God, she was a slob. And a lush.

It crossed her mind now and then that she should try to be one of the good wives. The ones who kept the house clean, and had dinner waiting for her husband when he came home. When they'd met, she'd actually been dressed as a 1950s housewife at a Halloween party, complete with martini glass, apron, and a copy of an old *Good Housekeeping* list of duties she was supposed to perform. He'd laughed, said she didn't look like the kind of woman who sat around waiting on a husband, and bought her a drink. They'd ended Halloween night with a few things that were not covered in the *Good Housekeeping* article. Fourteen months later they were married.

She gathered up the glasses and the plate. She could swing by her art studio in the back and grab the dishes there. There was definitely a plate next to her computer from today's lunch, possibly a wineglass from last night. She could rinse them in the sink, maybe.

As she reached the studio door, a faint rasp of sliding metal echoed from the front of the house. A key in a lock. There was a click, and then the hinge squeaked. They'd been trying to fix that damned thing for years.

The front door.

"Hey, babe," she called out, setting all the dishes down on the desk. "How was your flight?" Ah, well. He wouldn't notice them right away in the studio. And it wasn't like he didn't know her by now. She took a few steps toward the hall, then decided to take the back staircase. It was closer, and she'd probably meet him in the kitchen.

Something tickled her brain as her foot hit the first step. The lack of something. The usual chain of sounds she heard when Ben got home had been broken. She hadn't heard the hinge squeak again, or the door close. Or his keys hitting the table in the front hall.

"Babe?"

She lifted her foot from the step and walked back down the hall. From the top of the staircase she could see their front door. It sat open by almost a foot. She could smell the lawn outside and hear the traffic heading for the beltway.

Ben wasn't there. She didn't see his keys on the table. His briefcase wasn't shoved under the table where he always tossed it.

Becky took a few steps down the stairs. She peered over the banister to see if he was lurking in the hall. It wouldn't be the first time he'd leaped out to scare her.

The hallway was empty.

She walked downstairs to the front door. It hung open in a relaxed, casual way. The same way it did when she was heading out to grab the mail or to growl at Pat from down the street for letting her dog crap on their lawn.

Had she left the door open when she went out for the mail earlier? Maybe just enough for the wind to push it open? Had she imagined the sound of the key? Ben was due home any minute. She might've just heard the hinge squeak and added everything else.

She leaned out the door. It was cool. This late in the afternoon, the front of the house was in the shade.

Ben's car was in the driveway. It was right where it always landed, in front of the nearer garage door. She could see a faint shimmer of heat above the hood.

Becky pushed the door shut. The hinges squeaked. The latch clicked. "Are you in here, babe?"

Floorboards settled. The air in the house shifted. Someone was in the kitchen. She recognized the creak of the tiles near the dishwasher.

"Ben?" His name echoed in the house. She took a few strides toward the back of the house. "Where are you?"

The silence slowed her down, then brought her to a stop.

"If this is supposed to be funny, it's not."

Nothing.

She weighed her options. There was still a chance this was a trick. A joke gone bad. Ben would leap out and make her shriek and she'd hit him and then welcome him home.

It didn't feel like a trick. The house felt wrong. Ben's car might be in the driveway, but there was a stranger moving through their home.

They owned a gun. A Glock 17 or 19 or something. She'd taken four classes and gone shooting at the range three times. It was a badass, secret agent–level gun. That's what Ben had said. They'd probably never need it, but better to have it and not need it than need it and not . . .

The Glock was upstairs. In their bedroom. In the nightstand. She could take six long steps back and be at the main staircase.

Or take three steps forward and get a view into the kitchen.

She took two steps forward.

Ben's briefcase and travel bag sat in the hallway. It was a beat-up, gym bag sort of thing he'd had for years. He still used it because it held three or four days' worth of clothes, but it fit in an overhead compartment. Cut half an hour off his travel time to not be waiting on luggage.

"Babe, I swear to God, I'm calling the fucking cops in two minutes." Her voice echoed in the house. "This isn't funny."

A long groan sounded above her. The noise of stressed wood. The spot by her studio, close to the door. Neither of them had stepped on it in over a year because it was so damned loud.

Whoever was upstairs had stepped on it.

They were *upstairs*!

She looked up at the ceiling. Three seconds passed, and another board squeaked. She could almost see the footsteps through the plaster. Someone was circling around the house. Straight through to the kitchen, up the back staircase she'd had her foot on just five minutes ago, and into the upstairs hallway. They were near the bedroom.

Near the gun.

Jesus, why hadn't she grabbed the gun as soon as things got weird?

But why was Ben's luggage in the house? Why was his car in the driveway? Had someone grabbed him at the airport? Did he get carjacked?

There was a panic number she was supposed to call. In case something happened to him, if someone tried to get to him through her. He'd given it to her, and she'd never even put it in her phone.

It was in the desk in her studio. Of course.

Becky stepped into the kitchen and grabbed her cell phone from the counter. Then she grabbed a knife from the big block. A wedding present from one of Ben's old college friends. It was a great set. The blade of the butcher knife was almost fourteen inches long and sharp as hell. And the handle sat well in her hand.

They'd all laughed at the idea that knives were a bad-luck wedding gift.

She slid her fingers over the phone's screen and tapped in 911. She held off pressing CALL. There was still a chance this was a bad joke. Some stupid plan to get a scream or a laugh or excitement sex or something, but he sure as hell wasn't getting any off this.

And it wasn't his sort of thing.

She circled through the living room. It had a thick carpet, almost silent to walk across. Just make it through the house, give Ben one last time to admit he was an idiot, and then out the door. She'd call 911 from the front yard.

She was halfway across the living room when she heard the sound of metal sliding across metal. It was a fast, back-and-forth with a hard snap at the end. She'd heard it a lot at the range. She'd been the one making it.

She swallowed.

Becky looked down at her phone. Could she raise her voice enough to talk? Did the person upstairs know where she was in the house? What did 911 do when they got a silent call? Did they trace it and send a car? Did they hang up?

She had to get out of the house now.

The front door was closer, but it was a clear shot—bad choice of words—a clear *line of sight* for anyone in the upstairs hall. Almost straight from their bedroom door to the front door.

The back door was farther away, but there was more weaving and someone would have to get much closer to aim—to *see* her. She'd have a chance to make the call. But the backyard was a wall of fences around a pool they hadn't filled for the summer yet. She'd have to run back around to the side gate. And no one would be able to see her. Maybe not even hear her, with all the noise from that new house they were putting up one block over.

Plenty of time and opportunity for someone to grab her and drag her back into the house. It had to be the front door.

Becky gripped the knife, made sure her finger was still near the CALL button, and took three long strides across the living room. The carpet absorbed her footsteps, but she heard the fabric of her jeans and felt the air move around her.

Her foot hit the hall and she heard the creak of the second step from the top of the staircase. She froze. They were on the stairs. They'd see her going for the front door.

She should've gone out the back. She still could. But she'd have to be fast. They'd hear her for sure.

She ran for the door. Feet thumped on the stairs behind her. She reached for the knob.

"Stop!"

She turned and raised her knife. "You fuckhead," she gasped.

Ben stood on the staircase, four steps from the bottom. One foot was still on the fifth. He was wearing the charcoal suit with the cranberry shirt that looked so good on him. The Glock was in his hand, its barrel pointed in her direction. He clutched his own phone in his other hand.

"Put the knife down."

Becky's shoulders slumped and she tossed the knife on the table. It slid to a stop right where his keys usually landed. "You scared the piss out of me, you jerk. I thought someone was in the house."

He lowered himself to the next step. The pistol rose up. She could see enough of the muzzle to tell it was aimed at her.

"I've called the police," he hissed. "They're on the line right now."

She glanced past him up the staircase, then her eyes went back to the gun. Had they *both* been playing tag with an intruder? "Okay," she said. "Calm down and point that somewhere else."

Ben stared at her and came down two more steps. The pistol didn't waver. His wide eyes flitted to the knife, then past her to the front door, and over into the living room. "Where is she?"

"Babe," she said, her eyes on the pistol, "you're freaking me out with the—"

"Where is she?" he shouted. His voice echoed in the hall. The glass in the door trembled behind her.

She shrieked and her mind stumbled for a moment. "She? She who?"

Ben stepped off the staircase and glared at her. He raised the pistol. The barrel was just a black square with a hole in it. He was aiming it right between her eyes. "What have you done with her? What do you want with us?" He took a step toward her, and then another.

Becky couldn't tell if he was angry or sad. The black hole kept pulling her eyes away from his face. It was just a few feet away. She could see the little trembles and shifts as he squeezed the grip. "Babe," she pleaded, "what are you talking abou—"

"Who are you?" he yelled. "*Where the hell is my wife?*"

About the Author

PETER CLINES spent years toiling in the Hollywood trenches, working on such films and shows as *Veronica Mars, Psycho Beach Party,* and *Mystery Woman* while also writing articles, reviews, and interviews for *Creative Screenwriting* magazine, before finally turning his hand to writing fiction full-time. He is the author of the bestselling Ex-Heroes series and the novels *14* and *The Fold.* He lives in Southern California.

ALSO BY PETER CLINES

THE EX-HEROES SERIES

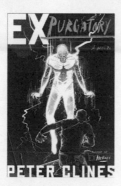

"*The Avengers* meets *The Walking Dead*,
with a large order of epic served on the side."

—Ernest Cline, *New York Times* bestselling author
of *Armada* and *Ready Player One*

B \ D \ W \ Y
Available wherever books are sold